MASTERPIECES OF MYSTERY AND THE UNKNOWN

ALSO BY AGATHA CHRISTIE FROM ST. MARTIN'S MINOTAUR

Masterpieces in Miniature
And Then There Were None
The Seven Dials Mystery
The Witness for the Prosecution and Other Stories
The Man in the Brown Suit
The Secret of Chimneys
The Sittaford Mystery
Murder Is Easy
Sparkling Cyanide
Towards Zero
Endless Night
Why Didn't They Ask Evans?
The Mysterious Mr. Quin
Death Comes as the End

Ordeal by Innocence
They Came to Baghdad
Parker Pyne Investigates
Crooked House
Double Sin and Other Stories
Destination Unknown
The Golden Ball and Other Stories
The Pale Horse
Passenger to Frankfurt
Three Blind Mice and Other Stories

BY AGATHA CHRISTIE, WRITING AS MARY WESTMACOTT

Absent in the Spring and Other Novels
A Daughter's a Daughter and Other Novels

BY AGATHA CHRISTIE, WRITTEN AS NOVELS BY CHARLES OSBORNE

Black Coffee
The Unexpected Guest
Spider's Web

MASTER

STORIES BY

AGATHA CHRISTIE

ST. MARTIN'S MINOTAUR NEW YORK

PIECES OF MYSTERY

AND THE UNKNOWN

www.minotaurbooks.com

Copyright acknowledgments appear on page vii.

Library of Congress Cataloging-in-Publication Data

Christie, Agatha, 1890–1976.

Masterpieces of mystery and the unknown : stories / by Agatha Christie.

p. cm.

ISBN 0-312-35148-8

EAN 978-0-312-35148-9

1. Detective and mystery stories, English. 2. Suspense fiction, English.
3. Supernatural—Fiction. I. Title.

PR6005.H66A6 2006

823'.912—dc22

2005044643

First Edition: March 2006

10 9 8 7 6 5 4 3 2 1

COPYRIGHT ACKNOWLEDGMENTS

CONTENTS

MASTERPIECES OF MYSTERY AND THE UNKNOWN

THE DRESSMAKER'S DOLL

The doll lay in the big velvet-covered chair. There was not much light in the room; the London skies were dark. In the gentle, grayish-green gloom, the sage-green coverings and the curtains and the rugs all blended with each other. The doll blended, too. She lay long and limp and sprawled in her green-velvet clothes and her velvet cap and the painted mask of her face. She was not a doll as children understand dolls. She was the Puppet Doll, the whim of Rich Women, the doll who lolls beside the telephone, or among the cushions of the divan. She sprawled there, eternally limp and yet strangely alive. She looked a decadent product of the twentieth century.

Sybil Fox, hurrying in with some patterns and a sketch, looked at the doll with a faint feeling of surprise and bewilderment. She wondered—but whatever she wondered did not get to the front of her mind. Instead, she thought to herself, "Now, what's happened to the pattern of the blue velvet? Wherever have I put it? I'm sure I had it here just now." She went out on the landing and called up to the workroom.

"Elspeth. Elspeth, have you the blue pattern up there? Mrs. Fellows-Brown will be here any minute now."

She went in again, switching on the lights. Again she glanced at the doll. "Now where on earth—ah, there it is." She picked the pattern up from where it had fallen from her hand. There was the usual creak outside on the landing as the elevator came to a halt and in a minute or two Mrs. Fellows-Brown, accompanied by her Pekinese, came puffing into the room rather like a fussy local train arriving at a wayside station.

"It's going to pour," she said, "simply *pour*!"

She threw off gloves and a fur. Alicia Coombe came in. She didn't always come in nowadays, only when special customers arrived, and Mrs. Fellows-Brown was such a customer.

Elspeth, the forewoman of the workroom, came down with the frock and Sybil pulled it over Mrs. Fellows-Brown's head.

"There," she said. "It really does suit you. It's a lovely color, isn't it?"

Alicia Coombe sat back a little in her chair, studying it.

"Yes," she said, "I think it's good. Yes, it's definitely a success."

Mrs. Fellows-Brown turned sideways and looked in the mirror.

"I must say," she said, "your clothes do *do* something to my behind."

"You're much thinner than you were three months ago," Sybil assured her.

"I'm really not," said Mrs. Fellows-Brown, "though I must say I *look* it in this. There's something about the way you cut, it really does minimize my behind. I almost look as though I hadn't got one—I mean only the usual kind that most people have." She sighed and gingerly smoothed the troublesome portion of her anatomy. "It's always been a bit of a trial to me," she said. "Of course, for years I could pull it in, you know, by sticking out my front. Well, I can't do that any longer because I've got a stomach now as well as a behind. And I mean—well, you can't pull it in both ways, can you?"

Alicia Coombe said, "You should see some of my customers!"

Mrs. Fellows-Brown experimented to and fro.

"A stomach is worse than a behind," she said. "It shows more. Or perhaps you think it does, because, I mean, when you're talking to people you're facing them and that's the moment they can't see your behind but they can notice your stomach. Anyway, I've made it a rule to pull in my stomach and let my behind look after itself." She craned her neck round still farther, then said suddenly, "Oh, that doll of yours! She gives me the creeps. How long have you had her?"

Sybil glanced uncertainly at Alicia Coombe who looked puzzled but vaguely distressed.

"I don't know exactly . . . some time I think—I never *can* remember things. It's awful nowadays—I simply *cannot* remember. Sybil, how long have we had her?"

Sybil said shortly, "I don't know."

"Well," said Mrs. Fellows-Brown, "she gives *me* the creeps. Uncanny! She looks, you know, as though she was watching us all, and perhaps laughing in that velvet sleeve of hers. I'd get rid of her if I were you." She gave a little shiver. Then she plunged once more into dressmaking details. Should she or should she not have the sleeves an inch shorter? And what about the length? When all these important points were settled satisfactorily, Mrs. Fellows-Brown resumed her own garments and prepared to leave. As she passed the doll, she turned her head again.

"No," she said, "I *don't* like that doll. She looks too much as though she *belonged* here. It isn't healthy."

"Now what did she mean by that?" demanded Sybil, as Mrs. Fellows-Brown departed down the stairs.

Before Alicia Coombe could answer, Mrs. Fellows-Brown returned, poking her head round the door.

"Good gracious, I forgot all about Fou-Ling. Where are you, ducksie? Well I never!"

She stared and the other two women stared, too. The Pekinese was sitting by the green-velvet chair, staring up at the limp doll sprawled on it. There was no expression, either of pleasure or resentment, on his small popeyed face. He was merely looking.

"Come along, mum's darling," said Mrs. Fellows-Brown.

Mum's darling paid no attention whatever.

"He gets more disobedient every day," said Mrs. Fellows-Brown, with the air of one cataloguing a virtue. "Come *on,* Fou-Ling. Dindins. Luffly liver."

Fou-Ling turned his head about an inch and a half toward his mistress, then with disdain resumed his appraisal of the doll.

"She certainly made an impression on him," said Mrs. Fellows-Brown. "I don't think he's ever noticed her before. *I* haven't either. Was she here last time I came?"

The two other women looked at each other. Sybil now had a frown on her face, and Alicia Coombe said, wrinkling up her forehead, "I told you—I simply can't remember anything nowadays. How long *have* we had her, Sybil?"

"Where did she come from?" demanded Mrs. Fellows-Brown. "Did you buy her?"

"Oh, no." Somehow Alicia Coombe was shocked at the idea. "Oh *no.* I suppose—I suppose someone gave her to me." She shook her head. "Maddening!" she exclaimed. "Absolutely maddening, when everything goes out of your head the very moment after it's happened."

"Now don't be stupid, Fou-Ling," said Mrs. Fellows-Brown sharply. "Come on. I'll have to pick you up."

She picked him up. Fou-Ling uttered a short bark of agonized protest. They went out of the room with Fou-Ling's popeyed face turned over his fluffy shoulder, still staring with enormous attention at the doll on the chair . . .

"That there doll," said Mrs. Groves, "fair gives me the creeps, it does."

Mrs. Groves was the cleaner. She had just finished a crablike progress backward along the floor. Now she was standing up and working slowly round the room with a duster.

"Funny thing," said Mrs. Groves, "never noticed it really until yesterday. And then it hit me all of a sudden, as you might say."

"You don't like it?" asked Sybil.

"I tell you, Mrs. Fox, it gives me the creeps," said the cleaning woman. "It ain't natural, if you know what I mean. All those long hanging legs and the way she's slouched down there and the cunning look she has in her eye. It doesn't look healthy, that's what I say."

"You've never said anything about her before," said Sybil.

"I tell you, I never noticed her—not till this morning . . . Of course I know she's been here some time but—" She stopped and a puzzled expression flitted across her face. "Sort of thing you might dream of at night," she said, and gathering up various cleaning implements she departed from the fitting room and walked across the landing to the room on the other side.

Sybil stared at the relaxed doll. An expression of bewilderment was growing on her face. Alicia Coombe entered and Sybil turned sharply.

"Miss Coombe, how long *have* you had this creature?"

"What, the doll? My dear, you know I can't remember things. Yesterday—why, it's too silly! I was going out to that lecture and I hadn't gone halfway down the street when I suddenly found I couldn't remember where I was going. I thought and I thought. Finally I told myself it *must* be Fortnums. I knew there was something I wanted to get at Fortnums. Well, you won't believe me, it wasn't till I actually got home and was having some tea that I remembered about the lecture. Of course, I've always heard that people go gaga as they get on in life, but it's happening to me much too fast. I've forgotten now where I've put my handbag—and my spectacles, too. Where did I put those spectacles? I had them just now—I was reading something in the *Times*."

"The spectacles are on the mantelpiece here," said Sybil, handing them to her. "How did you get the doll? Who gave her to you?"

"That's a blank, too," said Alicia Coombe. "*Somebody* gave her to me or sent her to me, I suppose . . . However she does seem to match the room very well, doesn't she?"

"Rather too well, I think," said Sybil. "Funny thing is, *I* can't remember when I first noticed her here."

"Now don't you get the same way as I am," Alicia Coombe admonished her. "After all, you're young still."

"But really, Miss Coombe, I don't remember. I mean I looked at her yesterday and thought there was something—well, Mrs. Groves is quite right—something creepy about her. And then I thought I'd already thought so, and then I tried to remember when I first thought so and—well, I just couldn't remember anything! In a way, it was as if I'd never seen her before—only it didn't feel like that. It felt as though she'd been here a long time but I'd only just noticed her."

"Perhaps she flew in through the window one day on a broomstick," said Alicia Coombe. "Anyway, she belongs here now all right." She looked round. "You could hardly imagine the room without her, could you?"

"No," said Sybil, with a slight shiver, "but I rather wish I could."

"Could what?"

"Imagine the room without her."

"Are we all going barmy about this doll?" demanded Alicia Coombe impatiently. "What's wrong with the poor thing? Looks like a decayed cabbage to me, but perhaps," she added, "that's because I haven't got my spectacles on." She put them on her nose and looked firmly at the doll. "Yes," she said, "I see what you mean. She *is* a little creepy. . . . Sad-looking but—well, sly and rather determined, too."

"Funny," said Sybil, "Mrs. Fellows-Brown taking such a violent dislike to her."

"She's one who never minds speaking her mind," said Alicia Coombe.

"But it's odd," persisted Sybil, "that this doll should make such an impression on her."

"Well, people do take dislikes very suddenly sometimes."

"Perhaps," said Sybil, with a little laugh, "that doll never *was* here until yesterday . . . Perhaps she just—flew in through the window as you say and settled herself here."

"No," said Alicia Coombe, "I'm sure she's been here some time. Perhaps she only became visible yesterday."

"That's what I feel, too," said Sybil, "that she's been here some time . . . but all the same I *don't* remember really seeing her till yesterday."

"Now, dear," said Alicia Coombe briskly, "do stop it. You're making me feel quite peculiar with shivers running up and down my spine. You're not going to work up a great deal of supernatural hoohah about that creature, are you?" She picked up the doll, shook it out, rearranged its shoulders, and sat it down again on another chair. Immediately the doll flopped slightly and relaxed.

"It's not a bit lifelike," said Alicia Coombe, staring at the doll. "And yet, in a funny way, she does seem alive, doesn't she?"

* * *

"OO, IT DID give me a turn," said Mrs. Groves, as she went round the showroom, dusting. "Such a turn as I hardly like to go into the fitting room any more."

"What's given you a turn?" demanded Miss Coombe, who was sitting at a writing table in the corner, busy with various accounts. "This woman," she added, more for her own benefit than that of Mrs. Groves, "thinks she can have two evening dresses, three cocktail dresses, and a suit every year without ever paying me a penny for them! Really, some people!"

"It's that doll," said Mrs. Groves.

"What, our doll again?"

"Yes, sitting up there at the desk, like a human. Oo, it didn't half give me a turn!"

"What are you talking about?"

Alicia Coombe got up, strode across the room, across the little landing outside, and into the room opposite—the fitting room. There was a small Sheraton desk in one corner of it, and there, sitting in a chair drawn up to it, her long floppy arms on the desk, sat the doll.

"Somebody seems to have been having fun," said Alicia Coombe. "Fancy sitting her up like that. Really, she looks quite natural."

Sybil Fox came down the stairs at this moment carrying a dress that was to be tried on that morning.

"Come here, Sybil. Look at our doll sitting at my private desk and writing letters now."

The two women looked.

"Really," said Alicia Coombe, "it's too ridiculous! I wonder who propped her up there. Did you?"

"No, I didn't," said Sybil. "It must have been one of the girls from upstairs."

"A silly sort of joke, really," said Alicia Coombe. She picked up the doll from the desk and threw her back on the sofa.

Sybil laid the dress over a chair carefully, then she went out and up the stairs to the workroom.

"You know the doll," she said, "the velvet doll in Miss Coombe's room downstairs—in the fitting room?"

The forewoman and three of the girls looked up.

"Yes, miss, of course we know."

"Who sat her up at the desk this morning for a joke?"

The three girls looked at her, then Elspeth, the forewoman, said, "Sat her up at the desk? *I* didn't."

"Nor did I," said one of the girls. "Did you, Marlene?" Marlene shook her head.

"This your bit of fun, Elspeth?"

"No, indeed," said Elspeth, a stern woman who looked as though her mouth should always be full of pins. "I've more to do than going about playing with dolls and sitting them up at desks."

"Look here," said Sybil, and to her surprise her voice shook slightly. "It was—it was quite a good joke, only I'd just like to know who did it."

The three girls bristled.

"We've told you, Mrs. Fox. None of us did it, did we, Marlene?"

"I didn't," said Marlene, "and if Nellie and Margaret say they didn't, well then none of us did."

"You've heard what *I* had to say," said Elspeth. "What's this all about anyway, Mrs. Fox?"

Sybil said slowly, "It just seemed so odd."

"Perhaps it was Mrs. Groves?" said Elspeth.

Sybil shook her head. "It wouldn't be Mrs. Groves. It gave *her* quite a turn."

"I'll come down and see for myself," said Elspeth.

"She's not there now," said Sybil. "Miss Coombe took her away from the desk and threw her back on the sofa. Well—" she paused, "what I mean is, someone must have stuck her up there in the chair at the writing desk—thinking it was funny, I suppose. And—and I don't see why they won't say so."

"I've told you twice, Mrs. Fox," said Margaret. "I don't see why you should go on accusing us of telling lies. None of us would do a silly thing like that."

"I'm sorry," said Sybil, "I didn't mean to upset you. But—but who else could possibly have done it?"

"Perhaps she got up and walked there herself," said Marlene, and giggled.

For some reason Sybil didn't like the suggestion.

"Oh, it's all a lot of nonsense, anyway," she said, and went down the stairs again.

Alicia Coombe was humming quite cheerfully. She looked round the room.

"I've lost my spectacles again," she said, "but it doesn't really matter. I don't want to see anything this moment. The trouble is, of course, when you're as blind as I am, that when you have lost your spectacles, unless you've got another pair to put on and find them with, well then you can't find them because you can't see to find them."

"I'll look round for you," said Sybil. "You had them just now."

"I went into the other room when you went upstairs. I expect I took them back in there."

She went across to the other room.

"It's such a bother," said Alicia Coombe. "I want to get on with these accounts. How can I if I haven't my spectacles?"

"I'll go up and get your second pair from the bedroom," said Sybil.

"I haven't got a second pair at present," said Alicia Coombe.

"Why, what's happened to them?"

"Well, I think I left them yesterday when I was out at lunch. I've rung up there, and I've rung up the two shops I went into, too."

"Oh, dear," said Sybil, "you'll have to get *three* pairs, I suppose."

"If I had three pairs of spectacles," said Alicia Coombe, "I should spend my whole life looking for one or the other of them. I really think it's best to have only *one*. Then you've *got* to look till you find it."

"Well, they must be somewhere," said Sybil. "You haven't been out of these two rooms. They're certainly not here, so you must have laid them down in the fitting room."

She went back, walking round, looking quite closely. Finally, as a last idea, she took up the doll from the sofa.

"I've got them," she called.

"Oh, where were they, Sybil?"

"Under our precious doll. I suppose you must have thrown them down when you put her back on the sofa."

"I didn't. I'm sure I didn't."

"Oh," said Sybil with exasperation. "Then I suppose the doll took them and was hiding them from you!"

"Really, you know," said Alicia, looking thoughtfully at the doll, "I wouldn't put it past her. She looks very intelligent, don't you think, Sybil?"

"I don't think I like her face," said Sybil. "She looks as though she knew something that we didn't."

"You don't think she looks sort of sad and sweet?" said Alicia Coombe, pleadingly, but without conviction.

"I don't think she's in the least sweet," said Sybil.

"No . . . perhaps you're right. . . . Oh, well, let's get on with things. Lady Lee will be here in another ten minutes. I just want to get these invoices done and posted."

"MRS. FOX. MRS. FOX."

"Yes, Margaret?" said Sybil. "What is it?"

Sybil was busy leaning over a table, cutting a piece of satin material.

"Oh, Mrs. Fox, it's that doll again. I took down the brown dress like you said, and there's that doll sitting up at the desk again. And it wasn't me—it wasn't any of us. Please, Mrs. Fox, we really wouldn't do such a thing."

Sybil's scissors slid a little.

"There," she said angrily, "look what you've made me do. Oh, well, it'll be all right, I suppose. Now, what's this about the doll?"

"She's sitting at the desk again."

Sybil went down and walked into the fitting room. The doll was sitting at the desk exactly as she had sat there before.

"You're very determined, aren't you?" said Sybil, speaking to the doll.

She picked her up unceremoniously and put her back on the sofa.

"That's your place, my girl," she said. "You stay there."

She walked across to the other room.

"Miss Coombe."

"Yes, Sybil?"

"Somebody *is* having a game with us, you know. That doll was sitting at the desk again."

"Who do you think it is?"

"It must be one of those three upstairs," said Sybil. "Thinks it's funny, I suppose. Of course they all swear to high heaven it wasn't them."

"Who do you think it is—Margaret?"

"No, I don't think it's Margaret. She looked quite queer when she came in and told me. I expect it's that giggling Marlene."

"Anyway, it's a very silly thing to do."

"Of course it is—idiotic," said Sybil. "However," she added grimly, "I'm going to put a stop to it."

"What are you going to do?"

"You'll see," said Sybil.

That night when she left, she locked the fitting-room door from the outside.

"I'm locking this door," she said, "and I'm taking the key with me."

"Oh, I see," said Alicia Coombe, with a faint air of amusement. "You're beginning to think it's me, are you? You think I'm so absent-minded that I go in there and think I'll write at the desk, but instead I pick the doll up and put her there to write for me. Is that the idea? And then I forget all about it?"

"Well, it's a possibility," Sybil admitted. "Anyway, I'm going to be quite sure that no silly practical joke is played tonight."

The following morning, her lips set grimly, the first thing Sybil did on arrival was to unlock the door of the fitting room and march in. Mrs. Groves, with an aggrieved expression and mop and duster in hand, had been waiting on the landing.

"*Now* we'll see!" said Sybil.

Then she drew back with a slight gasp.

The doll was sitting at the desk.

"Coo!" said Mrs. Groves behind her. "It's uncanny! That's what it is. Oh, there, Mrs. Fox, you look quite pale, as though you've come over queer. You need a little drop of something. Has Miss Coombe got a drop upstairs, do you know?"

"I'm quite all right," said Sybil.

She walked over to the doll, lifted her carefully, and crossed the room with her.

"Somebody's been playing a trick on you again," said Mrs. Groves.

"I don't see how they could have played a trick on me this time," said Sybil slowly. "I locked that door last night. You know yourself that no one could get in."

"Somebody's got another key, maybe," said Mrs. Groves helpfully.

"I don't think so," said Sybil. "We've never bothered to lock this door before. It's one of those old-fashioned keys and there's only one of them."

"Perhaps the other key fits it—the one to the door opposite."

In due course they tried all the keys in the shop, but none fitted the door of the fitting room.

"It *is* odd, Miss Coombe," said Sybil later, as they were having lunch together.

Alicia Coombe was looking rather pleased.

"My dear," she said. "I think it's simply extraordinary. I think we ought to write to the psychical research people about it. You know they might send an investigator—a medium or someone—to see if there's anything peculiar about the room."

"You don't seem to mind at all," said Sybil.

"Well, I rather enjoy it in a way," said Alicia Coombe. "I mean, at my age, it's rather fun when things happen! All the same—no," she added thoughtfully, "I don't think I do quite like it. I mean, that doll's getting rather above herself, isn't she?"

On that evening Sybil and Alicia Coombe locked the door once more on the outside.

"I still think," said Sybil, "that somebody might be playing a practical joke, though really, I don't see why . . ."

"Do you think she'll be at the desk again tomorrow morning?" demanded Alicia.

"Yes," said Sybil, "I do."

But they were wrong. The doll was not at the desk. Instead, she was on the window sill, looking out into the street. And again there was an extraordinary naturalness about her position.

"It's all frightfully silly, isn't it?" said Alicia Coombe, as they were snatching a quick cup of tea that afternoon. By common consent they were not having it in the fitting room, as they usually did, but in Alicia Coombe's own room opposite.

"Silly in what way?"

"Well, I mean, there's nothing you can get hold of. Just a doll that's always in a different place."

As day followed day it seemed a more and more apt observation. It was not only at night that the doll now moved. At any moment when they came into the fitting room, after they had been absent even a few minutes, they might find the doll in a different place. They could have left her on the sofa and find her on a chair. Then she'd be on a different chair. Sometimes she'd be in the window seat, sometimes at the desk again.

"She just moves about as she likes," said Alicia Coombe. "And I think, Sybil, I *think* it's amusing her."

The two women stood looking down at the inert sprawling figure in its limp, soft velvet, with its painted silk face.

"Some old bits of velvet and silk and a lick of paint, that's all it is," said Alicia Coombe. Her voice was strained. "I suppose, you know, we could—er—we could dispose of her."

"What do you mean, dispose of her?" asked Sybil. Her voice sounded almost shocked.

"Well," said Alicia Coombe, "we could put her in the fire, if there was a fire. Burn her, I mean, like a witch . . . Or of course," she added matter-of-factly, "we could just put her in the dustbin."

"I don't think that would do," said Sybil. "Somebody would probably take her out of the dustbin and bring her back to us."

"Or we could send her somewhere," said Alicia Coombe. "You know, to one of those societies who are always writing and asking for something—for a sale or a bazaar. I think that's the best idea."

"I don't know . . . ," said Sybil. "I'd be almost afraid to do that."

"Afraid?"

"Well, I think she'd come back," said Sybil.

"You mean, she'd come back *here?*"

"Yes."

"Like a homing pigeon?"

"Yes, that's what I mean."

"I suppose we're not going off our heads, are we?" said Alicia Coombe. "Perhaps I've really gone gaga and perhaps you're just humoring me, is that it?"

"No," said Sybil. "But I've got a nasty frightened feeling—a horrid feeling that she's too strong for us."

"What? That mess of rags?"

"Yes, that horrible limp mess of rags. Because, you see, she's so determined."

"Determined?"

"To have her own way? You mean, this is *her* room now!"

"Yes," said Alicia Coombe, looking round, "it is, isn't it? Of course, it always was, when you come to think of it—the colors and everything . . . I thought she fitted in here, but it's the room that fits her. I must say," added the dressmaker, with a touch of briskness in her voice, "it's rather absurd when a doll comes and takes possession of things like this. You know, Mrs. Groves won't come in here any longer and clean."

"Does she say she's frightened of the doll?"

"No. She just makes excuses of some kind or other." Then Alicia added with a hint of panic, "What are we going to do, Sybil? It's getting me down, you know. I haven't been able to design anything for weeks."

"I can't keep my mind on cutting out properly," Sybil confessed. "I make all sorts of silly mistakes. Perhaps," she said uncertainly, "your idea of writing to the psychical research people might do some good."

"Just make us look like a couple of fools," said Alicia Coombe. "I didn't seriously mean it. No, I suppose we'll just have to go on until—"

"Until what?"

"Oh, I don't know," said Alicia, and she laughed uncertainly.

On the following day Sybil, when she arrived, found the door of the fitting room locked.

"Miss Coombe, have you got the key? Did you lock this last night?"

"Yes," said Alicia Coombe, "I locked it and it's going to stay locked."

"What do you mean?"

"I just mean I've given up the room. The doll can have it. We don't need two rooms. We can fit in here."

"But it's your own private sitting room."

"Well, I don't want it any more. I've got a very nice bedroom. I can make a bed-sitting room out of that, can't I?"

"Do you mean you're really not going into that fitting room ever again?" said Sybil incredulously.

"That's exactly what I mean."

"But—what about cleaning? It'll get in a terrible state."

"Let it!" said Alicia Coombe. "If this place is suffering from some kind of possession by a doll, all right—let her keep possession. And clean the room herself." And she added, "She hates us, you know."

"What do you mean?" said Sybil. "The doll *hates* us?"

"Yes," said Alicia. "Didn't you know? You must have known. You must have seen it when you looked at her."

"Yes," said Sybil thoughtfully, "I suppose I did. I suppose I felt like that all along—that she hated us and wanted to get us out of there."

"She's a malicious little thing," said Alicia Coombe. "Anyway, she ought to be satisfied now."

Things went on rather more peacefully after that. Alicia Coombe announced to her staff that she was giving up the use of the fitting room for the present—it made too many rooms to dust and clean, she explained.

But it hardly helped her to overhear one of the work girls saying to another on the evening of the same day, "She really is batty, Miss Coombe is now. I always thought she was a bit queer—the way she lost things and forgot things. But it's really beyond anything now, isn't it? She's got a sort of thing about that doll downstairs."

"Ooo, you don't think she'll go really bats, do you?" said the other girl. "That she might knife us or something?"

They passed, chattering, and Alicia sat up indignantly in her chair. Going bats indeed! Then she added ruefully, to herself, "I suppose, if it wasn't for Sybil, I should think myself that I was going bats. But with me and Sybil and Mrs. Groves too, well, it does look as though there was *something* in it. But what I don't see is, how is it going to end?"

THREE WEEKS LATER, Sybil said to Alicia Coombe, "We've got to go into that room *sometime*."

"Why?"

"Well, I mean, it must be in a filthy state. Moths will be getting into things, and all that. We ought just to dust and sweep it and then lock it up again."

"I'd much rather keep it shut up and not go back in there," said Alicia Coombe.

Sybil said, "Really, you know, you're even more superstitious than I am."

"I suppose I am," said Alicia Coombe. "I was much more ready to believe in all this than you were, but to begin with, you know—I—well, I found it exciting in an odd sort of way. I don't know. I'm just scared, and I'd rather not go into that room again."

"Well, I want to," said Sybil, "and I'm going to."

"You know what's the matter with you?" said Alicia Coombe. "You're simply curious, that's all."

"All right, then I'm curious. I want to see what the doll's done."

"I still think it's much better to leave her alone," said Alicia.

"Now we've got out of that room, she's satisfied. You'd better leave her satisfied." She gave an exasperated sigh. "What nonsense we are talking!"

"Yes, I know we're talking nonsense, but if you tell me of any way of *not* talking nonsense—come on, now, give me that key."

"All right, all right."

"I believe you're afraid I'll let her out or something. I should think she was the kind that could pass through doors or windows."

Sybil unlocked the door and went in.

"How terribly odd," she said.

"What's odd?" said Alicia Coombe, peering over her shoulder.

"The room hardly seems dusty at all, does it? You'd think, after being shut up all this time—"

"Yes, it is odd."

"There she is," said Sybil.

The doll was on the sofa. She was not lying in her usual limp position. She was sitting upright, a cushion behind her back. She had the air of the mistress of the house, waiting to receive people.

"Well," said Alicia Coombe, "she seems at home all right, doesn't she? I almost feel I ought to apologize for coming in."

"Let's go," said Sybil.

She backed out, pulled the door to, and locked it again.

The two women gazed at each other.

"I wish I knew," said Alicia Coombe, "why it scares us so much . . ."

"My goodness, who wouldn't be scared?"

"Well, I mean, what *happens,* after all? It's nothing really—just a kind of puppet that gets moved around the room. I expect it isn't the puppet itself—it's a poltergeist."

"Now that *is* a good idea."

"Yes, but I don't really believe it. I think it's—it's that doll."

"Are you *sure* you don't know where she really came from?"

"I haven't the faintest idea," said Alicia. "And the more I think of it the more I'm perfectly certain that I didn't buy her, and that nobody gave her to me. I think she—well, she just came."

"Do you think she'll—ever go?"

"Really," said Alicia, "I don't see why she should . . . She's got all she wants."

But it seemed that the doll had not got all she wanted. The next day, when Sybil went into the showroom, she drew in her breath with a sudden gasp. Then she called up the stairs.

"Miss Coombe, Miss Coombe, come down here."

"What's the matter?"

Alicia Coombe, who had got up late, came down the stairs, hobbling a little precariously, for she had rheumatism in her right knee.

"What is the matter with you, Sybil?"

"Look. Look what's happened now."

They stood in the doorway of the showroom. Sitting on a sofa, sprawled easily over the arm of it, was the doll.

"She's got out," said Sybil. "*She's got out of that room!* She wants this room as well."

Alicia Coombe sat down by the door. "In the end," she said, "I suppose she'll want the whole shop."

"She might," said Sybil.

"You nasty, sly, malicious brute," said Alicia, addressing the doll. "What do you want to come and pester us so? We don't want you."

It seemed to her, and to Sybil too, that the doll moved very slightly. It was as though its limbs relaxed still further. A long limp arm was lying on the arm of the sofa and the half-hidden face looked as if it were peering from under the arm. And it was a sly, malicious look.

"Horrible creature," said Alicia. "I can't bear it! I can't bear it any longer."

Suddenly, taking Sybil completely by surprise, she dashed across the room, picked up the doll, ran to the window, opened it, and flung the doll out into the street. There was a gasp and a half cry of fear from Sybil.

"Oh, Alicia, you shouldn't have done that! I'm sure you shouldn't have done that!"

"I had to do something," said Alicia Coombe. "I just couldn't stand it any more."

Sybil joined her at the window. Down below on the pavement the doll lay, loose-limbed, face down.

"You've *killed* her," said Sybil.

"Don't be absurd . . . How can I kill something that's made of velvet and silk, bits and pieces. It's not real."

"It's horribly real," said Sybil.

Alicia caught her breath.

"Good heavens. That child—"

A small ragged girl was standing over the doll on the pavement. She looked up and down the street—a street that was not unduly crowded at this time of the morning though there was some automobile traffic; then, as though satisfied, the child bent, picked up the doll, and ran across the street.

"Stop, stop!" called Alicia.

She turned to Sybil.

"That child mustn't take the doll. She *mustn't!* That doll is dangerous—it's evil. We've got to stop her."

It was not they who stopped her. It was the traffic. At that moment three taxis came down one way and two tradesmen's vans in the other direction. The child was marooned on an island in the middle of the road. Sybil rushed down the stairs, Alicia Coombe following her. Dodging between a tradesman's van and a private car, Sybil, with Alicia Coombe directly behind her, arrived on the island before the child could get through the traffic on the opposite side.

"You can't take that doll," said Alicia Coombe. "Give her back to me."

The child looked at her. She was a skinny little girl about eight years old, with a slight squint. Her face was defiant.

"Why should I give 'er to you?" she said. "Pitched her out of the window, you did—I saw you. If you pushed her out of the window you don't want her, so now she's mine."

"I'll buy you another doll," said Alicia frantically. "We'll go to a toy shop—anywhere you like—and I'll buy you the best doll we can find. But give me back this one."

"Shan't," said the child.

Her arms went protectingly round the velvet doll.

"You *must* give her back," said Sybil. "She isn't yours."

She stretched out to take the doll from the child and at that moment the child stamped her foot, turned, and screamed at them.

"Shan't! Shan't! Shan't! She's my very own. I love her. *You* don't love her. You hate her. If you didn't hate her you wouldn't of pushed her out of the window. I love her, I tell you, and that's what she wants. She *wants* to be loved."

And then like an eel, sliding through the vehicles, the child ran across the street, down an alleyway, and out of sight before the two older women could decide to dodge the cars and follow.

"She's gone," said Alicia.

"She said the doll wanted to be loved," said Sybil.

"Perhaps," said Alicia, "perhaps that's what she wanted all along . . . to be loved . . ."

In the middle of the London traffic the two frightened women stared at each other.

THE LAST SÉANCE

Raoul Daubreuil crossed the Seine humming a little tune to himself. He was a good-looking young Frenchman of about thirty-two, with a fresh-colored face and a little black mustache. By profession he was an engineer. In due course he reached the Cardonet and turned in at the door of No. 17. The concierge looked out from her lair and gave him a grudging "Good-morning," to which he replied cheerfully. Then he mounted the stairs to the apartment on the third floor. As he stood there waiting for his ring at the bell to be answered he hummed once more his little tune. Raoul Daubreuil was feeling particularly cheerful this morning. The door was opened by an elderly Frenchwoman, whose wrinkled face broke into smiles when she saw who the visitor was.

"Good-morning, monsieur."

"Good-morning, Elise," said Raoul.

He passed into the vestibule, pulling off his gloves as he did so.

"Madame expects me, does she not?" he asked over his shoulder.

"Ah, yes, indeed, monsieur."

Elise shut the front door and turned toward him.

"If Monsieur will pass into the little salon, Madame will be with him in a few minutes. At the moment she reposes herself."

Raoul looked up sharply. "Is she not well?"

"Well!"

Elise gave a snort. She passed in front of Raoul and opened the door of the little salon for him. He went in and she followed him.

"Well!" she continued. "How should she be well, poor lamb? Séances, séances, and always séances! It is not right—not natural, not what the good God intended for us. For me, I say straight out, it is trafficking with the devil."

Raoul patted her on the shoulder reassuringly.

"There, there, Elise," he said soothingly, "do not excite yourself, and do not be too ready to see the devil in everything you do not understand."

Elise shook her head doubtingly.

"Ah, well," she grumbled under her breath, "Monsieur may say what he pleases, I don't like it. Look at Madame, every day she gets whiter and thinner, and the headaches!"

She held up her hands. "Ah, no, it is not good, all this spirit business. Spirits indeed! All the good spirits are in paradise, and the others are in purgatory."

"Your view of the life after death is refreshingly simple, Elise," said Raoul as he dropped into a chair.

The old woman drew herself up. "I am a good Catholic, monsieur."

She crossed herself, went toward the door, then paused, her hand on the handle.

"Afterward when you are married, monsieur," she said pleadingly, "it will not continue—all this?"

Raoul smiled at her affectionately.

"You are a good faithful creature, Elise," he said, "and devoted to your mistress. Have no fear, once she is my wife, all this 'spirit business' as you call it, will cease. For Madame Daubreuil there will be no more séances."

Elise's face broke into smiles.

"Is it true what you say?" she asked eagerly.

The other nodded gravely.

"Yes," he said, speaking almost more to himself than to her. "Yes, all this must end. Simone has a wonderful gift and she has used it freely, but now she has done her part. As you have justly observed, Elise, day by day she gets whiter and thinner. The life of a medium is a particularly trying and arduous one, involving a terrible nervous strain. All the same, Elise, your mistress is the most wonderful medium in Paris—more, in France. People from all over the world come to her because they know that with her there is no trickery, no deceit."

Elise gave a snort of contempt.

"Deceit! Ah, no, indeed. Madame could not deceive a new-born babe if she tried."

"She is an angel," said the young Frenchman with fervor. "And I—I shall do everything a man can to make her happy. You believe that?"

Elise drew herself up, and spoke with a certain simple dignity.

"I have served Madame for many years, monsieur. With all respect I may say that I love her. If I did not believe that you adored her as she deserves to be adored—*eh bien,* monsieur! I should be willing to tear you limb from limb."

Raoul laughed. "Bravo, Elise! You are a faithful friend, and you must approve of me now that I have told you Madame is going to give up the spirits."

He expected the old woman to receive this pleasantry with a laugh, but somewhat to his surprise she remained grave.

"Supposing, monsieur," she said hesitatingly, "the spirits will not give her up?"

Raoul stared at her. "Eh! What do you mean?"

"I said," repeated Elise, "supposing the spirits will not give her up?"

"I thought you didn't believe in the spirits, Elise?"

"No more I do," said Elise stubbornly. "It is foolish to believe in them. All the same . . ."

"Well?"

"It is difficult for me to explain, monsieur. You see, me, I always thought that these mediums, as they call themselves, were just clever cheats who imposed on the poor souls who had lost their dear ones.

But Madame is not like that. Madame is good. Madame is honest, and . . ."

She lowered her voice and spoke in a tone of awe.

"Things happen. It is not trickery, things happen, and that is why I am afraid. For I am sure of this, monsieur, it is not right. It is against nature and *le bon Dieu,* and somebody will have to pay."

Raoul got up from his chair and came and patted her on the shoulder.

"Calm yourself, my good Elise," he said, smiling. "See, I will give you some good news. Today is the last of these séances; after today there will be no more."

"There is one today, then?" asked the old woman suspiciously.

"The last, Elise, the last."

Elise shook her head disconsolately. "Madame is not fit . . . ," she began.

But her words were interrupted, the door opened and a tall, fair woman came in. She was slender and graceful, with the face of a Botticelli Madonna. Raoul's face lighted up, and Elise withdrew quickly and discreetly.

"Simone!"

He took both her long, white hands in his and kissed each in turn. She murmured his name very softly.

"Raoul, my dear one."

Again he kissed her hands and then looked intently into her face.

"Simone, how pale you are! Elise told me you were resting; you are not ill, my well-beloved?"

"No, not ill . . ." She hesitated.

He led her over to the sofa and sat down on it beside her.

"But tell me then."

The medium smiled faintly. "You will think me foolish," she murmured.

"I? Think you foolish? Never."

Simone withdrew her hand from his grasp. She sat perfectly still for a moment or two gazing down at the carpet. Then she spoke in a low, hurried voice.

"I am afraid, Raoul."

He waited for a minute or two expecting her to go on, but as she did not he said encouragingly:

"Yes, afraid of what?"

"Just afraid . . . that is all."

"But . . ."

He looked at her in perplexity, and she answered the look quickly.

"Yes, it is absurd, isn't it, and yet I feel just that. Afraid, nothing more. I don't know what of, or why, but all the time I am possessed with the idea that something terrible—terrible, is going to happen to me. . . ."

She stared out in front of her. Raoul put an arm gently round her.

"My dearest," he said, "come, you must not give way. I know what it is, the strain, Simone, the strain of a medium's life. All you need is rest—rest and quiet."

She looked at him gratefully. "Yes, Raoul, you are right. That is what I need, rest and quiet."

She closed her eyes and leaned back a little against his arm.

"And happiness," murmured Raoul in her ear.

His arm drew her closer. Simone, her eyes still closed, drew a deep breath.

"Yes," she murmured, "yes. When your arms are round me I feel safe. I forget my life—the terrible life—of a medium. You know much, Raoul, but even you do not know all it means."

He felt her body grow rigid in his embrace. Her eyes opened again, staring in front of her.

"One sits in the cabinet in the darkness, waiting, and the darkness is terrible, Raoul, for it is the darkness of emptiness, of nothingness. Deliberately one gives oneself up to be lost in it. After that one knows nothing, one feels nothing, but at last there comes the slow, painful return, the awakening out of sleep, but so tired—so terribly tired."

"I know," murmured Raoul, "I know."

"So tired," murmured Simone again. Her whole body seemed to droop as she repeated the words.

"But you are wonderful, Simone."

He took her hands in his, trying to rouse her to share his enthusiasm.

"You are unique—the greatest medium the world has ever known."

She shook her head, smiling a little at that.

"Yes, yes," Raoul insisted.

He drew two letters from his pocket.

"See here, from Professor Roche of the Salpetriere, and this one from Dr. Genir at Nancy, both imploring that you will continue to sit for them occasionally."

"Ah, no!"

Simone sprang suddenly to her feet.

"I will not, I will not. It is to be all finished—all done with. You promised me, Raoul."

Raoul stared at her in astonishment as she stood wavering, facing him almost like a creature at bay. He got up and took her hand.

"Yes, yes," he said. "Certainly it is finished, that is understood. But I am so proud of you, Simone, that is why I mentioned those letters."

She threw him a swift sideways glance of suspicion.

"It is not that you will ever want me to sit again?"

"No, no," said Raoul, "unless perhaps you yourself would care to, just occasionally for these old friends . . ."

But she interrupted him, speaking excitedly. "No, no, never again. There is danger. I tell you I can feel it, great danger."

She clasped her hands on her forehead a minute, then walked across to the window.

"Promise me never again," she said in a quieter voice over her shoulder.

Raoul followed her and put his arms round her shoulders.

"My dear one," he said tenderly, "I promise you after today you shall never sit again."

He felt the sudden start she gave.

"Today," she murmured. "Ah, yes—I had forgotten Madame Exe."

Raoul looked at his watch. "She is due any minute now; but perhaps, Simone, if you do not feel well . . ."

Simone hardly seemed to be listening to him; she was following out her own train of thought.

"She is—a strange woman, Raoul, a very strange woman. Do you know—I have almost a horror of her."

"Simone!"

There was reproach in his voice, and she was quick to feel it.

"Yes, yes, I know, you are like all Frenchmen, Raoul. To you a mother is sacred and it is unkind of me to feel like that about her when she grieves so for her lost child. But—I cannot explain it, she is so big and black, and her hands—have you ever noticed her hands, Raoul? Great big strong hands, as strong as a man's. Ah!"

She gave a little shiver and closed her eyes. Raoul withdrew his arm and spoke almost coldly.

"I really cannot understand you, Simone. Surely you, a woman, should have nothing but sympathy for another woman, a mother bereft of her only child."

Simone made a gesture of impatience. "Ah, it is you who do not understand, my friend! One cannot help these things. The first moment I saw her I felt . . ."

She flung her hand out. "Fear! You remember, it was a long time before I would consent to sit for her? I felt sure in some way she would bring me misfortune."

Raoul shrugged his shoulders. "Whereas, in actual fact, she brought you the exact opposite," he said dryly. "All the sittings have been attended with marked success. The spirit of the little Amelie was able to control you at once, and the materializations have really been striking. Professor Roche ought really to have been present at the last one."

"Materializations," said Simone in a low voice. "Tell me, Raoul (you know that I know nothing of what takes place while I am in the trance), are the materializations really so wonderful?"

He nodded enthusiastically. "At the first few sittings the figure of the child was visible in a kind of nebulous haze," he explained, "but at the last séance . . ."

"Yes?"

He spoke very softly. "Simone, the child that stood there was an actual living child of flesh and blood. I even touched her—but seeing that the touch was acutely painful to you, I would not permit Madame Exe to do the same. I was afraid that her self-control might break down, and that some harm to you might result."

Simone turned away again toward the window.

"I was terribly exhausted when I woke," she murmured. "Raoul, are you sure—are you really sure that all this is right? You know what dear old Elise thinks, that I am trafficking with the devil?" She laughed rather uncertainly.

"You know what I believe," said Raoul gravely. "In the handling of the unknown there must always be danger, but the cause is a noble one, for it is the cause of Science. All over the world there have been martyrs to Science, pioneers who have paid the price so that others may follow safely in their footsteps. For ten years now you have worked for Science at the cost of a terrific nervous strain. Now your part is done, from today onward you are free to be happy."

She smiled at him affectionately, her calm restored. Then she glanced quickly up at the clock.

"Madame Exe is late," she murmured. "She may not come."

"I think she will," said Raoul. "Your clock is a little fast, Simone."

Simone moved about the room, rearranging an ornament here and there.

"I wonder who she is, this Madame Exe?" she observed. "Where she comes from, who her people are? It is strange that we know nothing about her."

Raoul shrugged his shoulders. "Most people remain incognito if possible when they come to a medium," he observed. "It is an elementary precaution."

"I suppose so," agreed Simone listlessly.

A little china vase she was holding slipped from her fingers and broke to pieces on the tiles of the fireplace. She turned sharply on Raoul.

"You see," she murmured, "I am not myself. Raoul, would you think me very—very cowardly if I told Madame Exe I could not sit today?"

His look of pained astonishment made her redden.

"You promised, Simone . . . ," he began gently.

She backed against the wall. "I won't do it, Raoul. I won't do it."

And again that glance of his, tenderly reproachful, made her wince.

"It is not of the money I am thinking, Simone, though you must realize that the money this woman has offered you for a last sitting is enormous—simply enormous."

She interrupted him defiantly. "There are things that matter more than money."

"Certainly there are," he agreed warmly. "That is just what I am saying. Consider—this woman is a mother, a mother who has lost her only child. If you are not really ill, if it is only a whim on your part—you can deny a rich woman a caprice, but can you deny a mother one last sight of her child?"

The medium flung her hands out despairingly in front of her.

"Oh, you torture me," she murmured. "All the same you are right. I will do as you wish, but I know now what I am afraid of—it is the word 'mother.' "

"Simone!"

"There are certain primitive elementary forces, Raoul. Most of them have been destroyed by civilization, but motherhood stands where it stood at the beginning. Animals—human beings, they are all the same. A mother's love for her child is like nothing else in the world. It knows no law, no pity, it dares all things and crushes down remorselessly all that stands in its path."

She stopped, panting a little, then turned to him with a quick, disarming smile.

"I am foolish today, Raoul. I know it."

He took her hand in his. "Lie down for a minute or two," he urged. "Rest till she comes."

"Very well." She smiled at him and left the room. Raoul remained for a minute or two lost in thought, then he strode to the door, opened it, and crossed the little hall. He went into a room the other side of it, a sitting-room very much like the one he had left, but at one end was an alcove with a big armchair set in it. Heavy black velvet curtains were arranged so as to pull across the alcove. Elise was busy arranging the room. Close to the alcove she had set two chairs and a small round table. On the table was a tambourine, a horn, and some paper and pencils.

"The last time," murmured Elise with grim satisfaction. "Ah, monsieur, I wish it were over and done with."

The sharp ting of an electric bell sounded.

"There she is, that great *gendarme* of a woman," continued the old servant. "Why can't she go and pray decently for her little one's soul in a church, and burn a candle to Our Blessed Lady? Does not the good God know what is best for us?"

"Answer the bell, Elise," said Raoul peremptorily.

She threw him a look, but obeyed. In a minute or two she returned ushering in the visitor.

"I will tell my mistress you are here, madame."

Raoul came forward to shake hands with Madame Exe. Simone's words floated back to his memory.

"So big and so black."

She was a big woman, and the heavy black of French mourning seemed almost exaggerated in her case. Her voice when she spoke was very deep.

"I fear I am a little late, monsieur."

"A few minutes only," said Raoul, smiling. "Madame Simone is lying down. I am sorry to say she is far from well, very nervous and overwrought."

Her hand, which she was just withdrawing, closed on his suddenly like a vise.

"But she will sit?" she demanded sharply.

"Oh, yes, madame."

Madame Exe gave a sigh of relief, and sank into a chair, loosening one of the heavy black veils that floated round her.

"Ah, monsieur!" she murmured, "you cannot imagine, you cannot conceive the wonder and the joy of these séances to me! My little one! My Amelie! To see her, to hear her, even—perhaps—yes, perhaps to be even able to—stretch out my hand and touch her."

Raoul spoke quickly and peremptorily. "Madame Exe—how can

I explain?—on no account must you do anything except under my express directions, otherwise there is the gravest danger."

"Danger to me?"

"No, madame," said Raoul, "to the medium. You must understand that the phenomena that occur are explained by Science in a certain way. I will put the matter very simply, using no technical terms. A spirit, to manifest itself, has to use the actual physical substance of the medium. You have seen the vapor of fluid issuing from the lips of the medium. This finally condenses and is built up into the physical semblance of the spirit's dead body. But this ectoplasm we believe to be the actual substance of the medium. We hope to prove this some day by careful weighing and testing—but the great difficulty is the danger and pain which attends the medium on any handling of the phenomena. Were anyone to seize hold of the materialization roughly, the death of the medium might result."

Madame Exe had listened to him with close attention.

"That is very interesting, monsieur. Tell me, shall not a time come when the materialization shall advance so far that it shall be capable of detachment from its parent, the medium?"

"That is a fantastic speculation, madame."

She persisted. "But, on the facts, not impossible?"

"Quite impossible today."

"But perhaps in the future?"

He was saved from answering, for at that moment Simone entered. She looked languid and pale, but had evidently regained entire control of herself. She came forward and shook hands with Madame Exe, though Raoul noticed the faint shiver that passed through her as she did so.

"I regret, madame, to hear that you are indisposed," said Madame Exe.

"It is nothing," said Simone rather brusquely. "Shall we begin?"

She went to the alcove and sat down in the armchair. Suddenly Raoul in his turn felt a wave of fear pass over him.

"You are not strong enough," he exclaimed. "We had better cancel the séance. Madame Exe will understand."

"Monsieur!"

Madame Exe rose indignantly.

"Yes, yes, it is better not, I am sure of it."

"Madame Simone promised me one last sitting."

"That is so," agreed Simone quietly, "and I am prepared to carry out my promise."

"I hold you to it, madame," said the other woman.

"I do not break my word," said Simone coldly. "Do not fear, Raoul," she added gently, "after all, it is for the last time—the last time, thank God."

At a sign from her Raoul drew the heavy black curtains across the alcove. He also pulled the curtains of the window so that the room was in semi-obscurity. He indicated one of the chairs to Madame Exe and prepared himself to take the other. Madame Exe, however, hesitated.

"You will pardon me, monsieur, but—you understand I believe absolutely in your integrity and in that of Madame Simone. All the same, so that my testimony may be the more valuable, I took the liberty of bringing this with me."

From her handbag she drew a length of fine cord.

"Madame!" cried Raoul. "This is an insult!"

"A precaution."

"I repeat, it is an insult."

"I don't understand your objection, monsieur," said Madame Exe coldly. "If there is no trickery you have nothing to fear."

Raoul laughed scornfully. "I can assure you that I have nothing to fear, madame. Bind me hand and foot if you will."

His speech did not produce the effect he hoped, for Madame Exe merely murmured unemotionally:

"Thank you, monsieur," and advanced upon him with her roll of cord.

Suddenly Simone from behind the curtain gave a cry.

"No, no, Raoul, don't let her do it."

Madame Exe laughed derisively. "Madame is afraid," she observed sarcastically.

"Yes, I am afraid."

"Remember what you are saying, Simone," cried Raoul. "Madame Exe is apparently under the impression that we are charlatans."

"I must make sure," said Madame Exe grimly.

She went methodically about her task, binding Raoul securely to his chair.

"I must congratulate you on your knots, madame," he observed ironically when she had finished. "Are you satisfied now?"

Madame Exe did not reply. She walked round the room examining the paneling of the walls closely. Then she locked the door leading into the hall, and, removing the key, returned to her chair.

"Now," she said in an indescribable voice. "I am ready."

The minutes passed. From behind the curtain the sound of Simone's breathing became heavier and more stertorous. Then it died away altogether, to be succeeded by a series of moans. Then again there was silence for a little while, broken by the sudden clattering of the tambourine. The horn was caught up from the table and dashed to the ground. Ironic laughter was heard. The curtains of the alcove seemed to have been pulled back a little, the medium's figure was just visible through the opening, her head fallen forward on her breast. Suddenly Madame Exe drew in her breath sharply. A ribbon-like stream of mist was issuing from the medium's mouth. It condensed and began gradually to assume a shape, the shape of a little child.

"Amelie! My little Amelie!"

The hoarse whisper came from Madame Exe. The hazy figure condensed still further. Raoul stared almost incredulously. Never had there been a more successful materialization. Now, surely it was a real child, a real flesh and blood child standing there.

"Maman!" The soft childish voice spoke.

"My child!" cried Madame Exe. "My child!" She half-rose from her seat.

"Be careful, madame," cried Raoul warningly.

The materialization came hesitatingly through the curtains. It was a child. She stood there, her arms held out.

"Maman!"

"Ah!" cried Madame Exe. Again she half-rose from her seat.

"Madame," cried Raoul, alarmed, "the medium . . ."

"I must touch her," cried Madame Exe hoarsely.

She moved a step forward.

"For God's sake, madame, control yourself," cried Raoul.

He was really alarmed now.

"Sit down at once."

"My little one, I must touch her."

"Madame, I command you, sit down!"

He was writhing desperately with his bonds, but Madame Exe had done her work well; he was helpless. A terrible sense of impending disaster swept over him.

"In the name of God, madame, sit down!" he shouted. "Remember the medium."

Madame Exe paid no attention to him. She was like a woman transformed. Ecstasy and delight showed plainly in her face. Her outstretched hand touched the little figure that stood in the opening of the curtains. A terrible moan came from the medium.

"My God!" cried Raoul. "My God! This is terrible. The medium . . ."

Madame Exe turned on him with a harsh laugh.

"What do I care for your medium?" she cried. "I want my child."

"You are mad!"

"My child, I tell you. Mine! My own flesh and blood! My little one come back to me from the dead, alive and breathing."

Raoul opened his lips, but no words would come. She was terrible, this woman! Remorseless, savage, absorbed by her own passion. The baby lips parted, and for the third time the same word echoed:

"Maman!"

"Come then, my little one," cried Madame Exe.

With a sharp gesture she caught up the child in her arms. From behind the curtains came a long-drawn scream of utter anguish.

"Simone!" cried Raoul. "Simone!"

He was aware vaguely of Madame Exe rushing past him, of the unlocking of the door, of retreating footsteps down the stairs.

From behind the curtain there still sounded the terrible, high, long-drawn scream, such a scream, as Raoul had never heard. It died away in a horrible kind of gurgle. Then there came the thud of a body falling. . . .

Raoul was working like a maniac to free himself from his bonds. In his frenzy he accomplished the impossible, snapping the rope by sheer strength. As he struggled to his feet, Elise rushed in, crying, "Madame!"

"Simone!" cried Raoul.

Together they rushed forward and pulled the curtain. Raoul staggered back.

"My God!" he murmured. "Red—all red. . . ."

Elise's voice came beside him harsh and shaking.

"So Madame is dead. It is ended. But tell me, monsieur, what has happened. Why is Madame all shrunken away—why is she half her usual size? What has been happening here?"

"I do not know," said Raoul.

His voice rose to a scream.

"I do not know. I do not know. But I think—I am going mad. . . . Simone! Simone!"

THE WITNESS FOR THE PROSECUTION

Mr. Mayherne adjusted his pince-nez and cleared his throat with a little dry-as-dust cough that was wholly typical of him. Then he looked again at the man opposite him, the man charged with willful murder.

Mr. Mayherne was a small man, precise in manner, neatly, not to say foppishly dressed, with a pair of very shrewd and piercing gray eyes. By no means a fool. Indeed, as a solicitor, Mr. Mayherne's reputation stood very high. His voice, when he spoke to his client, was dry but not unsympathetic.

"I must impress upon you again that you are in very grave danger, and that the utmost frankness is necessary."

Leonard Vole, who had been staring in a dazed fashion at the blank wall in front of him, transferred his glance to the solicitor.

"I know," he said hopelessly. "You keep telling me so. But I can't seem to realize yet that I'm charged with murder—*murder.* And such a dastardly crime too."

Mr. Mayherne was practical, not emotional. He coughed again, took off his pince-nez, polished them carefully, and replaced them on his nose. Then he said:

"Yes, yes, yes. Now, my dear Mr. Vole, we're going to make a determined effort to get you off—and we shall succeed—we shall succeed. But I must have all the facts. I must know just how damaging the case against you is likely to be. Then we can fix upon the best line of defense."

Still the young man looked at him in the same dazed, hopeless fashion. To Mr. Mayherne the case had seemed black enough, and the guilt of the prisoner assured. Now, for the first time, he felt a doubt.

"You think I'm guilty," said Leonard Vole, in a low voice. "But, by God, I swear I'm not! It looks pretty black against me, I know that. I'm like a man caught in a net—the meshes of it all round me, entangling me whichever way I turn. But I didn't do it, Mr. Mayherne, I didn't do it!"

In such a position a man was bound to protest his innocence. Mr. Mayherne knew that. Yet, in spite of himself, he was impressed. It might be, after all, that Leonard Vole was innocent.

"You are right, Mr. Vole," he said gravely. "The case does look very black against you. Nevertheless, I accept your assurance. Now, let us get to facts. I want you to tell me in your own words exactly how you came to make the acquaintance of Miss Emily French."

"It was one day in Oxford Street. I saw an elderly lady crossing the road. She was carrying a lot of parcels. In the middle of the street she dropped them, tried to recover them, found a bus was almost on top of her and just managed to reach the curb safely, dazed and bewildered by people having shouted at her. I recovered her parcels, wiped the mud off them as best I could, retied the string of one, and returned them to her."

"There was no question of your having saved her life?"

"Oh, dear me, no! All I did was to perform a common act of courtesy. She was extremely grateful, thanked me warmly, and said something about my manners not being those of most of the younger generation—I can't remember the exact words. Then I lifted my hat and went on. I never expected to see her again. But life is full of coincidences. That very evening I came across her at a party at a friend's house. She recognized me at once and asked that I should be introduced to her. I then found out that she was a Miss Emily French and that she lived at Cricklewood. I talked to her for some time. She was, I imagine, an old lady who took sudden and violent fancies to people. She took one to me on the strength of a perfectly simple action which anyone might have performed. On leaving, she shook me warmly by the hand, and asked me to come and see her. I replied, of course, that I should be very pleased to do so, and she then urged me to name a day. I did not want particularly to go, but it would have seemed churlish to refuse, so I fixed on the following Saturday. After she had gone, I learned something about her from my friends. That she was rich, eccentric, lived alone with one maid, and owned no less than eight cats."

"I see," said Mr. Mayherne. "The question of her being well off came up as early as that?"

"If you mean that I inquired—," began Leonard Vole hotly, but Mr. Mayherne stilled him with a gesture.

"I have to look at the case as it will be presented by the other side. An ordinary observer would not have supposed Miss French to be a lady of means. She lived poorly, almost humbly. Unless you had been told the contrary, you would in all probability have considered her to be in poor circumstances—at any rate to begin with. Who was it exactly who told you that she was well off?"

"My friend, George Harvey, at whose house the party took place."

"Is he likely to remember having done so?"

"I really don't know. Of course it is some time ago now."

"Quite so, Mr. Vole. You see, the first aim of the prosecution will be to establish that you were in low water financially—that is true, is it not?"

Leonard Vole flushed.

"Yes," he said, in a low voice. "I'd been having a run of infernal bad luck just then."

"Quite so," said Mr. Mayherne again. "That being, as I say, in low water financially, you met this rich old lady and cultivated her acquaintance assiduously. Now if we are in a position to say that you had no idea she was well off, and that you visited her out of pure kindness of heart—"

"Which is the case."

"I dare say. I am not disputing the point. I am looking at it from the outside point of view. A great deal depends on the memory of Mr. Harvey. Is he likely to remember that conversation or is he not? Could he be confused by counsel into believing that it took place later?"

Leonard Vole reflected for some minutes. Then he said steadily enough, but with a rather paler face:

"I do not think that that line would be successful, Mr. Mayherne. Several of those present heard his remark, and one or two of them chaffed me about my conquest of a rich old lady."

The solicitor endeavored to hide his disappointment with a wave of the hand.

"Unfortunate," he said. "But I congratulate you upon your plain speaking, Mr. Vole. It is to you I look to guide me. Your judgment is quite right. To persist in the line I spoke of would have been disastrous. We must leave that point. You made the acquaintance of Miss French, you called upon her, the acquaintanceship progressed. We want a clear reason for all this. Why did you, a young man of thirty-three, good-looking, fond of sport, popular with your friends, devote so much of your time to an elderly woman with whom you could hardly have anything in common?"

Leonard Vole flung out his hands in a nervous gesture.

"I can't tell you—I really can't tell you. After the first visit, she pressed me to come again, spoke of being lonely and unhappy. She made it difficult for me to refuse. She showed so plainly her fondness and affection for me that I was placed in an awkward position. You see, Mr. Mayherne, I've got a weak nature—I drift—I'm one of those people who can't say 'No.' And believe me or not, as you like, after the third or fourth visit I paid her I found myself getting genuinely fond of the old thing. My mother died when I was young, an aunt brought me up, and she too died before I was fifteen. If I told you that I genuinely enjoyed being mothered and pampered, I dare say you'd only laugh."

Mr. Mayherne did not laugh. Instead he took off his pince-nez again and polished them, a sign with him that he was thinking deeply.

"I accept your explanation, Mr. Vole," he said at last. "I believe it to be psychologically probable. Whether a jury would take that view of it is another matter. Please continue your narrative. When was it that Miss French first asked you to look into her business affairs?"

"After my third or fourth visit to her. She understood very little of money matters, and was worried about some investments."

Mr. Mayherne looked up sharply.

"Be careful, Mr. Vole. The maid, Janet Mackenzie, declares that her mistress was a good woman of business and transacted all her own affairs, and this is borne out by the testimony of her bankers."

"I can't help that," said Vole earnestly. "That's what she said to me."

Mr. Mayherne looked at him for a moment or two in silence. Though he had no intention of saying so, his belief in Leonard Vole's innocence was at that moment strengthened. He knew something of the mentality of elderly ladies. He saw Miss French, infatuated with the good-looking young man, hunting about for pretexts that would bring him to the house. What more likely than that she should plead ignorance of business, and beg him to help her with her money affairs? She was enough of a woman of the world to realize that any man is slightly flattered by such an admission of his superiority. Leonard Vole had been flattered. Perhaps, too, she had not been averse to letting this young man know that she was wealthy. Emily French had been a strong-willed old woman, willing to pay her price for what she wanted. All this passed rapidly through Mr. Mayherne's mind, but he gave no indication of it, and asked instead a further question.

"And you did handle her affairs for her at request?"

"I did."

"Mr. Vole," said the solicitor, "I am going to ask you a very serious question, and one to which it is vital I should have a truthful answer. You were in low water financially. You had the handling of an old lady's affairs—an old lady who, according to her own statement, knew little or nothing of business. Did you at any time, or in any manner, convert to your own use the securities which you handled? Did you engage in any transaction for your own pecuniary advantage which will not bear the light of day?" He quelled the other's response. "Wait a minute before you answer. There are two courses open to us. Either we can make a feature of your probity and honesty in conducting her affairs while pointing out how unlikely it is that you would commit murder to obtain money which you might have obtained by such infinitely easier means. If, on the other hand, there is anything in your dealings which the prosecution will get hold of—if, to put it baldly, it can be proved that you swindled the old lady in any way, we must take the line that you had no motive for the murder, since she was already a profitable source of income to you. You perceive the distinction. Now, I beg of you, take your time before you reply."

But Leonard Vole took no time at all.

"My dealings with Miss French's affairs were all perfectly fair and above board. I acted for her interests to the very best of my ability, as any one will find who looks into the matter."

"Thank you," said Mr. Mayherne. "You relieve my mind very much. I pay you the compliment of believing that you are far too clever to lie to me over such an important matter."

"Surely," said Vole eagerly, "the strongest point in my favor is the lack of motive. Granted that I cultivated the acquaintanceship of a rich old lady in the hopes of getting money out of her—that, I gather, is the substance of what you have been saying—surely her death frustrates all my hopes?"

The solicitor looked at him steadily. Then, very deliberately, he repeated his unconscious trick with his pince-nez. It was not until they were firmly replaced on his nose that he spoke.

"Are you not aware, Mr. Vole, that Miss French left a will under which you are the principal beneficiary?"

"What?" The prisoner sprang to his feet. His dismay was obvious and unforced. "My God! What are you saying? She left her money to me?"

Mr. Mayherne nodded slowly. Vole sank down again, his head in his hands.

"You pretend you know nothing of this will?"

"Pretend? There's no pretense about it. I knew nothing about it."

"What would you say if I told you that the maid, Janet Mackenzie, swears that you *did* know? That her mistress told her distinctly that she had consulted you in the matter, and told you of her intentions?"

"Say? That she's lying! No, I go too fast. Janet is an elderly woman. She was a faithful watchdog to her mistress, and she didn't like me. She was jealous and suspicious. I should say that Miss French confided her intentions to Janet, and that Janet either mistook something she said, or else was convinced in her own mind that I had persuaded the old lady into doing it. I dare say that she herself believes now that Miss French actually told her so."

"You don't think she dislikes you enough to lie deliberately about the matter?"

Leonard Vole looked shocked and startled.

"No, indeed! Why should she?"

"I don't know," said Mr. Mayherne thoughtfully. "But she's very bitter against you."

The wretched young man groaned again.

"I'm beginning to see," he muttered. "It's frightful. I made up to her, that's what they'll say, I got her to make a will leaving her money to me, and then I go there that night, and there's nobody in the house—they find her the next day—oh! my God, it's awful!"

"You are wrong about there being nobody in the house," said Mr. Mayherne. "Janet, as you remember, was to go out for the evening. She went, but about half-past nine she returned to fetch the pattern of a blouse sleeve which she had promised to a friend. She let herself in by the back door, went upstairs and fetched it, and went out again. She heard voices in the sitting-room, though she could not distinguish what they said, but she will swear that one of them was Miss French's and one was a man's."

"At half-past nine," said Leonard Vole. "At half-past nine. . . ." He sprang to his feet. "But then I'm saved—saved—"

"What do you mean, saved?" cried Mr. Mayherne, astonished.

"By half-past nine I was at home again! My wife can prove that. I left Miss French about five minutes to nine. I arrived home about twenty past nine. My wife was there waiting for me. Oh, thank God—thank God! And bless Janet Mackenzie's sleeve pattern."

In his exuberance, he hardly noticed that the grave expression on the solicitor's face had not altered. But the latter's words brought him down to earth with a bump.

"Who, then, in your opinion, murdered Miss French?"

"Why, a burglar, of course, as was thought at first. The window was forced, you remember. She was killed with a heavy blow from a crowbar, and the crowbar was found lying on the floor beside the body. And several articles were missing. But for Janet's absurd suspicions and dislike of me, the police would never have swerved from the right track."

"That will hardly do, Mr. Vole," said the solicitor. "The things that were missing were mere trifles of no value, taken as a blind. And the marks on the window were not at all conclusive. Besides, think for yourself. You say you were no longer in the house by half-past nine. Who, then, was the man Janet heard talking to Miss French in the sitting-room? She would hardly be having an amicable conversation with a burglar?"

"No," said Vole. "No—" He looked puzzled and discouraged. "But, anyway," he added with reviving spirit, "it lets me out. I've got an alibi. You must see Romaine—my wife—at once."

"Certainly," acquiesced the lawyer. "I should already have seen Mrs. Vole but for her being absent when you were arrested. I wired to Scotland at once, and I understand that she arrives back tonight. I am going to call upon her immediately I leave here."

Vole nodded, a great expression of satisfaction settling down over his face.

"Yes, Romaine will tell you. My God! it's a lucky chance that."

"Excuse me, Mr. Vole, but you are very fond of your wife?"

"Of course."

"And she of you?"

"Romaine is devoted to me. She'd do anything in the world for me."

He spoke enthusiastically, but the solicitor's heart sank a little lower. The testimony of a devoted wife—would it gain credence?

"Was there anyone else who saw you return at nine-twenty. A maid, for instance?"

"We have no maid."

"Did you meet anyone in the street on the way back?"

"Nobody I knew. I rode part of the way in a bus. The conductor might remember."

Mr. Mayherne shook his head doubtfully.

"There is no one, then, who can confirm your wife's testimony?"

"No. But it isn't necessary, surely?"

"I dare say not. I dare say not," said Mr. Mayherne hastily. "Now there's just one thing more. Did Miss French know that you were a married man?"

"Oh, yes."

"Yet you never took your wife to see her. Why was that?"

For the first time, Leonard Vole's answer came halting and uncertain.

"Well—I don't know."

"Are you aware that Janet Mackenzie says her mistress believed you to be single, and contemplated marrying you in the future?"

Vole laughed.

"Absurd! There was forty years' difference in age between us."

"It has been done," said the solicitor dryly. "The fact remains. Your wife never met Miss French?"

"No—" Again the constraint.

"You will permit me to say," said the lawyer, "that I hardly understand your attitude in the matter."

Vole flushed, hesitated, and then spoke.

"I'll make a clean breast of it. I was hard up, as you know. I hoped that Miss French might lend me some money. She was fond of me, but she wasn't at all interested in the struggles of a young couple. Early on, I found that she had taken it for granted that my wife and I didn't get on—were living apart. Mr. Mayherne—I wanted the money—for Romaine's sake. I said nothing, and allowed the old lady to think what she chose. She spoke of my being an adopted son to her. There was never any question of marriage—that must be just Janet's imagination."

"And that is all?"

"Yes—that is all."

Was there just a shade of hesitation in the words? The lawyer fancied so. He rose and held out his hand.

"Good-bye, Mr. Vole." He looked into the haggard young face and spoke with an unusual impulse. "I believe in your innocence in spite of the multitude of facts arrayed against you. I hope to prove it and vindicate you completely."

Vole smiled back at him.

"You'll find the alibi is all right," he said cheerfully.

Again he hardly noticed that the other did not respond.

"The whole thing hinges a good deal on the testimony of Janet Mackenzie," said Mr. Mayherne. "She hates you. That much is clear."

"She can hardly hate me," protested the young man.

The solicitor shook his head as he went out.

"Now for Mrs. Vole," he said to himself.

He was seriously disturbed by the way the thing was shaping.

The Voles lived in a small shabby house near Paddington Green. It was to this house that Mr. Mayherne went.

In answer to his ring, a big slatternly woman, obviously a charwoman, answered the door.

"Mrs. Vole? Has she returned yet?"

"Got back an hour ago. But I dunno if you can see her."

"If you will take my card to her," said Mr. Mayherne quietly, "I am quite sure that she will do so."

The woman looked at him doubtfully, wiped her hand on her apron and took the card. Then she closed the door in his face and left him on the step outside.

In a few minutes, however, she returned with a slightly altered manner.

"Come inside, please."

She ushered him into a tiny drawing-room. Mr. Mayherne, examining a drawing on the wall, started up suddenly to face a tall, pale woman who had entered so quietly that he had not heard her.

"Mr. Mayherne? You are my husband's solicitor, are you not? You have come from him? Will you please sit down?"

Until she spoke he had not realized that she was not English. Now, observing her more closely, he noticed the high cheekbones, the dense blue-black of the hair, and an occasional very slight movement of the hands that was distinctly foreign. A strange woman, very quiet. So quiet as to make one uneasy. From the very first Mr. Mayherne was conscious that he was up against something that he did not understand.

"Now, my dear Mrs. Vole," he began, "you must not give way—"

He stopped. It was so very obvious that Romaine Vole had not the slightest intention of giving way. She was perfectly calm and composed.

"Will you please tell me about it?" she said. "I must know everything. Do not think to spare me. I want to know the worst." She hesitated, then repeated in a lower tone, with a curious emphasis which the lawyer did not understand: "I want to know the worst."

Mr. Mayherne went over his interview with Leonard Vole. She listened attentively, nodding her head now and then.

"I see," she said, when he had finished. "He wants me to say that he came in at twenty minutes past nine that night?"

"He did come in at that time?" said Mr. Mayherne sharply.

"That is not the point," she said coldly. "Will my saying so acquit him? Will they believe me?"

Mr. Mayherne was taken aback. She had gone so quickly to the core of the matter.

"That is what I want to know," she said. "Will it be enough? Is there anyone else who can support my evidence?"

There was a suppressed eagerness in her manner that made him vaguely uneasy.

"So far there is no one else," he said reluctantly.

"I see," said Romaine Vole.

She sat for a minute or two perfectly still. A little smile played over her lips.

The lawyer's feeling of alarm grew stronger and stronger.

"Mrs. Vole—," he began. "I know what you must feel—"

"Do you?" she asked. "I wonder."

"In the circumstances—"

"In the circumstances—I intend to play a lone hand."

He looked at her in dismay.

"But, my dear Mrs. Vole—you are overwrought. Being so devoted to your husband—"

"I beg your pardon?"

The sharpness of her voice made him start. He repeated in a hesitating manner:

"Being so devoted to your husband—"

Romaine Vole nodded slowly, the same strange smile on her lips.

"Did he tell you that I was devoted to him?" she asked softly. "Ah! yes, I can see he did. How stupid men are! Stupid—stupid—stupid—"

She rose suddenly to her feet. All the intense emotion that the lawyer had been conscious of in the atmosphere was now concentrated in her tone.

"I hate him, I tell you! I hate him. I hate him. I hate him! I would like to see him hanged by the neck till he is dead."

The lawyer recoiled before her and the smoldering passion in her eyes.

She advanced a step nearer, and continued vehemently:

"Perhaps I shall see it. Supposing I tell you that he did not come in that night at twenty past nine, but at twenty past ten? You say that he tells you he knew nothing about the money coming to him. Supposing I tell you he knew all about it, and counted on it, and committed murder to get it? Supposing I tell you that he admitted to me that night when he came in what he had done? That there was blood on his coat? What then? Supposing that I stand up in court and say all these things?"

Her eyes seemed to challenge him. With an effort, he concealed his growing dismay, and endeavored to speak in a rational tone.

"You cannot be asked to give evidence against your husband—"

"He is not my husband!"

The words came out so quickly that he fancied he had misunderstood her.

"I beg your pardon? I—"

"He is not my husband."

The silence was so intense that you could have heard a pin drop.

"I was an actress in Vienna. My husband is alive but in a madhouse. So we could not marry. I am glad now."

She nodded defiantly.

"I should like you to tell me one thing," said Mr. Mayherne. He contrived to appear as cool and unemotional as ever. "Why are you so bitter against Leonard Vole?"

She shook her head, smiling a little.

"Yes, you would like to know. But I shall not tell you. I will keep my secret. . . ."

Mr. Mayherne gave his dry little cough and rose.

"There seems no point in prolonging this interview," he remarked. "You will hear from me again after I have communicated with my client."

She came closer to him, looking into his eyes with her own wonderful dark ones.

"Tell me," she said, "did you believe—honestly—that he was innocent when you came here today?"

"I did," said Mr. Mayherne.

"You poor little man," she laughed.

"And I believe so still," finished the lawyer. "Good evening, madam."

He went out of the room, taking with him the memory of her startled face.

"This is going to be the devil of a business," said Mr. Mayherne to himself as he strode along the street.

Extraordinary, the whole thing. An extraordinary woman. A very dangerous woman. Women were the devil when they got their knife into you.

What was to be done? That wretched young man hadn't a leg to stand upon. Of course, possibly he did commit the crime. . . .

"No," said Mr. Mayherne to himself. "No—there's almost too much evidence against him. I don't believe this woman. She was trumping up the whole story. But she'll never bring it into court."

He wished he felt more conviction on the point.

* * *

THE POLICE COURT proceedings were brief and dramatic. The principal witnesses for the prosecution were Janet Mackenzie, maid to the dead woman, and Romaine Heilger, Austrian subject, the mistress of the prisoner.

Mr. Mayherne sat in court and listened to the damning story that the latter told. It was on the lines she had indicated to him in their interview.

The prisoner reserved his defense and was committed for trial.

Mr. Mayherne was at his wits' end. The case against Leonard Vole was black beyond words. Even the famous K. C. who was engaged for the defense held out little hope.

"If we can shake that Austrian woman's testimony, we might do something," he said dubiously. "But it's a bad business."

Mr. Mayherne had concentrated his energies on one single point. Assuming Leonard Vole to be speaking the truth, and to have left the murdered woman's house at nine o'clock, who was the man Janet heard talking to Miss French at half-past nine?

The only ray of light was in the shape of a scapegrace nephew who had in bygone days cajoled and threatened his aunt out of various sums of money. Janet Mackenzie, the solicitor learned, had always been attached to this young man, and had never ceased urging his claims upon her mistress. It certainly seemed possible that it was this nephew who had been with Miss French after Leonard Vole left, especially as he was not to be found in any of his old haunts.

In all other directions, the lawyer's researches had been negative in their result. No one had seen Leonard Vole entering his own house, or leaving that of Miss French. No one had seen any other man enter or leave the house in Cricklewood. All inquiries drew blank.

It was the eve of the trial when Mr. Mayherne received the letter which was to lead his thoughts in an entirely new direction.

It came by the six o'clock post. An illiterate scrawl, written on common paper and enclosed in a dirty envelope with the stamp stuck on crooked.

Mr. Mayherne read it through once or twice before he grasped its meaning.

DEAR MISTER:

Youre the lawyer chap wot acts for the young feller. If you want that painted foreign hussy showd up for wot she is an her pack of lies you come to 16 Shaw's Rents Stepney to-night It ull cawst you 2 hundred quid Arsk for Misses Mogson.

The solicitor read and reread this strange epistle. It might, of course, be a hoax, but when he thought it over, he became increasingly convinced that it was genuine, and also convinced that it was the one hope for the prisoner. The evidence of Romaine Heilger damned him completely, and the line the defense meant to pursue, the line that the evidence of a woman who had admittedly lived an immoral life was not to be trusted, was at best a weak one.

Mr. Mayherne's mind was made up. It was his duty to save his client at all costs. He must go to Shaw's Rents.

He had some difficulty in finding the place, a ramshackle building in an evil-smelling slum, but at last he did so, and on inquiry for Mrs. Mogson was sent up to a room on the third floor. On this door he knocked, and getting no answer, knocked again.

At this second knock, he heard a shuffling sound inside, and presently the door was opened cautiously half an inch and a bent figure peered out.

Suddenly the woman, for it was a woman, gave a chuckle and opened the door wider.

"So it's you, dearie," she said, in a wheezy voice. "Nobody with you, is there? No playing tricks? That's right. You can come in—you can come in."

With some reluctance the lawyer stepped across the threshold into the small dirty room, with its flickering gas jet. There was an untidy unmade bed in a corner, a plain deal table and two rickety chairs. For the first time Mr. Mayherne had a full view of the tenant of this unsavory apartment. She was a woman of middle age, bent in figure, with a mass of untidy gray hair and a scarf wound tightly round her face. She saw him looking at this and laughed again, the same curious, toneless chuckle.

"Wondering why I hide my beauty, dear? He, he, he. Afraid it may tempt you, eh? But you shall see—you shall see."

She drew aside the scarf and the lawyer recoiled involuntarily before the almost formless blur of scarlet. She replaced the scarf again.

"So you're not wanting to kiss me, dearie? He, he, I don't wonder. And yet I was a pretty girl once—not so long ago as you'd think, either. Vitriol, dearie, vitriol—that's what did that. Ah! but I'll be even with 'em—"

She burst into a hideous torrent of profanity which Mr. Mayherne tried vainly to quell. She fell silent at last, her hands clenching and unclenching themselves nervously.

"Enough of that," said the lawyer sternly. "I've come here because I have reason to believe you can give me information which will clear my client, Leonard Vole. Is that the case?"

Her eyes leered at him cunningly.

"What about the money, dearie?" she wheezed. "Two hundred quid, you remember."

"It is your duty to give evidence, and you can be called upon to do so."

"That won't do, dearie. I'm an old woman, and I know nothing. But you give me two hundred quid, and perhaps I can give you a hint or two. See?"

"What kind of hint?"

"What should you say to a letter? A letter from *her.* Never mind how I got hold of it. That's my business. It'll do the trick. But I want my two hundred quid."

Mr. Mayherne looked at her coldly, and made up his mind.

"I'll give you ten pounds, nothing more. And only that if this letter is what you say it is."

"Ten pounds?" She screamed and raved at him.

"Twenty," said Mr. Mayherne, "and that's my last word."

He rose as if to go. Then, watching her closely, he drew out a pocketbook, and counted out twenty one-pound notes.

"You see," he said. "That is all I have with me. You can take it or leave it."

But already he knew that the sight of the money was too much for her. She cursed and raved impotently, but at last she gave in. Going over to the bed, she drew something out from beneath the tattered mattress.

"Here you are, damn you!" she snarled. "It's the top one you want."

It was a bundle of letters that she threw to him, and Mr. Mayherne untied them and scanned them in his usual cool, methodical manner. The woman, watching him eagerly, could gain no clue from his impassive face.

He read each letter through, then returned again to the top one and read it a second time. Then he tied the whole bundle up again carefully.

They were love letters, written by Romaine Heilger, and the man they were written to was not Leonard Vole. The top letter was dated the day of the latter's arrest.

"I spoke true, dearie, didn't I?" whined the woman. "It'll do for her, that letter?"

Mr. Mayherne put the letters in his pocket, then he asked a question.

"How did you get hold of this correspondence?"

"That's telling," she said with a leer. "But I know something more. I heard in court what that hussy said. Find out where she was at twenty past ten, the time she says she was at home. Ask at the Lion Road Cinema. They'll remember—a fine upstanding girl like that—curse her!"

"Who is the man?" asked Mr. Mayherne. "There's only a Christian name here."

The other's voice grew thick and hoarse, her hands clenched and unclenched. Finally she lifted one to her face.

"He's the man that did this to me. Many years ago now. She took him away from me—a chit of a girl she was then. And when I went after him—and went for him too—he threw the cursed stuff at me! And she laughed—damn her! I've had it in for her for years. Followed her, I have, spied upon her. And now I've got her! She'll suffer for this, won't she, Mr. Lawyer? She'll suffer?"

"She will probably be sentenced to a term of imprisonment for perjury," said Mr. Mayherne quietly.

"Shut away—that's what I want. You're going, are you? Where's my money? Where's that good money?"

Without a word, Mr. Mayherne put down the notes on the table. Then, drawing a deep breath, he turned and left the squalid room. Looking back, he saw the old woman crooning over the money.

He wasted no time. He found the cinema in Lion Road easily enough, and, shown a photograph of Romaine Heilger, the commissionaire recognized her at once. She had arrived at the cinema with a man some time after ten o'clock on the evening in question. He had not noticed her escort particularly, but he remembered the lady who had spoken to him about the picture that was showing. They stayed until the end, about an hour later.

Mr. Mayherne was satisfied. Romaine Heilger's evidence was a tissue of lies from beginning to end. She had evolved it out of her passionate hatred. The lawyer wondered whether he would ever know what lay behind that hatred. What had Leonard Vole done to her? He had seemed dumbfounded when the solicitor had reported her attitude to him. He had declared earnestly that such a thing was incredible—yet it had seemed to Mr. Mayherne that after the first astonishment his protests had lacked sincerity.

He did know. Mr. Mayherne was convinced of it. He knew, but he had no intention of revealing the fact. The secret between those two remained a secret. Mr. Mayherne wondered if some day he should come to learn what it was.

The solicitor glanced at his watch. It was late, but time was everything. He hailed a taxi and gave an address.

"Sir Charles must know of this at once," he murmured to himself as he got in.

THE TRIAL OF Leonard Vole for the murder of Emily French aroused widespread interest. In the first place the prisoner was young and good-looking, then he was accused of a particularly dastardly crime, and there was the further interest of Romaine Heilger, the principal witness for the prosecution. There had been pictures of her in many papers, and several fictitious stories as to her origin and history.

The proceedings opened quietly enough. Various technical evidence came first. Then Janet Mackenzie was called. She told substantially the same story as before. In cross-examination counsel for the defense succeeded in getting her to contradict herself once or twice over her account of Vole's association with Miss French; he emphasized the fact that though she had heard a man's voice in the sitting-room that night, there was nothing to show that it was Vole who was there, and he managed to drive home a feeling that jealousy and dislike of the prisoner were at the bottom of a good deal of her evidence.

Then the next witness was called.

"Your name is Romaine Heilger?"

"Yes."

"You are an Austrian subject?"

"Yes."

"For the last three years you have lived with the prisoner and passed yourself off as his wife?"

Just for a moment Romaine Heilger's eyes met those of the man in the dock. Her expression held something curious and unfathomable.

"Yes."

The questions went on. Word by word the damning facts came out. On the night in question the prisoner had taken out a crowbar with him. He had returned at twenty minutes past ten, and had confessed to having killed the old lady. His cuffs had been stained with blood, and he had burned them in the kitchen stove. He had terrorized her into silence by means of threats.

As the story proceeded, the feeling of the court which had, to begin with, been slightly favorable to the prisoner, now set dead against him. He himself sat with downcast head and moody air, as though he knew he were doomed.

Yet it might have been noted that her own counsel sought to restrain Romaine's animosity. He would have preferred her to be more unbiased.

Formidable and ponderous, counsel for the defense arose.

He put it to her that her story was a malicious fabrication from start to finish, that she had not even been in her own house at the time in question, that she was in love with another man and was deliberately seeking to send Vole to his death for a crime he did not commit.

Romaine denied these allegations with superb insolence.

Then came the surprising denouement, the production of the letter. It was read aloud in court in the midst of a breathless stillness.

> Max, beloved, the Fates have delivered him into our hands! He has been arrested for murder—but, yes, the murder of an old lady! Leonard, who would not hurt a fly! At last I shall have my revenge. The poor chicken! I shall say that he came in that night with blood upon him—that he confessed to me. I shall hang him, Max—and when he hangs he will know and realize that it was Romaine who sent him to his death. And then—happiness, Beloved! Happiness at last!

There were experts present ready to swear that the handwriting was that of Romaine Heilger, but they were not needed. Confronted with the letter, Romaine broke down utterly and confessed everything. Leonard Vole had returned to the house at the time he said, twenty past nine. She had invented the whole story to ruin him.

With the collapse of Romaine Heilger, the case for the Crown collapsed also. Sir Charles called his few witnesses, the prisoner himself went into the box and told his story in a manly straightforward manner, unshaken by cross-examination.

The prosecution endeavored to rally, but without great success. The judge's summing up was not wholly favorable to the prisoner, but a reaction had set in and the jury needed little time to consider their verdict.

"We find the prisoner not guilty."

Leonard Vole was free!

Little Mr. Mayherne hurried from his seat. He must congratulate his client.

He found himself polishing his pince-nez vigorously, and checked himself. His wife had told him only the night before that he was getting a habit of it. Curious things, habits. People themselves never knew they had them.

An interesting case—a very interesting case. That woman, now, Romaine Heilger.

The case was dominated for him still by the exotic figure of Romaine Heilger. She had seemed a pale, quiet woman in the house at Paddington, but in court she had flamed out against the sober background, flaunting herself like a tropical flower.

If he closed his eyes he could see her now, tall and vehement, her exquisite body bent forward a little, her right hand clenching and unclenching itself unconsciously all the time.

Curious things, habits. That gesture of hers with the hand was her habit, he supposed. Yet he had seen someone else do it quite lately. Who was it now? Quite lately—

He drew in his breath with a gasp as it came back to him. The woman in Shaw's Rents. . . .

He stood still, his head whirling. It was impossible—impossible—Yet, Romaine Heilger was an actress.

The K. C. came up behind him and clapped him on the shoulder.

"Congratulated our man yet? He's had a narrow shave, you know. Come along and see him."

But the little lawyer shook off the other's hand.

He wanted one thing only—to see Romaine Heilger face to face.

He did not see her until some time later, and the place of their meeting is not relevant.

"So you guessed," she said, when he had told her all that was in his mind. "The face? Oh! that was easy enough, and the light of that gas jet was too bad for you to see the makeup."

"But why—why—"

"Why did I play a lone hand?" She smiled a little, remembering the last time she had used the words.

"Such an elaborate comedy!"

"My friend—I had to save him. The evidence of a woman devoted to him would not have been enough—you hinted as much yourself. But I know something of the psychology of crowds. Let my evidence be wrung from me, as an admission, damning me in the eyes of the law, and a reaction in favor of the prisoner would immediately set in."

"And the bundle of letters?"

"One alone, the vital one, might have seemed like a—what do you call it?—put-up job."

"Then the man called Max?"

"Never existed, my friend."

"I still think," said little Mr. Mayherne, in an aggrieved manner, "that we could have got him off by the—er—normal procedure."

"I dared not risk it. You see you thought he was innocent—"

"And you knew it? I see," said little Mr. Mayherne.

"My dear Mr. Mayherne," said Romaine, "you do not see at all. I knew—he was guilty!"

THE RED SIGNAL

"No, but how too thrilling," said pretty Mrs. Eversleigh, opening her lovely, but slightly vacant, blue eyes very wide. "They always say women have a sixth sense; do you think it's true, Sir Alington?"

The famous alienist smiled sardonically. He had an unbounded contempt for the foolish pretty type, such as his fellow guest. Alington West was the supreme authority on mental disease, and he was fully alive to his own position and importance. A slightly pompous man of full figure.

"A great deal of nonsense is talked, I know that, Mrs. Eversleigh. What does the term mean—a sixth sense?"

"You scientific men are always so severe. And it really is extraordinary the way one seems to positively know things sometimes—just know them, feel them, I mean—quite uncanny—it really is. Claire knows what I mean, don't you, Claire?"

She appealed to her hostess with a slight pout, and a tilted shoulder.

Claire Trent did not reply at once. It was a small dinner party—she and her husband, Violet Eversleigh, Sir Alington West, and his nephew Dermot West, who was an old friend of Jack Trent's. Jack

Trent himself, a somewhat heavy florid man, with a good-humored smile, and a pleasant lazy laugh, took up the thread.

"Bunkum, Violet! Your best friend is killed in a railway accident. Straight away you remember that you dreamed of a black cat last Tuesday—marvelous, you felt all along that something was going to happen!"

"Oh, no, Jack, you're mixing up premonitions with intuition now. Come, now, Sir Alington, you must admit that premonitions are real?"

"To a certain extent, perhaps," admitted the physician cautiously. "But coincidence accounts for a good deal, and then there is the invariable tendency to make the most of a story afterward."

"I don't think there is any such thing as premonition," said Claire Trent, rather abruptly. "Or intuition, or a sixth sense, or any of the things we talk about so glibly. We go through life like a train rushing through the darkness to an unknown destination."

"That's hardly a good simile, Mrs. Trent," said Dermot West, lifting his head for the first time and taking part in the discussion. There was a curious glitter in the clear gray eyes that shone out rather oddly from the deeply tanned face. "You've forgotten the signals, you see."

"The signals?"

"Yes, green if it's all right, and red—for danger!"

"Red—for danger—how thrilling!" breathed Violet Eversleigh.

Dermot turned from her rather impatiently.

"That's just a way of describing it, of course."

Trent stared at him curiously.

"You speak as though it were an actual experience, Dermot, old boy."

"So it is—has been, I mean."

"Give us the yarn."

"I can give you one instance. Out in Mesopotamia, just after the Armistice, I came into my tent one evening with the feeling strong upon me. Danger! Look out! Hadn't the ghost of a notion what it was all about. I made a round of the camp, fussed unnecessarily, took all precautions against an attack by hostile Arabs. Then I went back to my tent. As soon as I got inside, the feeling popped up again stronger than ever. Danger! In the end I took a blanket outside, rolled myself up in it and slept there."

"Well?"

"The next morning, when I went inside the tent, first thing I saw was a great knife arrangement—about half a yard long—struck down through my bunk, just where I would have lain. I soon found out about it—one of the Arab servants. His son had been shot as a spy. What have you got to say to that, Uncle Alington, as an example of what I call the red signal?"

The specialist smiled noncommittally.

"A very interesting story, my dear Dermot."

"But not one that you accept unreservedly?"

"Yes, yes, I have no doubt but that you had the premonition of danger, just as you state. But it is the origin of the premonition I dispute. According to you, it came from without, impressed by some outside source upon your mentality. But nowadays we find that nearly everything comes from within—from our subconscious self.

"I suggest that by some glance or look this Arab had betrayed himself. Your conscious self did not notice or remember, but with your subconscious self it was otherwise. The subconscious never forgets. We believe, too, that it can reason and deduce quite independently of the higher or conscious will. Your subconscious self, then, believed that an attempt might be made to assassinate you, and succeeded in forcing its fear upon your conscious realization."

"That sounds very convincing, I admit," said Dermot, smiling.

"But not nearly so exciting," pouted Mrs. Eversleigh.

"It is also possible that you may have been subconsciously aware of the hate felt by the man toward you. What in old days used to be called telepathy certainly exists, though the conditions governing it are very little understood."

"Have there been any other instances?" asked Claire of Dermot.

"Oh! yes, but nothing very pictorial—and I suppose they could all be explained under the heading of coincidence. I refused an invitation to a country house once, for no other reason than the 'red signal.' The place was burned out during the week. By the way, Uncle Alington, where does the subconscious come in there?"

"I'm afraid it doesn't," said Sir Alington, smiling.

"But you've got an equally good explanation. Come, now. No need to be tactful with near relatives."

"Well, then, nephew, I venture to suggest that you refused the invitation for the ordinary reason that you didn't much want to go, and that after the fire, you suggested to yourself that you had had a warning of danger, which explanation you now believe implicitly."

"It's hopeless," laughed Dermot. "It's heads you win, tails I lose."

"Never mind, Mr. West," cried Violet Eversleigh. "I believe in your Red Signal. Is the time in Mesopotamia the last time you had it?"

"Yes—until—"

"I beg your pardon?"

"Nothing."

Dermot sat silent. The words which had nearly left his lips were: "Yes, until tonight." They had come quite unbidden to his lips, voicing a thought which had as yet not been consciously realized, but he was aware at once that they were true. The Red Signal was looming up out of the darkness. Danger! Danger close at hand!

But why? What conceivable danger could there be here? Here in the house of his friends? At least—well, yes, there was that kind of danger. He looked at Claire Trent—her whiteness, her slenderness, the exquisite droop of her golden head. But that danger had been there for some time—it was never likely to get acute. For Jack Trent was his best friend, and more than his best friend, the man who had saved his life in Flanders and been recommended for the V.C. for doing so. A good fellow, Jack, one of the best. Damned bad luck that he should have fallen in love with Jack's wife. He'd get over it some day, he supposed. A thing couldn't go on hurting like this forever. One could starve it out—that was it, starve it out. It was not as though she would ever guess—and if she did guess, there was no danger of her caring. A statue, a beautiful statue, a thing of gold and ivory and pale pink coral . . . a toy for a king, not a real woman. . . .

Claire . . . the very thought of her name, uttered silently, hurt him. . . . He must get over it. He'd cared for women before. . . . "But not like this!" said something. "Not like this." Well, there it was. No danger there—heartache, yes, but not danger. Not the danger of the Red Signal. That was for something else.

He looked round the table and it struck him for the first time that it was rather an unusual little gathering. His uncle, for instance, seldom dined out in this small, informal way. It was not as though the Trents were old friends; until this evening Dermot had not been aware that he knew them at all.

To be sure, there was an excuse. A rather notorious medium was coming after dinner to give a séance. Sir Alington professed to be mildly interested in spiritualism. Yes, that was an excuse, certainly.

The word forced itself on his notice. An excuse. Was the séance just an excuse to make the specialist's presence at dinner natural? If so, what was the real object of his being here? A host of details came rushing into Dermot's mind, trifles unnoticed at the time, or, as his uncle would have said, unnoticed by the conscious mind.

The great physician had looked oddly, very oddly, at Claire more than once. He seemed to be watching her. She was uneasy under his scrutiny. She made little twitching motions with her hands. She was nervous, horribly nervous, and was it, could it be, frightened? Why was she frightened?

With a jerk he came back to the conversation round the table. Mrs. Eversleigh had got the great man talking upon his own subject.

"My dear lady," he was saying, "what *is* madness? I can assure you that the more we study the subject, the more difficult we find it to pronounce. We all practice a certain amount of self-deception, and when we carry it so far as to believe we are the Czar of Russia, we are shut up or restrained. But there is a long road before we reach that point. At what particular spot on it shall we erect a post and say, 'On this side sanity, on the other madness'? It can't be done, you know. And I will tell you this: if the man suffering from a delusion happened to hold his tongue about it, in all probability we should never be able to distinguish him from a normal individual. The extraordinary sanity of the insane is an interesting subject."

Sir Alington sipped his wine with appreciation and beamed upon the company.

"I've always heard they are very cunning," remarked Mrs. Eversleigh. "Loonies, I mean."

"Remarkably so. And suppression of one's particular delusion has a disastrous effect very often. All suppressions are dangerous, as psychoanalysis has taught us. The man who has a harmless eccentricity, and can indulge it as such, seldom goes over the border-line. But the man"—he paused—"or woman who is to all appearance perfectly normal, may be in reality a poignant source of danger to the community."

His gaze traveled gently down the table to Claire, and then back again.

A horrible fear shook Dermot. Was that what he meant? Was that what he was driving at? Impossible, but—

"And all from suppressing oneself," sighed Mrs. Eversleigh. "I quite see that one should be very careful always to—to express one's personality. The dangers of the other are frightful."

"My dear Mrs. Eversleigh," expostulated the physician, "you have quite misunderstood me. The cause of the mischief is in the physical matter of the brain—sometimes arising from some outward agency such as a blow; sometimes, alas, congenital."

"Heredity is so sad," sighed the lady vaguely. "Consumption and all that."

"Tuberculosis is not hereditary," said Sir Alington dryly.

"Isn't it? I always thought it was. But madness is! How dreadful. What else?"

"Gout," said Sir Alington, smiling. "And color blindness—the latter is rather interesting. It is transmitted direct to males, but is latent in females. So, while there are many color blind men, for a woman to be color blind, it must have been latent in her mother as well as present in her father—rather an unusual state of things to occur. That is what is called sex limited heredity."

"How interesting. But madness is not like that, is it?"

"Madness can be handed down to men or women equally," said the physician gravely.

Claire rose suddenly, pushing back her chair so abruptly that it overturned and fell to the ground. She was very pale and the nervous motions of her fingers were very apparent.

"You—you will not be long, will you?" she begged. "Mrs. Thompson will be here in a few minutes now."

"One glass of port, and I will be with you," declared Sir Alington. "To see this wonderful Mrs. Thompson's performance is what I have come for, is it not? Ha, ha! Not that I needed any inducement." He bowed.

Claire gave a faint smile of acknowledgment and passed out of the room with Mrs. Eversleigh.

"Afraid I've been talking shop," remarked the physician as he resumed his seat. "Forgive me, my dear fellow."

"Not at all," said Trent perfunctorily.

He looked strained and worried. For the first time Dermot felt an outsider in the company of his friend. Between these two was a secret that even an old friend might not share. And yet the whole thing was fantastic and incredible. What had he to go upon? Nothing but a couple of glances and a woman's nervousness.

They lingered over their wine but a very short time, and arrived up in the drawing room just as Mrs. Thompson was announced.

The medium was a plump middle-aged woman, atrociously dressed in magenta velvet, with a loud, rather common voice.

"Hope I'm not late, Mrs. Trent," she said cheerily. "You did say nine o'clock, didn't you?"

"You are quite punctual, Mrs. Thompson," said Claire in her sweet, slightly husky voice. "This is our little circle."

No further introductions were made, as was evidently the custom. The medium swept them all with a shrewd, penetrating eye.

"I hope we shall get some good results," she remarked briskly. "I can't tell you how I hate it when I go out and I can't give satisfaction, so to speak. It just makes me mad. But I think Shiromako (my Japanese control, you know) will be able to get through all right tonight. I'm feeling ever so fit, and I refused the welsh rarebit, fond of cheese though I am."

Dermot listened, half-amused, half-disgusted. How prosaic the whole thing was! And yet, was he not judging foolishly? Everything, after all, was natural—the powers claimed by mediums were natural powers, as yet imperfectly understood. A great surgeon might be wary of indigestion on the eve of a delicate operation. Why not Mrs. Thompson?

Chairs were arranged in a circle, lights so that they could conveniently be raised and lowered. Dermot noticed that there was no question of tests, or of Sir Alington satisfying himself as to the conditions of the séance. No, this business of Mrs. Thompson was only a blind. Sir Alington was here for quite another purpose. Claire's mother, Dermot remembered, had died abroad. There had been some mystery about her. . . . Hereditary. . . .

With a jerk he forced his mind back to the surroundings of the moment.

Everyone took their places, and the lights were turned out, all but a small red-shaded one on a far table.

For a while nothing was heard but the low, even breathing of the medium. Gradually it grew more and more stertorous. Then, with a suddenness that made Dermot jump, a loud rap came from the far end of the room. It was repeated from the other side. Then a perfect crescendo of raps was heard. They died away, and a sudden high peal of mocking laughter rang through the room.

Then silence, broken by a voice utterly unlike that of Mrs. Thompson, a high-pitched, quaintly inflected voice.

"I am here, gentlemen," it said. "Yess, I am here. You wish ask me things?"

"Who are you? Shiromako?"

"Yess. I Shiromako. I pass over long ago. I work. I very happy."

Further details of Shiromako's life followed. It was all very flat and uninteresting, and Dermot had heard it often before. Everyone was happy, very happy. Messages were given from vaguely described relatives, the description being so loosely worded as to fit almost any contingency. An elderly lady, the mother of someone present, held the floor for some time, imparting copybook maxims with an air of refreshing novelty hardly borne out by her subject matter.

"Someone else want to get through now," announced Shiromako. "Got a very important message for one of the gentlemen."

There was a pause, and then a new voice spoke, prefacing its remarks with an evil demoniacal chuckle.

"Ha, ha! Ha, ha, ha! Better not go home. Take my advice."

"Who are you speaking to?" asked Trent.

"One of you three. I shouldn't go home if I were him. Danger! Blood! Not very much blood—quite enough. No, don't go home." The voice grew fainter. *"Don't go home!"*

It died away completely. Dermot felt his blood tingling. He was convinced that the warning was meant for him. Somehow or other, there was danger abroad tonight.

There was a sigh from the medium, and then a groan. She was coming round. The lights were turned on, and presently she sat upright, her eyes blinking a little.

"Go off well, my dear? I hope so."

"Very good indeed, thank you, Mrs. Thompson."

"Shiromako, I suppose?"

"Yes, and others."

Mrs. Thompson yawned.

"I'm dead beat. Absolutely down and out. Does fairly take it out of you. Well, I'm glad it was a success. I was a bit afraid something disagreeable might happen. There's a queer feel about this room tonight."

She glanced over each ample shoulder in turn, and then shrugged them uncomfortably.

"I don't like it," she said. "Any sudden deaths among any of you people lately?"

"What do you mean—among us?"

"Near relatives—dear friends? No? Well, if I wanted to be melodramatic, I'd say that there was death in the air tonight. There, it's only my nonsense. Good-bye, Mrs. Trent. I'm glad you've been satisfied."

Mrs. Thompson in her magenta velvet gown went out.

"I hope you've been interested, Sir Alington," murmured Claire.

"A most interesting evening, my dear lady. Many thanks for the opportunity. Let me wish you good night. You are all going on to a dance, are you not?"

"Won't you come with us?"

"No, no. I make it a rule to be in bed by half-past eleven. Good night. Good night, Mrs. Eversleigh. Ah, Dermot, I rather want to have a word with you. Can you come with me now? You can rejoin the others at the Grafton Galleries."

"Certainly, Uncle. I'll meet you there then, Trent."

Very few words were exchanged between uncle and nephew during the short drive to Harley Street. Sir Alington made a semi-apology for dragging Dermot away, and assured him that he would only detain him a few minutes.

"Shall I keep the car for you, my boy?" he asked, as they alighted.

"Oh, don't bother, Uncle. I'll pick up a taxi."

"Very good. I don't like to keep Charlson up later than I can help. Good night, Charlson. Now where the devil did I put my key?"

The car glided away as Sir Alington stood on the steps searching his pockets.

"Must have left it in my other coat," he said at length. "Ring the bell, will you? Johnson is still up, I dare say."

The imperturbable Johnson did indeed open the door within sixty seconds.

"Mislaid my key, Johnson," explained Sir Alington. "Bring a couple of whiskies and sodas into the library."

"Very good, Sir Alington."

The physician strode on into the library and turned on the lights. He motioned to Dermot to close the door.

"I won't keep you long, Dermot, but there's just something I want to say to you. Is it my fancy, or have you a certain—*tendresse,* shall we say, for Mrs. Jack Trent?"

The blood rushed to Dermot's face.

"Jack Trent is my best friend."

"Pardon me, but that is hardly answering my question. I dare say that you consider my views on divorce and such matters highly puritanical, but I must remind you that you are my only near relative and my heir."

"There is no question of a divorce," said Dermot angrily.

"There certainly is not, for a reason which I understand perhaps better than you do. That particular reason I cannot give you now, but I do wish to warn you. She is not for you."

The young man faced his uncle's gaze steadily.

"I do understand—and permit me to say, perhaps better than you think. I know the reason for your presence at dinner tonight."

"Eh?" The physician was clearly startled. "How did you know that?"

"Call it a guess, sir. I am right, am I not, when I say that you were there in your—professional capacity."

Sir Alington strode up and down.

"You are quite right, Dermot. I could not, of course, have told you so myself, though I am afraid it will soon be common property."

Dermot's heart contracted.

"You mean that you have—made up your mind?"

"Yes, there is insanity in the family—on the mother's side. A sad case—a very sad case."

"I can't believe it, sir."

"I dare say not. To the layman there are few if any signs apparent."

"And to the expert?"

"The evidence is conclusive. In such a case the patient must be placed under restraint as soon as possible."

"My God!" breathed Dermot. "But you can't shut anyone up for nothing at all."

"My dear Dermot! Cases are only placed under restraint when their being at large would result in danger to the community."

"Danger?"

"Very grave danger. In all probability a peculiar form of homicidal mania. It was so in the mother's case."

Dermot turned away with a groan, burying his face in his hands. Claire—white and golden Claire!

"In the circumstances," continued the physician comfortably, "I felt it incumbent on me to warn you."

"Claire," murmured Dermot. "My poor Claire."

"Yes, indeed, we must all pity her."

Suddenly Dermot raised his head.

"I say I don't believe it. Doctors make mistakes. Everyone knows that. And they're always keen on their own specialty."

"My dear Dermot," cried Sir Alington angrily.

"I tell you I don't believe it—and anyway, even if it is so, I don't care. I love Claire. If she will come with me, I shall take her away—far away—out of the reach of meddling physicians. I shall guard her, care for her, shelter her with my love."

"You will do nothing of the sort. Are you mad?" Dermot laughed scornfully.

"*You* would say so."

"Understand me, Dermot." Sir Alington's face was red with suppressed passion. "If you do this thing—this shameful thing—I shall withdraw the allowance I am now making you, and I shall make a new will leaving all I possess to various hospitals."

"Do as you please with your damned money," said Dermot in a low voice. "I shall have the woman I love."

"A woman who—"

"Say a word against her and, by God, I'll kill you!" cried Dermot.

A slight chink of glasses made them both swing round. Unheard by them in the heat of their argument, Johnson had entered with a tray of glasses. His face was the imperturbable one of the good servant, but Dermot wondered just exactly how much he had overheard.

"That'll do, Johnson," said Sir Alington curtly. "You can go to bed."

"Thank you, sir. Good night, sir."

Johnson withdrew.

The two men looked at each other. The momentary interruption had calmed the storm.

"Uncle," said Dermot. "I shouldn't have spoken to you as I did. I can quite see that from your point of view you are perfectly right. But I have loved Claire Trent for a long time. The fact that Jack Trent is my best friend has hitherto stood in the way of my ever speaking of love to Claire herself. But in these circumstances that fact no longer counts. The idea that any monetary conditions can deter me is absurd. I think we've both said all there is to be said. Good night."

"Dermot—"

"It is really no good arguing further. Good night, Uncle Alington."

He went out quickly, shutting the door behind him. The hall was in darkness. He passed through it, opened the front door and emerged into the street, banging the door behind him.

A taxi had just deposited a fare at a house farther along the street and Dermot hailed it, and drove to the Grafton Galleries.

In the door of the ballroom he stood for a minute, bewildered, his head spinning. The raucous jazz music, the smiling women—it was as though he had stepped into another world.

Had he dreamed it all? Impossible that that grim conversation with his uncle should have really taken place. There was Claire floating past, like a lily in her white and silver gown that fitted sheathlike to her slenderness. She smiled at him, her face calm and serene. Surely it was all a dream.

The dance had stopped. Presently she was near him, smiling up into his face. As in a dream he asked her to dance. She was in his arms now, the raucous melodies had begun again.

He felt her flag a little.

"Tired? Do you want to stop?"

"If you don't mind. Can we go somewhere where we can talk? There is something I want to say to you."

Not a dream. He came back to earth with a bump. Could he ever have thought her face calm and serene? It was haunted with anxiety, with dread. How much did she know?

He found a quiet corner, and they sat down side by side.

"Well," he said, assuming a lightness he did not feel, "you said you had something you wanted to say to me?"

"Yes." Her eyes were cast down. She was playing nervously with the tassel of her gown. "It's difficult—"

"Tell me, Claire."

"It's just this. I want you to—to go away for a time."

He was astonished. Whatever he had expected, it was not this.

"You want me to go away? Why?"

"It's best to be honest, isn't it? I know that you are a—a gentleman and my friend. I want you to go away because I—I have let myself get fond of you."

"Claire."

Her words left him dumb—tongue-tied.

"Please do not think that I am conceited enough to fancy that you—would ever be likely to fall in love with me. It is only that—I am not very happy—and—oh! I would rather you went away."

"Claire, don't you know that I have cared—cared damnably—ever since I met you?"

She lifted startled eyes to his face.

"You cared? You have cared a long time?"

"Since the beginning."

"Oh!" she cried. "Why didn't you tell me? Then? When I could have come to you! Why tell me now when it's too late. No, I'm mad—I don't know what I'm saying. I could never have come to you."

"Claire, what did you mean when you said 'now that it's too late'? Is it—is it because of my uncle? What he knows?"

She nodded, the tears running down her face.

"Listen, Claire, you're not to believe all that. You're not to think about it. Instead, you will come away with me. I will look after you—keep you safe always."

His arms went round her. He drew her to him, felt her tremble at his touch. Then suddenly she wrenched herself free.

"Oh, no, please. Can't you see? I couldn't now. It would be ugly—ugly—ugly. All along I've wanted to be good—and now—it would be ugly as well."

He hesitated, baffled by her words. She looked at him appealingly.

"Please," she said. "I want to be good. . . ."

Without a word, Dermot got up and left her. For the moment he was touched and racked by her words beyond argument. He went for his hat and coat, running into Trent as he did so.

"Hallo, Dermot, you're off early."

"Yes, I'm not in the mood for dancing tonight."

"It's a rotten night," said Trent gloomily. "But you haven't got my worries."

Dermot had a sudden panic that Trent might be going to confide in him. Not that—anything but that!

"Well, so long," he said hurriedly. "I'm off home."

"Home, eh? What about the warning of the spirits?"

"I'll risk that. Good night, Jack."

Dermot's flat was not far away. He walked there, feeling the need of the cool night air to calm his fevered brain. He let himself in with his key and switched on the light in the bedroom.

And all at once, for the second time that night, the feeling of the Red Signal surged over him. So overpowering was it that for the moment it swept even Claire from his mind.

Danger! He was in danger. At this very moment, in this very room!

He tried in vain to ridicule himself free of the fear. Perhaps his efforts were secretly halfhearted. So far, the Red Signal had given him timely warning which had enabled him to avoid disaster. Smiling a little at his own superstition, he made a careful tour of the flat. It was possible that some malefactor had got in and was lying concealed there. But his search revealed nothing. His man, Milson, was away, and the flat was absolutely empty.

He returned to his bedroom and undressed slowly, frowning to himself. The sense of danger was acute as ever. He went to a drawer to get out a handkerchief, and suddenly stood stock still. There was an unfamiliar lump in the middle of the drawer.

His quick nervous fingers tore aside the handkerchiefs and took out the object concealed beneath them.

It was a revolver.

With the utmost astonishment Dermot examined it keenly. It was of a somewhat unfamiliar pattern, and one shot had been fired from it lately. Beyond that he could make nothing of it. Someone had placed it in that drawer that very evening. It had not been there when he dressed for dinner—he was sure of that.

He was about to replace it in the drawer, when he was startled by a bell ringing. It rang again and again, sounding unusually loud in the quietness of the empty flat.

Who could be coming to the front door at this hour? And only one answer came to the question—an answer instinctive and persistent.

Danger—danger—danger.

Led by some instinct for which he did not account, Dermot switched off his light, slipped on an overcoat that lay across a chair, and opened the hall door.

Two men stood outside. Beyond them Dermot caught sight of a blue uniform. A policeman!

"Mr. West?" asked one of the two men.

It seemed to Dermot that ages elapsed before he answered. In reality it was only a few seconds before he replied in a very fair imitation of his servant's expressionless voice:

"Mr. West hasn't come in yet."

"Hasn't come in yet, eh? Very well, then, I think we'd better come in and wait for him."

"No, you don't."

"See here, my man, I'm inspector Verall of Scotland Yard, and I've got a warrant for the arrest of your master. You can see it if you like."

Dermot perused the proffered paper, or pretended to do so, asking in a dazed voice:

"What for? What's he done?"

"Murder. Sir Alington West of Harley Street."

His brain in a whirl, Dermot fell back before his redoubtable visitors. He went into the sitting-room and switched on the light. The inspector followed him.

"Have a search round," he directed the other man. Then he turned to Dermot.

"You stay here, my man. No slipping off to warn your master. What's your name, by the way?"

"Milson, sir."

"What time do you expect your master in, Milson?"

"I don't know, sir, he was going to a dance, I believe. At the Grafton Galleries."

"He left there just under an hour ago. Sure he's not been back here?"

"I don't think so, sir. I fancy I should have heard him come in."

At this moment the second man came in from the adjoining room. In his hand he carried the revolver. He took it across to the inspector in some excitement. An expression of satisfaction flitted across the latter's face.

"That settles it," he remarked. "Must have slipped in and out without your hearing him. He's hooked it by now. I'd better be off. Cawley, you stay here, in case he should come back again, and you can keep an eye on this fellow. He may know more about his master than he pretends."

The inspector bustled off. Dermot endeavored to get the details of the affair from Cawley, who was quite ready to be talkative.

"Pretty clear case," he vouchsafed. "The murder was discovered almost immediately. Johnson, the manservant, had only just gone up to bed when he fancied he heard a shot, and came down again. Found Sir Alington dead, shot through the heart. He rang us up at once and we came along and heard his story."

"Which made it a pretty clear case?" ventured Dermot.

"Absolutely. This young West came in with his uncle and they were quarreling when Johnson brought in the drinks. The old boy was threatening to make a new will, and your master was talking about shooting him. Not five minutes later the shot was heard. Oh, yes, clear enough."

Clear enough indeed. Dermot's heart sank as he realized the overwhelming evidence against him. And no way out save flight. He set his wits to work. Presently he suggested making a cup of tea. Cawley assented readily enough. He had already searched the flat and knew there was no back entrance.

Dermot was permitted to depart to the kitchen. Once there he put the kettle on, and chinked cups and saucers industriously. Then he stole swiftly to the window and lifted the sash. The flat was on the second floor, and outside the window was the small wire lift used by tradesmen which ran up and down on its steel cable.

Like a flash Dermot was outside the window and swinging himself down the wire rope. It cut into his hands, making them bleed, but he went on desperately.

A few minutes later he was emerging cautiously from the back of the block. Turning the corner, he cannoned into a figure standing by the sidewalk. To his utter amazement he recognized Jack Trent. Trent was fully alive to the perils of the situation.

"My God! Dermot! Quick, don't hang about here."

Taking him by the arm, he led him down a side street, then down another. A lonely taxi was sighted and hailed and they jumped in, Trent giving the man his own address.

"Safest place for the moment. There we can decide what to do next to put those fools off the track. I came round here, hoping to be able to warn you before the police got here."

"I didn't even know that you had heard of it. Jack, you don't believe—"

"Of course not, old fellow, not for one minute. I know you far too well. All the same, it's a nasty business for you. They came round asking questions—what time you got to the Grafton Galleries, when you left, and so on. Dermot, who could have done the old boy in?"

"I can't imagine. Whoever did it put the revolver in my drawer, I suppose. Must have been watching us pretty closely."

"That séance business was damned funny. 'Don't go home.' Meant for poor old West. He did go home, and got shot."

"It applies to me, too," said Dermot. "I went home and found a planted revolver and a police inspector."

"Well, I hope it doesn't get me, too," said Trent. "Here we are."

He paid the taxi, opened the door with his latchkey, and guided Dermot up the dark stairs to his den, a small room on the first floor.

He threw open the door and Dermot walked in, while Trent switched on the light, and came to join him.

"Pretty safe here for the time being," he remarked. "Now we can get our heads together and decide what is best to be done."

"I've made a fool of myself," said Dermot suddenly. "I ought to have faced it out. I see more clearly now. The whole thing's a plot. What the devil are you laughing at?"

For Trent was leaning back in his chair, shaking with unrestrained mirth. There was something horrible in the sound—something horrible, too, about the man altogether.

There was a curious light in his eyes.

"A damned clever plot," he gasped out. "Dermot, you're done for."

He drew the telephone toward him.

"What are you going to do?" asked Dermot.

"Ring up Scotland Yard. Tell 'em their bird's here—safe under lock and key. Yes, I locked the door when I came in and the key's in my pocket. No good looking at that other door behind me. That leads into Claire's room, and she always locks it on her side. She's afraid of me, you know. Been afraid of me a long time. She always knows when I'm thinking about that knife—a long sharp knife. No, you don't—"

Dermot had been about to make a rush at him, but the other had suddenly produced a revolver.

"That's the second of them," chuckled Trent. "I put the first in your drawer—after shooting old West with it—What are you looking at over my head? That door? It's no use, even if Claire were to open it—and she might to you—I'd shoot you before you got there. Not in the heart—not to kill, just wing you, so that you couldn't get away. I'm a jolly good shot, you know. I saved your life once. More fool I. No, no; I want you hanged—yes, hanged. It isn't you I want the knife for. It's Claire—pretty Claire, so white and soft. Old West knew. That's what he was here for tonight, to see if I were mad or not. He wanted to shut me up—so that I shouldn't get at Claire with a knife. I was very cunning. I took his latchkey and yours, too. I slipped away from the dance as soon as I got there. I saw you come out of his house, and I went in. I shot him and came away at once. Then I went to your place and left the revolver. I was at the Grafton Galleries again almost as soon as you were, and I put the latchkey back in your coat pocket when I was saying good night to you. I don't mind telling you all this. There's no one else to hear, and when you're being hanged I'd like you to know I did it. . . . There's not a loophole of escape. It makes me laugh . . . God, how it makes me laugh! What are you thinking of? What the devil are you looking at?"

"I'm thinking of some words you quoted just now. You'd have done better, Trent, not to come home."

"What do you mean?"

"Look behind you!"

Trent spun round. In the doorway of the communicating room stood Claire—and Inspector Verall. . . .

Trent was quick. The revolver spoke just once—and found its mark. He fell forward across the table. The inspector sprang to his side, as Dermot stared at Claire in a dream. Thoughts flashed through his brain disjointedly. His uncle—their quarrel—the colossal misunderstanding—the divorce laws of England which would never free Claire from an insane husband—"we must all pity her"—the plot between her and Sir Alington which the cunning of Trent had seen through—her cry to him, "Ugly—ugly—ugly!" Yes, but now—

The inspector straightened up.

"Dead," he said vexedly.

"Yes," Dermot heard himself saying, "he was always a good shot. . . ."

THE FOURTH MAN

Canon Parfitt panted a little. Running for trains was not much of a business for a man of his age. For one thing his figure was not what it was and with the loss of his slender silhouette went an increasing tendency to be short of breath. This tendency the Canon himself always referred to, with dignity, as "My heart, you know!"

He sank into the corner of the first-class carriage with a sigh of relief. The warmth of the heated carriage was most agreeable to him. Outside the snow was falling. Lucky to get a corner seat on a long night journey. Miserable business if you didn't. There ought to be a sleeper on this train.

The other three corners were already occupied, and noting this fact Canon Parfitt became aware that the man in the far corner was smiling at him in gentle recognition. He was a clean-shaven man with a quizzical face and hair just turning gray on the temples. His profession was so clearly the law that no one could have mistaken him for anything else for a moment. Sir George Durand was, indeed, a very famous lawyer.

"Well, Parfitt," he remarked genially, "you had a run for it, didn't you?"

"Very bad for my heart, I'm afraid," said the Canon. "Quite a coincidence meeting you, Sir George. Are you going far north?"

"Newcastle," said Sir George laconically. "By the way," he added, "do you know Dr. Campbell Clark?"

The man sitting on the same side of the carriage as the Canon inclined his head pleasantly.

"We met on the platform," continued the lawyer. "Another coincidence."

Canon Parfitt looked at Dr. Campbell Clark with a good deal of interest. It was a name of which he had often heard. Dr. Clark was in the forefront as a physician and mental specialist, and his last book, *The Problem of the Unconscious Mind,* had been the most discussed book of the year.

Canon Parfitt saw a square jaw, very steady blue eyes, and reddish hair untouched by gray, but thinning rapidly. And he received also the impression of a very forceful personality.

By a perfectly natural association of ideas the Canon looked across to the seat opposite him, half-expecting to receive a glance of recognition there also, but the fourth occupant of the carriage proved to be a total stranger—a foreigner, the Canon fancied. He was a slight dark man, rather insignificant in appearance. Hunched in a big overcoat, he appeared to be fast asleep.

"Canon Parfitt of Bradchester?" inquired Dr. Campbell Clark in a pleasant voice.

The Canon looked flattered. Those "scientific sermons" of his had really made a great hit—especially since the press had taken them up. Well, that was what the Church needed—good modern up-to-date stuff.

"I have read your book with great interest, Dr. Campbell Clark," he said. "Though it's a bit too technical here and there for me to follow."

Durand broke in.

"Are you for talking or sleeping, Canon?" he asked. "I'll confess at once that I suffer from insomnia and that therefore I'm in favor of the former."

"Oh, certainly! By all means," said the Canon. "I seldom sleep on these night journeys and the book I have with me is a very dull one."

"We are at any rate a representative gathering," remarked the doctor with a smile. "The Church, the law, the medical profession."

"Not much we couldn't give an opinion on between us, eh?" laughed Durand. "The Church for the spiritual view, myself for the purely worldly and legal view, and you, doctor, with the widest field of all, ranging from the purely pathological to the—super-psychological! Among the three of us we should cover any ground pretty completely, I fancy."

"Not so completely as you imagine, I think," said Dr. Clark. "There's another point of view, you know, that you left out, and that's rather an important one."

"Meaning?" queried the lawyer.

"The point of view of the man in the street."

"Is that so important? Isn't the man in the street usually wrong?"

"Oh, almost always! But he has the thing that all expert opinion must lack—the personal point of view. In the end, you know, you can't get away from personal relationships. I've found that in my profession. For every patient who comes to me genuinely ill, at least five come who have nothing whatever the matter with them except an inability to live happily with the inmates of the same house. They call it everything—from housemaid's knee to writer's cramp, but it's all the same thing, the raw surface produced by mind rubbing against mind."

"You have a lot of patients with 'nerves,' I suppose," the Canon remarked disparagingly. His own nerves were excellent.

"Ah, and what do you mean by that?" The other swung round on him, quick as a flash. "Nerves! People use that word and laugh after it, just as you did. 'Nothing the matter with so and so,' they say. 'Just nerves.' But, good God, man, you've got the crux of everything there! You can get at a mere bodily ailment and heal it. But at this day we know very little more about the obscure causes of the hundred and one forms of nervous disease than we did in—well, the reign of Queen Elizabeth!"

"Dear me," said Canon Parfitt, a little bewildered by this onslaught. "Is that so?"

"Mind you, it's a sign of grace," Dr. Campbell Clark went on. "In the old days we considered man a simple animal, body and soul—with stress laid on the former."

"Body, soul and spirit," corrected the clergyman mildly.

"Spirit?" The doctor smiled oddly. "What do you parsons mean exactly by spirit? You've never been very clear about it, you know. All down the ages you've funked an exact definition."

The Canon cleared his throat in preparation for speech, but to his chagrin he was given no opportunity. The doctor went on.

"Are we even sure the word is spirit—might it not be spirits?"

"Spirits?" Sir George Durand questioned, his eyebrows raised quizzically.

"Yes." Campbell Clark's gaze transferred itself to him. He leaned forward and tapped the other man lightly on the breast. "Are you so sure," he said gravely, "that there is only one occupant of this structure—for that is all it is, you know—this desirable residence to be let furnished—for seven, twenty-one, forty-one, seventy-one—whatever it may be!—years? And in the end the tenant moves his things out—little by little—and then goes out of the house altogether—and down comes the house, a mass of ruin and decay. You're the master of the house, we'll admit that, but aren't you ever conscious of the presence of others—soft-footed servants, hardly noticed, except for the work they do—work that you're not conscious of having done? Or friends—moods that take hold of you and make you, for the time being, a 'different man,' as the saying goes? You're the king of the castle, right enough, but be very sure the 'dirty rascal' is there too."

"My dear Clark," drawled the lawyer, "you make me positively uncomfortable. Is my mind really a battleground of conflicting personalities? Is that Science's latest?"

It was the doctor's turn to shrug his shoulders.

"Your body is," he said dryly. "If the body, why not the mind?"

"Very interesting," said Canon Parfitt. "Ah! Wonderful science—wonderful science."

And inwardly he thought to himself: "I can get a most arresting sermon out of the idea."

But Dr. Campbell Clark had leaned back again in his seat, his momentary excitement spent.

"As a matter of fact," he remarked in a dry, professional manner, "it is a case of dual personality that takes me to Newcastle tonight. Very interesting case. Neurotic subject, of course. But quite genuine."

"Dual personality," said Sir George Durand thoughtfully. "It's not so very rare, I believe. There's loss of memory as well, isn't there? I know the matter cropped up in a case in the Probate Court the other day."

Dr. Clark nodded.

"The classic case, of course," he said, "was that of Felicie Bault. You may remember hearing of it?"

"Of course," said Canon Parfitt. "I remember reading about it in the papers—but quite a long time ago—seven years at least."

Dr. Campbell Clark nodded.

"That girl became one of the most famous figures in France. Scientists from all over the world came to see her. She had no less than four distinct personalities. They were known as Felicie 1, Felicie 2, Felicie 3, etc."

"Wasn't there some suggestion of deliberate trickery?" asked Sir George alertly.

"The personalities of Felicie 3 and Felicie 4 were a little open to doubt," admitted the doctor. "But the main facts remain. Felicie Bault was a Brittany peasant girl. She was the third of a family of five, the daughter of a drunken father and a mentally defective mother. In one of his drinking bouts the father strangled the mother and was, if I remember rightly, transported for life. Felicie was then five years of age. Some charitable people interested themselves in the children and Felicie was brought up and educated by an English maiden lady who had a kind of home for destitute children. She could make very little of Felicie, however. She describes the girl as abnormally slow and stupid, taught to read and write only with the greatest difficulty, and clumsy with her hands. This lady, Miss Slater, tried to fit the girl for domestic service, and did indeed find her several places when she was of an age to take them. But she never stayed long anywhere owing to her stupidity and also her intense laziness."

The doctor paused for a minute, and the Canon, recrossing his legs and arranging his traveling rug more closely round him, was suddenly aware that the man opposite him had moved very slightly. His eyes, which had formerly been shut, were now open, and something in them, something mocking and indefinable, startled the worthy Canon. It was as though the man were listening and gloating secretly over what he heard.

"There is a photograph taken of Felicie Bault at the age of seventeen," continued the doctor. "It shows her as a loutish peasant girl, heavy of build. There is nothing in that picture to indicate that she was soon to be one of the most famous persons in France.

"Five years later, when she was 22, Felicie Bault had a severe nervous illness, and on recovery the strange phenomena began to manifest themselves. The following are facts attested to by many eminent scientists. The personality called Felicie 1 was indistinguishable from the Felicie Bault of the last twenty-two years. Felicie 1 wrote French badly and haltingly, spoke no foreign languages, and was unable to play the piano. Felicie 2, on the contrary, spoke Italian fluently and German moderately. Her handwriting was quite different from that of Felicie 1, and she wrote fluent and expressive French. She could discuss politics and art and she was passionately fond of playing the piano. Felicie 3 had many points in common with Felicie 2. She was intelligent and apparently well educated, but in moral character she was a total contrast. She appeared, in fact, an utterly depraved creature—but depraved in a Parisian and not a provincial way. She knew all the Paris *argot,* and the expressions of the chic *demi monde*. Her language was filthy and she would rail against religion and so-called 'good people' in the most blasphemous terms. Finally there was Felicie 4—a dreamy, almost half-witted creature, distinctly pious and professedly clairvoyant, but this fourth personality was very unsatisfactory and elusive, and has been sometimes thought to be a deliberate trickery on the part of Felicie 3—a kind of joke played by her on a credulous public. I may say that (with the possible exception of Felicie 4) each personality was distinct and separate and had no knowledge of the others. Felicie 2 was undoubtedly the most predominant and would last sometimes for a fortnight at a time, then Felicie 1 would appear abruptly for a day or two. After that, perhaps, Felicie 3 or 4, but the two latter seldom remained in command for more than a few hours. Each change was accompanied by severe headache and heavy sleep, and in each case there was complete loss of memory of the other states, the personality in question taking up life where she had left it, unconscious of the passage of time."

"Remarkable," murmured the Canon. "Very remarkable. As yet we know next to nothing of the marvels of the universe."

"We know that there are some very astute impostors in it," remarked the lawyer dryly.

"The case of Felicie Bault was investigated by lawyers as well as by doctors and scientists," said Dr. Campbell Clark quickly. "Maître Quimbellier, you remember, made the most thorough investigation and confirmed the views of the scientists. And after all, why should it surprise us so much? We come across the double-yolked egg, do we not? And the twin banana? Why not the double soul—or in this case the quadruple soul—in the single body?"

"The double soul?" protested the Canon.

Dr. Campbell Clark turned his piercing blue eyes on him.

"What else can we call it? That is to say—if the personality is the soul?"

"It is a good thing such a state of affairs is only in the nature of a 'freak,'" remarked Sir George. "If the case were common, it would give rise to pretty complications."

"The condition is, of course, quite abnormal," agreed the doctor. "It was a great pity that a longer study could not have been made, but all that was put an end to by Felicie's unexpected death."

"There was something queer about that, if I remember rightly," said the lawyer slowly.

Dr. Campbell Clark nodded.

"A most unaccountable business. The girl was found one morning dead in bed. She had clearly been strangled. But to everyone's stupefaction it was presently proved beyond doubt that she had actually strangled herself. The marks on her neck were those of her own fingers. A method of suicide which, though not physically impossible, must have necessitated terrific muscular strength and almost superhuman will power. What had driven the girl to such straits has never been found out. Of course her mental balance must always have been precarious. Still, there it is. The curtain has been rung down forever on the mystery of Felicie Bault."

It was then that the man in the far corner laughed.

The other three men jumped as though shot. They had totally forgotten the existence of the fourth among them. As they stared toward the place where he sat, still hunched in his overcoat, he laughed again.

"You must excuse me, gentlemen," he said, in perfect English that had, nevertheless, a foreign flavor.

He sat up, displaying a pale face with a small jet-black mustache.

"Yes, you must excuse me," he said, with a mock bow. "But really! in science, is the last word ever said?"

"You know something of the case we have been discussing?" asked the doctor courteously.

"Of the case? No. But I knew her."

"Felicie Bault?"

"Yes. And Annette Ravel also. You have not heard of Annette Ravel, I see? And yet the story of the one is the story of the other. Believe me, you know nothing of Felicie Bault if you do not also know the history of Annette Ravel."

He drew out a watch and looked at it.

"Just half an hour before the next stop. I have time to tell you the story—that is, if you care to hear it?"

"Please tell it to us," said the doctor quietly.

"Delighted," said the Canon. "Delighted."

Sir George Durand merely composed himself in an attitude of keen attention.

"My name, gentlemen," began their strange traveling companion, "is Raoul Letardeau. You have spoken just now of an English lady, Miss Slater, who interested herself in works of charity. I was born in that Brittany fishing village, and when my parents were both killed in a railway accident it was Miss Slater who came to the rescue and saved me from the equivalent of your English workhouse. There were some twenty children under her care, girls and boys. Among these children were Felicie Bault and Annette Ravel. If I cannot make you understand the personality of Annette, gentlemen, you will understand nothing. She was the child of what you call a *fille de joie* who had died of consumption abandoned by her lover. The mother had been a dancer, and Annette, too, had the desire to dance. When I saw her first she was eleven years old, a little shrimp of a thing with eyes that alternately mocked and promised—a little creature all fire and life. And at once—yes, at once—she made me her slave. It was 'Raoul, do this for me.' 'Raoul, do that for me.' And me, I obeyed. Already I worshipped her, and she knew it.

"We would go down to the shore together, we three—for Felicie would come with us. And there Annette would pull off her shoes and stockings and dance on the sand. And then when she sank down breathless, she would tell us of what she meant to do and be.

" 'See you, I shall be famous. Yes, exceedingly famous. I will have hundreds and thousands of silk stockings—the finest silk. And I shall live in an exquisite apartment. All my lovers shall be young and handsome as well as being rich. And when I dance all Paris shall come to see me. They will yell and call and shout and go mad over my dancing. And in the winters I shall not dance, I shall go south to the sunlight. There are villas there with orange trees. I shall have one of them. I shall lie in the sun on silk cushions, eating oranges. As for you, Raoul, I will never forget you, however great and rich and famous I shall be. I will protect you and advance your career. Felicie here shall be my maid—no, her hands are too clumsy. Look at them, how large and coarse they are.'

"Felicie would grow angry at that. And then Annette would go on teasing her.

" 'She is so ladylike, Felicie—so elegant, so refined. She is a princess in disguise—ha, ha.'

" 'My father and mother were married, which is more than yours were,' Felicie would growl out spitefully.

" 'Yes, and your father killed your mother. A pretty thing, to be a murderer's daughter.'

" 'Your father left your mother to rot,' Felicie would rejoin.

"'Ah! yes.' Annette became thoughtful. '*Pauvre Maman*. One must keep strong and well. It is everything to keep strong and well.'

"'I am as strong as a horse,' Felicie boasted.

"And indeed she was. She had twice the strength of any other girl in the Home. And she was never ill.

"But she was stupid, you comprehend, stupid like a brute beast. I often wondered why she followed Annette round as she did. It was, with her, a kind of fascination. Sometimes, I think, she actually hated Annette, and indeed Annette was not kind to her. She jeered at her slowness and stupidity, and baited her in front of the others. I have seen Felicie grow quite white with rage. Sometimes I have thought that she would fasten her fingers round Annette's neck and choke the life out of her. She was not nimble-witted enough to reply to Annette's taunts, but she did learn in time to make one retort which never failed. That was the reference to her own health and strength. She had learned (what I had always known) that Annette envied her her strong physique, and she struck instinctively at the weak spot in her enemy's armor.

"One day Annette came to me in great glee.

"'Raoul,' she said, 'we shall have fun today with that stupid Felicie.'

"'What are you going to do?'

"'Come behind the little shed and I will tell you.'

"It seemed that Annette had got hold of some book. Part of it she did not understand, and indeed the whole thing was much over her head. It was an early work on hypnotism.

"'A bright object, they say. The brass knob of my bed, it twirls round. I made Felicie look at it last night. "Look at it steadily," I said. "Do not take your eyes off it." And then I twirled it. Raoul, I was frightened. Her eyes looked so queer—so queer. "Felicie, you will do what I say always," I said. "I will do what you say always, Annette," she answered. And then—and then—I said: "Tomorrow you will bring a tallow candle out into the playground at twelve o'clock and start to eat it. And if anyone asks you, you will say that it is the best *galette* you ever tasted." Oh! Raoul, think of it!'

"'But she'll never do such a thing,' I objected.

"'The book says so. Not that I can quite believe it—but, oh! Raoul, if the book is all true, how we shall amuse ourselves!'

"I, too, thought the idea very funny. We passed word round to the comrades and at twelve o'clock we were all in the playground. Punctual to the minute, out came Felicie with a stump of candle in her hand. Will you believe me, Messieurs, she began solemnly to nibble at it. We were all in hysterics! Every now and then one or another of the children would go up to her and say solemnly: 'It is good, what you eat there, eh, Felicie?' And she would answer. 'But, yes, it is the best *galette* I ever tasted.' And then we would shriek with laughter. We laughed at last so loud that the noise seemed to wake up Felicie to a realization of what she was doing. She blinked her eyes in a puzzled way, looked at the candle, then at us. She passed her hand over her forehead.

"'But what is it that I do here?' she muttered.

"'You are eating a candle,' we screamed.

"'*I* made you do it. *I* made you do it,' cried Annette, dancing about.

"Felicie stared for a moment. Then she went slowly up to Annette.

"'So it is you—it is you who have made me ridiculous? I seem to remember. Ah! I will kill you for this.'

"She spoke in a very quiet tone, but Annette rushed suddenly away and hid behind me.

"'Save me, Raoul! I am afraid of Felicie. It was only a joke, Felicie. Only a joke.'

"'I do not like these jokes,' said Felicie. 'You understand? I hate you. I hate you all.'

"She suddenly burst out crying and rushed away.

"Annette was, I think, scared by the result of her experiment, and did not try to repeat it. But from that day on her ascendancy over Felicie seemed to grow stronger.

"Felicie, I now believe, always hated her, but nevertheless she could not keep away from her. She used to follow Annette around like a dog.

"Soon after that, Messieurs, employment was found for me, and I only came to the Home for occasional holidays. Annette's desire to become a dancer was not taken seriously, but she developed a very pretty singing voice as she grew older and Miss Slater consented to her being trained as a singer.

"She was not lazy, Annette. She worked feverishly, without rest. Miss Slater was obliged to prevent her doing too much. She spoke to me once about her.

" 'You have always been fond of Annette,' she said. 'Persuade her not to work too hard. She has a little cough lately that I do not like.'

"My work took me far afield soon afterward. I received one or two letters from Annette at first, but then came silence. For five years after that I was abroad.

"Quite by chance, when I returned to Paris, my attention was caught by a poster advertising Annette Ravelli with a picture of the lady. I recognized her at once. That night I went to the theater in question. Annette sang in French and Italian. On the stage she was wonderful. Afterward I went to her dressing room. She received me at once.

" 'Why, Raoul,' she cried, stretching out her whitened hands to me. "This is splendid! Where have you been all these years?'

"I would have told her, but she did not really want to listen.

" 'You see, I have very nearly arrived!'

"She waved a triumphant hand round the room filled with bouquets.

" 'The good Miss Slater must be proud of your success.'

" 'That old one? No, indeed. She designed me, you know, for the Conservatoire. Decorous concert singing. But me, I am an artist. It is here, on the variety stage, that I can express myself.'

"Just then a handsome middle-aged man came in. He was very distinguished. By his manner I soon saw that he was Annette's protector. He looked sideways at me, and Annette explained.

" 'A friend of my infancy. He passes through Paris, sees my picture on a poster, *et voilà!*'

"The man was then very affable and courteous. In my presence he produced a ruby and diamond bracelet and clasped it on Annette's wrist. As I rose to go, she threw me a glance of triumph and a whisper.

"'I arrive, do I not? You see? All the world is before me.'

"But as I left the room, I heard her cough, a sharp dry cough. I knew what it meant, that cough. It was the legacy of her consumptive mother.

"I saw her next two years later. She had gone for refuge to Miss Slater. Her career had broken down. She was in a state of advanced consumption for which the doctors said nothing could be done.

"Ah! I shall never forget her as I saw her then! She was lying in a kind of shelter in the garden. She was kept outdoors night and day. Her cheeks were hollow and flushed, her eyes bright and feverish.

"She greeted me with a kind of desperation that startled me.

"'It is good to see you, Raoul. You know what they say—that I may not get well? They say it behind my back, you understand. To me they are soothing and consolatory. But it is not true, Raoul, it is not true! I shall not permit myself to die. Die? With beautiful life stretching in front of me? It is the will to live that matters. All the great doctors say that nowadays. I am not one of the feeble ones who let go. Already I feel myself infinitely better—infinitely better, do you hear?'

"She raised herself on her elbow to drive her words home, then fell back, attacked by a fit of coughing that racked her thin body.

"'The cough—it is nothing,' she gasped. 'And hemorrhages do not frighten me. I shall surprise the doctors. It is the will that counts. Remember, Raoul, I am going to live.'

"It was pitiful, you understand, pitiful.

"Just then, Felicie Bault came out with a tray. A glass of hot milk. She gave it to Annette and watched her drink it with an expression that I could not fathom. There was a kind of smug satisfaction in it.

"Annette, too, caught the look. She flung the glass down angrily, so that it smashed to bits.

"'You see her? That is how she always looks at me. She is glad I am going to die! Yes, she gloats over it. She who is well and strong. Look at her—never a day's illness, that one! And all for nothing. What good is that great carcass of hers to her? What can she make of it?'

"Felicie stooped and picked up the broken fragments of glass.

"'I do not mind what she says,' she observed in a singsong voice.

'What does it matter? I am a respectable girl, I am. As for her. She will be knowing the fires of Purgatory before very long. I am a Christian. I say nothing.'

"'You hate me!' cried Annette. 'You have always hated me. Ah! but I can charm you, all the same. I can make you do what I want. See now, if I asked you to, you would go down on your knees before me now on the grass.'

"'You are absurd,' said Felicie uneasily.

"'But, yes, you will do it. You will. To please me. Down on your knees. I ask it of you, I, Annette. Down on your knees, Felicie.'

"Whether it was the wonderful pleading in the voice, or some deeper motive, Felicie obeyed. She sank slowly on to her knees, her arms spread wide, her face vacant and stupid.

"Annette flung back her head and laughed—peal upon peal of laughter.

"'Look at her, with her stupid face! How ridiculous she looks. You can get up now, Felicie, thank you! It is of no use to scowl at me. I am your mistress. You have to do what I say.'

"She lay back on her pillows exhausted. Felicie picked up the tray and moved slowly away. Once she looked back over her shoulder, and the smoldering resentment in her eyes startled me.

"I was not there when Annette died. But it was terrible, it seems. She clung to life. She fought against death like a madwoman. Again and again she gasped out: 'I will not die—do you hear me? I will not die. I will live—live—'

"Miss Slater told me all this when I came to see her six months later.

"'My poor Raoul,' she said kindly. 'You loved her, did you not?'"

"'Always—always. But of what use could I be to her? Let us not talk of it. She is dead—she so brilliant, so full of burning life. . . .'

"Miss Slater was a sympathetic woman. She went on to talk of other things. She was very worried about Felicie, so she told me. The girl had had a queer sort of nervous breakdown and ever since she had been very strange in manner.

"'You know,' said Miss Slater, after a momentary hesitation, 'that she is learning the piano?'

"I did not know it and was very much surprised to hear it. Felicie—learning the piano! I would have declared the girl would not know one note from another.

"'She has talent, they say,' continued Miss Slater. 'I can't understand it. I have always put her down as—well, Raoul, you know yourself, she was always a stupid girl.'

"I nodded.

"'She is so strange in her manner I don't know what to make of it.'

"A few minutes later I entered the Salle de Lecture. Felicie was playing the piano. She was playing the air that I had heard Annette sing in Paris. You understand, Messieurs, it gave me quite a turn. And then, hearing me, she broke off suddenly and looked round at me, her eyes full of mockery and intelligence. For a moment I thought—Well, I will not tell you what I thought.

"'*Tiens!*' she said. 'So it is you—Monsieur Raoul.'

"I cannot describe the way she said it. To Annette I had never ceased to be Raoul. But Felicie, since we had met as grown-ups, always addressed me as Monsieur Raoul. But the way she said it now was different—as though the *Monsieur,* slightly stressed, was somehow amusing.

"'Why, Felicie,' I stammered, 'you look quite different today.'

"'Do I?' she said reflectively. 'It is odd, that. But do not be so solemn, Raoul—decidedly I shall call you Raoul—did we not play together as children?—Life was made for laughter. Let us talk of the poor Annette—she who is dead and buried. Is she in Purgatory, I wonder, or where?'

"And she hummed a snatch of song—untunefully enough, but the words caught my attention.

"'Felicie!' I cried. 'You speak Italian?'

"'Why not, Raoul? I am not as stupid as I pretend to be, perhaps.' She laughed at my mystification.

"'I don't understand—,' I began.

"'But I will tell you. I am a very fine actress, though no one suspects it. I can play many parts—and play them very well.'

"She laughed again and ran quickly out of the room before I could stop her.

"I saw her again before I left. She was asleep in an armchair. She was snoring heavily. I stood and watched her, fascinated, yet repelled. Suddenly she woke with a start. Her eyes, dull and lifeless, met mine.

"'Monsieur Raoul,' she muttered mechanically.

"'Yes, Felicie. I am going now. Will you play for me again before I go?'

"'I? Play? You are laughing at me, Monsieur Raoul.'

"'Don't you remember playing for me this morning?'

"She shook her head.

"'I play? How can a poor girl like me play?'

"She paused for a minute as though in thought, then beckoned me nearer.

"'Monsieur Raoul, there are things going on in this house! They play tricks upon you. They alter the clocks. Yes, yes, I know what I am saying. And it is all her doing.'

"'Whose doing?' I asked, startled.

"'That Annette's. That wicked one's. When she was alive she always tormented me. Now that she is dead, she comes back from the dead to torment me.'

"I stared at Felicie. I could see now that she was in an extremity of terror, her eyes starting from her head.

"'She is bad, that one. She is bad, I tell you. She would take the bread from your mouth, the clothes from your back, the soul from your body. . . .'

"She clutched me suddenly.

"'I am afraid, I tell you—afraid. I hear her voice—not in my ear—no, not in my ear. Here, in my head—' She tapped her forehead. 'She will drive me away—drive me away altogether, and then what shall I do, what will become of me?'

"Her voice rose almost to a shriek. She had in her eyes the look of the terrified beast at bay. . . .

"Suddenly she smiled, a pleasant smile, full of cunning, with something in it that made me shiver.

"'If it should come to it, Monsieur Raoul, I am very strong with my hands—very strong with my hands.'

"I had never noticed her hands particularly before. I looked at them now and shuddered in spite of myself. Squat brutal fingers, and as Felicie had said, terribly strong. . . . I cannot explain to you the nausea that swept over me. With hands such as these her father must have strangled her mother. . . .

"That was the last time I ever saw Felicie Bault. Immediately afterward I went abroad—to South America. I returned from there two years after her death. Something I had read in the newspapers of her life and sudden death. I have heard fuller details tonight—from you. Felicie 3 and Felicie 4—I wonder? She was a good actress, you know!"

The train suddenly slackened speed. The man in the corner sat erect and buttoned his overcoat more closely.

"What is your theory?" asked the lawyer, leaning forward.

"I can hardly believe—," began Canon Parfitt, and stopped.

The doctor said nothing. He was gazing steadily at Raoul Letardeau.

"The clothes from your back, the soul from your body," quoted the Frenchman lightly. He stood up. "I say to you, Messieurs, that the history of Felicie Bault is the history of Annette Ravel. You did not know her, gentlemen. I did. She was very fond of life. . . ."

His hand on the door, ready to spring out, he turned suddenly and bending down tapped Canon Parfitt on the chest.

"M. le docteur over there, he said just now that all this"—his hand smote the Canon's stomach, and the Canon winced—"was only a residence. Tell me, if you find a burglar in your house what do you do? Shoot him, do you not?"

"No," cried the Canon. "No, indeed—I mean—not in this country."

But he spoke the last words to empty air. The carriage door banged.

The clergyman, the lawyer, and the doctor were alone. The fourth corner was vacant.

S.O.S.

"Ah!" said Mr. Dinsmead appreciatively. He stepped back and surveyed the round table with approval. The firelight gleamed on the coarse white tablecloth, the knives and forks, and the other table appointments.

"Is—is everything ready?" asked Mrs. Dinsmead hesitatingly. She was a little faded woman, with a colorless face, meager hair scraped back from her forehead, and a perpetually nervous manner.

"Everything's ready," said her husband with a kind of ferocious geniality.

He was a big man, with stooping shoulders and a broad red face. He had little pig's eyes that twinkled under his bushy brows, and a big jowl devoid of hair.

"Lemonade?" suggested Mrs. Dinsmead, almost in a whisper.

Her husband shook his head.

"Tea. Much better in every way. Look at the weather, streaming and blowing. A nice cup of hot tea is what's needed for supper on an evening like this."

He winked facetiously, then fell to surveying the table again.

"A good dish of eggs, cold corned beef, and bread and cheese.

That's my order for supper. So come along and get it ready, Mother. Charlotte's in the kitchen waiting to give you a hand."

Mrs. Dinsmead rose, carefully winding up the ball of her knitting.

"She's grown a very good-looking girl," she murmured.

"Ah!" said Mr. Dinsmead. "The mortal image of her ma! So go along with you, and don't let's waste any more time."

He strolled about the room humming to himself for a minute or two. Once he approached the window and looked out.

"Wild weather," he murmured to himself. "Not much likelihood of our having visitors tonight."

Then he too left the room.

About ten minutes later Mrs. Dinsmead entered bearing a dish of fried eggs. Her two daughters followed, bringing the rest of the provisions. Mr. Dinsmead and his son Johnnie brought up the rear. The former seated himself at the head of the table.

"And for what we are to receive, et cetera," he remarked humorously. "And blessings on the man who first thought of tinned foods. What would we do, I should like to know, miles from anywhere, if we hadn't a tin now and then to fall back upon when the butcher forgets his weekly call?"

He proceeded to carve corned beef dexterously.

"I wonder who ever thought of building a house like this, miles from anywhere," said his daughter Magdalen, pettishly. "We never see a soul."

"No," said her father. "Never a soul."

"I can't think what made you take it, Father," said Charlotte.

"Can't you, my girl? Well, I had my reasons—I had my reasons."

His eyes sought his wife's furtively, but she frowned.

"And haunted, too," said Charlotte. "I wouldn't sleep alone here for anything."

"Pack of nonsense," said her father. "Never seen anything, have you?"

"Not seen anything perhaps, but—"

"But what?"

Charlotte did not reply, but she shivered a little. A great surge of rain came driving against the window-pane, and Mrs. Dinsmead dropped a spoon with a tinkle on the tray.

"Not nervous, are you, Mother?" said Mr. Dinsmead. "It's a wild night, that's all. Don't you worry, we're safe here by our fireside, and not a soul from outside likely to disturb us. Why, it would be a miracle if anyone did. And miracles don't happen. No," he added as though to himself, with a kind of peculiar satisfaction, "miracles don't happen."

As the words left his lips there came a sudden knocking at the door. Mr. Dinsmead stayed as though petrified.

"What's that?" he muttered. His jaw fell.

Mrs. Dinsmead gave a little whimpering cry and pulled her shawl up round her. The color came into Magdalen's face and she leaned forward and spoke to her father.

"The miracle has happened," she said. "You'd better go and let whoever it is in."

TWENTY MINUTES EARLIER Mortimer Cleveland had stood in the driving rain and mist surveying his car. It was really cursed bad luck. Two punctures within ten minutes of each other, and here he was, stranded, miles from anywhere, in the midst of these bare Wiltshire Downs with night coming on and no prospect of shelter. Serve him right for trying to take a short cut. If only he had stuck to the main road! Now he was lost on what seemed a mere cart-track on the hillside, with no possibility of getting the car farther, and with no idea if there were even a village anywhere near.

He looked round him perplexedly, and his eye was caught by a gleam of light on the hillside above him. A second later the mist obscured it once more but, waiting patiently, he presently got a second glimpse of it. After a moment's cogitation, he left the car and struck up the side of the hill.

Soon he was out of the mist, and he recognized the light as shining from the lighted window of a small cottage. Here, at any rate, was shelter. Mortimer Cleveland quickened his pace, bending his head to meet the furious onslaught of wind and rain trying its best to drive him back.

Cleveland was, in his own way, something of a celebrity, though doubtless the majority of folks would have displayed complete ignorance of his name and achievements. He was an authority on mental science and had written two excellent text books on the subconscious. He was also a member of the Psychical Research Society and a student of the occult in so far as it affected his own conclusions and line of research.

He was by nature peculiarly susceptible to atmosphere, and by deliberate training he had increased his own natural gift. When he had at last reached the cottage and rapped at the door, he was conscious of an excitement, a quickening of interest, as though all his faculties had suddenly been sharpened.

The murmur of voices within had been plainly audible to him. Upon his knock there came a sudden silence, then the sound of a chair being pushed back along the floor. In another minute the door was flung open by a boy of about fifteen. Cleveland could look straight over his shoulder upon the scene within.

It reminded him of an interior by some Dutch painter. A round table spread for a meal, a family party sitting round it, one or two flickering candles and the firelight's glow over all. The father, a big man, sat at one side of the table, a little gray woman with a frightened face sat opposite him. Facing the door, looking straight at Cleveland, was a girl. Her startled eyes looked straight into his, her hand with a cup in it was arrested halfway to her lips.

She was, Cleveland saw at once, a beautiful girl of an extremely uncommon type. Her hair, red gold, stood out round her face like a mist; her eyes, very far apart, were a pure gray. She had the mouth and chin of an early Italian Madonna.

There was a moment's dead silence. Then Cleveland stepped into the room and explained his predicament. He brought his trite story to a close, and there was another pause harder to understand. At last, as though with an effort, the father rose.

"Come in, sir—Mr. Cleveland, did you say?"

"That is my name," said Mortimer, smiling.

"Ah, yes. Come in, Mr. Cleveland. Not weather for a dog outside, is it? Come in by the fire. Shut the door, can't you, Johnnie? Don't stand there half the night."

Cleveland came forward and sat on a wooden stool by the fire. The boy Johnnie shut the door.

"Dinsmead, that's my name," said the other man. He was all geniality now. "This is the Missus, and these are my two daughters, Charlotte and Magdalen."

For the first time, Cleveland saw the face of the girl who had been sitting with her back to him, and saw that, in a totally different way, she was quite as beautiful as her sister. Very dark, with a face of marble pallor, a delicate aquiline nose, and a grave mouth. It was a kind of frozen beauty, austere and almost forbidding. She acknowledged her father's introduction by bending her head, and she looked at him with an intent gaze that was searching in character. It was as though she were summing him up, weighing him in the balance of her clear young judgment.

"A drop of something to drink, eh, Mr. Cleveland?"

"Thank you," said Mortimer. "A cup of tea will meet the case admirably."

Mr. Dinsmead hesitated a minute, then he picked up the five cups, one after another, from the table and emptied them into the slop bowl.

"This tea's cold," he said brusquely. "Make us some more, will you, Mother?"

Mrs. Dinsmead got up quickly and hurried off with the teapot. Mortimer had an idea that she was glad to get out of the room.

The fresh tea soon came, and the unexpected guest was plied with viands.

Mr. Dinsmead talked and talked. He was expansive, genial, loquacious. He told the stranger all about himself. He'd lately retired from the building trade—yes, made quite a good thing out of it. He and the Missus thought they'd like a bit of country air—never lived in the country before. Wrong time of year to choose, of course, October and November, but they didn't want to wait "Life's uncertain, you know, sir." So they had taken this cottage. Eight miles from anywhere, and nineteen miles from anything you could call a town. No, they didn't complain. The girls found it a bit dull, but he and Mother enjoyed the quiet.

So he talked on, leaving Mortimer almost hypnotized by the easy flow. Nothing here, surely, but rather commonplace domesticity. And yet, at that first glimpse of the interior, he had diagnosed something else, some tension, some strain, emanating from one of those four people—he didn't know which. Mere foolishness, his nerves were all awry! They were startled by his sudden appearance—that was all.

He broached the question of a night's lodging, and was met with a ready response.

"You'll have to stop with us, Mr. Cleveland. Nothing else for miles around. We can give you a bedroom, and though my pajamas may be a bit roomy, why, they're better than nothing, and your own clothes will be dry by morning."

"It's very good of you."

"Not at all," said the other genially. "As I said just now, one couldn't turn away a dog on a night like this. Magdalen, Charlotte, go up and see to the room."

The two girls left the room. Presently Mortimer heard them moving about overhead.

"I can quite understand that two attractive young ladies like your daughters might find it dull here," said Cleveland.

"Good lookers, aren't they?" said Mr. Dinsmead with fatherly pride. "Not much like their mother or myself. We're a homely pair, but much attached to each other, I'll tell you that, Mr. Cleveland. Eh, Maggie, isn't that so?"

Mrs. Dinsmead smiled primly. She had started knitting again. The needles clicked busily. She was a fast knitter.

Presently the room was announced ready, and Mortimer, expressing thanks once more, declared his intention of turning in.

"Did you put a hot-water bottle in the bed?" demanded Mrs. Dinsmead, suddenly mindful of her house pride.

"Yes, Mother, two."

"That's right," said Dinsmead. "Go up with him, girls, and see that every thing is all right."

Magdalen preceded him up the staircase, her candle held aloft. Charlotte came behind.

The room was quite a pleasant one, small and with a sloping roof, but the bed looked comfortable, and the few pieces of somewhat dusty furniture were of old mahogany. A large can of hot water stood in the basin, a pair of pink pajamas of ample proportions were laid over a chair, and the bed was made and turned down.

Magdalen went over to the window and saw that the fastenings were secure. Charlotte cast a final eye over the washstand appointments. Then they both lingered by the door.

"Good night, Mr. Cleveland. You are sure there is everything?"

"Yes, thank you, Miss Magdalen. I am sorry to have given you both so much trouble. Good night."

"Good night."

They went out, shutting the door behind them. Mortimer Cleveland was alone. He undressed slowly and thoughtfully. When he had donned Mr. Dinsmead's pink pajamas, he gathered up his own wet clothes and put them outside the door as his host had bade him. From downstairs he could hear the rumble of Dinsmead's voice.

What a talker the man was! Altogether an odd personality—but indeed there was something odd about the whole family, or was it his imagination?

He went slowly back into his room and shut the door. He stood by the bed lost in thought. And then he started—

The mahogany table by the bed was smothered in dust. Written in the dust were three letters, clearly visible. *S.O.S.*

Mortimer stared as if he could hardly believe his eyes. It was a confirmation of all his vague surmises and forebodings. He was right, then. Something was wrong in this house.

S.O.S. A call for help. But whose finger had written it in the dust? Magdalen's or Charlotte's? They had both stood there, he remembered, for a moment or two, before going out of the room.

Whose hand had secretly dropped to the table and traced out those three letters?

The faces of the two girls came up before him. Magdalen's, dark and aloof, and Charlotte's, as he had seen it first, wide-eyed, startled, with an unfathomable something in her glance.

He went again to the door and opened it. The boom of Mr. Dinsmead's voice was no longer to be heard. The house was silent.

He thought to himself.

"I can do nothing tonight. Tomorrow—well, we shall see."

CLEVELAND WOKE EARLY. He went down through the living room, and out into the garden. The morning was fresh and beautiful after the rain. Someone else was up early, too. At the bottom of the garden Charlotte was leaning on the fence staring out over the Downs. His pulses quickened a little as he went down to join her. All along he had been secretly convinced that it was Charlotte who had written the message. As he came up to her, she turned and wished him "Good morning." Her eyes were direct and childlike, with no hint of a secret understanding in them.

"A very good morning," said Mortimer, smiling. "The weather this morning is a contrast to last night's."

"It is indeed."

Mortimer broke off a twig from a tree near by. With it he began idly to draw on the smooth, sandy patch at his feet. He traced an S, then an O, then an S, watching the girl narrowly as he did so. But again he could detect no gleam of comprehension.

"Do you know what these letters represent?" he said abruptly.

Charlotte frowned a little. "Aren't they what boats send out when they are in distress?" she asked.

Mortimer nodded. "Someone wrote that on the table by my bed last night," he said quietly. "I thought perhaps you might have done so."

She looked at him in wide-eyed astonishment.

"I? Oh, no."

He was wrong then. A sharp pang of disappointment shot through him. He had been so sure—so sure. It was not often that his intuitions led him astray.

"You are quite certain?" he persisted.

"Oh, yes."

They turned and went slowly together toward the house. Charlotte seemed preoccupied about something. She replied at random to the few observations he made. Suddenly she burst out in a low, hurried voice.

"It—it's odd your asking that about those letters, *S.O.S.* I didn't write them, of course, but—I so easily might have."

He stopped and looked at her, and she went on quickly: "It sounds silly, I know, but I have been so frightened, so dreadfully frightened, and when you came in last night, it seemed like an—an answer to something."

"What are you frightened of?" he asked quickly.

"I don't know."

"You don't know?"

"I think—it's the house. Ever since we came here it has been growing and growing. Everyone seems different somehow. Father, Mother, and Magdalen, they all seem different."

Mortimer did not speak at once, and before he could do so, Charlotte went on again.

"You know this house is supposed to be haunted?"

"What?" All his interest was quickened.

"Yes, a man murdered his wife in it, oh, some years ago now. We only found out about it after we got here. Father says ghosts are all nonsense, but I—don't know."

Mortimer was thinking rapidly.

"Tell me," he said in a businesslike tone, "was this murder committed in the room I had last night?"

"I don't know anything about that," said Charlotte.

"I wonder now," said Mortimer half to himself, "yes, that may be it."

Charlotte looked at him uncomprehendingly.

"Miss Dinsmead," said Mortimer, gently, "Have you ever had any reason to believe that you are mediumistic?"

She stared at him.

"I think you know that you did write *S.O.S.* last night," he said quietly. "Oh! quite unconsciously, of course. A crime stains the atmosphere, so to speak. A sensitive mind such as yours might be acted upon in such a manner. You have been reproducing the sensations and impressions of the victim. Many years ago *she* may have written *S.O.S.* on that table, and you unconsciously reproduced her act last night."

Charlotte's face brightened.

"I see," she said. "You think that is the explanation?"

A voice called her from the house, and she went in, leaving Mortimer to pace up and down the garden paths. Was he satisfied with his own explanation? Did it cover the facts as he knew them? Did it account for the tension he had felt on entering the house last night?

Perhaps, and yet he still had the odd feeling that his sudden appearance had produced something very like consternation. He thought to himself.

"I must not be carried away by the psychic explanation. It might account for Charlotte—but not for the others. My coming as I did upset them horribly, all except Johnnie. Whatever it is that's the matter, Johnnie is out of it."

He was quite sure of that; strange that he should be so positive, but there it was.

At that minute Johnnie himself came out of the cottage and approached the guest.

"Breakfast's ready," he said awkwardly. "Will you come in?"

Mortimer noticed that the lad's fingers were much stained. Johnnie felt his glance and laughed ruefully.

"I'm always messing about with chemicals, you know," he said. "It makes Dad awfully wild sometimes. He wants me to go into building, but I want to do chemistry and research work."

Mr. Dinsmead appeared at the window ahead of them, broad, jovial, smiling, and at sight of him all Mortimer's distrust and antagonism reawakened. Mrs. Dinsmead was already seated at the table. She wished him "Good morning" in her colorless voice, and he had again the impression that for some reason or other, she was afraid of him.

Magdalen came in last. She gave him a brief nod and took her seat opposite him.

"Did you sleep well?" she asked abruptly. "Was your bed comfortable?"

She looked at him very earnestly, and when he replied courteously in the affirmative he noticed something very like a flicker of disappointment pass over her face. What had she expected him to say, he wondered?

He turned to his host.

"This lad of yours is interested in chemistry, it seems," he said pleasantly.

There was a crash. Mrs. Dinsmead had dropped her tea cup.

"Now then, Maggie, now then," said her husband.

It seemed to Mortimer that there was admonition, warning, in his voice. He turned to his guest and spoke fluently of the advantages of the building trade, and of not letting young boys get above themselves.

After breakfast he went out in the garden by himself, and smoked. The time was clearly at hand when he must leave the cottage. A night's shelter was one thing; to prolong it was difficult without an excuse, and what possible excuse could he offer? And yet he was singularly loath to depart.

Turning the thing over and over in his mind, he took a path that led round the other side of the house. His shoes were soled with crepe rubber, and made little or no noise. He was passing the kitchen window when he heard Dinsmead's words from within, and the words attracted his attention immediately.

"It's a fair lump of money, it is."

Mrs. Dinsmead's voice answered. It was too faint in tone for Mortimer to hear the words, but Dinsmead replied:

"Nigh on £60,000, the lawyer said."

Mortimer had no intention of eavesdropping, but he retraced his steps very thoughtfully. The mention of money seemed to crystallize the situation. Somewhere or other there was a question of £60,000. It made the thing clearer—and uglier.

Magdalen came out of the house, but her father's voice called her almost immediately, and she went in again. Presently Dinsmead himself joined his guest.

"Rare good morning," he said genially. "I hope your car will be none the worse."

"Wants to find out when I'm going," thought Mortimer to himself.

Aloud he thanked Mr. Dinsmead once more for his timely hospitality.

"Not at all, not at all," said the other.

Magdalen and Charlotte came together out of the house and strolled arm in arm to a rustic seat some little distance away. The dark head and the golden one made a pleasant contrast together and on an impulse Mortimer said:

"Your daughters are very unlike, Mr. Dinsmead."

The other who was just lighting his pipe gave a sharp jerk of the wrist and dropped the match.

"Do you think so?" he asked. "Yes, well, I suppose they are."

Mortimer had a flash of intuition.

"But of course they are not both your daughters," he said smoothly.

He saw Dinsmead look at him, hesitate for a moment, and then make up his mind.

"That's very clever of you, sir," he said. "No, one of them is a foundling; we took her in as a baby and we have brought her up as our own. She herself has not the least idea of the truth, but she'll have to know soon." He sighed.

"A question of inheritance?" suggested Mortimer quietly.

The other flashed a suspicious look at him.

Then he decided that frankness was best; his manner became almost aggressively frank and open.

"It's odd you should say that, sir."

"A case of telepathy, eh?" said Mortimer, and smiled.

"It is like this, sir. We took her in to oblige the mother—for a consideration, as at the time I was just starting in the building trade.

A few months ago I noticed an advertisement in the papers, and it seemed to me that the child in question must be our Magdalen. I went to see the lawyers, and there has been a lot of talk one way and another. They were suspicious—naturally, as you might say—but everything is cleared up now. I am taking the girl herself to London next week—she doesn't know anything about it so far. Her father, it seems, was a very rich man. He only learned of the child's existence a few months before his death. He hired agents to try and trace her, and left all his money to her when she should be found."

Mortimer listened with close attention. He had no reason to doubt Mr. Dinsmead's story. It explained Magdalen's dark beauty; explained too, perhaps, her aloof manner. Nevertheless, though the story itself might be true, something lay undivulged behind it.

But Mortimer had no intention of rousing the other's suspicions. Instead, he must go out of his way to allay them.

"A very interesting story, Mr. Dinsmead," he said. "I congratulate Miss Magdalen. An heiress and a beauty, she has a great future ahead."

"She has that," agreed her father warmly, "and she's a rare good girl too, Mr. Cleveland."

There was every evidence of hearty warmth in his manner.

"Well," said Mortimer, "I must be pushing along now, I suppose. I have got to thank you once more, Mr. Dinsmead, for your singularly well-timed hospitality."

Accompanied by his host, he went into the house to bid farewell to Mrs. Dinsmead. She was standing by the window with her back to them, and did not hear them enter. At her husband's jovial, "Here's Mr. Cleveland come to say good-bye," she started nervously and swung round, dropping something which she held in her hand. Mortimer picked it up for her. It was a miniature of Charlotte done in the style of some twenty-five years ago. Mortimer repeated to her the thanks he had already proffered to her husband. He noticed again her look of fear and the furtive glances that she shot at him beneath her eyelids.

The two girls were not in evidence, but it was not part of Mortimer's policy to seem anxious to see them; also he had his own idea, which was shortly to prove correct.

He had gone about half a mile from the house on his way down to where he had left the car the night before, when the bushes on one side of the path were thrust aside, and Magdalen came out on the track ahead of him.

"I had to see you," she said.

"I expected you," said Mortimer. "It was you who wrote S.O.S. on the table in my room last night, wasn't it?"

Magdalen nodded.

"Why?" asked Mortimer gently.

The girl turned aside and began pulling off leaves from a bush.

"I don't know," she said. "Honestly, I don't know."

"Tell me," said Mortimer.

Magdalen drew a deep breath.

"I am a practical person," she said, "not the kind of person who imagines things or fancies them. You, I think, believe in ghosts and spirits. I don't, and when I tell you that there is something very wrong in that house," she pointed up the hill, "I mean that there is something tangibly wrong—it's not just an echo of the past. It has been coming on ever since we've been there. Every day it grows worse. Father is different, Mother is different, Charlotte is different."

Mortimer interposed. "Is Johnnie different?" he asked.

Magdalen looked at him, a dawning appreciation in her eyes. "No," she said, "now I come to think of it. Johnnie is not different. He is the only one who's—who's untouched by it all. He was untouched last night at tea."

"And you?" asked Mortimer.

"I was afraid—horribly afraid, just like a child—without knowing what it was I was afraid of. And Father was—queer, there's no other word for it. He talked about miracles and then I prayed—actually prayed for a miracle, and *you* knocked on the door."

She stopped abruptly, staring at him. "I seem mad to you, I suppose," she said defiantly.

"No," said Mortimer, "on the contrary you seem extremely sane. All sane people have a premonition of danger if it is near them."

"You don't understand," said Magdalen. "I was not afraid—for myself."

"For whom, then?"

But again Magdalen shook her head in a puzzled fashion. "I don't know."

She went on: "I wrote *S.O.S.* on an impulse. I had an idea—absurd, no doubt—that they would not let me speak to you—the rest of them, I mean. I don't know what it was I meant to ask you to do. I don't know now."

"Never mind," said Mortimer. "I shall do it."

"What can you do?"

Mortimer smiled a little.

"I can think."

She looked at him doubtfully.

"Yes," said Mortimer, "a lot can be done that way, more than you would ever believe. Tell me, was there any chance word or phrase that attracted your attention just before that meal last evening?"

Magdalen frowned. "I don't think so," she said.

"At least I heard Father saying something to Mother about Charlotte being the living image of her, and he laughed in a very queer way, but—there's nothing odd in that, is there?"

"No," said Mortimer slowly, "except that Charlotte is not like your mother."

He remained lost in thought for a minute or two, then looked up to find Magdalen watching him uncertainly.

"Go home, child," he said, "and don't worry. Leave it in my hands."

She went obediently up the path toward the cottage. Mortimer strolled on a little farther, then threw himself from conscious thought or effort, and let a series of pictures flit at will across the surface of his mind.

Johnnie! He always came back to Johnnie. Johnnie, completely innocent, utterly free from all the network of suspicion and intrigue, but nevertheless the pivot around which everything turned. He remembered the crash of Mrs. Dinsmead's cup on her saucer at breakfast that morning. What had caused her agitation? A chance reference on his part to the lad's fondness for chemicals? At the moment he had not been conscious of Mr. Dinsmead, but he saw him now clearly, as he sat, his teacup poised halfway to his lips.

That took him back to Charlotte, as he had seen her when the door opened last night. She had sat staring at him over the rim of her teacup. And swiftly on that followed another memory. Mr. Dinsmead emptying teacups one after the other, and saying, "This tea's cold."

He remembered the steam that went up. Surely the tea had not been so very cold after all?

Something began to stir in his brain. A memory of something read not so very long ago, within a month perhaps. Some account of a whole family poisoned by a lad's carelessness. A packet of arsenic left in the larder had sifted through to the bread below. He had read it in the paper. Probably Mr. Dinsmead had read it too.

Things began to grow clearer. . . .

Half an hour later, Mortimer Cleveland rose briskly to his feet.

IT WAS EVENING once more in the cottage. The eggs were poached tonight and there was a tin of brawn. Presently Mrs. Dinsmead came in from the kitchen bearing the big teapot. The family took their places round the table.

Mrs. Dinsmead filled the cups and handed them round the table. Then, as she put the teapot down, she gave a sudden little cry and pressed her hand to her throat. Mr. Dinsmead swung round in his chair, following the direction of her terrified eyes. Mortimer Cleveland was standing in the doorway.

He came forward. His manner was pleasant and apologetic.

"I'm afraid I startled you," he said. "I had to come back for something."

"Back for something," cried Mr. Dinsmead. His face was purple, his veins swelling. "Back for what, I should like to know?"

"Some tea," said Mortimer.

With a swift gesture he took something from his pocket and taking up one of the teacups from the table, emptied some of its contents into a little test-tube he held in his left hand.

"What—what are you doing?" gasped Mr. Dinsmead. His face

had gone chalky-white, the purple dying out as if by magic. Mrs. Dinsmead gave a thin, high, frightened cry.

"You read the papers, Mr. Dinsmead? I am sure you do. Sometimes one reads accounts of a whole family being poisoned—some of them recover, some do not. In this case, one would not. The first explanation would be the tinned brawn you were eating, but supposing the doctor to be a suspicious man, not easily taken in by the tinned food theory? There is a packet of arsenic in your larder. On the shelf below it is a packet of tea. There is a convenient hole in the top shelf. What more natural to suppose than that the arsenic found its way into the tea by accident? Your son Johnnie might be blamed for carelessness, nothing more."

"I—I don't know what you mean," gasped Dinsmead.

"I think you do." Mortimer took up a second teacup and filled a second test-tube. He fixed a red label to one and a blue label to the other.

"The red-labeled one," he said, "contains tea from your daughter Charlotte's cup, the other from your daughter Magdalen's. I am prepared to swear that in the first I shall find four or five times the amount of arsenic than in the latter."

"You are mad!" said Dinsmead.

"Oh, dear me, no. I am nothing of the kind. You told me today, Mr. Dinsmead, that Magdalen was not your own daughter. You lied to me. Magdalen *is* your daughter. Charlotte was the child you adopted, the child who was so like her mother that when I held a miniature of that mother in my hand today I mistook it for one of Charlotte herself. You wanted your own daughter to inherit the fortune, and since it might be impossible to keep Charlotte out of sight, and someone who knew her mother might have realized the truth of the resemblance, you decided on, well—sufficient white arsenic at the bottom of a teacup."

Mrs. Dinsmead gave a sudden high cackle, rocking herself to and fro in violent hysterics.

"Tea," she squeaked, "that's what he said, tea, not lemonade."

"Hold your tongue, can't you?" roared her husband wrathfully.

Mortimer saw Charlotte looking at him, wide-eyed, wondering, across the table. Then he felt a hand on his arm, and Magdalen dragged him out of earshot.

"Those," she pointed at the vials—"Daddy. You won't—"

Mortimer laid his hand on her shoulder. "My child," he said, "you don't believe in the past. I do. I believe in the atmosphere of this house. If he had not come to this particular house, perhaps—I say *perhaps*—your father might not have conceived the plan he did. I will keep these two test-tubes to safeguard Charlotte now and in the future. Apart from that, I shall do nothing—in gratitude, if you will, to the hand that wrote *S.O.S.*"

WHERE THERE'S A WILL

"Above all, avoid worry and excitement," said Dr. Meynell, in the comfortable fashion affected by doctors.

Mrs. Harter, as is often the case with people hearing these soothing but meaningless words, seemed more doubtful than relieved.

"There is a certain cardiac weakness," continued the doctor fluently, "but nothing to be alarmed about. I can assure you of that. All the same," he added, "it might be as well to have an elevator installed. Eh? What about it?"

Mrs. Harter looked worried.

Dr. Meynell, on the contrary, looked pleased with himself. The reason he liked attending rich patients rather than poor ones was that he could exercise his active imagination in prescribing for their ailments.

"Yes, an elevator," said Dr. Meynell, trying to think of something else even more dashing—and failing. "Then we shall avoid all undue exertion. Daily exercise on the level on a fine day, but avoid walking up hills. And, above all, plenty of distraction for the mind. Don't dwell on your health."

To the old lady's nephew, Charles Ridgeway, the doctor was slightly more explicit.

"Do not misunderstand me," he said. "Your aunt may live for years, probably will. At the same time, shock or overexertion might carry her off like that!" He snapped his fingers. "She must lead a very quiet life. No exertion. No fatigue. But, of course, she must not be allowed to brood. She must be kept cheerful and the mind well distracted."

"Distracted," said Charles Ridgeway thoughtfully.

Charles was a thoughtful young man. He was also a young man who believed in furthering his own inclinations whenever possible.

That evening he suggested the installation of a radio set.

Mrs. Harter, already seriously upset at the thought of the elevator, was disturbed and unwilling. Charles was persuasive.

"I do not know that I care for these new-fangled things," said Mrs. Harter piteously. "The waves, you know—the electric waves. They might affect me."

Charles, in a superior and kindly fashion, pointed out the futility of this idea.

Mrs. Harter, whose knowledge of the subject was of the vaguest but who was tenacious of her own opinion, remained unconvinced.

"All that electricity," she murmured timorously. "You may say what you like, Charles, but some people are affected by electricity. I always have a terrible headache before a thunderstorm. I know that."

She nodded her head triumphantly.

Charles was a patient young man. He was also persistent.

"My dear Aunt Mary," he said, "let me make the thing clear to you."

He was something of an authority on the subject. He delivered quite a lecture on the theme; warming to his task, he spoke of bright-emitter tubes, of dull-emitter tubes, of high frequency and low frequency, of amplification and of condensers.

Mrs. Harter, submerged in a sea of words that she did not understand, surrendered.

"Of course, Charles," she murmured, "if you really think—"

"My dear Aunt Mary," said Charles enthusiastically, "it is the very thing for you, to keep you from moping and all that."

The elevator prescribed by Dr. Meynell was installed shortly afterward and was very nearly the death of Mrs. Harter since, like many other old ladies, she had a rooted objection to strange men in the house. She suspected them one and all of having designs on her old silver.

After the elevator the radio set arrived. Mrs. Harter was left to contemplate the, to her, repellent object—a large, ungainly-looking box, studded with knobs.

It took all Charles's enthusiasm to reconcile her to it, but Charles was in his element, turning knobs and discoursing eloquently.

Mrs. Harter sat in her high-backed chair, patient and polite, with a rooted conviction in her own mind that these new-fangled notions were neither more nor less than unmitigated nuisances.

"Listen, Aunt Mary, we are on to Berlin! Isn't that splendid? Can you hear the fellow?"

"I can't hear anything except a good deal of buzzing and clicking," said Mrs. Harter.

Charles continued to twirl knobs. "Brussels," he announced with enthusiasm.

"It is really?" said Mrs. Harter with no more than a trace of interest.

Charles again turned knobs and an unearthly howl echoed forth into the room.

"Now we seem to be on to the Dogs' Home," said Mrs. Harter, who was an old lady with a certain amount of spirit.

"Ha, ha!" said Charles, "you will have your joke, won't you, Aunt Mary? Very good that!"

Mrs. Harter could not help smiling at him. She was very fond of Charles. For some years a niece, Miriam Harter, had lived with her. She had intended to make the girl her heiress, but Miriam had not been a success. She was impatient and obviously bored by her aunt's society. She was always out, "gadding about" as Mrs. Harter called it. In the end she had entangled herself with a young man of whom her aunt thoroughly disapproved. Miriam had been returned to her mother with a curt note much as if she had been goods on approval.

She had married the young man in question and Mrs. Harter usually sent her a handkerchief case or a table center at Christmas.

Having found nieces disappointing, Mrs. Harter turned her attention to nephews. Charles, from the first, had been an unqualified success. He was always pleasantly deferential to his aunt and listened with an appearance of intense interest to the reminiscences of her youth. In this he was a great contrast to Miriam who had been frankly bored and showed it. Charles was never bored; he was always good-tempered, always gay. He told his aunt many times a day that she was a perfectly marvelous old lady.

Highly satisfied with her new acquisition, Mrs. Harter had written to her lawyer with instructions as to the making of a new will. This was sent to her, duly approved by her, and signed.

And now even in the matter of the radio, Charles was soon proved to have won fresh laurels.

Mrs. Harter, at first antagonistic, became tolerant and finally fascinated. She enjoyed it very much better when Charles was out. The trouble with Charles was that he could not leave the thing alone. Mrs. Harter would be seated in her chair comfortably listening to a symphony concert or a lecture on Lucrezia Borgia or Pond Life, quite happy and at peace with the world. Not so Charles. The harmony would be shattered by discordant shrieks while he enthusiastically attempted to get foreign stations. But on those evenings when Charles was dining out with friends, Mrs. Harter enjoyed the radio very much indeed. She would turn on two switches, sit in her high-backed chair, and enjoy the program of the evening.

It was about three months after the radio had been installed that the first eerie happening occurred. Charles was absent at a bridge party.

The program for that evening was a ballad concert. A well-known soprano was singing "Annie Laurie," and in the middle of "Annie Laurie" a strange thing happened. There was a sudden break, the music ceased for a moment, the buzzing, clicking noise continued, and then that too died away. There was silence, and then very faintly a low buzzing sound was heard.

Mrs. Harter got the impression, why she did not know, that the machine was tuned into somewhere very far away, and then, clearly and distinctly, a voice spoke, a man's voice with a faint Irish accent.

"Mary—can you hear me, Mary? It is Patrick speaking. . . . I am coming for you soon. You will be ready, won't you, Mary?"

Then, almost immediately, the strains of "Annie Laurie" once more filled the room.

Mrs. Harter sat rigid in her chair, her hands clenched on each arm of it. Had she been dreaming? Patrick! Patrick's voice! Patrick's voice in this very room, speaking to her. No, it must be a dream, a hallucination perhaps. She must just have dropped off to sleep for a minute or two. A curious thing to have dreamed—that her dead husband's voice should speak to her over the ether. It frightened her just a little. What were the words he had said?

"I am coming for you soon. You will be ready, won't you, Mary?"

Was it, could it be a premonition? Cardiac weakness. Her heart. After all, she was getting on in years.

"It's a warning—that's what it is," said Mrs. Harter, rising slowly and painfully from her chair, and added characteristically, "All that money wasted on putting in an elevator!"

She said nothing of her experience to anyone, but for the next day or two she was thoughtful and a little preoccupied.

And then came the second occasion. Again she was alone in the room. The radio, which had been playing an orchestral selection, died away with the same suddenness as before. Again there was silence, the sense of distance, and finally Patrick's voice, not as it had been in life—but a voice rarefied, far-away, with a strange unearthly quality.

"Patrick speaking to you, Mary. I will be coming for you very soon now. . . ."

Then click, buzz, and the orchestral selection was in full swing again.

Mrs. Harter glanced at the clock. No, she had not been asleep this time. Awake and in full possession of her faculties, she had heard Patrick's voice speaking. It was no hallucination, she was sure of that. In a confused way she tried to think over all that Charles had explained to her of the theory of ether waves.

Could it be that Patrick had really spoken to her? That his actual voice had been wafted through space? There were missing wave lengths or something of that kind. She remembered Charles speaking of "gaps in the scale." Perhaps the missing waves explained all the so-called psychological phenomena? No, there was nothing inherently impossible in the idea. Patrick had spoken to her. He had availed himself of modern science to prepare her for what must soon be coming.

Mrs. Harter rang the bell for her maid, Elizabeth.

Elizabeth was a tall, gaunt woman of sixty. Beneath an unbending exterior she concealed a wealth of affection and tenderness for her mistress.

"Elizabeth," said Mrs. Harter when her faithful retainer had appeared, "you remember what I told you? The top left-hand drawer of my bureau. It is locked—the long key with the white label. Everything there is ready."

"Ready, ma'am?"

"For my burial," snorted Mrs. Harter. "You know perfectly well what I mean, Elizabeth. You helped me to put the things there yourself."

Elizabeth's face began to work strangely.

"Oh, ma'am," she wailed, "don't dwell on such things. I thought you was a sight better."

"We have all got to go sometime or another," said Mrs. Harter practically. "I am over my three score years and ten, Elizabeth. There, there, don't make a fool of yourself. If you must cry, go and cry somewhere else."

Elizabeth retired, still sniffing.

Mrs. Harter looked after her with a good deal of affection.

"Silly old fool, but faithful," she said, "very faithful. Let me see, was it a hundred pounds, or only fifty I left her? It ought to be a hundred."

The point worried the old lady and the next day she sat down and wrote to her lawyer asking if he would send her her will so that she might look it over. It was that same day that Charles startled her by something he said at lunch.

"By the way, Aunt Mary," he said, "who is that funny old josser up in the spare room? The picture over the mantelpiece, I mean. The old johnny with the beaver and sidewhiskers?"

Mrs. Harter looked at him austerely.

"That is your Uncle Patrick as a young man," she said.

"Oh, I say, Aunt Mary, I am awfully sorry. I didn't mean to be rude."

Mrs. Harter accepted the apology with a dignified bend of the head.

Charles went on rather uncertainly, "I just wondered. You see—"

He stopped undecidedly and Mrs. Harter said sharply:

"Well? What were you going to say?"

"Nothing," said Charles hastily. "Nothing that makes sense, I mean."

For the moment the old lady said nothing more, but later that day, when they were alone together, she returned to the subject.

"I wish you would tell me, Charles, what it was that made you ask me about the picture of your uncle."

Charles looked embarrassed.

"I told you, Aunt Mary. It was nothing but a silly fancy of mine—quite absurd."

"Charles," said Mrs. Harter in her most autocratic voice, "I insist upon knowing."

"Well, my dear aunt, if you will have it, I fancied I saw him—the man in the picture, I mean—looking out of the end window when I was coming up the drive last night. Some effect of the light, I suppose. I wondered who on earth he could be, the face so—early Victorian, if you know what I mean. And then Elizabeth said there was no one, no visitor or stranger in the house, and later in the evening I happened to drift into the spare room, and there was the picture over the mantelpiece. My man to the life! It is quite easily explained, really, I expect. Subconscious and all that. Must have noticed the picture before without realizing that I had noticed it, and then just fancied the face at the window."

"The end window?" said Mrs. Harter sharply.

"Yes, why?"

"Nothing," said Mrs. Harter.

But she was startled all the same. That room had been her husband's dressing room.

That same evening, Charles again being absent, Mrs. Harter sat listening to the wireless with feverish impatience. If for the third time she heard the mysterious voice, it would prove to her finally and without a shadow of doubt that she was really in communication with some other world.

Although her heart beat faster, she was not surprised when the same break occurred, and after the usual interval of deathly silence the faint far-away Irish voice spoke once more.

"Mary—you are prepared now. . . . On Friday I shall come for you. . . . Friday at half-past nine. . . . Do not be afraid—there will be no pain. . . . Be ready. . . ."

Then, almost cutting short the last word, the music of the orchestra broke out again, clamorous and discordant.

Mrs. Harter sat very still for a minute or two. Her face had gone white and she looked blue and pinched round the lips.

Presently she got up and sat down at her writing desk. In a somewhat shaky hand she wrote the following lines:

> Tonight, at 9:15, I have distinctly heard the voice of my dead husband. He told me that he would come for me on Friday night at 9:30. If I should die on that day and at that hour I should like the facts made known so as to prove beyond question the possibility of communicating with the spirit world.
>
> —MARY HARTER

Mrs. Harter read over what she had written, enclosed it in an envelope, and addressed the envelope. Then she rang the bell, which was promptly answered by Elizabeth. Mrs. Harter got up from her desk and gave the note she had just written to the old woman.

"Elizabeth," she said, "if I should die on Friday night I should like that note given to Dr. Meynell. No"—as Elizabeth appeared about to protest—"do not argue with me. You have often told me you believe in premonitions. I have a premonition now. There is one thing more. I have left you in my will £50. I should like you to have £100. If I am not able to go to the bank myself before I die, Mr. Charles will see to it."

As before, Mrs. Harter cut short Elizabeth's tearful protests. In pursuance of her determination the old lady spoke to her nephew on the subject the following morning.

"Remember, Charles, that if anything should happen to me, Elizabeth is to have an extra £50."

"You are very gloomy these days, Aunt Mary," said Charles cheerfully. "What is going to happen to you? According to Dr. Meynell, we shall be celebrating your hundredth birthday in twenty years or so!"

Mrs. Harter smiled affectionately at him but did not answer. After a minute or two she said:

"What are you doing on Friday evening, Charles?"

Charles looked a trifle surprised.

"As a matter of fact, the Ewings asked me to go in and play bridge, but if you would rather I stayed at home—"

"No," said Mrs. Harter with determination. "Certainly not. I mean it, Charles. On that night of all nights I should much rather be alone."

Charles looked at her curiously, but Mrs. Harter vouchsafed no further information. She was an old lady of courage and determination. She felt that she must go through with her strange experience single-handed.

Friday evening found the house very silent. Mrs. Harter sat as usual in her straight-backed chair drawn up to the fireplace. All her preparations were made. That morning she had been to the bank, had drawn out £50 in notes, and had handed them over to Elizabeth despite the latter's tearful protests. She had sorted and arranged all her personal belongings and had labeled one or two pieces of jewelry with the names of friends or relations. She had also written out a list of instructions for Charles. The Worcester tea service was to go to Cousin Emma, the Sevres jars to young William, and so on.

Now she looked at the long envelope she held in her hand and drew from it a folded document. This was her will sent to her by Mr.

Hopkinson in accordance with her instructions. She had already read it carefully, but now she looked over it once more to refresh her memory. It was a short, concise document. A bequest of £50 to Elizabeth Marshall in consideration of faithful service; two bequests of £500 to a sister and a first cousin; and the remainder to her beloved nephew Charles Ridgeway.

Mrs. Harter nodded her head several times. Charles would be a very rich man when she was dead. Well, he had been a dear good boy to her. Always kind, always affectionate, and with a merry tongue which never failed to please her.

She looked at the clock. Three minutes to the half-hour. Well, she was ready. And she was calm—quite calm. Although she repeated these last words to herself several times, her heart beat strangely and unevenly. She hardly realized it herself, but she was strung up to a fine point of over-wrought nerves.

Half-past nine. The wireless was switched on. What would she hear? A familiar voice announcing the weather forecast or that faraway voice belonging to a man who had died twenty-five years before?

But she heard neither. Instead there came a familiar sound, a sound she knew well but which tonight made her feel as though an icy hand were laid on her heart. A fumbling at the front door. . . .

It came again. And then a cold blast seemed to sweep through the room. Mrs. Harter had now no doubt what her sensations were. She was afraid. . . . She was more than afraid—she was terrified. . . .

And suddenly there came to her the thought: *"Twenty-five years is a long time. Patrick is a stranger to me now."*

Terror! That was what was invading her.

A soft step outside the door—a soft halting footstep. Then the door swung silently open. . . .

Mrs. Harter staggered to her feet, swaying slightly from side to side, her eyes fixed on the open doorway. Something slipped from her fingers into the grate.

She gave a strangled cry which died in her throat. In the dim light of the doorway stood a familiar figure with chestnut beard and whiskers and an old-fashioned Victorian coat.

Patrick had come for her!

Her heart gave one terrified leap and stood still. She slipped to the ground in a crumpled heap.

THERE ELIZABETH FOUND her, an hour later.

Dr. Meynell was called at once and Charles Ridgeway was hastily summoned from his bridge party. But nothing could be done. Mrs. Harter was beyond human aid.

It was not until two days later that Elizabeth remembered the note given to her by her mistress. Dr. Meynell read it with great interest and showed it to Charles Ridgeway.

"A very curious coincidence," he said. "It seems clear that your aunt had been having hallucinations about her dead husband's voice. She must have strung herself up to such a point that the excitement was fatal, and when the time actually came she died of the shock."

"Auto-suggestion?" asked Charles.

"Something of the sort. I will let you know the result of the autopsy as soon as possible, though I have no doubt of it myself. In the circumstances an autopsy is desirable, though purely as a matter of form."

Charles nodded comprehendingly.

On the preceding night, when the household was in bed, he had removed a certain wire which ran from the back of the radio cabinet to his bedroom on the floor above. Also, since the evening had been a chilly one, he had asked Elizabeth to light a fire in his room, and in that fire he had burned a chestnut beard and whiskers. Some Victorian clothing belonging to his late uncle he replaced in the camphor-scented chest in the attic.

As far as he could see, he was perfectly safe. His plan, the shadowy outline of which had first formed in his brain when Doctor Meynell had told him that his aunt might with due care live for many years, had succeeded admirably. A sudden shock, Dr. Meynell had said. Charles, that affectionate young man, beloved of old ladies, smiled to himself.

When the doctor had departed, Charles went about his duties

mechanically. Certain funeral arrangements had to be finally settled. Relatives coming from a distance had to have trains looked out for them. In one or two cases they would have to stay the night. Charles went about it all efficiently and methodically, to the accompaniment of an undercurrent of his own thoughts.

A very good stroke of business! That was the burden of them. Nobody, least of all his dead aunt, had known in what perilous straits Charles stood. His activities, carefully concealed from the world, had landed him where the shadow of a prison loomed ahead.

Exposure and ruin had stared him in the face unless he could in a few short months raise a considerable sum of money. Well—that was all right now. Charles smiled to himself. Thanks to—yes, call it a practical joke—nothing criminal about *that*—he was saved. He was now a very rich man. He had no anxieties on the subject, for Mrs. Harter had never made any secret of her intentions.

Chiming in very appositely with these thoughts, Elizabeth put her head round the door and informed him that Mr. Hopkinson was here and would like to see him.

About time, too, Charles thought. Repressing a tendency to whistle, he composed his face to one of suitable gravity and went to the library. There he greeted the precise old gentleman who had been for over a quarter of a century the late Mrs. Harter's legal adviser.

The lawyer seated himself at Charles's invitation and with a dry little cough entered upon business matters.

"I did not quite understand your letter to me, Mr. Ridgeway. You seemed to be under the impression that the late Mrs. Harter's will was in our keeping?"

Charles stared at him.

"But surely—I've heard my aunt say as much."

"Oh! quite so, quite so. It *was* in our keeping."

"Was?"

"That is what I said. Mrs. Harter wrote to us, asking that it might be forwarded to her on Tuesday last."

An uneasy feeling crept over Charles. He felt a far-off premonition of unpleasantness.

"Doubtless it will come to light among her papers," continued the lawyer smoothly.

Charles said nothing. He was afraid to trust his tongue. He had already been through Mrs. Harter's papers pretty thoroughly, well enough to be quite certain that no will was among them. In a minute or two, when he had regained control of himself, he said so. His voice sounded unreal to himself, and he had a sensation as of cold water trickling down his back.

"Has anyone been through her personal effects?" asked the lawyer.

Charles replied that the maid, Elizabeth, had done so. At Mr. Hopkinson's suggestion Elizabeth was sent for. She came promptly, grim and upright, and answered the questions put to her.

She had been through all her mistress's clothes and personal belongings. She was quite sure that there had been no legal document such as a will among them. She knew what the will looked like—her poor mistress had had it in her hand only the morning of her death.

"You are sure of that?" asked the lawyer sharply.

"Yes, sir. She told me so. And she made me take fifty pounds in notes. The will was in a long blue envelope."

"Quite right," said Mr. Hopkinson.

"Now I come to think of it," continued Elizabeth, "that same blue envelope was lying on this table the morning after—but empty. I laid it on the desk."

"I remember seeing it there," said Charles.

He got up and went over to the desk. In a minute or two he turned round with an envelope in his hand which he handed to Mr. Hopkinson. The latter examined it and nodded his head.

"That is the envelope in which I dispatched the will on Tuesday last."

Both men looked hard at Elizabeth.

"Is there anything more, sir?" she inquired respectfully.

"Not at present, thank you."

Elizabeth went toward the door.

"One minute," said the lawyer. "Was there a fire in the grate that evening?"

"Yes, sir, there was always a fire."

"Thank you, that will do."

Elizabeth went out. Charles leaned forward, resting a shaking hand on the table.

"What do you think? What are you driving at?"

Mr. Hopkinson shook his head.

"We must still hope the will may turn up. If it does not—"

"Well, if it does not?"

"I am afraid there is only one conclusion possible. Your aunt sent for that will in order to destroy it. Not wishing Elizabeth to lose by that, she gave her the amount of her legacy in cash."

"But why?" cried Charles wildly. "Why?"

Mr. Hopkinson coughed. A dry cough.

"You have had no—er—disagreement with your aunt, Mr. Ridgeway?" he murmured.

Charles gasped.

"No, indeed," he cried warmly. "We were on the kindliest, most affectionate terms, right up to the end."

"Ah!" said Mr. Hopkinson, not looking at him.

It came to Charles with a shock that the lawyer did not believe him. Who knew what this dry old stick might not have heard? Rumors of Charles's doings might have come round to him. What more natural than that he should suppose that these same rumors had come to Mrs. Harter, and that aunt and nephew should have had an altercation on the subject?

But it wasn't so! Charles knew one of the bitterest moments of his career. His lies had been believed. Now that he spoke the truth, belief was withheld. The irony of it!

Of course his aunt had never burned the will! Of course—

His thoughts came to a sudden check. What was that picture rising before his eyes? An old lady with one hand clasped to her heart . . . something slipping . . . a paper . . . falling on the red-hot embers. . . .

Charles's face grew livid. He heard a hoarse voice—his own—asking:

"If that will's never found—?"

"There is a former will of Mrs. Harter's still extant. Dated September, 1920. By it Mrs. Harter leaves everything to her niece, Miriam Harter, now Miriam Robinson."

What was the old fool saying? Miriam? Miriam with her nondescript husband, and her four whining brats. All his cleverness—for Miriam!

The telephone rang sharply at his elbow. He took up the receiver. It was the doctor's voice, hearty and kindly.

"That you, Ridgeway? Thought you'd like to know. The autopsy's just concluded. Cause of death as I surmised. But as a matter of fact the cardiac trouble was much more serious than I suspected when she was alive. With the utmost care she couldn't have lived longer than two months at the outside. Thought you'd like to know. Might console you more or less."

"Excuse me," said Charles, "would you mind saying that again?"

"She couldn't have lived longer than two months," said the doctor in a slightly louder tone. "All things work out for the best, you know, my dear fellow—"

But Charles had slammed back the receiver on its hook. He was conscious of the lawyer's voice speaking from a long way off.

"Dear me, Mr. Ridgeway, are you ill?"

Damn them all! The smug-faced lawyer. That poisonous old ass Meynell. No hope in front of him—only the shadow of the prison wall. . . .

He felt that Somebody had been playing with him—playing with him like a cat with a mouse. Somebody must be laughing. . . .

THE MYSTERY OF THE BLUE JAR

Jack Hartington surveyed his topped drive ruefully. Standing by the ball, he looked back to the tee, measuring the distance. His face was eloquent of the disgusted contempt which he felt. With a sigh he drew out his iron, executed two vicious swings with it, annihilating in turn a dandelion and a tuft of grass, and then addressed himself firmly to the ball.

It is hard when you are twenty-four years of age, and your one ambition in life is to reduce your handicap at golf, to be forced to give time and attention to the problem of earning your living. Five and a half days out of the seven saw Jack imprisoned in a kind of mahogany tomb in the city. Saturday afternoon and Sunday were religiously devoted to the real business of life, and in an excess of zeal he had taken rooms at the small hotel near Stourton Heath links, and rose daily at the hour of six A.M. to get in an hour's practice before catching the 8:46 to town.

The only disadvantage to the plan was that he seemed constitutionally unable to hit anything at that hour in the morning. A foozled iron succeeded a muffed drive. His mashie shots ran merrily along the ground, and four putts seemed to be the minimum on any green.

Jack sighed, grasped his iron firmly, and repeated to himself the magic words, "Left arm right through, and don't look up."

He swung back—and then stopped, petrified, as a shrill cry rent the silence of the summer's morning.

"Murder," it called. "Help! Murder!"

It was a woman's voice, and it died away at the end into a sort of gurgling sigh.

Jack flung down his club and ran in the direction of the sound. It had come from somewhere quite near at hand. This particular part of the course was quite wild country, and there were few houses about. In fact, there was only one near at hand, a small picturesque cottage, which Jack had often noticed for its air of Old World daintiness. It was toward this cottage that he ran. It was hidden from him by a heather-covered slope, but he rounded this and in less than a minute was standing with his hand on the small latched gate.

There was a girl standing in the garden, and for a moment Jack jumped to the natural conclusion that it was she who had uttered the cry for help. But he quickly changed his mind.

She had a little basket in her hand, half-full of weeds, and had evidently just straightened herself up from weeding a wide border of pansies. Her eyes, Jack noticed, were just like pansies themselves, velvety and soft and dark, and more violet than blue. She was like a pansy altogether, in her straight purple linen gown.

The girl was looking at Jack with an expression midway between annoyance and surprise.

"I beg your pardon," said the young man. "But did you cry out just now?"

"I? No, indeed."

Her surprise was so genuine that Jack felt confused. Her voice was very soft and pretty with a slight foreign inflection.

"But you must have heard it," he exclaimed. "It came from somewhere just near here."

She stared at him.

"I heard nothing at all."

Jack in his turn stared at her. It was perfectly incredible that she should not have heard that agonized appeal for help. And yet her calmness was so evident that he could not believe she was lying to him.

"It came from somewhere close at hand," he insisted.

She was looking at him suspiciously now.

"What did it say?" she asked.

"Murder—help! Murder!"

"Murder—help, murder," repeated the girl. "Somebody has played a trick on you, Monsieur. Who could be murdered here?"

Jack looked about him with a confused idea of discovering a dead body upon a garden path. Yet he was still perfectly sure that the cry he had heard was real and not a product of his imagination. He looked up at the cottage windows. Everything seemed perfectly still and peaceful.

"Do you want to search our house?" asked the girl dryly.

She was so clearly skeptical that Jack's confusion grew deeper than ever. He turned away.

"I'm sorry," he said. "It must have come from higher up in the woods."

He raised his cap and retreated. Glancing back over his shoulder, he saw that the girl had calmly resumed her weeding.

For some time he hunted through the woods, but could find no sign of anything unusual having occurred. Yet he was as positive as ever that he had really heard the cry. In the end, he gave up the search and hurried home to bolt his breakfast and catch the 8:46 by the usual narrow margin of a second or so. His conscience pricked him a little as he sat in the train. Ought he not to have immediately reported what he had heard to the police? That he had not done so was solely owing to the pansy girl's incredulity. She had clearly suspected him of romancing—possibly the police might do the same. Was he absolutely certain that he had heard the cry?

By now he was not nearly so positive as he had been—the natural result of trying to recapture a lost sensation. Was it some bird's cry in the distance that he had twisted into the resemblance of a woman's voice?

But he rejected the suggestion angrily. It was a woman's voice, and he had heard it. He remembered looking at his watch just before the cry had come. As nearly as possible it must have been five and twenty minutes past seven when he had heard the call. That might be a fact useful to the police if—if anything should be discovered.

Going home that evening, he scanned the evening papers anxiously to see if there were any mention of a crime having been committed. But there was nothing, and he hardly knew whether to be relieved or disappointed.

The following morning was wet—so wet that even the most ardent golfer might have his enthusiasm damped. Jack rose at the last possible moment, gulped his breakfast, ran for the train, and again eagerly scanned the papers. Still no mention of any gruesome discovery having been made. The evening papers told the same tale.

"Queer," said Jack to himself, "but there it is. Probably some blinking little boys having a game together up in the woods."

He was out early the following morning. As he passed the cottage, he noted out of the tail of his eye that the girl was out in the garden again weeding. Evidently a habit of hers. He did a particularly good approach shot, and hoped that she had noticed it. As he teed up on the next tee, he glanced at his watch.

"Just five and twenty past seven," he murmured. "I wonder—"

The words were frozen on his lips. From behind him came the same cry which had so startled him before. A woman's voice, in dire distress.

"Murder—help, murder!"

Jack raced back. The pansy girl was standing by the gate. She looked startled, and Jack ran up to her triumphantly, crying out:

"You heard it this time, anyway."

Her eyes were wide with some emotion he could not fathom but he noticed that she shrank back from him as he approached, and even glanced back at the house, as though she meditated running to it for shelter.

She shook her head, staring at him.

"I heard nothing at all," she said wonderingly.

It was as though she had struck him a blow between the eyes. Her sincerity was so evident that he could not disbelieve her. Yet he couldn't have imagined it—he couldn't—he couldn't—

He heard her voice speaking gently—almost with sympathy.

"You have had the shell-shock, yes?"

In a flash he understood her look of fear, her glance back at the house. She thought that he suffered from delusions. . . .

And then, like a douche of cold water, came the horrible thought, was she right? Did he suffer from delusions? Obsessed by the horror of the thought, he turned and stumbled away without vouchsafing a word. The girl watched him go, sighed, shook her head, and bent down to her weeding again.

Jack endeavored to reason matters out with himself. "If I hear the damned thing again, at twenty-five minutes past seven," he said to himself, "it's clear that I've got hold of a hallucination of some sort. But I won't hear it."

He was nervous all day, and went to bed early, determined to put the matter to the proof the following morning.

As was perhaps natural in such a case, he remained awake half the night and finally overslept himself. It was twenty past seven by the time he was clear of the hotel and running toward the links. He realized that he would not be able to get to the fatal spot by twenty-five past, but surely, if the voice were a hallucination pure and simple, he would hear it anywhere. He ran on, his eyes fixed on the hands of his watch.

Twenty-five past. From far off came the echo of a woman's voice, calling. The words could not be distinguished, but he was convinced that it was the same cry he had heard before, and that it came from the same spot, somewhere in the neighborhood of the cottage.

Strangely enough, that fact reassured him. It might, after all, be a hoax. Unlikely as it seemed, the girl herself might be playing a trick on him. He set his shoulders resolutely, and took out a club from his golf bag. He would play the few holes up to the cottage.

The girl was in the garden as usual. She looked up this morning, and when he raised his cap to her, said good morning rather shyly. . . . She looked, he thought, lovelier than ever.

"Nice day, isn't it?" Jack called out cheerily, cursing the unavoidable banality of the observation.

"Yes, indeed, it is lovely."

"Good for the garden, I expect?"

The girl smiled a little, disclosing a fascinating dimple.

"Alas, no! For my flowers the rain is needed. See, they are all dried up."

Jack accepted the invitation of her gesture, and came up to the low hedge dividing the garden from the course, looking over it into the garden.

"They seem all right," he remarked awkwardly, conscious as he spoke of the girl's slightly pitying glance running over him.

"The sun is good, is it not?" she said. "For the flowers one can always water them. But the sun gives strength and repairs the health. Monsieur is much better today, I can see."

Her encouraging tone annoyed Jack intensely.

"Curse it all," he said to himself. "I believe she's trying to cure me by suggestion.

"I'm perfectly well," he said irritably.

"That is good then," returned the girl, quickly and soothingly.

Jack had the irritating feeling that she didn't believe him.

He played a few more holes and hurried back to breakfast. As he ate it, he was conscious, not for the first time, of the close scrutiny of a man who sat at the table next to him. He was a man of middle-age, with a powerful, forceful face. He had a small dark beard and very piercing gray eyes, and an ease and assurance of manner which placed him among the higher ranks of the professional classes. His name, Jack knew, was Lavington, and he had heard vague rumors as to his being a well-known medical specialist, but as Jack was not a frequenter of Harley Street, the name had conveyed little or nothing to him.

But this morning he was very conscious of the quiet observation under which he was being kept, and it frightened him a little. Was his secret written plainly in his face for all to see? Did this man, by reason of his professional calling, know that there was something amiss in the hidden gray matter?

Jack shivered at the thought. Was it true? Was he really going mad? Was the whole thing a hallucination, or was it a gigantic hoax?

And suddenly a very simple way of testing the solution occurred to him. He had hitherto been alone on his round. Supposing someone else was with him? Then one out of three things might happen. The voice might be silent. They might both hear it. Or—he only might hear it.

That evening he proceeded to carry his plan into effect. Lavington was the man he wanted with him. They fell into conversation easily enough—the older man might have been waiting for such an opening. It was clear that for some reason or other Jack interested him. The latter was able to come quite easily and naturally to the suggestion that they might play a few holes together before breakfast. The arrangement was made for the following morning.

They started out a little before seven. It was a perfect day, still and cloudless, but not too warm. The doctor was playing well, Jack wretchedly. His whole mind was intent on the forthcoming crisis. He kept glancing surreptitiously at his watch. They reached the seventh tee, between which and the hole the cottage was situated, about twenty past seven.

The girl, as usual, was in the garden as they passed. She did not look up as they passed.

The two balls lay on the green, Jack's near the hole, the doctor's some little distance away.

"I've got this for it," said Lavington. "I must go for it, I suppose."

He bent down, judging the line he should take. Jack stood rigid, his eyes glued on his watch. It was exactly twenty-five minutes past seven.

The ball ran swiftly along the grass, stopped on the edge of the hole, hesitated, and dropped in.

"Good putt," said Jack. His voice sounded hoarse and unlike himself. . . . He shoved his wrist watch farther up his arm with a sigh of overwhelming relief. Nothing had happened. The spell was broken.

"If you don't mind waiting a minute," he said, "I think I'll have a pipe."

They paused a while on the eighth tee. Jack filled and lit the pipe with fingers that trembled a little in spite of himself. An enormous weight seemed to have lifted from his mind.

"Lord, what a good day it is," he remarked, staring at the prospect ahead of him with great contentment.

"Go on, Lavington, your swipe."

And then it came. Just at the very instant the doctor was hitting. A woman's voice, high and agonized.

"Murder—Help! Murder!"

The pipe fell from Jack's nerveless hand, as he spun round in the direction of the sound, and then, remembering, gazed breathlessly at his companion.

Lavington was looking down the course, shading his eyes.

"A bit short—just cleared the bunker, though, I think."

He had heard nothing.

The world seemed to spin round with Jack. He took a step or two, lurching heavily. When he recovered himself, he was lying on the short turf, and Lavington was bending over him.

"There, take it easy now, take it easy."

"What did I do?"

"You fainted, young man—or gave a very good try at it."

"My God!" said Jack, and groaned.

"What's the trouble? Something on your mind?"

"I'll tell you in one minute, but I'd like to ask you something first."

The doctor lit his own pipe and settled himself on the bank.

"Ask anything you like," he said comfortably.

"You've been watching me for the last day or two. Why?"

Lavington's eyes twinkled a little.

"That's rather an awkward question. A cat can look at a king, you know."

"Don't put me off. I'm in earnest. Why was it? I've a vital reason for asking."

Lavington's face grew serious.

"I'll answer you quite honestly. I recognized in you all the signs of a man laboring under a sense of acute strain, and it intrigued me what that strain could be."

"I can tell you that easily enough," said Jack bitterly. "I'm going mad."

He stopped dramatically, but his statement not seeming to arouse the interest and consternation he expected, he repeated it.

"I tell you I'm going mad."

"Very curious," murmured Lavington. "Very curious indeed."

Jack felt indignant.

"I suppose that's all it does seem to you. Doctors are so damned callous."

"Come, come, my young friend, you're talking at random. To begin with, although I have taken my degree, I do not practice medicine. Strictly speaking, I am not a doctor—not a doctor of the body, that is."

Jack looked at him keenly.

"Of the mind?"

"Yes, in a sense, but more truly I call myself a doctor of the soul."

"Oh!"

"I perceive the disparagement in your tone, and yet we must use some word to denote the active principle which can be separated and exist independently of its fleshy home, the body. You've got to come to terms with the soul, you know, young man; it isn't just a religious term invented by clergymen. But we'll call it the mind, or the subconscious self, or any term that suits you better. You took offense at my tone just now, but I can assure you that it really did strike me as very curious that such a well-balanced and perfectly normal young man as yourself should suffer from the delusion that he was going out of his mind."

"I'm out of my mind all right. Absolutely balmy."

"You will forgive me for saying so, but I don't believe it."

"I suffer from delusions."

"After dinner?"

"No, in the morning."

"Can't be done," said the doctor, relighting his pipe which had gone out.

"I tell you I hear things that no one else hears."

"One man in a thousand can see the moons of Jupiter. Because the other nine hundred and ninety-nine can't see them there's no reason to doubt that the moons of Jupiter exist, and certainly no reason for calling the thousandth man a lunatic."

"The moons of Jupiter are a proved scientific fact."

"It's quite possible that the delusions of today may be the proved scientific facts of tomorrow."

In spite of himself, Lavington's matter-of-fact manner was having its effect upon Jack. He felt immeasurably soothed and cheered. The doctor looked at him attentively for a minute or two and then nodded.

"That's better," he said. "The trouble with you young fellows is that you're so cocksure nothing can exist outside your own philosophy that you get the wind up when something occurs to jolt you out of that opinion. Let's hear your grounds for believing that you're going mad, and we'll decide whether or not to lock you up afterward."

As faithfully as he could, Jack narrated the whole series of occurrences.

"But what I can't understand," he ended, "is why this morning it should come at half-past seven—five minutes late."

Lavington thought for a minute or two. Then—

"What's the time now by your watch?" he asked.

"Quarter to eight," replied Jack, consulting it.

"That's simple enough, then. Mine says twenty to eight. Your watch is five minutes fast. That's a very interesting and important point—to me. In fact, it's invaluable."

"In what way?"

Jack was beginning to get interested.

"Well, the obvious explanation is that on the first morning you *did* hear some such cry—may have been a joke, may not. On the following mornings, you suggestioned yourself to hear it exactly the same time."

"I'm sure I didn't."

"Not consciously, of course, but the subconscious plays us some funny tricks, you know. But, anyway, that explanation won't wash. If it were a case of suggestion, you would have heard the cry at twenty-five minutes past seven by your watch, and you could never have heard it when the time, as you thought, was past."

"Well, then?"

"Well—it's obvious, isn't it? This cry for help occupies a perfectly definite place and time in space. The place is the vicinity of that cottage and the time is twenty-five minutes past seven."

"Yes, but why should I be the one to hear it? I don't believe in ghosts and all that spook stuff—spirits rapping and all the rest of it. Why should I hear the damned thing?"

"Ah! that we can't tell at present. It's a curious thing that many of the best mediums are made out of confirmed skeptics. It isn't the people who are interested in occult phenomena who get the manifestations. Some people see and hear things that other people don't—we don't know why, and nine times out of ten they don't want to see or hear them, and are convinced that they are suffering from delusions—just as you were. It's like electricity. Some substances are good conductors, and for a long time we didn't know why, and had to be content just to accept the fact. Nowadays we do know why. Some day, no doubt, we shall know why you hear this thing and I and the girl don't. Everything's governed by natural law, you know—there's no such thing really as the supernatural. Finding out the laws that govern so-called psychic phenomena is going to be a tough job—but every little helps."

"But what am I going to do?" asked Jack.

Lavington chuckled.

"Practical, I see. Well, my young friend, you are going to have a good breakfast and get off to the city without worrying your head further about things you don't understand. I, on the other hand, am going to poke about, and see what I can find out about that cottage back there. That's where the mystery centers, I dare swear."

Jack rose to his feet.

"Right, sir. I'm on, but, I say—"

"Yes?"

Jack flushed awkwardly.

"I'm sure the girl's all right," he muttered.

Lavington looked amused.

"You didn't tell me she was a pretty girl! Well, cheer up, I think the mystery started before her time."

Jack arrived home that evening in a perfect fever of curiosity. He was by now pinning his faith blindly to Lavington. The doctor had accepted the matter so naturally, had been so matter-of-fact and unperturbed by it, that Jack was impressed.

He found his new friend waiting for him in the hall when he came down for dinner, and the doctor suggested that they should dine together at the same table.

"Any news, sir?" asked Jack anxiously.

"I've collected the life history of Heather Cottage all right. It was tenanted first by an old gardener and his wife. The old man died, and the old woman went to her daughter. Then a builder got hold of it, and modernized it with great success, selling it to a city gentleman who used it for week ends. About a year ago, he sold it to some people called Turner—Mr. and Mrs. Turner. They seem to have been rather a curious couple from all I can make out. He was an Englishman, his wife was popularly supposed to be partly Russian, and was a very handsome, exotic-looking woman. They lived very quietly, seeing no one, and hardly ever going outside the cottage garden. The local rumor goes that they were afraid of something—but I don't think we ought to rely on that.

"And then suddenly one day they departed, cleared out one morning early, and never came back. The agents here got a letter from Mr. Turner, written from London, instructing him to sell the place as quickly as possible. The furniture was sold off, and the house itself was sold to a Mr. Mauleverer. He only actually lived in it a fortnight—then he advertised it to be let furnished. The people who have it now are a consumptive French professor and his daughter. They have been there just ten days."

Jack digested this in silence.

"I don't see that that gets us any forrader," he said at last. "Do you?"

"I rather want to know more about the Turners," said Lavington quietly. "They left very early in the morning, you remember. As far as I can make out, nobody actually saw them go. Mr. Turner has been seen since—but I can't find anybody who has seen Mrs. Turner."

Jack paled.

"It can't be—you don't mean—"

"Don't excite yourself, young man. The influence of anyone at the point of death—and especially of violent death—upon their surroundings is very strong. Those surroundings might conceivably absorb that influence, transmitting it in turn to a suitably tuned receiver—in this case yourself."

"But why me?" murmured Jack rebelliously. "Why not someone who could do some good?"

"You are regarding the force as intelligent and purposeful, instead of blind and mechanical. I do not believe myself in earthbound spirits, haunting a spot for one particular purpose. But the thing I have seen, again and again, until I can hardly believe it to be pure coincidence, is a kind of blind groping toward justice—a subterranean moving of blind forces, always working obscurely toward that end. . . ."

He shook himself, as though casting off some obsession that preoccupied him, and turned to Jack with a ready smile.

"Let us banish the subject—for tonight at all events," he suggested.

Jack agreed readily enough, but did not find it so easy to banish the subject from his own mind.

During the week end, he made vigorous inquiries of his own, but succeeded in eliciting little more than the doctor had done. He had definitely given up playing golf before breakfast.

The next link in the chain came from an unexpected quarter. On getting back one day, Jack was informed that a young lady was waiting to see him. To his intense surprise it proved to be the girl of the garden—the pansy girl, as he always called her in his own mind. She was very nervous and confused.

"You will forgive me, Monsieur, for coming to seek you like this? But there is something I want to tell you—I—"

She looked around uncertainly.

"Come in here," said Jack promptly, leading the way into the now deserted "Ladies' Drawing-room" of the hotel, a dreary apartment, with a good deal of red plush about it. "Now, sit down, Miss, Miss—"

"Marchaud, Monsieur. Felise Marchaud."

"Sit down, Mademoiselle Marchaud, and tell me all about it."

Felise sat down obediently. She was dressed in dark green today, and the beauty and charm of the proud little face was more evident than ever. Jack's heart beat faster as he sat down beside her.

"It is like this," explained Felise. "We have been here but a short time, and from the beginning we hear the house—our so sweet little house—is haunted. No servant will stay in it. That does not matter so much—me, I can do the *ménage* and cook easily enough."

"Angel," thought the infatuated young man. "She's wonderful."

But he maintained an outward semblance of business-like attention.

"This talk of ghosts, I think it is all folly—that is until four days ago. Monsieur, four nights running, I have had the same dream. A lady stands there—she is beautiful, tall and very fair. In her hands she holds a blue china jar. She is distressed—very distressed, and continually she holds out the jar to me, as though imploring me to do something with it. But alas! she cannot speak, and I—I do not know what she asks. That was the dream for the first two nights—but the night before last, there was more of it. She and the blue jar faded away, and suddenly I heard her voice crying out—I know it is her voice, you comprehend—and, oh! Monsieur, the words she says are those you spoke to me that morning. 'Murder—help! Murder!' I awoke in terror. I say to myself—it is a nightmare, the words you heard are an accident. But last night the dream came again. Monsieur, what is it? You too have heard. What shall we do?"

Felise's face was terrified. Her small hands clasped themselves together, and she gazed appealingly at Jack. The latter affected an unconcern he did not feel.

"That's all right, Mademoiselle Marchaud. You mustn't worry. I tell you what I'd like you to do, if you don't mind. Repeat the whole story to a friend of mine who is staying here, a Dr. Lavington."

Felise signified her willingness to adopt this course, and Jack went off in search of Lavington. He returned with him a few minutes later.

Lavington gave the girl a keen scrutiny as he acknowledged Jack's hurried introductions. With a few reassuring words, he soon put the girl at her ease, and he, in his turn, listened attentively to her story.

"Very curious," he said, when she had finished. "You have told your father this?"

Felise shook her head.

"I have not liked to worry him. He is very ill still"—her eyes filled with tears—"I keep from him anything that might excite or agitate him."

"I understand," said Lavington kindly. "And I am glad you came to us, Mademoiselle Marchaud. Hartington here, as you know, had an experience something similar to yours. I think I may say that we are well on the track now. There is nothing else that you can think of?"

Felise gave a quick movement.

"Of course! How stupid I am. It is the point of the whole story. Look, Monsieur, at what I found at the back of one of the cupboards where it had slipped behind the shelf."

She held out to them a dirty piece of drawing-paper on which was executed roughly in water colors a sketch of a woman. It was a mere daub, but the likeness was probably good enough. It represented a tall fair woman, with something subtly un-English in her face. She was standing by a table on which was standing a blue china jar.

"I only found it this morning," explained Felise. "Monsieur le docteur, that is the face of the woman I saw in my dream, and that is the identical blue jar."

"Extraordinary," commented Lavington. "The key to the mystery is evidently the blue jar. It looks like a Chinese jar to me, probably an old one. It seems to have a curious raised pattern over it."

"It is Chinese," declared Jack. "I have seen an exactly similar one in my uncle's collection—he is a great collector of Chinese porcelain, you know, and I remember noticing a jar just like this a short time ago."

"The Chinese jar," mused Lavington. He remained a minute or two lost in thought, then raised his head suddenly, a curious light shining in his eyes. "Hartington, how long has your uncle had that jar?"

"How long? I really don't know."

"Think. Did he buy it lately?"

"I don't know—yes, I believe he did, now I come to think of it. I'm not very interested in porcelain myself, but I remember his showing me his 'recent acquisitions,' and this was one of them."

"Less than two months ago? The Turners left Heather Cottage just two months ago."

"Yes, I believe it was."

"Your uncle attends country sales sometimes?"

"He's always tooling round to sales."

"Then there is no inherent improbability in our assuming that he bought this particular piece of porcelain at the sale of the Turners' things. A curious coincidence—or perhaps what I call the groping of blind justice. Hartington, you must find out from your uncle at once where he bought this jar."

Jack's face fell.

"I'm afraid that's impossible. Uncle George is away on the Continent. I don't even know where to write to him."

"How long will he be away?"

"Three weeks to a month at least."

There was a silence. Felise sat looking anxiously from one man to the other.

"Is there nothing that we can do?" she asked timidly.

"Yes, there is one thing," said Lavington, in a tone of suppressed excitement. "It is unusual, perhaps, but I believe that it will succeed. Hartington, you must get hold of that jar. Bring it down here and, if Mademoiselle permits, we will spend a night in Heather Cottage, taking the blue jar with us."

Jack felt his skin creep uncomfortably.

"What do you think will happen?" he asked uneasily.

"I have not the slightest idea—but I honestly believe that the mystery will be solved and the ghost laid. Quite possibly there may be a false bottom to the jar and something is concealed inside it. If no phenomenon occurs, we must use our own ingenuity."

Felise clasped her hands.

"It is a wonderful idea," she exclaimed.

Her eyes were alight with enthusiasm. Jack did not feel nearly so enthusiastic—in fact, he was inwardly funking it badly, but nothing would have induced him to admit the fact before Felise. The doctor acted as though his suggestion were the most natural one in the world.

"When can you get the jar?" asked Felise, turning to Jack.

"Tomorrow," said the latter, unwillingly.

He had to go through with it now, but the memory of that frenzied cry for help that had haunted him each morning was something to be ruthlessly thrust down and not thought about more than could be helped.

He went to his uncle's house the following evening, and took away the jar in question. He was more than ever convinced when he saw it again that it was the identical one pictured in the water color sketch, but carefully as he looked it over he could see no sign that it contained a secret receptacle of any kind.

It was eleven o'clock when he and Lavington arrived at Heather Cottage. Felise was on the lookout for them, and opened the door softly before they had time to knock.

"Come in," she whispered. "My father is asleep upstairs, and we must not wake him. I have made coffee for you in here."

She led the way into a small cozy sitting-room. A spirit lamp stood in the grate, and bending over it, she brewed them both some fragrant coffee.

Then Jack unfastened the Chinese jar from its many wrappings. Felise gasped as her eyes fell on it.

"But yes, but yes," she cried eagerly. "That is it—I would know it anywhere."

Meanwhile Lavington was making his own preparations. He removed all the ornaments from a small table and set it in the middle of the room. Round it he placed three chairs. Then, taking the blue jar from Jack, he placed it in the center of the table.

"Now," he said, "we are ready. Turn off the lights, and let us sit round the table in the darkness."

The others obeyed him. Lavington's voice spoke again out of the darkness.

"Think of nothing—or of everything. Do not force the mind. It is possible that one of us has mediumistic powers. If so, that person will go into a trance. Remember, there is nothing to fear. Cast out fear from your hearts, and drift—drift—"

His voice died away and there was silence. Minute by minute, the silence seemed to grow more pregnant with possibilities. It was all very well for Lavington to say "Cast out fear." It was not fear that Jack felt—it was panic. And he was almost certain that Felise felt the same way. Suddenly he heard her voice, low and terrified.

"Something terrible is going to happen. I feel it."

"Cast out fear," said Lavington. "Do not fight against the influence."

The darkness seemed to get darker and the silence more acute. And nearer and nearer came that indefinable sense of menace.

Jack felt himself choking—stifling—the evil thing was very near. . . .

And then the moment of conflict passed. He was drifting—drifting downstream—his lids closed—peace—darkness. . . .

JACK STIRRED SLIGHTLY. His head was heavy—heavy as lead. Where was he?

Sunshine . . . birds. . . . He lay staring up at the sky.

Then it all came back to him. The sitting. The little room. Felise and the doctor. What had happened?

He sat up, his head throbbing unpleasantly, and looked round him. He was lying in a little copse not far from the cottage. No one else was near him. He took out his watch. To his amazement it registered half-past twelve.

Jack struggled to his feet, and ran as fast as he could in the direction of the cottage. They must have been alarmed by his failure to come out of the trance, and carried him out into the open air.

Arrived at the cottage, he knocked loudly on the door. But there was no answer, and no signs of life about it. They must have gone off to get help. Or else—Jack felt an indefinable fear invade him. What had happened last night?

He made his way back to the hotel as quickly as possible. He was about to make some inquiries at the office, when he was diverted by a colossal punch in the ribs which nearly knocked him off his feet. Turning in some indignation, he beheld a white-haired old gentleman wheezing with mirth.

"Didn't expect me, my boy. Didn't expect me, hey?" said this individual.

"Why, Uncle George, I thought you were miles away—in Italy somewhere."

"Ah! but I wasn't. Landed at Dover last night. Thought I'd motor up to town and stop here to see you on the way. And what did I find. Out all night, hey? Nice goings on—"

"Uncle George," Jack checked him firmly. "I've got the most extraordinary story to tell you. I dare say you won't believe it."

He narrated the whole story.

"And God knows what's become of them," he ended.

His uncle seemed on the verge of apoplexy.

"The jar," he managed to ejaculate at last. "THE BLUE JAR! What's become of that?"

Jack stared at him in non-comprehension, but submerged in the torrent of words that followed he began to understand.

It came with a rush: "Ming—unique—gem of my collection—worth ten thousand pounds at least—offer from Hoggenheimer, the American millionaire—only one of its kind in the world.—Confound it, sir, what have you done with my BLUE JAR?"

Jack rushed to the office. He must find Lavington. The young lady in the office eyed him coldly.

"Dr. Lavington left late last night—by motor. He left a note for you."

Jack tore it open. It was short and to the point.

MY DEAR YOUNG FRIEND:

Is the day of the supernatural over? Not quite—especially when tricked out in new scientific language. Kindest regards from Felise, invalid father, and myself. We have twelve hours start, which ought to be ample.

Yours ever,
Ambrose Lavington,
Doctor of the Soul

SING A SONG OF SIXPENCE

Sir Edward Palliser, K. C., lived at No. 9 Queen Anne's Close. Queen Anne's Close is a cul-de-sac. In the very heart of Westminster it manages to have a peaceful Old World atmosphere far removed from the turmoil of the twentieth century. It suited Sir Edward Palliser admirably.

Sir Edward had been one of the most eminent criminal barristers of his day and now that he no longer practiced at the bar he had amused himself by amassing a very fine criminological library. He was also the author of a volume of Reminiscences of Eminent Criminals.

On this particular evening Sir Edward was sitting in front of his library fire, sipping some very excellent black coffee and shaking his head over a volume of Lombroso. Such ingenious theories and so completely out of date!

The door opened almost noiselessly and his well-trained manservant approached over the thick pile carpet, and murmured discreetly:

"A young lady wishes to see you, sir."

"A young lady?"

Sir Edward was surprised. Here was something quite out of the usual course of events. Then he reflected that it might be his niece, Ethel—but no, in that case Armor would have said so.

He inquired cautiously. "The lady did not give her name?"

"No, sir, but she said she was quite sure you would wish to see her."

"Show her in," said Sir Edward Palliser. He felt pleasurably intrigued.

A tall, dark girl of close on thirty, wearing a black coat and skirt, well cut, and a little black hat, came to Sir Edward with outstretched hand and a look of eager recognition on her face. Armor withdrew, closing the door noiselessly behind him.

"Sir Edward—you do know me, don't you? I'm Magdalen Vaughan."

"Why, of course." He pressed the outstretched hand warmly.

He remembered her perfectly now. That trip home from America on the *Siluric!* This charming child—for she had been little more than a child. He had made love to her, he remembered, in a discreet, elderly man-of-the-world fashion. She had been so adorably young—so eager—so full of admiration and hero-worship—just made to captivate the heart of a man near sixty. The remembrance brought additional warmth into the pressure of his hand.

"This is most delightful of you. Sit down, won't you." He arranged an armchair for her, talking easily and evenly, wondering all the time why she had come. When at last he brought the easy flow of small talk to an end, there was a silence.

Her hand closed and unclosed on the arm of the chair, she moistened her lips. Suddenly she spoke—abruptly.

"Sir Edward—I want you to help me."

He was surprised and murmured mechanically: "Yes?"

She went on, speaking more intensely: "You said that if ever I needed help—that if there were anything in the world you could do for me—you would do it."

Yes, he had said that. It was the sort of thing one did say—particularly at the moment of parting. He could recall the break in his voice—the way he had raised her hand to his lips.

"If there is ever anything I can do—remember, I mean it. . . ."

Yes, one said that sort of thing. . . . But very, very rarely did one have to fulfill one's words! And certainly not after—how many?—

nine or ten years. He flashed a quick glance at her—she was still a very good-looking girl, but she had lost what had been to him her charm—that look of dewy untouched youth. It was a more interesting face now, perhaps—a younger man might have thought so—but Sir Edward was far from feeling the tide of warmth and emotion that had been his at the end of that Atlantic voyage.

His face became legal and cautious. He said in a rather brisk way: "Certainly, my dear young lady, I shall be delighted to do anything in my power—though I doubt if I can be very helpful to anyone in these days."

If he were preparing his way of retreat she did not notice it. She was of the type that can only see one thing at a time and what she was seeing at this moment was her own need. She took Sir Edward's willingness to help for granted.

"We are in terrible trouble, Sir Edward."

"We? You are married?"

"No—I meant my brother and I. Oh, and William and Emily, too, for that matter. But I must explain. I have—I had an aunt—Miss Crabtree. You may have read about her in the papers? It was horrible. She was killed—murdered."

"Ah!" A flash of interest lit up Sir Edward's face. "About a month ago, wasn't it?"

The girl nodded. "Rather less than that—three weeks."

"Yes, I remember. She was hit on the head in her own house. They didn't get the fellow who did it."

Again Magdalen Vaughan nodded. "They didn't get the man—I don't believe they ever will get the man. You see—there mightn't be any man to get."

"What?"

"Yes—it's awful. Nothing's come out about it in the papers. But that's what the police think. They know nobody came to the house that night."

"You mean—?"

"That it's one of us four. It must be. They don't know which—and we don't know which. . . . We don't know. And we sit there every day looking at each other surreptitiously and wondering. Oh! if only it could have been someone from outside—but I don't see how it can . . ."

Sir Edward stared at her, his interest rising.

"You mean that the members of the family are under suspicion?"

"Yes, that's what I mean. The police haven't said so, of course. They've been quite polite and nice. But they've ransacked the house, they've questioned us all, and Martha again and again. . . . And because they don't know which, they're holding their hand. I'm so frightened—so horribly frightened. . . ."

"My dear child. Come now, surely you are exaggerating."

"I'm not. It's one of us four—it must be."

"Who are the four to whom you refer?"

Magdalen sat up straight and spoke more composedly.

"There's myself and Matthew. Aunt Lily was our great aunt. She was my grandmother's sister. We've lived with her ever since we were fourteen (we're twins, you know). Then there was William Crabtree. He was her nephew—her brother's child. He lived there, too, with his wife, Emily."

"She supported them?"

"More or less. He has a little money of his own, but he's not strong and has to live at home. He's a quiet, dreamy sort of man. I'm sure it would have been impossible for him to have—oh! it's awful of me to think of it even!"

"I am still very far from understanding the position. Perhaps you would not mind running over the facts—if it does not distress you too much."

"Oh, no! I want to tell you. And it's all quite clear in my mind still—horribly clear. We'd had tea, you understand, and we'd all gone off to do things of our own. I to do some dressmaking, Matthew to type an article—he does a little journalism; William to do his stamps. Emily hadn't been down to tea. She'd taken a headache powder and was lying down. So there we were, all of us, busy and occupied. And when Martha went in to lay supper at half-past seven, there Aunt Lily was—dead. Her head—oh, it's horrible!—all crushed in."

"The weapon was found, I think?"

"Yes. It was a heavy paper weight that always lay on the table by the door. The police tested it for fingerprints, but there were none. It had been wiped clean."

"And your first surmise?"

"We thought, of course, it was a burglar. There were two or three drawers of the bureau pulled out, as though a thief had been looking for something. Of course we thought it was a burglar! And then the police came—and they said she had been dead at least an Hour, and asked Martha who had been to the house, and Martha said nobody. And all the windows were fastened on the inside, and there seemed no signs of anything having been tampered with. And then they began to ask us questions . . ."

She stopped. Her breast heaved. Her eyes, frightened and imploring, sought Sir Edward's in search of reassurance.

"For instance, who benefited by your aunt's death?"

"That's simple. We all benefit equally. She left her money to be divided in equal shares among the four of us."

"And what was the value of her estate?"

"The lawyer told us it will come to about eighty thousand pounds after the death duties are paid."

Sir Edward opened his eyes in some slight surprise.

"That is quite a considerable sum. You knew, I suppose, the total of your aunt's fortune?"

Magdalen shook her head.

"No—it came quite as a surprise to us. Aunt Lily was always terribly careful about money. She kept just the one servant and always talked a lot about economy."

Sir Edward nodded thoughtfully. Magdalen leaned forward a little in her chair.

"You will help me—you will?"

Her words came to Sir Edward as an unpleasant shock just at the moment when he was becoming interested in her story for its own sake.

"My dear young lady—what can I possibly do? If you want good legal advice, I can give you the name—"

She interrupted him. "Oh! I don't want that sort of thing! I want you to help me personally—as a friend."

"That's very charming of you, but—"

"I want you to come to our house. I want you to ask questions. I want you to see and judge for yourself."

"But my dear young—"

"Remember, you promised. Anywhere—any time—you said, if I wanted help . . ."

Her eyes, pleading yet confident, looked into his. He felt ashamed and strangely touched. That terrific sincerity of hers, that absolute belief in an idle promise, ten years old, as a sacred binding thing. How many men had not said those self-same words—a cliché almost!—and how few of them had ever been called upon to make good.

He said rather weakly: "I'm sure there are many people who would advise you better than I could."

"I've got lots of friends—naturally." (He was amused by the naive self-assurance of that.) "But, you see, none of them are clever. Not like you. You're used to questioning people. And with all your experience you must know."

"Know what?"

"Whether they're innocent or guilty."

He smiled rather grimly to himself. He flattered himself that, on the whole, he usually had known! Though, on many occasions, his private opinion had not been that of the jury.

Magdalen pushed back her hat from her forehead with a nervous gesture, looked round the room, and said: "How quiet it is here. Don't you sometimes long for some noise?"

The cul-de-sac! All unwittingly her words, spoken at random, touched him on the raw. A cul-de-sac. Yes, but there was always a way out—the way you had come—the way back into the world. . . . Something impetuous and youthful stirred in him. Her simple trust appealed to the best side of his nature—and the condition of her problem appealed to something else—the innate criminologist in him. He wanted to see these people of whom she spoke. He wanted to form his own judgment.

He said: "If you are really convinced I can be of any use. . . . Mind, I guarantee nothing."

He expected her to be overwhelmed with delight, but she took it very calmly.

"I knew you would do it. I've always thought of you as a real friend. Will you come back with me now?"

"No. I think if I pay you a visit tomorrow it will be more satisfactory. Will you give me the name and address of Miss Crabtree's lawyer? I may want to ask him a few questions."

She wrote it down and handed it to him. Then she got up and said rather shyly: "I—I'm really most awfully grateful. Good-bye."

"And your own address?"

"How stupid of me. 18 Palatine Walk, Chelsea."

IT WAS THREE O'CLOCK on the following afternoon when Sir Edward Palliser approached 18 Palatine Walk with a sober, measured tread. In the interval he had found out several things. He had paid a visit that morning to Scotland Yard, where the Assistant Commissioner was an old friend of his, and he had also had an interview with the late Miss Crabtree's lawyer. As a result he had a clearer vision of the circumstances. Miss Crabtree's arrangements in regard to money had been somewhat peculiar. She never made use of a check book. Instead she was in the habit of writing to her lawyer and asking him to have a certain sum in five-pound notes waiting for her. It was nearly always the same sum. Three hundred pounds four times a year. She came to fetch it herself in a four-wheeler, which she regarded as the only safe means of conveyance. At other times she never left the house.

At Scotland Yard Sir Edward learned that the question of finance had been gone into very carefully. Miss Crabtree had been almost due for her next instalment of money. Presumably the previous three hundred had been spent—or almost spent. But this was exactly the point that had not been easy to ascertain. By checking the household expenditure, it was soon evident that Miss Crabtree's expenditure per quarter fell a good deal short of the three hundred. On the other hand, she was in the habit of sending five-pound notes to needy friends and relatives. Whether there had been much or little money in the house at the time of her death was a debatable point. None had been found.

It was this particular point which Sir Edward was revolving in his mind as he approached Palatine Walk.

The door of the house (which was a non-basement one) was opened to him by a small elderly woman with an alert gaze. He was shown into a big double room on the left of the small hallway and there Magdalen came to him. More clearly than before, he saw the traces of nervous strain in her face.

"You told me to ask questions, and I have come to do so," said Sir Edward, smiling as he shook hands. "First of all, I want to know who last saw your aunt and exactly what time that was?"

"It was after tea—five o'clock. Martha was the last person with her. She had been paying the books that afternoon, and brought Aunt Lily the change and the accounts."

"You trust Martha?"

"Oh, absolutely. She was with Aunt Lily for—oh, thirty years, I suppose. She's honest as the day."

Sir Edward nodded.

"Another question. Why did your cousin, Mrs. Crabtree, take a headache powder?"

"Well, because she had a headache."

"Naturally, but was there any particular reason why she should have a headache?"

"Well, yes, in a way. There was rather a scene at lunch. Emily is very excitable and highly strung. She and Aunt Lily used to have rows sometimes."

"And they had one at lunch?"

"Yes. Aunt Lily was rather trying about little things. It all started out of nothing—and then they were at it hammer and tongs—with Emily saying all sorts of things she couldn't possibly have meant—that she'd leave the house and never come back—that she was grudged every mouthful she ate—oh, all sorts of silly things. And Aunt Lily said the sooner she and her husband packed their boxes and went the better. But it all meant nothing, really."

"Because Mr. and Mrs. Crabtree couldn't afford to pack up and go?"

"Oh, not only that. William was fond of Aunt Emily. He really was."

"It wasn't a day of quarrels, by any chance?"

Magdalen's color heightened.

"You mean me? The fuss about my wanting to be a manikin?"

"Your aunt wouldn't agree?"

"No."

"Why did you want to be a manikin, Miss Magdalen? Does the life strike you as a very attractive one?"

"No, but anything would be better than going on living here."

"Yes, then. But now you will have a comfortable income, won't you?"

"Oh, yes, it's quite different now."

She made the admission with the utmost simplicity.

He smiled but pursued the subject no further. Instead he said: "And your brother? Did he have a quarrel, too?"

"Matthew? Oh, no."

"Then no one can say he had a motive for wishing his aunt out of the way?"

He was quick to seize on the momentary dismay that showed in her face.

"I forgot," he said casually. "He owed a good deal of money, didn't he?"

"Yes; poor old Matthew."

"Still, that will be all right now."

"Yes—" She sighed. "It is a relief."

And still she saw nothing! He changed the subject hastily.

"Your cousins and your brother are at home?"

"Yes; I told them you were coming. They are all so anxious to help. Oh, Sir Edward—I feel, somehow, that you are going to find out that everything is all right—that none of us had anything to do with it—that, after all, it was an outsider."

"I can't do miracles. I may be able to find out the truth, but I can't make the truth be what you want it to be."

"Can't you? I feel that you could do anything—anything."

She left the room. He thought, disturbed, "What did she mean by that? Does she want me to suggest a line of defense? For whom?"

His meditations were interrupted by the entrance of a man about fifty years of age. He had a naturally powerful frame, but stooped slightly. His clothes were untidy and his hair carelessly brushed. He looked good-natured but vague.

"Sir Edward Palliser? Oh, how do you do? Magdalen sent me along, It's very good of you, I'm sure, to wish to help us, though I don't think anybody will ever be really discovered. I mean, they won't catch the fellow.

"You think it was a burglar, then—someone from outside?"

"Well, it must have been. It couldn't be one of the family. These fellows are very clever nowadays, they climb like cats and they get in and out as they like."

"Where were you, Mr. Crabtree, when the tragedy occurred?"

"I was busy with my stamps—in my little sitting-room upstairs."

"You didn't hear anything?"

"No—but then I never do hear anything when I'm absorbed. Very foolish of me, but there it is."

"Is the sitting-room you refer to over this room?"

"No, it's at the back."

Again the door opened. A small, fair woman entered. Her hands were twitching nervously. She looked fretful and excited.

"William, why didn't you wait for me? I said 'wait.'"

"Sorry, my dear, I forgot. Sir Edward Palliser—my wife."

"How do you do, Mrs. Crabtree? I hope you don't mind my coming here to ask a few questions. I know how anxious you must all be to have things cleared up."

"Naturally. But I can't tell you anything—can I, William? I was asleep—on my bed—I only woke up when Martha screamed."

Her hands continued to twitch.

"Where is your room, Mrs. Crabtree?"

"It's over this. But I didn't hear anything—how could I? I was asleep."

He could get nothing out of her but that. She knew nothing—

she had heard nothing—she had been asleep. She reiterated it with the obstinacy of a frightened woman. Yet Sir Edward knew very well that it might easily be—probably was—the bare truth.

He excused himself at last—said he would like to put a few questions to Martha. William Crabtree volunteered to take him to the kitchen. In the hall Sir Edward nearly collided with a tall, dark young man who was striding toward the front door.

"Mr. Matthew Vaughan?"

"Yes—but, look here, I can't wait. I've got an appointment."

"Matthew!" It was his sister's voice from the stairs. "Oh, Matthew, you promised—"

"I know, sis. But I can't. Got to meet a fellow. And, anyway, what's the good of talking about the damned thing over and over again. We have enough of that with the police. I'm fed up with the whole show."

The front door banged. Mr. Matthew Vaughan had made his exit.

Sir Edward was introduced into the kitchen. Martha was ironing. She paused, iron in hand. Sir Edward shut the door behind him.

"Miss Vaughan has asked me to help her," he said. "I hope you won't object to my asking you a few questions."

She looked at him, then shook her head.

"None of them did it, sir. I know what you're thinking, but it isn't so. As nice a set of ladies and gentlemen as you could wish to see."

"I've no doubt of it. But their niceness isn't what we call evidence, you know."

"Perhaps not, sir. The law's a funny thing. But there is evidence—as you call it, sir. None of them could have done it without my knowing."

"But surely—"

"I know what I'm talking about, sir. There, listen to that—"

"That" was a creaking sound above their heads.

"The stairs, sir. Every time anyone goes up or down, the stairs creak something awful. It doesn't matter how quiet you go. Mrs. Crabtree, she was lying on her bed, and Mr. Crabtree was fiddling about with them wretched stamps of his, and Miss Magdalen she was up above, working her sewing machine, and if any one of those three had come down the stairs I should have known it. And they didn't!"

She spoke with a positive assurance which impressed the barrister. He thought: "A good witness. She'd carry weight."

"You mightn't have noticed."

"Yes, I would. I'd have noticed without noticing, so to speak. Like you notice when a door shuts and somebody goes out."

Sir Edward shifted his ground.

"That is three of them accounted for, but there is a fourth. Was Mr. Matthew Vaughan upstairs also?"

"No, but he was in the little room downstairs. Next door. And he was typewriting. You can hear it plain in here. His machine never stopped for a moment. Not for a moment, sir. I can swear to it. A nasty, irritating tap-tapping noise it is, too."

Sir Edward paused a minute.

"It was you who found her, wasn't it?"

"Yes, sir, it was. Lying there with blood on her poor hair. And no one hearing a sound on account of the tap-tapping of Mr. Matthew's typewriter."

"I understand you are positive that no one came to the house?"

"How could they, sir, without my knowing? The bell rings in here. And there's only the one door."

He looked at her straight in the face.

"You were attached to Miss Crabtree?"

A warm glow—genuine—unmistakable—came into her face.

"Yes, indeed, I was, sir. But for Miss Crabtree—well, I'm getting on and I don't mind speaking of it now. I got into trouble, sir, when I was a girl, and Miss Crabtree stood by me—took me back into her service, she did, when it was all over. I'd have died for her—I would indeed."

Sir Edward knew sincerity when he heard it. Martha was sincere.

"As far as you know, no one came to the door—?"

"No one could have come."

"I said as far as you know. But if Miss Crabtree had been expecting someone—if she opened the door to that someone herself . . ."

"Oh!" Martha seemed taken back.

"That's possible, I suppose?" Sir Edward urged.

"It's possible—yes—but it isn't very likely. I mean . . ."

She was clearly taken aback. She couldn't deny and yet she wanted to do so. Why? Because she knew that the truth lay elsewhere. Was that it? The four people in the house—one of them guilty? Did Martha want to shield that guilty party? Had the stairs creaked? Had someone come stealthily down and did Martha know who that someone was?

She herself was honest—Sir Edward was convinced of that.

He pressed his point, watching her.

"Miss Crabtree might have done that, I suppose? The window of that room faces the street. She might have seen whoever it was she was waiting for from the window and gone out into the hall and let him—or her—in. She might even have wished that no one should see the person."

Martha looked troubled. She said at last reluctantly:

"Yes, you may be right, sir. I never thought of that. That she was expecting a gentleman—yes, it well might be."

It was as though she began to perceive advantages in the idea.

"You were the last person to see her, were you not?"

"Yes, sir. After I'd cleared away the tea. I took the receipted books to her and the change from the money she'd given me."

"Had she given the money to you in five-pound notes?"

"A five-pound note, sir," said Martha in a shocked voice. "The books never came up as high as five pounds. I'm very careful."

"Where did she keep her money?"

"I don't rightly know, sir. I should say that she carried it about with her—in her black velvet bag. But of course she may have kept it in one of the drawers in her bedroom that were locked. She was very fond of locking up things, though prone to lose her keys."

Sir Edward nodded. "You don't know how much money she had—in five-pound notes, I mean?"

"No, sir, I couldn't say what the exact amount was."

"And she said nothing to you that could lead you to believe that she was expecting anybody?"

"No, sir."

"You're quite sure? What exactly did she say?"

"Well," Martha considered, "she said the butcher was nothing more than a rogue and a cheat, and she said I'd had in a quarter of a pound of tea more than I ought, and she said Mrs. Crabtree was full of nonsense for not liking to eat margarine, and she didn't like one of the sixpences I'd brought her back—one of the new ones with oak leaves on it—she said it was bad, and I had a lot of trouble to convince her. And she said—oh, that the fishmonger had sent haddocks instead of whitings, and had I told him about it, and I said I had—and, really, I think that's all, sir."

Martha's speech had made the deceased lady loom clear to Sir Edward as a detailed description would never have done. He said casually: "Rather a difficult mistress to please, eh?"

"A bit fussy, but there, poor dear, she didn't often get out, and staying cooped up she had to have something to amuse herself like. She was pernickety but kindhearted—never a beggar sent away from the door without something. Fussy she may have been, but a real charitable lady."

"I am glad, Martha, that she leaves one person to regret her."

The old servant caught her breath.

"You mean—oh, but they were all fond of her—really—underneath. They all had words with her now and again, but it didn't mean anything."

Sir Edward lifted his head. There was a crack above.

"That's Miss Magdalen coming down."

"How do you know?" he shot at her.

The old woman flushed. "I know her step," she muttered.

Sir Edward left the kitchen rapidly. Martha had been right. Magdalen had just reached the bottom stair. She looked at him hopefully.

"Not very far on as yet," said Sir Edward, answering her look, and added, "You don't happen to know what letters your aunt received on the day of her death?"

"They are all together. The police have been through them, of course."

She led the way to the big double drawing-room and, unlocking a drawer, took out a large black velvet bag with an old-fashioned silver clasp.

"This is Aunt's bag. Everything is in here just as it was on the day of her death. I've kept it like that."

Sir Edward thanked her and proceeded to turn out the contents of the bag on the table. It was, he fancied, a fair specimen of an eccentric elderly lady's handbag.

There were some odd silver change, two ginger nuts, three newspaper cuttings about Joanna South-cott's box, a trashy, printed poem about the unemployed, an *Old Moore's Almanack,* a large piece of camphor, some spectacles, and three letters. A spidery one from someone called "Cousin Lucy," a bill for mending a watch, and an appeal from a charitable institution.

Sir Edward went through everything very carefully, then repacked the bag and handed it to Magdalen with a sigh.

"Thank you, Miss Magdalen. I'm afraid there isn't much there."

He rose, observed that the window commanded a good view of the front door steps, then took Magdalen's hand in his.

"You are going?"

"Yes."

"But it's—it's going to be all right?"

"Nobody connected with the law ever commits himself to a rash statement like that," said Sir Edward solemnly, and made his escape.

He walked along the street, lost in thought. The puzzle was there under his hand—and he had not solved it. It needed something—some little thing. Just to point the way.

A hand fell on his shoulder and he started. It was Matthew Vaughan, somewhat out of breath.

"I've been chasing you, Sir Edward. I want to apologize. For my rotten manners half an hour ago. But I've not got the best temper in the world, I'm afraid. It's awfully good of you to bother about this business. Please ask me whatever you like. If there's anything I can do to help—"

Suddenly Sir Edward stiffened. His glance was fixed—not on Matthew—but across the street. Somewhat bewildered, Matthew repeated: "If there's anything I can do to help—"

"You have already done it, my dear young man," said Sir Edward. "By stopping me at this particular spot and so fixing my attention on something I might otherwise have missed."

He pointed across the street to a small restaurant opposite.

"The Four and Twenty Blackbirds?" asked Matthew in a puzzled voice.

"Exactly."

"It's an odd name—but you get quite decent food there, I believe."

"I shall not take the risk of experimenting," said Sir Edward. "Being further from my nursery days than you are, my young friend, I probably remember my nursery rhymes better. There is a classic that runs thus, if I remember rightly: *'Sing a song of sixpence, a pocket full of rye, Four and twenty blackbirds baked in a pie'*—and so on. The rest of it does not concern us."

He wheeled round sharply.

"Where are you going?" asked Matthew Vaughan.

"Back to your house, my friend."

They walked there in silence, Matthew Vaughan shooting puzzled glances at his companion. Sir Edward entered, strode to a drawer, lifted out a velvet bag, and opened it. He looked at Matthew and the young man reluctantly left the room.

Sir Edward tumbled out the silver change on the table. Then he nodded. His memory had not been at fault.

He got up and rang the bell, slipping something into the palm of his hand as he did so.

Martha answered the bell.

"You told me, Martha, if I remember rightly, that you had a slight altercation with your late mistress over one of the new sixpences."

"Yes, sir."

"Ah! but the curious thing is, Martha, that among this loose change, there is no new sixpence. There are two sixpences, but they are both old ones."

She stared at him in a puzzled fashion.

"You see what that means? Someone did come to the house that evening—someone to whom your mistress gave sixpence. . . . I think she gave it to him in exchange for this. . . ."

With a swift movement he shot his hand forward, holding out the doggerel verse about unemployment.

One glance at her face was enough.

"The game is up, Martha—you see, I know. You may as well tell me everything."

She sank down on a chair—the tears raced down her face.

"It's true—it's true—the bell didn't ring properly—I wasn't sure, and then I thought I'd better go and see. I got to the door just as he struck her down. The roll of five-pound notes was on the table in front of her—it was the sight of them as made him do it—that and thinking she was alone in the house as she'd let him in. I couldn't scream. I was too paralyzed and then he turned—and I saw it was my boy. . . .

"Oh, he's been a bad one always. I gave him all the money I could. He's been in jail twice. He must have come around to see me, and then Miss Crabtree, seeing as I didn't answer the door, went to answer it herself, and he was taken aback and pulled out one of those unemployment leaflets, and the mistress being kind of charitable, told him to come in, and got out a sixpence. And all the time that roll of notes was lying on the table where it had been when I was giving her the change. And the devil got into my Ben and he got behind her and struck her down."

"And then?" asked Sir Edward.

"Oh, sir, what could I do? My own flesh and blood. His father was a bad one, and Ben takes after him—but he was my own son. I hustled him out, and I went back to the kitchen, and I went to lay for supper at the usual time. Do you think it was very wicked of me, sir? I tried to tell you no lies when you was asking me questions."

Sir Edward rose.

"My poor woman," he said with feeling in his voice. "I am very sorry for you. All the same, the law will have to take its course, you know."

"He's fled the country, sir. I don't know where he is."

"There's a chance, then, that he may escape the gallows, but don't build upon it. Will you send Miss Magdalen to me?"

"Oh, Sir Edward. How wonderful of you—how wonderful you

are," said Magdalen when he had finished his brief recital. "You've saved us all. How can I ever thank you?"

Sir Edward smiled down at her and patted her hand gently. He was very much the great man. Little Magdalen had been very charming on the *Siluric*. That bloom of seventeen—wonderful! She had completely lost it now, of course.

"Next time you need a friend—," he said.

"I'll come straight to you."

"No, no," cried Sir Edward in alarm. "That's just what I don't want you to do. Go to a younger man."

He extricated himself with dexterity from the grateful household and hailing a taxi sank into it with a sigh of relief. Even the charm of a dewy seventeen seemed doubtful.

It could not really compare with a really well-stocked library on criminology.

The taxi turned into Queen Anne's Close.

His cul-de-sac.

THE MYSTERY OF THE SPANISH SHAWL

Mr. Eastwood looked at the ceiling. Then he looked down at the floor. From the floor his gaze traveled slowly up the right-hand wall. Then, with a sudden stern effort, he focused his gaze once more upon the typewriter before him.

The virgin white of the sheet of paper was defaced by a title written in capital letters.

"THE MYSTERY OF THE SECOND CUCUMBER," so it ran. A pleasing title. Anthony Eastwood felt that anyone reading that title would be at once intrigued and arrested by it. "The Mystery of the Second Cucumber," they would say. "What can that be about? A cucumber? The second cucumber? I must certainly read that story." And they would be thrilled and charmed by the consummate ease with which this master of detective fiction had woven an exciting plot round this simple vegetable.

That was all very well. Anthony Eastwood knew as well as anyone what the story ought to be like—the bother was that somehow or other he couldn't get on with it. The two essentials for a story were a title and a plot—the rest was mere spade-work; sometimes the title led to a plot all by itself, as it were, and then all was plain sailing—

but in this case the title continued to adorn the top of the page, and not the vestige of a plot was forthcoming.

Again Anthony Eastwood's gaze sought inspiration from the ceiling, the floor, and the wallpaper, and still nothing materialized.

"I shall call the heroine Sonia," said Anthony, to urge himself on. "Sonia or possibly Dolores—she shall have a skin of ivory pallor—the kind that's not due to ill-health, and eyes like fathomless pools. The hero shall be called George, or possibly John—something short and British. Then the gardener—I suppose there will have to be a gardener, we've got to drag that beastly cucumber in somehow or other—the gardener might be Scottish, and amusingly pessimistic about the early frosts."

This method sometimes worked, but it didn't seem to be going to this morning. Although Anthony could see Sonia and George and the comic gardener quite clearly, they didn't show any willingness to be active and do things.

"I could make it a banana, of course," thought Anthony desperately. "Or a lettuce, or a Brussels sprout—Brussels sprout, now, how about that? Really a cryptogram for Brussels—stolen bearer bonds—sinister Belgian baron."

For a moment a gleam of light seemed to show, but it died down again. The Belgian baron wouldn't materialize, and Anthony suddenly remembered that early frosts and cucumbers were incompatible, which seemed to put the lid on the amusing remarks of the Scottish gardener.

"Oh! Damn!" said Mr. Eastwood.

He rose and seized the *Daily Mail.* It was just possible that someone or other had been done to death in such a way as to lend inspiration to a perspiring author. But the news this morning was mainly political and foreign. Mr. Eastwood cast down the paper in disgust.

Next seizing a novel from the table, he closed his eyes and dabbed his finger down on one of the pages. The word thus indicated by fate was "sheep." Immediately, with startling brilliance, a whole story unrolled itself in Mr. Eastwood's brain. Lovely girl—lover killed in the war, her brain unhinged—tends sheep on the Scottish mountains—mystic meeting with dead lover, final effect of sheep and moonlight like Academy picture, with girl lying dead in the snow, and two trails of footsteps. . . .

It was a beautiful story. Anthony came out of its conception with a sigh and a sad shake of the head. He knew only too well that the editor in question did not want that kind of story—beautiful though it might be. The kind of story he wanted, and insisted on having (and incidentally paid handsomely for getting), was all about mysterious dark women, stabbed to the heart, a young hero unjustly suspected, and the sudden unraveling of the mystery and fixing of the guilt on the least likely person, by means of wholly inadequate clues—in fact, "THE MYSTERY OF THE SECOND CUCUMBER."

"Although," reflected Anthony, "ten to one he'll alter the title and call it something rotten, like *'Murder Most Foul,'* without so much as asking me! Oh, curse that telephone."

He strode angrily to it, and took down the receiver. Twice already in the last hour he had been summoned to it—once for a wrong number, and once to be roped in for dinner by a skittish society dame whom he hated bitterly, but who had been too pertinacious to defeat.

"Hallo!" he growled into the receiver.

A woman's voice answered him, a soft, caressing voice with a trace of foreign accent.

"Is that you, beloved?" it said.

"Well—er—I don't know," said Mr. Eastwood cautiously. "Who's speaking?"

"It is I. Carmen. Listen, beloved. I am pursued—in danger—you must come at once. It is life or death now."

"I beg your pardon," said Mr. Eastwood politely. "I'm afraid you've got the wrong—"

She broke in before he could complete the sentence.

"*Madre de Dios!* They are coming. If they find out what I am doing, they will kill me. Do not fail me. Come at once. It is death for me if you don't come. You know, 320 Kirk Street. The word is cucumber. . . . Hush. . . ."

He heard the faint click as she hung up the receiver at the other end. "Well, I'm damned," said Mr. Eastwood, very much astonished. He crossed over to his tobacco jar, and filled his pipe carefully.

"I suppose," he mused, "that that was some curious effect of my subconscious self. She can't have said cucumber. The whole thing is very extraordinary. Did she say cucumber, or didn't she?"

He strolled up and down irresolutely.

"320 Kirk Street. I wonder what it's all about? She'll be expecting the other man to turn up. I wish I could have explained. 320 Kirk Street. The word is cucumber—oh, impossible, absurd—hallucination of a busy brain."

He glanced malevolently at the typewriter.

"What good are you, I should like to know? I've been looking at you all the morning, and a lot of good it's done me. An author should get his plots from life—from life, do you hear? I'm going out to get one now."

He clapped a hat on his head, gazed affectionately at his priceless collection of old enamels, and left the flat.

Kirk Street, as most Londoners know, is a long, straggling thoroughfare, chiefly devoted to antique shops, where all kinds of spurious goods are offered at fancy prices. There are also old brass shops, glass shops, decayed secondhand shops, and secondhand clothes dealers.

No. 320 was devoted to the sale of old glass. Glassware of all kinds filled it to overflowing. It was necessary for Anthony to move gingerly as he advanced up a center aisle flanked by wine glasses and with lusters and chandeliers swaying and twinkling over his head.

A very old lady was sitting at the back of the shop. She had a budding mustache that many an undergraduate might have envied, and a truculent manner.

She looked at Anthony and said, "Well?" in a forbidding voice.

Anthony was a young man somewhat easily discomposed. He immediately inquired the price of some hock glasses.

"Forty-five shillings for half a dozen."

"Oh, really," said Anthony. "Rather nice, aren't they? How much are these things?"

"Beautiful, they are, old Waterford. Let you have the pair for eighteen guineas."

Mr. Eastwood felt that he was laying up trouble for himself. In another minute he would be buying something, hypnotized by this fierce old woman's eye. And yet he could not bring himself to leave the shop.

"What about that?" he asked, and pointed to a chandelier.

"Thirty-five guineas."

"Ah!" said Mr. Eastwood regretfully. "That's rather more than I can afford."

"What do you want?" asked the old lady. "Something for a wedding present?"

"That's it," said Anthony, snatching at the explanation. "But they're very difficult to suit."

"Ah, well," said the lady, rising with an air of determination. "A nice piece of old glass comes amiss to nobody. I've got a couple of old decanters here—and there's a nice little liqueur set, just the thing for a bride—"

For the next ten minutes Anthony endured agonies. The lady had him firmly in hand. Every conceivable specimen of the glass maker's art was paraded before his eyes. He became desperate.

"Beautiful, beautiful," he exclaimed in a perfunctory manner, as he put down a large goblet that was being forced on his attention. Then blurted out hurriedly, "I say, are you on the telephone here?"

"No, we're not. There's a call office at the post office just opposite. Now, what do you say, the goblet—or these fine old rummers?"

Not being a woman, Anthony was quite unversed in the gentle art of getting out of a shop without buying anything.

"I'd better have the liqueur set," he said gloomily.

It seemed the smallest thing. He was terrified of being landed with the chandelier.

With bitterness in his heart he paid for his purchase. And then, as the old lady was wrapping up the parcel, courage suddenly returned to him. After all, she would only think him eccentric, and, anyway, what the devil did it matter what she thought?

"Cucumber," he said, clearly and firmly.

The old crone paused abruptly in her wrapping operations.

"Eh? What did you say?"

"Nothing," lied Anthony hastily.

"Oh! I thought you said cucumber."

"So I did," said Anthony defiantly.

"Well," said the old lady. "Why ever didn't you say that before? Wasting my time. Through that door there and upstairs. She's waiting for you."

As though in a dream, Anthony passed through the door indicated, and climbed some extremely dirty stairs. At the top of them a door stood ajar displaying a tiny sitting-room.

Sitting on a chair, her eyes fixed on the door, and an expression of eager expectancy on her face, was a girl.

Such a girl! She really had the ivory pallor that Anthony had so often written about. And her eyes! Such eyes! She was not English, that could be seen at a glance. She had a foreign exotic quality which showed itself even in the costly simplicity of her dress.

Anthony paused in the doorway, somewhat abashed. The moment of explanations seemed to have arrived. But with a cry of delight the girl rose and flew into his arms.

"You have come," she cried. "You have come. Oh, the saints and the Holy Madonna be praised."

Anthony, never one to miss opportunities, echoed her fervently. She drew away at last, and looked up in his face with a charming shyness.

"I should never have known you," she declared. "Indeed I should not."

"Wouldn't you?" said Anthony feebly.

"No, even your eyes seem different—and you are ten times handsomer than I ever thought you would be."

"Am I?"

To himself Anthony was saying, "Keep calm, my boy, keep calm. The situation is developing very nicely, but don't lose your head."

"I may kiss you again, yes?"

"Of course you can," said Anthony heartily. "As often as you like."

There was a very pleasant interlude.

"I wonder who the devil I am?" thought Anthony. "I hope to goodness the real fellow won't turn up. What a perfect darling she is."

Suddenly the girl drew away from him, and terror showed in her face.

"You were not followed here?"

"Lord, no."

"Ah, but they are very cunning. You do not know them as I do. Boris, he is a fiend."

"I'll soon settle Boris for you."

"You are a lion—yes, but a lion. As for them, they are *canaille*—all of them. Listen, I have *it!* They would have killed me had they known. I was afraid—I did not know what to do, and then I thought of you. . . . Hush, what was that?"

It was a sound in the shop below. Motioning to him to remain where he was, she tiptoed out on to the stairs. She returned with a white face and staring eyes.

"*Madre de Dios!* It is the police. They are coming up here. You have a knife? A revolver? Which?"

"My dear girl, you don't seriously expect me to murder a policeman?"

"Oh, but you are mad—mad! They will take you away and hang you by the neck until you're dead."

"They'll what?" said Mr. Eastwood, with a very unpleasant feeling going up and down his spine.

Steps sounded on the stair.

"Here they come," whispered the girl. "Deny everything. It is the only hope."

"That's easy enough," muttered Mr. Eastwood, *sotto voce*.

In another minute two men had entered the room. They were in plain clothes, but they had an official bearing that spoke of long training. The smaller of the two, a little dark man with quiet gray eyes, was the spokesman.

"I arrest you, Conrad Fleckman," he said, "for the murder of Anna Rosenberg. Anything you say will be used in evidence against you. Here is my warrant and you will do well to come quietly."

A half-strangled scream burst from the girl's lips. Anthony stepped forward with a composed smile.

"You are making a mistake, officer," he said pleasantly. "My name is Anthony Eastwood."

The two detectives seemed completely unimpressed by his statement.

"We'll see about that later," said one of them, the one who had not spoken before. "In the meantime, you come along with us."

"Conrad," wailed the girl. "Conrad, do not let them take you."

Anthony looked at the detectives.

"You will permit me, I am sure, to say good-bye to this young lady?"

With more decency of feeling than he had expected, the two men moved toward the door. Anthony drew the girl into the corner by the window, and spoke to her in a rapid undertone.

"Listen to me. What I said was true. I am not Conrad Fleckman. When you rang up this morning, they must have given you the wrong number. My name is Anthony Eastwood. I came in answer to your appeal because—well, I came."

She stared at him incredulously.

"You are not Conrad Fleckman?"

"No."

"Oh!" she cried, with a deep accent of distress. "And I kissed you!"

"That's all right," Mr. Eastwood assured her. "The early Christians made a practice of that sort of thing. Jolly sensible. Now, look here. I'll tool off these people. I shall soon prove my identity. In the meantime, they won't worry you, and you can warn this precious Conrad of yours. Afterward—"

"Yes?"

"Well—just this. My telephone number is Northwestern 1743—and mind they don't give you the wrong one."

She gave him an enchanting glance, half-tears, half a smile.

"I shall not forget—indeed, I shall not forget."

"That's all right then. Good-bye. I say—"

"Yes?"

"Talking of the early Christians—once more wouldn't matter, would it?"

She flung her arms round his neck. Her lips just touched his.

"I do like you—yes, I do like you. You will remember that, whatever happens, won't you?"

Anthony disengaged himself reluctantly and approached his captors.

"I am ready to come with you. You don't want to detain this young lady, I suppose?"

"No, sir, that will be quite all right," said the small man civilly.

"Decent fellows, these Scotland Yard men," thought Anthony to himself, as he followed them down the narrow stairway.

There was no sign of the old woman in the shop, but Anthony caught a heavy breathing from a door at the rear, and guessed that she stood behind it, cautiously observing events.

Once out in the dinginess of Kirk Street, Anthony drew a long breath, and addressed the smaller of the two men.

"Now, then, Inspector—you are an inspector, I suppose?"

"Yes, sir. Detective-Inspector Verrall. This is Detective-Sergeant Carter."

"Well, Inspector Verrall, the time has come to talk sense—and to listen to it, too. I'm not Conrad What's-his-name. My name is Anthony Eastwood, as I told you, and I am a writer by profession. If you will accompany me to my flat, I think that I shall be able to satisfy you of my identity."

Something in the matter-of-fact way Anthony spoke seemed to impress the detectives. For the first time an expression of doubt passed over Verrall's face.

Carter, apparently, was harder to convince.

"I dare say," he sneered. "But you'll remember the young lady was calling you 'Conrad' all right."

"Ah! that's another matter. I don't mind admitting to you both that for—er—reasons of my own, I was passing myself off upon that lady as a person called Conrad. A private matter, you understand."

"Likely story, isn't it?" observed Carter. "No, sir, you come along with us. Hail that taxi, Joe."

A passing taxi was stopped, and the three men got inside. Anthony made a last attempt, addressing himself to Verrall as the more easily convinced of the two.

"Look here, my dear Inspector, what harm is it going to do you to come along to my flat and see if I'm speaking the truth? You can keep the taxi if you like—there's a generous offer! It won't make five minutes' difference either way."

Verall looked at him searchingly.

"I'll do it," he said suddenly. "Strange as it appears, I believe you're speaking the truth. We don't want to make fools of ourselves at the station by arresting the wrong man. What's the address?"

"Forty-eight Brandenburg Mansions."

Verrall leaned out and shouted the address to the taxi driver. All three sat in silence until they arrived at their destination, when Carter sprang out, and Verrall motioned to Anthony to follow him.

"No need for any unpleasantness," he explained, as he too descended. "We'll go in friendly like, as though Mr. Eastwood was bringing a couple of pals home."

Anthony felt extremely grateful for the suggestion and his opinion of the Criminal Investigation Department rose every minute.

In the hallway they were fortunate enough to meet Rogers, the porter. Anthony stopped.

"Ah! Good evening, Rogers," he remarked casually.

"Good evening, Mr. Eastwood," replied the porter respectfully.

He was attached to Anthony, who set an example of liberality not always followed by his neighbors.

Anthony paused with his foot on the bottom step of the stairs.

"By the way, Rogers," he said casually, "how long have I been living here? I was just having a little discussion about it with these friends of mine."

"Let me see, sir, it must be getting on for close on four years now."

"Just what I thought."

Anthony flung a glance of triumph at the two detectives. Carter grunted, but Verrall was smiling broadly.

"Good, but not good enough, sir," he remarked. "Shall we go up?"

Anthony opened the door of the flat with his latchkey. He was thankful to remember that Seamark, his man, was out. The fewer witnesses of this catastrophe the better.

The typewriter was as he had left it. Carter strode across to the table and read the headline on the paper.

"THE MYSTERY OF THE SECOND CUCUMBER?" he announced in a gloomy voice.

"A story of mine," exclaimed Anthony nonchalantly.

"That's another good point, sir," said Verall nodding his head, his eyes twinkling. "By the way, sir, what was it about? What was the mystery of the second cucumber?"

"Ah, there you have me," said Anthony. "It's that second cucumber that's at the bottom of this trouble."

Carter was looking at him intently. Suddenly he shook his head and tapped his forehead significantly.

"Balmy, poor young fellow," he murmured in an audible aside.

"Now, gentlemen," said Mr. Eastwood briskly, "to business. Here are letters addressed to me, my bankbook, communications from editors. What more do you want?"

Verall examined the papers that Anthony thrust upon him.

"Speaking for myself, sir," he said respectfully, "I want nothing more. I'm quite convinced. But I can't take the responsibility of releasing you upon myself. You see, although it seems positive that you have been residing here as Mr. Eastwood for some years, yet it is possible that Conrad Fleckman and Anthony Eastwood are one and the same person. I must make a thorough search of the flat, take your fingerprints, and telephone to headquarters."

"That seems a comprehensive program," remarked Anthony. "I can assure you that you're welcome to any guilty secrets of mine you may lay your hands on."

The inspector grinned. For a detective he was a singularly human person.

"Will you go into the little end room, sir, with Carter, while I'm getting busy?"

"All right," said Anthony unwillingly. "I suppose it couldn't be the other way about, could it?"

"Meaning?"

"That you and I and a couple of whiskies and sodas should occupy the end room while our friend, the sergeant, does the heavy searching."

"If you prefer it, sir?"

"I do prefer it."

They left Carter investigating the contents of the desk with business-like dexterity. As they passed out of the room, they heard him take down the telephone and call up Scotland Yard.

"This isn't so bad," said Anthony, settling himself with a whiskey and soda by his side, having hospitably attended to the wants of Inspector Verrall. "Shall I drink first, just to show you that the whiskey isn't poisoned?"

The inspector smiled.

"Very irregular, all this," he remarked. "But we know a thing or two in our profession. I realized right from the start that we'd made a mistake. But of course one had to observe all the usual forms. You can't get away from red tape, can you, sir?"

"I suppose not," said Anthony regretfully. "The sergeant doesn't seem very matey yet, though, does he?"

"Ah, he's a fine man, Detective-Sergeant Carter. You wouldn't find it easy to put anything over on him."

"I've noticed that," said Anthony. "By the way, Inspector," he added, "is there any objection to my hearing something about myself?"

"In what way, sir?"

"Come, now, don't you realize that I'm devoured by curiosity? Who was Anna Rosenberg, and why did I murder her?"

"You'll read all about it in the newspapers tomorrow, sir."

"'Tomorrow I may be Myself with Yesterday's ten thousand years,'" quoted Anthony. "I really think you might satisfy my perfectly legitimate curiosity, Inspector. Cast aside your official reticence, and tell me all."

"It's quite irregular, sir."

"My dear Inspector, when we are becoming such fast friends?"

"Well, sir, Anna Rosenberg was a German who lived at Hampstead. With no visible means of livelihood, she grew yearly richer and richer."

"I'm just the opposite," commented Anthony. "I have a visible means of livelihood and I get yearly poorer and poorer. Perhaps I should do better if I lived in Hampstead. I've always heard Hampstead is very bracing."

"At one time," continued Verrall, "she was a secondhand clothes dealer—"

"That explains it," interrupted Anthony. "I remember selling my uniform after the war—not khaki, the other stuff. The whole flat was full of red trousers and gold lace, spread out to best advantage. A fat man in a check suit arrived in a Rolls Royce with a factotum complete with bag. He bid one pound ten for the lot. In the end I threw in a hunting coat and some Zeiss glasses and at a given signal the factotum opened the bag and shoveled the goods inside, and the fat man tendered me a ten-pound note and asked me for change."

"About ten years ago," continued the inspector, "there were several Spanish political refugees in London—among them a certain Don Fernando Ferrarez with his young wife and child. They were very poor, and the wife was ill. Anna Rosenberg visited the place where they were lodging and asked if they had anything to sell. Don Fernando was out, and his wife decided to part with a very wonderful Spanish shawl, embroidered in a marvelous manner, which had been one of her husband's last presents to her before flying from Spain. When Don Fernando returned, he flew into a terrible rage on hearing the shawl had been sold, and tried vainly to recover it. When he at last succeeded in finding the secondhand clothes woman in question, she declared that she had resold the shawl to a woman whose name she did not know. Don Fernando was in despair. Two months later he was stabbed in the street and died as a result of his wounds. From that time onward, Anna Rosenberg seemed suspiciously flush of money. In the ten years that followed, her house at Hampstead was burgled no less than eight times. Four of the attempts were frustrated and nothing was taken; on the other four occasions, an embroidered shawl of some kind was among the booty."

The inspector paused, and then went on in obedience to an urgent gesture from Anthony.

"A week ago, Carmen Ferrarez, the young daughter of Don Fernando, arrived in this country from a convent in France. Her first action was to seek out Anna Rosenberg at Hampstead. There she is reported to have had a violent scene with the old woman, and her words at leaving were overheard by one of the servants.

"'You have it still,' she cried. 'All these years you have grown rich on it—but I say to you solemnly that in the end it will bring you bad luck. You have no moral right to it, and the day will come when you will wish you had never seen the Shawl of the Thousand Flowers.'

"Three days after that, Carmen Ferrarez, disappeared mysteriously from the hotel where she was staying. In her room was found a name and address—the name of Conrad Fleckman, and also a note from a man purporting to be an antique dealer asking if she were disposed to part with a certain embroidered shawl which he believed she had in her possession. The address given on the note was a false one.

"It is clear that the shawl is the center of the whole mystery. Yesterday morning Conrad Fleckman called upon Anna Rosenberg. She was shut up with him for an hour or more, and when he left she was obliged to go to bed, so white and shaken was she by the interview. But she gave orders that if he came to see her again he was always to be admitted. Last night she got up and went out about nine o'clock, and did not return. She was found this morning in the house occupied by Conrad Fleckman, stabbed through the heart. On the floor beside her was—what do you think?"

"The shawl?" breathed Anthony. "The Shawl of a Thousand Flowers."

"Something far more gruesome than that. Something which explained the whole mysterious business of the shawl and made its hidden value clear. . . . Excuse me, I fancy that's the chief—"

There had indeed been a ring at the bell. Anthony contained his impatience as best he could, and waited for the inspector to return. He was pretty well at ease about his own position now. As soon as they took his fingerprints they would realize their mistake.

And then, perhaps, Carmen would ring up. . . .

The Shawl of a Thousand Flowers! What a strange story—just the kind of story to make an appropriate setting for the girl's exquisite dark beauty.

Carmen Ferrarez. . . .

He jerked himself back from daydreaming. What a time that inspector fellow was. He rose and pulled the door open. The flat was strangely silent. Could they have gone? Surely not without a word to him.

He strode out into the next room. It was empty—so was the sitting-room. Strangely empty! It had a bare, disheveled appearance. Good heavens! His enamels—the silver!

He rushed wildly through the flat. It was the same tale everywhere. The place had been denuded. Every single thing of value, and Anthony had a very pretty collector's taste in small things, had been taken.

With a groan Anthony staggered to a chair, his head in his hands. He was aroused by the ringing of the front door bell. He opened it to confront Rogers.

"You'll excuse me, sir," said Rogers. "But the gentlemen fancied you might be wanting something."

"The gentlemen?"

"Those two friends of yours, sir. I helped them with the packing as best I could. Very fortunately I happened to have them two good cases in the basement." His eyes dropped to the floor. "I've swept up the straw as best I could, sir."

"You packed the things in here?" groaned Anthony.

"Yes, sir. Was that not your wishes, sir? It was the tall gentlemen told me to do so, sir, and seeing as you were busy talking to the other gentleman in the little end room, I didn't like to disturb you."

"I wasn't talking to him," said Anthony. "He was talking to me—curse him."

Rogers coughed.

"I'm sure I'm very sorry for the necessity, sir," he murmured.

"Necessity?"

"Of parting with your little treasures, sir."

"Eh? Oh, yes. Ha, ha!" He gave a mirthless laugh. "They've driven off by now, I suppose. Those—those friends of mine, I mean?"

"Oh, yes, sir, some time ago. I put the cases on the taxi and the tall gentleman went upstairs again, and then they both came running down and drove off at once. . . . Excuse me, sir, but is anything wrong, sir?"

Rogers might well ask. The hollow groan which Anthony emitted would have aroused surmise anywhere.

"Everything is wrong, thank you, Rogers. But I see clearly that you were not to blame. Leave me, I would commune a while with my telephone."

Five minutes later saw Anthony pouring his tale into the ears of Inspector Driver, who sat opposite to him, notebook in hand. An unsympathetic man, Inspector Driver, and not (Anthony reflected) nearly so like a real inspector! Distinctly stagey, in fact. Another striking example of the superiority of Art over Nature.

Anthony reached the end of his tale. The inspector shut up his notebook.

"Well?" said Anthony anxiously.

"Clear as paint," said the inspector. "It's the Patterson gang. They've done a lot of smart work lately. Big fair man, small dark man, and the girl."

"The girl?"

"Yes, dark and mighty good-looking. Acts as decoy usually."

"A—a Spanish girl?"

"She might call herself that. She was born in Hampstead."

"I said it was a bracing place," murmured Anthony.

"Yes, it's clear enough," said the inspector, rising to depart. "She got you on the phone and pitched you a tale—she guessed you'd come along all right. Then she goes along to old Mother Gibson's, who isn't above accepting a tip for the use of her room for them as finds it awkward to meet in public—lovers, you understand, nothing criminal. You fall for it all right, they get you back here, and while one of them pitches you a tale, the other gets away with the swag. It's the Pattersons all right—just their touch."

"And my things?" asked Anthony anxiously.

"We'll do what we can, sir. But the Pattersons are uncommon sharp."

"They seem to be," said Anthony bitterly.

The inspector departed, and scarcely had he gone before there came a ring at the door. Anthony opened it. A small boy stood there, holding a package.

"Parcel for you, sir."

Anthony took it with some surprise. He was not expecting a parcel of any kind. Returning to the sitting-room with it, he cut the string.

It was a liqueur set!

"Damn!" said Anthony.

Then he noticed that at the bottom of one of the glasses there was a tiny artificial rose. His mind flew back to the upper room in Kirk Street.

"I do like you—yes, I do like you. You will remember that whatever happens, won't you?"

That was what she had said. Whatever happens. . . . Did she mean—

Anthony took hold of himself sternly.

"This won't do," he admonished himself.

His eye fell on the typewriter, and he sat down with a resolute face.

THE MYSTERY OF THE SECOND CUCUMBER

His face grew dreamy again. The Shawl of a Thousand Flowers. What was it that was found on the floor beside the dead body? The gruesome thing that explained the whole mystery?

Nothing, of course, since it was only a trumped-up tale to hold his attention, and the teller had used the old Arabian Nights' trick of breaking off at the most interesting point. But couldn't there be a gruesome thing that explained the whole mystery? Couldn't there? If one gave one's mind to it?

Anthony tore the sheet of paper from his typewriter and substituted another. He typed a headline:

THE MYSTERY OF THE SPANISH SHAWL

He surveyed it for a moment or two in silence. Then he began to type rapidly. . . .

PHILOMEL COTTAGE

"Good-bye, darling."

"Good-bye, sweetheart."

Alix Martin stood leaning over the small rustic gate, watching the retreating figure of her husband, as he walked down the road in the direction of the village.

Presently he turned a bend and was lost to sight, but Alix still stayed in the same position, absentmindedly smoothing a lock of the rich brown hair which had blown across her face, her eyes far-away and dreamy.

Alix Martin was not beautiful, nor even, strictly speaking, pretty. But her face, the face of a woman no longer in her first youth, was irradiated and softened until her former colleagues of the old office days would hardly have recognized her. Miss Alix King had been a trim business-like young woman, efficient, slightly brusque in manner, obviously capable and matter-of-fact. She had made the least, not the most, of her beautiful brown hair. Her mouth, not ungenerous in its lines, had always been severely compressed. Her clothes had been neat and suitable, without a hint of coquetry.

Alix had graduated in a hard school. For fifteen years, from the age of eighteen until she was thirty-three, she had kept herself (and for seven years of the time, an invalid mother) by her work as a shorthand-typist. It was the struggle for existence which had hardened the soft lines of her girlish face.

True, there had been romance—of a kind. Dick Windyford, a fellow clerk. Very much of a woman at heart, Alix had always known without seeming to know that he cared. Outwardly they had been friends, nothing more. Out of his slender salary, Dick had been hard put to it to provide for the schooling of a younger brother. For the moment, he could not think of marriage. Nevertheless, when Alix envisaged the future, it was with the half-acknowledged certainty that she would one day be Dick's wife. They cared for one another, so she would have put it, but they were both sensible people. Plenty of time, no need to do anything rash. So the years had gone on.

And then suddenly deliverance from daily toil had come to the girl in the most unexpected manner. A distant cousin had died leaving her money to Alix. A few thousand pounds, enough to bring in a couple of hundred a year. To Alix, it was freedom, life, independence. Now she and Dick need wait no longer.

But Dick reacted unexpectedly. He had never directly spoken of his love to Alix, now he seemed less inclined to do so than ever. He avoided her, became morose and gloomy. Alix was quick to realize the truth. She had become a woman of means. Delicacy and pride stood in the way of Dick's asking her to be his wife.

She liked him none the worse for it and was indeed deliberating as to whether she herself might not take the first step when for the second time the unexpected descended upon her.

She met Gerald Martin at a friend's house. He fell violently in love with her and within a week they were engaged. Alix, who had always considered herself "not the falling-in-love kind," was swept clean off her feet.

Unwittingly she had found the way to arouse her former lover. Dick Windyford had come to her stammering with rage and anger.

"The man's a perfect stranger to you. You know nothing about him."

"I know that I love him."

"How can you know—in a week?"

"It doesn't take everyone eleven years to find out that they're in love with a girl," cried Alix angrily.

His face went white.

"I've cared for you ever since I met you. I thought that you cared also."

Alix was truthful.

"I thought so, too," she admitted. "But that was because I didn't know what love was."

Then Dick had burst out again. Prayers, entreaties, even threats. Threats against the man who had supplanted him. It was amazing to Alix to see the volcano that existed beneath the reserved exterior of the man she thought she knew so well. Also, it frightened her a little. . . . Dick, of course, couldn't possibly mean the things he was saying, the threats of vengeance against Gerald Martin. He was angry, that was all. . . .

Her thoughts had gone back to that interview now, on this sunny morning, as she leaned on the gate of the cottage. She had been married a month, and she was idyllically happy. Yet, in the momentary absence of the husband who was everything to her, a tinge of anxiety invaded her perfect happiness, and the cause of that anxiety was Dick Windyford.

Three times since her marriage she had dreamed the same dream. The environment differed, but the main facts were always the same. She saw her husband lying dead and Dick Windyford standing over him, and she knew clearly and distinctly that his was the hand which had dealt the fatal blow.

But horrible though that was, there was something more horrible still—horrible that was, on awakening, for in the dream it seemed perfectly natural and inevitable. *She, Alix Martin, was glad that her husband was dead*—she stretched out grateful hands to the murderer, sometimes she thanked him. The dream always ended the same way, with herself clasped in Dick Windyford's arms.

She had said nothing of this dream to her husband, but secretly it had perturbed her more than she liked to admit. Was it a warning—a warning against Dick Windyford? Had he some secret power which he was trying to establish over her at a distance? She did not know much about hypnotism, but surely she had always heard that persons could not be hypnotized against their will.

Alix was roused from her thoughts by the sharp ringing of the telephone bell from within the house. She entered the cottage, and picked up the receiver. Suddenly she swayed, and put out a hand to keep herself from falling.

"Who did you say was speaking?"

"Why, Alix, what's the matter with your voice? I wouldn't have known it. It's Dick."

"Oh!" said Alix—"Oh! Where are you?"

"At the Travelers Arms—that's the right name, isn't it? Or don't you even know of the existence of your village pub? I'm on my holiday—doing a bit of fishing here. Any objection to my looking you two good people up this evening after dinner?"

"No," said Alix sharply. "You mustn't come."

There was a pause, and Dick's voice, with a subtle alteration in it, spoke again.

"I beg your pardon," he said formally. "Of course I won't bother you—"

Alix broke in hastily. Of course he must think her behavior too extraordinary. It was extraordinary. Her nerves must be all to pieces. It wasn't Dick's fault that she had these dreams.

"I only meant that we were—engaged tonight," she explained, trying to make her voice sound as natural as possible. "Won't you—won't you come to dinner tomorrow night?"

But Dick evidently noticed the lack of cordiality in her tone.

"Thanks very much," he said, in the same formal voice. "But I may be moving on any time. Depends upon whether a pal of mine turns up or not. Good-bye, Alix." He paused, and then added hastily, in a different tone, "Best of luck to you, my dear."

Alix hung up the receiver with a feeling of relief.

"He mustn't come here," she repeated to herself. "He mustn't come here. Oh! what a fool I am! To imagine myself into a state like this. All the same, I'm glad he's not coming."

She caught up a rustic rush hat from a table, and passed out into the garden again, pausing to look up at the name carved over the porch, Philomel Cottage.

"Isn't it a very fanciful name?" she had said to Gerald once before they were married. He had laughed.

"You little Cockney," he had said, affectionately. "I don't believe you have ever heard a nightingale. I'm glad you haven't. Nightingales should sing only for lovers. We'll hear them together on a summer's evening outside our own home."

And at the remembrance of how they had indeed heard them, Alix, standing in the doorway of her home, blushed happily.

It was Gerald who had found Philomel Cottage. He had come to Alix bursting with excitement. He had found the very spot for them—unique—a gem—the chance of a lifetime. And when Alix had seen it, she too was captivated. It was true that the situation was rather lonely—they were two miles from the nearest village—but the cottage itself was so exquisite with its Old World appearance, and its solid comfort of bathrooms, hot-water system, electric light and telephone, that she fell a victim to its charm immediately. And then a hitch occurred. The owner, a rich man who had made it his whim, declined to rent it. He would only sell.

Gerald Martin, though possessed of a good income, was unable to touch his capital. He could raise at most a thousand pounds. The owner was asking three. But Alix, who had set her heart on the place, came to the rescue. Her own capital was easily realized, being in bearer bonds. She would contribute half of it to the purchase of the home. So Philomel Cottage became their very own, and never for a minute had Alix regretted the choice. It was true that servants did not appreciate the rural solitude—indeed at the moment they had none at all—but Alix, who had been starved of domestic life, thoroughly enjoyed cooking dainty little meals and looking after the house.

The garden which was magnificently stocked with flowers was attended to by an old man from the village who came twice a week, and Gerald Martin, who was keen on gardening, spent most of his time there.

As she rounded the corner of the house, Alix was surprised to see the old gardener in question busy over the flower beds. She was surprised because his days for work were Mondays and Fridays, and today was Wednesday.

"Why, George, what are you doing here?" she asked, as she came toward him.

The old man straightened up with a chuckle, touching the brim of an aged cap.

"I thought as how you'd be surprised, ma'am. But 'tis this way. There be a fête over to Squire's on Friday, and I sez to myself, I sez, neith Mr. Martin nor yet his good lady won't take it amiss if I comes for once on a Wednesday instead of a Friday."

"That's quite all right," said Alix. "I hope you'll enjoy yourself at the fête."

"I reckon to," said George simply. "It's a fine thing to be able to eat your fill and know all the time as it's not you as is paying for it. Squire allus has a proper sit-down tea for 'is tenants. Then I thought too, ma'am, as I might as well see you before you goes away so as to learn your wishes for the borders. You'll have no idea when you'll be back, ma'am, I suppose?"

"But I'm not going away."

George stared at her.

"Bain't you going to Lunnon tomorrow?"

"No. What put such an idea into your head?"

George jerked his head over his shoulder.

"Met Maister down to village yesterday. He told me you was both going away to Lunnon tomorrow, and it was uncertain when you'd be back again."

"Nonsense," said Alix, laughing. "You must have misunderstood him."

All the same, she wondered exactly what it could have been that Gerald had said to lead the old man into such a curious mistake. Going to London? She never wanted to go to London again.

"I hate London," she said suddenly and harshly.

"Ah!" said George placidly. "I must have been mistook somehow, and yet he said it plain enough it seemed to me. I'm glad you're stopping on here—I don't hold with all this gallivanting about, and I don't think nothing of Lunnon. I've never needed to go there. Too many moty cars—that's the trouble nowadays. Once people have got a moty car, blessed if they can stay still anywheres. Mr. Ames, wot used to have this house—nice peaceful sort of gentleman he was until he bought one of them things. Hadn't 'ad it a month before he put up this cottage for sale. A tidy lot he'd spent on it, too, with taps in all the bedrooms, and the electric light and all. 'You'll never see your money back,' I sez to him. 'It's not everyone as'll have your fad for washing themselves in every room in the house, in a manner of speaking.' But 'George,' he sez to me, 'I'll get every penny of two thousand pounds for this house.' And sure enough, he did."

"He got three thousand," said Alix, smiling.

"Two thousand," repeated George. "The sum he was asking was talked of at the time. And a very high figure it was thought to be."

"It really was three thousand," said Alix.

"Women never understand figures," said George, unconvinced. "You'll not tell me that Mr. Ames had the face to stand up to you, and say three thousand brazen like in a loud voice."

"He didn't say it to me," said Alix. "He said it to my husband."

George stooped again to his flower bed.

"The price was two thousand," he said obstinately.

Alix did not trouble to argue with him. Moving to one of the further beds, she began to pick an armful of flowers. The sunshine, the scent of the flowers, the faint hum of hurrying bees, all conspired to make the day a perfect thing.

As she moved with her fragrant posy toward the house, Alix noticed a small dark green object, peeping from between some leaves in one of the beds. She stooped and picked it up, recognizing it for her husband's pocket diary. It must have fallen from his pocket when he was weeding.

She opened it, scanning the entries with some amusement. Almost from the beginning of their married life, she had realized that the impulsive and emotional Gerald had the uncharacteristic virtues of neatness and method. He was extremely fussy about meals being punctual, and always planned his day ahead with the accuracy of a time table. This morning, for instance, he had announced that he should start for the village after breakfast—at 10:15. And at 10:15 to the minute he had left the house.

Looking through the diary, she was amused to notice the entry on the date of May 14th. "Marry Alix St. Peter's 2:30."

"The big silly," murmured Alix to herself, turning the pages.

Suddenly she stopped.

"Thursday, June 18th—why that's today."

In the space for that day was written in Gerald's neat precise hand: "9 P.M." Nothing else. What had Gerald planned to do at 9 P.M. Alix wondered. She smiled to herself as she realized that had this been a story, like those she had so often read, the diary would doubtless have furnished her with some sensational revelation. It would have had in it for certain the name of another woman. She fluttered the back pages idly. There were dates, appointments, cryptic references to business deals, but only one woman's name—her own.

Yet as she slipped the book into her pocket and went on with her flowers to the house, she was aware of a vague uneasiness. Those words of Dick Windyford's recurred to her, almost as though he had been at her elbow repeating them: "The man's a perfect stranger to you. You know nothing about him."

It was true. What did she know about him. After all, Gerald was forty. In forty years there must have been women in his life. . . .

Alix shook herself impatiently. She must not give way to these thoughts. She had a far more instant preoccupation to deal with. Should she, or should she not, tell her husband that Dick Windyford had rung her up?

There was the possibility to be considered that Gerald might have already run across him in the village. But in that case he would be sure to mention it to her immediately upon his return and matters would be taken out of her hands. Otherwise—what? Alix was aware of a distinct desire to say nothing about it. Gerald had always shown himself kindly disposed toward the other. "Poor devil," he had said once, "I believe he's just as keen on you as I am. Hard luck on him to be shelved." He had had no doubts of Alix's own feelings.

If she told him, he was sure to suggest asking Dick Windyford to Philomel Cottage. Then she would have to explain that Dick had proposed it himself, and that she had made an excuse to prevent his coming. And when he asked her why she had done so, what could she say? Tell him her dream? But he would only laugh—or worse, see that she attached an importance to it which he did not. Then he would think—oh! he might think anything!

In the end, rather shamefacedly, Alix decided to say nothing. It was the first secret she had ever kept from her husband, and the consciousness of it made her feel ill at ease.

When she heard Gerald returning from the village shortly before lunch, she hurried into the kitchen and pretended to be busy with the cooking so as to hide her confusion.

It was evident at once that Gerald had seen nothing of Dick Windyford. Alix felt at once relieved and embarrassed. She was definitely committed now to a policy of concealment. For the rest of the day she was nervous and absentminded, starting at every sound, but her husband seemed to notice nothing. He himself seemed to have his thoughts far away, and once or twice she had to speak a second time before he answered some trivial remark of hers.

It was not until after their simple evening meal, when they were sitting in the oak beamed living room with the windows thrown open to let in the sweet night air scented with the perfume of the mauve and white stocks that grew outside, that Alix remembered the pocket diary, and seized upon it gladly to distract her thoughts from their doubt and perplexity.

"Here's something you've been watering the flowers with," she said, and threw it into his lap.

"Dropped it in the border, did I?"

"Yes, I know all your secrets now."

"Not guilty," said Gerald, shaking his head.

"What about your assignation at nine o'clock tonight?"

"Oh! that—" he seemed taken back for a moment, then he smiled as though something afforded him particular amusement. "It's an assignation with a particularly nice girl, Alix. She's got brown hair and blue eyes and she's particularly like you."

"I don't understand," said Alix, with mock severity. "You're evading the point."

"No, I'm not. As a matter of fact, that's a reminder that I'm going to develop some negatives tonight, and I want you to help me."

Gerald Martin was an enthusiastic photographer. He had a somewhat old-fashioned camera, but with an excellent lens, and he developed his own plates in a small cellar which he had fitted up as a dark room. He was never tired of posing Alix in different positions.

"And it must be done at nine o'clock precisely," said Alix teasingly.

Gerald looked a little vexed.

"My dear girl," he said, with a shade of testiness in his manner, "one should always plan a thing for a definite time. Then one gets through one's work properly."

Alix sat for a minute or two in silence watching her husband as he lay in his chair smoking, his dark head flung back and the clear-cut lines of his clean-shaven face showing up against the somber background. And suddenly, from some unknown source, a wave of panic surged over her, so that she cried out before she could stop herself. "Oh! Gerald, I wish I knew more about you."

Her husband turned an astonished face upon her.

"But, my dear Alix, you do know all about me. I've told you of my boyhood in Northumberland, of my life in South Africa, and these last ten years in Canada which have brought me success."

"Oh, business!"

Gerald laughed suddenly.

"I know what you mean—love affairs. You women are all the same. Nothing interests you but the personal element."

Alix felt her throat go dry, as she muttered indistinctly: "Well, but there must have been—love affairs. I mean—If I only knew—"

There was silence again for a minute or two. Gerald Martin was frowning, a look of indecision on his face. When he spoke, it was gravely, without a trace of his former bantering manner.

"Do you think it wise, Alix—this Bluebeard's chamber business? There have been women in my life, yes. I don't deny it. You wouldn't believe me if I did deny it. But I can swear to you truthfully that not one of them meant anything to me."

There was a ring of sincerity in his voice which comforted the listening wife.

"Satisfied, Alix?" he asked, with a smile. Then he looked at her with a shade of curiosity.

"What has turned your mind onto these unpleasant subjects tonight of all nights? You never mentioned them before."

Alix got up and began to walk about restlessly.

"Oh! I don't know," she said. "I've been nervy all day."

"That's odd," said Gerald, in a low voice, as though speaking to himself. "That's very odd."

"Why is it odd?"

"Oh, my dear girl, don't flash out at me so. I only said it was odd because as a rule you're so sweet and serene."

Alix forced a smile.

"Everything's conspired to annoy me today," she confessed. "Even old George had got some ridiculous idea into his head that we were going away to London. He said you had told him so."

"Where did you see him?" asked Gerald sharply.

"He came to work today instead of Friday."

"The old fool," said Gerald angrily.

Alix stared in surprise. Her husband's face was convulsed with rage. She had never seen him so angry. Seeing her astonishment, Gerald made an effort to regain control of himself.

"Well, he *is* a stupid old fool," he protested.

"What can you have said to make him think that?"

"I? I never said anything. At least—Oh, yes, I remember. I made some weak joke about being 'off to London in the morning' and I suppose he took it seriously. Or else he didn't hear properly. You undeceived him, of course?"

He waited anxiously for her reply.

"Of course, but he's the sort of old man who if once he gets an idea in his head—well, it isn't so easy to get it out again."

Then she told him of the gardener's insistence on the sum asked for the cottage.

Gerald was silent for a minute or two, then he said slowly:

"Ames was willing to take two thousand in cash and the remaining thousand on mortgage. That's the origin of that mistake, I fancy."

"Very likely," agreed Alix.

Then she looked up at the clock, and pointed to it with a mischievous finger.

"We ought to be getting down to it, Gerald. Five minutes behind schedule."

A very peculiar smile came over Gerald Martin's face.

"I've changed my mind," he said quietly. "I shall not do any photography tonight."

A WOMAN'S MIND is a curious thing. When she went to bed that Thursday night, Alix's mind was contented and at rest. Her momentarily assailed happiness reasserted itself, triumphant as of yore.

But by the evening of the following day, she realized that some subtle forces were at work undermining it. Dick Windyford had not rung up again, nevertheless she felt what she supposed to be his influence at work. Again and again those words of his recurred to her. "The man's a perfect stranger. You know nothing about him." And with them came the memory of her husband's face, photographed clearly on her brain as he said: "Do you think it wise, Alix, this Bluebeard's chamber business?" Why had he said that? What had he meant by those words?

There had been warning in them—a hint of menace. It was as though he had said in effect—"You had better not pry into my life, Alix. You may get a nasty shock if you do." True, a few minutes later, he had sworn to her that there had been no woman in his life that mattered—but Alix tried in vain to recapture her sense of his sincerity. Was he not bound to swear that?

By Friday morning, Alix had convinced herself that there had been a woman in Gerald's life—a Bluebeard's chamber that he had sedulously sought to conceal from her. Her jealousy, slow to awaken, was now rampant.

Was it a woman he had been going to meet that night, at 9 P.M.? Was his story of photographs to develop a lie invented upon the spur of the moment? With a queer sense of shock Alix realized that ever since she had found that pocket diary she had been in torment. And there had been nothing in it? That was the irony of the whole thing.

Three days ago she would have sworn that she knew her husband through and through. Now it seemed to her that he was a stranger of whom she knew nothing. She remembered his unreasonable anger against old George, so at variance with his usual good-tempered manner. A small thing, perhaps, but it showed her that she did not really know the man who was her husband.

There were several little things required on Friday from the village to carry them over the week-end. In the afternoon Alix suggested that she should go for them while Gerald remained in the garden, but somewhat to her surprise he opposed this plan vehemently, and insisted on going himself while she remained at home. Alix was forced to give way to him, but his insistence surprised and alarmed her. Why was he so anxious to prevent her going to the village?

Suddenly an explanation suggested itself to her which made the whole thing clear. Was it not possible that, while saying nothing to her, Gerald had indeed come across Dick Windyford? Her own jealousy, entirely dormant at the time of their marriage, had only developed afterward. Might it not be the same with Gerald? Might he not be anxious to prevent her seeing Dick Windyford again? This explanation was so consistent with the facts, and so comforting to Alix's perturbed mind, that she embraced it eagerly.

Yet when tea time had come and past, she was restless and ill at ease. She was struggling with a temptation that had assailed her ever since Gerald's departure. Finally, pacifying her conscience with the assurance that the room did need a thorough tidying, she went upstairs to her husband's dressing room. She took a duster with her to keep up the pretense of housewifery.

"If I were only sure," she repeated to herself. "If I could only be sure."

In vain she told herself that anything compromising would have been destroyed ages ago. Against that she argued that men do sometimes keep the most damning piece of evidence through an exaggerated sentimentality.

In the end Alix succumbed. Her cheeks burning with the shame of her action, she hunted breathlessly through packets of letters and documents, turned out the drawers, even went through the pockets of her husband's clothes. Only two drawers eluded her—the lower drawer of the chest of drawers and the small right-hand drawer of the writing desk were both locked. But Alix was by now lost to all shame. In one of those drawers she was convinced that she would find evidence of this imaginary woman of the past who obsessed her.

She remembered that Gerald had left his keys lying carelessly on the sideboard downstairs. She fetched them and tried them one by one. The third key fitted the writing table drawer. Alix pulled it open eagerly. There was a check book and a wallet well stuffed with notes, and at the back of the drawer a packet of letters tied up with a piece of tape.

Her breath coming unevenly, Alix untied the tape. Then a deep burning blush overspread her face, and she dropped the letters back into the drawer, closing and relocking it. For the letters were her own, written to Gerald Martin before she married him.

She turned now to the chest of drawers, more with a wish to feel that she had left nothing undone, than from any expectation of finding what she sought. She was ashamed and almost convinced of the madness of her obsession.

To her annoyance none of the keys on Gerald's bunch fitted the drawer in question. Not to be defeated, Alix went into the other rooms and brought back a selection of keys with her. To her satisfaction, the key of the spare room wardrobe also fitted the chest of drawers. She unlocked the drawer and pulled it open. But there was nothing in it but a roll of newspaper clippings already dirty and discolored with age.

Alix breathed a sigh of relief. Nevertheless she glanced at the clippings, curious to know what subject had interested Gerald so much that he had taken the trouble to keep the dusty roll. They were nearly all American papers, dated some seven years ago, and dealing with the trail of the notorious swindler and bigamist, Charles LeMaitre. LeMaitre had been suspected of doing away with his women victims. A skeleton had been found beneath the floor of one of the houses he had rented, and most of the women he had "married" had never been heard of again.

He had defended himself from the charge with consummate skill, aided by some of the best legal talent in the United States. The Scottish verdict of "Non proven" might perhaps have stated the case best. In its absence, he was found Not Guilty on the capital charge, though sentenced to a long term of imprisonment on the other charges preferred against him.

Alix remembered the excitement caused by the case at the time, and also the sensation aroused by the escape of LeMaitre some three years later. He had never been recaptured. The personality of the man and his extraordinary power over women had been discussed at great length in the English papers at the time, together with an account of his excitability in court, his passionate protestations, and his occasional sudden physical collapses, due to the fact that he had a weak heart, though the ignorant accredited it to his dramatic powers.

There was a picture of him in one of the clippings Alix held, and she studied it with some interest—a long-bearded, scholarly looking gentleman. It reminded her of someone, but for the moment she could not tell who that someone was. She had never known that Gerald took an interest in crime and famous trials, though she knew that it was a hobby with many men.

Who was it the face reminded her of? Suddenly, with a shock, she realized that it was Gerald himself. The eyes and brows bore a strong resemblance to him. Perhaps he had kept the cutting for that reason. Her eyes went on to the paragraph beside the picture. Certain dates, it seemed, had been entered in the accused's pocketbook, and it was contended that these were dates when he had done away with his victims. Then a woman gave evidence and identified the prisoner positively by the fact that he had a mole on his left wrist, just below the palm of the left hand.

Alix dropped the papers from a nerveless hand, and swayed as she stood. *On his left wrist, just below the palm, Gerald had a small scar. . . .*

The room whirled round her. . . . Afterward it struck her as strange that she should have leaped at once to such absolute certainty. Gerald Martin was Charles LeMaitre! She knew it and accepted it in a flash. Disjointed fragments whirled through her brain, like pieces of a jigsaw puzzle fitting into place.

The money paid for the house—her money—her money only. The bearer bonds she had entrusted to his keeping. Even her dream appeared in its true significance. Deep down in her, her subconscious self had always feared Gerald Martin and wished to escape from him. And it was to Dick Windyford this self of hers had looked for help. That, too, was why she was able to accept the truth so easily, without doubt or hesitation. She was to have been another of LeMaitre's victims. Very soon, perhaps.

A half cry escaped her as she remembered something. Thursday 9 P.M. The cellar, with the flagstones that were so easily raised. Once before, he had buried one of his victims in a cellar. It had been all planned for Thursday night. But to write it down beforehand in that methodical manner—insanity! No, it was logical. Gerald always made a memorandum of his engagements—murder was, to him, a business proposition like any other.

But what had saved her? What could possibly have saved her? Had he relented at the last minute? No—in a flash the answer came to her. Old George. She understood now her husband's uncontrollable anger. Doubtless he had paved the way by telling everyone he met that they were going to London the next day. Then George had come to work unexpectedly, had mentioned London to her, and she had contradicted the story. Too risky to do away with her that night, with old George repeating that conversation. But what an escape! If she had not happened to mention that trivial matter—Alix shuddered.

But there was no time to be lost. She must get away at once—before he came back. For nothing on earth would she spend another night under the same roof with him. She hurriedly replaced the roll of clippings in the drawer, shut it to and locked it.

And then she stayed motionless as though frozen to stone. She had heard the creak of the gate into the road. Her husband had returned.

For a moment Alix stayed as though petrified, then she crept on tiptoe to the window, looking out from behind the shelter of the curtain.

Yes, it was her husband. He was smiling to himself and humming a little tune. In his hand he held an object which almost made the terrified girl's heart stop beating. It was a brand new spade.

Alix leaped to a knowledge born of instinct. *It was to be tonight. . . .*

But there was still a chance. Gerald, still humming his little tune, went round to the back of the house.

"He's going to put it in the cellar—ready," thought Alix with a shiver.

Without hesitating a moment, she ran down the stairs and out of the cottage. But just as she emerged from the door, her husband came round the other side of the house.

"Hullo," he said. "Where are you running off to in such a hurry?"

Alix strove desperately to appear calm and as usual. Her chance was gone for the moment, but if she was careful not to arouse his suspicions, it would come again later. Even now, perhaps. . . .

"I was going to walk to the end of the lane and back," she said, in a voice that sounded weak and uncertain to her own ears.

"Right," said Gerald, "I'll come with you."

"No—please, Gerald. I'm—nervy, headachy—I'd rather go alone."

He looked at her attentively. She fancied a momentary suspicion gleamed in his eye.

"What's the matter with you, Alix? You're pale—trembling."

"Nothing," she forced herself to be brusque—smiling. "I've got a headache, that's all. A walk will do me good."

"Well, it's no good you're saying you don't want me," declared Gerald with his easy laugh. "I'm coming whether you want me or not."

She dared not protest further. If he suspected that she knew—

With an effort she managed to regain something of her normal manner. Yet she had an uneasy feeling that he looked at her sideways every now and then, as though not quite satisfied. She felt that his suspicions were not completely allayed.

When they returned to the house, he insisted on her lying down, and brought some eau de cologne to bathe her temples. He was, as ever, the devoted husband, yet Alix felt herself as helpless as though bound hand and foot in a trap.

Not for a minute would he leave her alone. He went with her into the kitchen and helped her to bring in the simple cold dishes she had already prepared. Supper was a meal that choked her, yet she forced herself to eat, and even to appear gay and natural. She knew now that she was fighting for her life. She was alone with this man, miles from help, absolutely at his mercy. Her only chance was so to lull his suspicions that he would leave her alone for a few moments—long enough for her to get to the telephone in the hall and summon assistance. That was her only hope now. He would overtake her if she took to flight long before she could reach assistance.

A momentary hope flashed over her as she remembered how he had abandoned his plan before. Suppose she told him that Dick Windyford was coming up to see them that evening?

The words trembled on her lips—then she rejected them hastily. This man would not be balked a second time. There was a determination, an elation underneath his calm bearing that sickened her. She would only precipitate the crime. He would murder her there and then, and calmly ring up Dick Windyford with a tale of having been suddenly called away. Oh! if only Dick Windyford were coming to the house this evening. If Dick—

A sudden idea flashed into her mind. She looked sharply sideways at her husband as though she feared that he might read her mind. With the forming of a plan, her courage was reinforced. She became so completely natural in manner that she marveled at herself. She felt that Gerald now was completely reassured.

She made the coffee and took it out to the porch where they often sat on fine evenings.

"By the way," said Gerald suddenly, "we'll do those photographs later."

Alix felt a shiver run through her, but she replied nonchalantly:

"Can't you manage alone? I'm rather tired tonight."

"It won't take long." He smiled to himself. "And I can promise you you won't be tired afterward."

The words seemed to amuse him. Alix shuddered. Now or never was the time to carry out her plan.

She rose to her feet.

"I'm just going to telephone to the butcher," she announced nonchalantly. "Don't you bother to move."

"To the butcher? At this time of night?"

"His shop's shut, of course, silly. But he's in his house all right. And tomorrow's Saturday, and I want him to bring me some veal cutlets early, before someone else grabs them from him. The old dear will do anything for me."

She passed quickly into the house, closing the door behind her. She heard Gerald say, "Don't shut the door," and was quick with her light reply. "It keeps the moths out. I hate moths. Are you afraid I'm going to make love to the butcher, silly?"

Once inside she snatched down the telephone receiver and gave the number of the Travelers Arms. She was put through at once.

"Mr. Windyford? Is he still there? May I speak to him?"

Then her heart gave a sickening thump. The door was pushed open and her husband came into the hall.

"Do go away, Gerald," she said pettishly. "I hate anyone listening when I'm telephoning."

He merely laughed and threw himself into a chair.

"Sure it really is the butcher you're telephoning to?" he quizzed.

Alix was in despair. Her plan had failed. In a minute Dick Windyford would come to the phone. Should she risk all and cry out an appeal for help. Would he grasp what she meant before Gerald wrenched her away from the phone. Or would he merely treat it as a practical joke.

And then as she nervously depressed and released the little key in the receiver she was holding, which permits the voice to be heard or not heard at the other end, another plan flashed into her head.

"It will be difficult," she thought. "It means keeping my head, and thinking of the right words, and not faltering for a moment, but I believe I could do it. I *must* do it."

And at that minute she heard Dick Windyford's voice at the other end of the phone.

Alix drew a deep breath. Then she depressed the key firmly and spoke.

"Mrs. Martin speaking—from Philomel Cottage. *Please come* (she released the key) tomorrow morning with six nice veal cutlets (she depressed the key again) *It's very important* (she released the key) Thank you so much, Mr. Hexworthy, you don't mind my ringing you up so late, I hope, but those veal cutlets are really a matter of (she depressed the key again) *life or death* . . . (she released it) Very well—tomorrow morning—(she depressed it) *as soon as possible* . . ."

She replaced the receiver on the hook and turned to face her husband, breathing hard.

"So that's how you talk to your butcher, is it?" said Gerald.

"It's the feminine touch," said Alix lightly.

She was simmering with excitement. He had suspected nothing. Surely Dick, even if he didn't understand, would come.

She passed into the sitting room and switched on the electric light. Gerald followed her.

"You seem very full of spirits now," he said, watching her curiously.

"Yes," said Alix, "my headache's gone."

She sat down in her usual seat and smiled at her husband, as he sank into his own chair opposite her. She was saved. It was only five and twenty past eight. Long before nine o'clock Dick would have arrived.

"I didn't think much of that coffee you gave me," complained Gerald. "It tasted very bitter."

"It's a new kind I was trying. We won't have it again if you don't like it, dear."

Alix took up a piece of needlework and began to stitch. She felt complete confidence in her own ability to keep up the part of the devoted wife. Gerald read a few pages of his book. Then he glanced up at the clock and tossed the book away.

"Half-past eight. Time to go down to the cellar and start work."

The work slipped from Alix's fingers.

"Oh! not yet. Let us wait until nine o'clock."

"No, my girl, half-past eight. That's the time I fixed. You'll be able to get to bed all the earlier."

"But I'd rather wait until nine."

"Half-past eight," said Gerald obstinately. "You know when I fix a time, I always stick to it. Come along, Alix. I'm not going to wait a minute longer."

Alix looked up at him, and in spite of herself she felt a wave of terror slide over her. The mask had been lifted; Gerald's hands were twitching; his eyes were shining with excitement; he was continually passing his tongue over his dry lips. He no longer cared to conceal his excitement.

Alix thought: "It's true—he can't wait—he's like a madman."

He strode over to her, and jerked her onto her feet with a hand on her shoulder.

"Come on, my girl—or I'll carry you there."

His tone was gay, but there was an undisguised ferocity behind it that appalled her. With a supreme effort she jerked herself free and clung cowering against the wall. She was powerless. She couldn't get away—she couldn't do anything—and he was coming toward her.

"Now, Alix——"

"No—no."

She screamed, her hands held out impotently to ward him off.

"Gerald—stop—I've got something to tell you, something to confess . . ."

He did stop.

"To confess?" he said curiously.

"Yes, to confess." She went on desperately, seeking to hold his arrested attention. "Something I ought to have told you before."

A look of contempt swept over his face. The spell was broken.

"A former lover, I suppose," he sneered.

"No," said Alix. "Something else. You'd call it, I expect—yes, you'd call it a crime."

And at once she saw that she had struck the right note. Again his attention was arrested, held. Seeing that, her nerve came back to her. She felt mistress of the situation once more.

"You had better sit down again," she said quietly.

She herself crossed the room to her old chair and sat down. She even stooped and picked up her needlework. But behind her calmness she was thinking and inventing feverishly. For the story she invented must hold his interest until help arrived.

"I told you," she said, "that I had been a shorthand typist for fifteen years. That was not entirely true. There were two intervals. The first occurred when I was twenty-two. I came across a man, an elderly man with a little property. He fell in love with me and asked me to marry him. I accepted. We were married." She paused. "I induced him to insure his life in my favor."

She saw a sudden keen interest spring up in her husband's face, and went on with renewed assurance.

"During the war I worked for a time in a Hospital Dispensary. There I had the handling of all kinds of rare drugs and poisons. Yes, poisons."

She paused reflectively. He was keenly interested now, not a doubt of it. The murderer is bound to have an interest in murder. She had gambled on that, and succeeded. She stole a glance at the clock. It was five and twenty to nine.

"There is one poison—it is a little white powder. A pinch of it means death. You know something about poisons perhaps?"

She put the question in some trepidation. If he did, she would have to be careful.

"No," said Gerald, "I know very little about them."

She drew a breath of relief. This made her task easier.

"You have heard of hyoscine, of course? This is a drug that acts much the same way, but it is absolutely untraceable. Any doctor would give a certificate of heart failure. I stole a small quantity of this drug and kept it by me."

She paused, marshaling her forces.

"Go on," said Gerald.

"No. I'm afraid. I can't tell you. Another time."

"Now," he said impatiently. "I want to hear."

"We had been married a month. I was very good to my elderly husband, very kind and devoted. He spoke in praise of me to all the neighbors. Everyone knew what a devoted wife I was. I always made his coffee myself every evening. One evening, when we were alone together, I put a pinch of the deadly alkaloid in his cup."

Alix paused, and carefully rethreaded her needle. She, who had never acted in her life, rivaled the greatest actress in the world at this moment. She was actually living the part of the cold-blooded poisoner.

"It was very peaceful. I sat watching him. Once he gasped a little and asked for air. I opened the window. Then he said he could not move from his chair. Presently he died."

She stopped, smiling. It was a quarter to nine. Surely they would come soon.

"How much," said Gerald, "was the insurance money?"

"About two thousand pounds. I speculated with it, and lost it. I went back to my office work. But I never meant to remain there long. Then I met another man. I had stuck to my maiden name at the office. He didn't know I had been married before. He was a younger man, rather good-looking, and quite well off. We were married quietly in Sussex. He didn't want to insure his life, but of course he made a will in my favor. He liked me to make his coffee myself also, just as my first husband had done."

Alix smiled reflectively, and added simply:

"I make very good coffee."

Then she went on.

"I had several friends in the village where we were living. They were very sorry for me, with my husband dying suddenly of heart failure one evening after dinner. I didn't quite like the doctor. I don't think he suspected me, but he was certainly very surprised at my husband's sudden death. I don't quite know why I drifted back to the office again. Habit, I suppose. My second husband left about four thousand pounds. I didn't speculate with it this time. I invested it. Then, you see—"

But she was interrupted. Gerald Martin, his face suffused with blood, half choking, was pointing a shaking forefinger at her.

"The coffee—my God! the coffee!"

She stared at him.

"I understand now why it was bitter. You devil. You've poisoned me."

His hands gripped the arms of his chair. He was ready to spring upon her.

"You've poisoned me."

Alix had retreated from him to the fireplace. Now, terrified, she opened her lips to deny—and then paused. In another minute he would spring upon her. She summoned all her strength. Her eyes held his steadily, compellingly.

"Yes," she said, "I poisoned you. Already the poison is working. At this minute you can't move from your chair—you can't move—"

If she could keep him there—even a few minutes—

Ah! what was that? Footsteps on the road. The creak of the gate. Then footsteps on the path outside. The door of the hall opened—

"You can't move," she said again.

Then she slipped past him and fled headlong from the room to fall, half fainting, into Dick Windyford's arms.

"My God! Alix!" he cried.

Then he turned to the man with him, a tall stalwart figure in policeman's uniform.

"Go and see what's been happening in that room."

He laid Alix carefully down on a couch and bent over her.

"My little girl," he murmured. "My poor little girl. What have they been doing to you?"

Her eyelids fluttered and her lips just murmured his name.

Dick was aroused from tumultuous thoughts by the policeman's touching him on the arm.

"There's nothing in that room, sir, but a man sitting in a chair. Looks as though he'd had some kind of bad fright, and—"

"Yes?"

"Well, sir, he's—dead."

They were startled by hearing Alix's voice. She spoke as though in some kind of dream.

"And presently," she said, almost as though she were quoting from something, "he died. . . ."

ACCIDENT

"And I tell you this—it's the same woman—not a doubt of it!" Captain Haydock looked into the eager, vehement face of his friend and sighed. He wished Evans would not be so positive and so jubilant. In the course of a career spent at sea, the old sea captain had learned to leave things that did not concern him well alone. His friend Evans, late C.I.D. Inspector, had a different philosophy of life. "Acting on information received—" had been his motto in early days, and he had improved upon it to the extent of finding out his own information. Inspector Evans had been a very smart, wide-awake officer, and had justly earned the promotion which had been his. Even now, when he had retired from the force, and had settled down in the country cottage of his dreams, his professional instinct was still active.

"Don't often forget a face," he reiterated complacently. "Mrs. Anthony—yes, it's Mrs. Anthony right enough. When you said Mrs. Merrowdene—I knew her at once."

Captain Haydock stirred uneasily. The Merrowdenes were his nearest neighbors, barring Evans himself, and this identifying of Mrs. Merrowdene with a former heroine of a *cause célèbre* distressed him.

"It's a long time ago," he said rather weakly.

"Nine years," said Evans, accurate as ever. "Nine years and three months. You remember the case?"

"In a vague sort of way."

"Anthony turned out to be an arsenic eater," said Evans, "so they acquitted her."

"Well, why shouldn't they?"

"No reason in the world. Only verdict they could give on the evidence. Absolutely correct."

"Then, that's all right," said Haydock. "And I don't see what we're bothering about."

"Who's bothering?"

"I thought you were."

"Not at all."

"The thing's over and done with," summed up the Captain. "If Mrs. Merrowdene at one time of her life was unfortunate enough to be tried and acquitted of murder—"

"It's not usually considered unfortunate to be acquitted," put in Evans.

"You know what I mean," said Captain Haydock, irritably. "If the poor lady has been through that harrowing experience, it's no business of ours to rake it up, is it?"

Evans did not answer.

"Come now, Evans. The lady was innocent—you've just said so."

"I didn't say she was innocent. I said she was acquitted."

"It's the same thing."

"Not always."

Captain Haydock, who had commenced to tap his pipe out against the side of his chair, stopped, and sat up with a very alert expression:

"Hullo-ullo-ullo," he said. "The wind's in that quarter, is it? You think she wasn't innocent?"

"I wouldn't say that. I just—don't know. Anthony was in the habit of taking arsenic. His wife got it for him. One day, by mistake, he takes far too much. Was the mistake his or his wife's? Nobody could tell, and the jury very properly gave her the benefit of the doubt. That's all quite right and I'm not finding fault with it. All the same—I'd like to know."

Captain Haydock transferred his attention to his pipe once more.

"Well," he said comfortably, "it's none of our business."

"I'm not so sure. . . ."

"But, surely—"

"Listen to me a minute. This man, Merrowdene—in his laboratory this evening, fiddling round with tests—you remember—"

"Yes. He mentioned Marsh's test for arsenic. Said you would know all about it—it was in your line—and chuckled. He wouldn't have said that if he'd thought for one moment—"

Evans interrupted him.

"You mean he wouldn't have said that if he knew. They've been married how long—six years, you told me? I bet you anything he has no idea his wife is the once notorious Mrs. Anthony."

"And he will certainly not know it from me," said Captain Haydock stiffly.

Evans paid no attention, but went on.

"You interrupted me just now. After Marsh's test, Merrowdene heated a substance in a test tube, the metallic residue he dissolved in water and then precipitated it by adding silver nitrate. That was a test for chlorates. A neat, unassuming little test. But I chanced to read these words in a book that stood open on the table. *H_2So_4 decomposes chlorates with evolution of Cl_2O_4. If heated, violent explosions occur, the mixture ought therefore to be kept cool and only very small quantities used.*"

Haydock stared at his friend.

"Well, what about it?"

"Just this. In my profession we've got tests, too—tests for murder. There's adding up the facts—weighing them, dissecting the residue when you've allowed for prejudice and the general inaccuracy of witnesses. But there's another test for murder—one that is fairly accurate, but rather—dangerous! A murderer is seldom content with one crime. Give him time and a lack of suspicion and he'll commit another. You catch a man—has he murdered his wife or hasn't he?—perhaps the case isn't very black against him. Look into his past—if you find that he's had several wives—and that they've all died, shall we say—rather curiously?—then you know! I'm not speaking legally, you understand. I'm speaking of moral certainty. Once you know, you can go ahead looking for evidence."

"Well?"

"I'm coming to the point. That's all right if there is a past to look into. But suppose you catch your murderer at his or her first crime? Then that test will be one from which you get no reaction. But the prisoner acquitted—starting life under another name.

Will or will not the murderer repeat the crime?"

"That's a horrible idea."

"Do you still say it's none of our business?"

"Yes, I do. You've no reason to think that Mrs. Merrowdene is anything but a perfectly innocent woman."

The ex-Inspector was silent for a moment. Then he said slowly:

"I told you that we looked into her past and found nothing. That's not quite true. There was a stepfather. As a girl of eighteen she had a fancy for some young man—and her stepfather exerted his authority to keep them apart. She and her stepfather went for a walk along a rather dangerous part of the cliff. There was an accident—the stepfather went too near the edge—it gave way and he went over and was killed."

"You don't think—"

"It was an accident. Accident! Anthony's overdose of arsenic was an accident. She'd never have been tried if it hadn't transpired that there was another man—he sheered off, by the way. Looked as though he weren't satisfied even if the jury were. I tell you, Haydock, where that woman is concerned I'm afraid of another—accident!"

The old Captain shrugged his shoulders.

"Well, I don't know how you're going to guard against that."

"Neither do I," said Evans ruefully.

"I should leave well enough alone," said Captain Haydock. "No good ever came of butting into other people's affairs."

But that advice was not palatable to the ex-Inspector. He was a man of patience but determination. Taking leave of his friend, he sauntered down to the village, revolving in his mind the possibilities of some kind of successful action.

Turning into the post office to buy some stamps, he ran into the object of his solicitude, George Merrowdene. The ex-chemistry professor was a small, dreamy-looking man, gentle and kindly in manner, and usually completely absent-minded. He recognized the other and greeted him amicably, stooping to recover the letters that the impact had caused him to drop on the ground. Evans stooped also and, more rapid in his movements than the other, secured them first, handing them back to their owner with an apology.

He glanced down at them in doing so, and the address on the topmost suddenly awakened all his suspicions anew. It bore the name of a well-known insurance firm.

Instantly his mind was made up. The guileless George Merrowdene hardly realized how it came about that he and the ex-Inspector were strolling down the village together, and still less could he have said how it came about that the conversation should come round to the subject of life insurance.

Evans had no difficulty in attaining his object. Merrowdene of his own accord volunteered the information that he had just insured his life for his wife's benefit, and asked Evans's opinion of the company in question.

"I made some rather unwise investments," he explained. "As a result, my income has diminished. If anything were to happen to me, my wife would be left very badly off. This insurance will put things right."

"She didn't object to the idea?" inquired Evans casually. "Some ladies do, you know. Feel it's unlucky—that sort of thing."

"Oh, Margaret is very practical," said Merrowdene, smiling. "Not at all superstitious. In fact, I believe it was her idea originally. She didn't like my being so worried."

Evans had got the information he wanted. He left the other shortly afterward, and his lips were set in a grim line. The late Mr. Anthony had insured his life in his wife's favor a few weeks before his death.

Accustomed to rely on his instincts, he was perfectly sure in his own mind. But how to act was another matter. He wanted, not to arrest a criminal red-handed, but to prevent a crime being committed and that was a very different and a very much more difficult thing.

All day he was very thoughtful. There was a Primrose League Fête that afternoon held in the grounds of the local squire, and he went to it, indulging in the penny dip, guessing the weight of a pig, and shying at coconuts, all with the same look of abstracted concentration on his face. He even indulged in half a crown's worth of Zara the Crystal Gazer, smiling a little to himself as he did so, remembering his own activities against fortune-tellers in his official days.

He did not pay very much heed to her singsong, droning voice till the end of a sentence held his attention.

"—and you will very shortly—very shortly indeed—be engaged on a matter of life or death—life or death to one person."

"Eh—what's that?" he asked abruptly.

"A decision—you have a decision to make. You must be very careful—very, very careful. . . . If you were to make a mistake—the smallest mistake—"

"Yes?"

The fortune-teller shivered. Inspector Evans knew it was all nonsense, but he was nevertheless impressed.

"I warn you—you must not make a mistake. If you do, I see the result clearly, a death. . . ."

Odd, damned odd! A death. Fancy her lighting upon that!

"If I make a mistake a death will result? Is that it?"

"Yes."

"In that case," said Evans, rising to his feet and handing over half a crown, "I mustn't make a mistake, eh?"

He spoke lightly enough, but as he went out of the tent, his jaw set determinedly. Easy to say—not so easy to be sure of doing. He mustn't make a slip. A life, a valuable human life depended on it.

And there was no one to help him. He looked across at the figure of his friend Haydock in the distance. No help there. "Leave things alone," was Haydock's motto. And that wouldn't do here.

Haydock was talking to a woman. She moved away from him and came toward Evans, and the Inspector recognized her. It was Mrs. Merrowdene. On an impulse he put himself deliberately in her path.

Mrs. Merrowdene was rather a fine-looking woman. She had a broad serene brow, very beautiful brown eyes, and a placid expression. She had the look of an Italian Madonna which she heightened by parting her hair in the middle and looping it over her ears. She had a deep, rather sleepy voice.

She smiled up at Evans, a contented, welcoming smile.

"I thought it was you, Mrs. Anthony—I mean Mrs. Merrowdene," he said glibly.

He made the slip deliberately, watching her without seeming to do so. He saw her eyes widen, heard the quick intake of her breath. But her eyes did not falter. She gazed at him steadily and proudly.

"I was looking for my husband," she said quietly. "Have you seen him anywhere about?"

"He was over in that direction when I last saw him."

They went side by side in the direction indicated, chatting quietly and pleasantly. The Inspector felt his admiration mounting. What a woman! What self-command! What wonderful poise! A remarkable woman—and a very dangerous one. He felt sure—a very dangerous one.

He still felt very uneasy, though he was satisfied with his initial step. He had let her know that he recognized her. That would put her on her guard. She would not dare attempt anything rash. There was the question of Merrowdene. If he could be warned. . . .

They found the little man absently contemplating a china doll which had fallen to his share in the penny dip. His wife suggested home and he agreed eagerly. Mrs. Merrowdene turned to the Inspector.

"Won't you come back with us and have a quiet cup of tea, Mr. Evans?"

Was there a faint note of challenge in her voice? He thought there was.

"Thank you, Mrs. Merrowdene. I should like to very much."

They walked there, talking together of pleasant ordinary things. The sun shone, a breeze blew gently, everything around them was pleasant and ordinary.

Their maid was out at the Fête, Mrs. Merrowdene explained, when they arrived at the charming Old World cottage. She went into her room to remove her hat, returning to set out tea and boil the kettle on a little silver lamp. From a shelf near the fireplace she took three small bowls and saucers.

"We have some very special Chinese tea," she explained. "And we always drink it in the Chinese manner—out of bowls, not cups."

She broke off, peered into a cup, and exchanged it for another, with an exclamation of annoyance.

"George—it's too bad of you. You've been taking these bowls again."

"I'm sorry, dear," said the professor apologetically. "They're such a convenient size. The ones I ordered haven't come."

"One of these days you'll poison us all," said his wife with a half laugh. "Mary finds them in the laboratory and brings them back here and never troubles to wash them out unless they've something very noticeable in them. Why, you were using one of them for potassium cyanide the other day. Really, George, it's frightfully dangerous."

Merrowdene looked a little irritated.

"Mary's no business to remove things from the laboratory. She's not to touch anything there."

"But we often leave our teacups there after tea. How is she to know? Be reasonable, dear."

The professor went into his laboratory, murmuring to himself, and with a smile. Mrs. Merrowdene poured boiling water on the tea and blew out the flame of the little silver lamp.

Evans was puzzled. Yet a glimmering of light penetrated to him. For some reason or other, Mrs. Merrowdene was showing her hand. Was this to be the "accident"? Was she speaking of all this so as deliberately to prepare her alibi beforehand. So that when, one day, the "accident" happened, he would be forced to give evidence in her favor. Stupid of her, if so, because before that—

Suddenly he drew in his breath. She had poured the tea into the three bowls. One she set before him, one before herself, the other she placed on a little table by the fire near the chair her husband usually sat in, and it was as she placed this last one on the table that a little strange smile curved round her lips. It was the smile that did it.

He knew!

A remarkable woman—a dangerous woman. No waiting—no preparation. This afternoon—this very afternoon—with him here as witness. The boldness of it took his breath away.

It was clever—it was damnably clever. He would be able to prove nothing. She counted on his not suspecting—simply because it was "so soon." A woman of lightning rapidity of thought and action.

He drew a deep breath and leaned forward.

"Mrs. Merrowdene, I'm a man of queer whims. Will you be very kind and indulge me in one of them?"

She looked inquiring but unsuspicious.

He rose, took the bowl from in front of her, and crossed to the little table, where he substituted it for the other. This other he brought back and placed in front of her.

"I want to see you drink this."

Her eyes met his. They were steady, unfathomable. The color slowly drained from her face.

She stretched out her hand, raised the cup. He held his breath.

Supposing all along he had made a mistake.

She raised it to her lips—at the last moment, with a shudder she leaned forward and quickly poured it into a pot containing a fern. Then she sat back and gazed at him defiantly.

He drew a long sigh of relief, and sat down again.

"Well?" she said.

Her voice had altered. It was slightly mocking—defiant.

He answered her soberly and quietly.

"You are a very clever woman, Mrs. Merrowdene. I think you understand me. There must be no—repetition. You know what I mean?"

"I know what you mean."

Her voice was even, devoid of expression. He nodded his head, satisfied. She was a clever woman, and she didn't want to be hanged.

"To your long life and to that of your husband," he said significantly and raised his tea to his lips.

Then his face changed. It contorted horribly . . . he tried to rise—to cry out. . . . His body stiffened—his face went purple. He fell back sprawling over the chair—his limbs convulsed.

Mrs. Merrowdene leaned forward, watching him. A little smile crossed her lips. She spoke to him—very softly and gently.

"You made a mistake, Mr. Evans. You thought I wanted to kill George. . . . How stupid of you—how very stupid."

She sat there a minute longer looking at the dead man, the third man who had threatened to cross her path and separate her from the man she loved. . . .

Her smile broadened. She looked more than ever like a Madonna. Then she raised her voice and called.

"George—George. . . . Oh! Do come here. I'm afraid there's been the most dreadful accident. . . . Poor Mr. Evans. . . ."

THE LISTERDALE MYSTERY

Mrs. St. Vincent was adding up figures. Once or twice she sighed, and her hand stole to her aching forehead. She had always disliked arithmetic. It was unfortunate that nowadays her life should seem to be composed entirely of one particular kind of sum, the ceaseless adding together of small necessary items of expenditure making a total that never failed to surprise and alarm her.

Surely it couldn't come to *that!* She went back over the figures. She had made a trifling error in the pence, but otherwise the figures were correct.

Mrs. St. Vincent sighed again. Her headache by now was very bad indeed. She looked up as the door opened and her daughter Barbara came into the room. Barbara St. Vincent was a very pretty girl; she had her mother's delicate features, and the same proud turn of the head, but her eyes were dark instead of blue, and she had a different mouth, a sulky red mouth not without attraction.

"Oh, Mother!" she cried. "Still juggling with those horrid old accounts? Throw them all into the fire."

"We must know where we are," said Mrs. St. Vincent uncertainly.

The girl shrugged her shoulders.

"We're always in the same boat," she said dryly. "Damned hard up. Down to the last penny as usual."

Mrs. St. Vincent sighed.

"I wish—" she began, and then stopped.

"I must find something to do," said Barbara in hard tones. "And find it quickly. After all, I have taken that shorthand and typing course. So have about one million other girls from all I can see! 'What experience?' 'None, but—' 'Oh! Thank you, good morning. We'll let you know.' But they never do! I must find some other kind of a job—*any* job."

"Not yet, dear," pleaded her mother. "Wait a little longer."

Barbara went to the window and stood looking out with unseeing eyes that took no note of the dingy line of houses opposite.

"Sometimes," she said slowly, "I'm sorry Cousin Amy took me with her to Egypt last winter. Oh! I know I had fun—about the only fun I've ever had or am likely to have in my life. I *did* enjoy myself—enjoyed myself thoroughly. But it was very unsettling. I mean—coming back to *this.*"

She swept a hand round the room. Mrs. St. Vincent followed it with her eyes and winced. The room was typical of cheap furnished lodgings. A dusty aspidistra, showily ornamental furniture, a gaudy wallpaper faded in patches. There were signs that the personality of the tenants had struggled with that of the landlady; one or two pieces of good china, much cracked and mended, so that their saleable value was *nil,* a piece of embroidery thrown over the back of the sofa, a water color sketch of a young girl in the fashion of twenty years ago, near enough still to Mrs. St. Vincent not to be mistaken.

"It wouldn't matter," continued Barbara, "if we'd never known anything else. But to think of Ansteys—"

She broke off, not trusting herself to speak of that dearly loved home which had belonged to the St. Vincent family for centuries and which was now in the hands of strangers.

"If only Father—hadn't speculated—and borrowed—"

"My dear," said Mrs. St. Vincent. "Your father was never, in any sense of the word, a businessman."

She said it with a graceful kind of finality, and Barbara came over and gave her an aimless sort of kiss as she murmured, "Poor old Mums. I won't say anything."

Mrs. St. Vincent took up her pen again and bent over her desk. Barbara went back to the window. Presently the girl said:

"Mother. I heard from—from Jim Masterton this morning. He wants to come and see me."

Mrs. St. Vincent laid down her pen and looked up sharply.

"Here?" she exclaimed.

"Well, we can't ask him to dinner at the Ritz very well," sneered Barbara.

Her mother looked unhappy. Again she looked round the room with innate distaste.

"You're right," said Barbara. "It's a disgusting place. Genteel poverty! Sounds all right—a whitewashed cottage in the country, shabby chintzes of good design, bowls of roses, crown Derby tea service that you wash up yourself. That's what it's like in books. In real life, with a son starting on the bottom rung of office life, it means London. Frowsy landladies, dirty children on the stairs, haddocks for breakfasts that aren't quite—quite and so on."

"If only—" began Mrs. St. Vincent. "But, really, I'm beginning to be afraid we can't afford even this room much longer."

"That means a bed-sitting-room—horror!—for you and me," said Barbara. "And a cupboard under the tiles for Rupert. And when Jim comes to call, I'll receive him in that dreadful room downstairs with tabbies all round the walls knitting, and staring at us, and coughing that dreadful kind of gulping cough they have!"

There was a pause.

"Barbara," said Mrs. St. Vincent at last. "Do you—I mean—would you—?"

She stopped, flushing a little.

"You needn't be delicate, Mother," said Barbara. "Nobody is nowadays. Marry Jim, I suppose you mean? I would like a shot if he asked me. But I'm so awfully afraid he won't."

"Oh! Barbara, dear."

"Well, it's one thing seeing me out there with Cousin Amy, moving (as they say in novelettes) in the best society. He *did* take a fancy to me. Now he'll come here and see me in *this!* And he's a funny creature, you know, fastidious and old-fashioned. I—I rather like him for that. It reminds me of Ansteys and the village—everything a hundred years behind the times, but so—so—oh! I don't know—so fragrant. Like lavender!"

She laughed, half-ashamed of her eagerness. Mrs. St. Vincent spoke with a kind of earnest simplicity.

"I should like you to marry Jim Masterton," she said. "He is—one of us. He is very well off, also, but that I don't mind about so much."

"I do," said Barbara. "I'm sick of being hard up."

"But, Barbara, it isn't—"

"Only for that? No. I do really. I—oh! Mother, can't you *see* I do?"

Mrs. St. Vincent looked very unhappy.

"I wish he could see you in your proper setting, darling," she said wistfully.

"Oh, well!" said Barbara. "Why worry? We might as well try and be cheerful about things. Sorry I've had such a grouch. Cheer up, darling."

She bent over her mother, kissed her forehead lightly, and went out. Mrs. St. Vincent, relinquishing all attempts at finance, sat down on the uncomfortable sofa. Her thoughts ran round in circles like squirrels in a cage.

"One may say what one likes, appearances *do* put a man off. Not later—not if they were really engaged. He'd know then what a sweet, dear girl she is. But it's so easy for young people to take the tone of their surroundings. Rupert, now, he's quite different from what he used to be. Not that I want my children to be stuck-up. That's not it a bit. But I should hate it if Rupert got engaged to that dreadful girl in the tobacconist's. I daresay she may be a very nice girl, really. But she's not our kind. It's all so difficult. Poor little Babs. If I could do anything—anything. But where's the money to come from? We've sold everything to give Rupert his start. We really can't even afford this."

To distract herself Mrs. St. Vincent picked up the *Morning Post* and glanced down the advertisements on the front page. Most of them she knew by heart. People who wanted capital, people who had capital and were anxious to dispose of it on note of hand alone, people who wanted to buy teeth (she always wondered why), people who wanted to sell furs and gowns and who had optimistic ideas on the subject of price.

Suddenly she stiffened to attention. Again and again she read the printed words.

"To gentlepeople only. Small house in Westminster, exquisitely furnished, offered to those who would really care for it. Rent purely nominal. No agents."

A very ordinary advertisement. She had read many the same or—well, nearly the same. Nominal rent, that was where the trap lay.

Yet, since she was restless and anxious to escape from her thoughts, she put on her hat straightaway and took a convenient bus to the address given in the advertisement.

It proved to be that of a firm of house agents. Not a new bustling firm—a rather decrepit, old-fashioned place. Rather timidly she produced the advertisement, which she had torn out, and asked for particulars.

The white-haired old gentleman who was attending to her stroked his chin thoughtfully.

"Perfectly. Yes, perfectly, madam. That house, the house mentioned in the advertisement, is No. 7 Cheviot Place. You would like an order?"

"I should like to know the rent first?" said Mrs. St. Vincent.

"Ah! The rent. The exact figure is not settled, but I can assure you that it is purely nominal."

"Ideas of what is purely nominal can vary," said Mrs. St. Vincent.

The old gentleman permitted himself to chuckle a little.

"Yes, that's an old trick—an old trick. But you can take my word for it, it isn't so in this case. Two or three guineas a week, perhaps, not more."

Mrs. St. Vincent decided to have the order. Not, of course, that there was any real likelihood of her being able to afford the place. But, after all, she might just *see* it. There must be some grave disadvantage attaching to it, to be offered at such a price.

But her heart gave a little throb as she looked up at the outside of 7 Cheviot Place. A gem of a house. Queen Anne, and in perfect condition! A butler answered the door. He had gray hair and little side whiskers, and the meditative calm of an archbishop. A kindly archbishop, Mrs. St. Vincent thought.

He accepted the order with a benevolent air.

"Certainly, madam, I will show you over. The house is ready for occupation."

He went before her, opening doors, announcing rooms.

"The drawing room, the white study, a powder closet through here, madam."

It was perfect—a dream. The furniture all of the period, each piece with signs of wear, but polished with loving care. The loose rugs were of beautiful dim old colors. In each room were bowls of fresh flowers. The back of the house looked over the Green Park. The whole place radiated an old-world charm.

The tears came into Mrs. St. Vincent's eyes, and she fought them back with difficulty. So had Ansteys looked—Ansteys . . .

She wondered whether the butler had noticed her emotion. If so, he was too much the perfectly trained servant to show it. She liked these old servants, one felt safe with them, at ease. They were like friends.

"It is a beautiful house," she said softly. "Very beautiful. I am glad to have seen it."

"Is it for yourself alone, madam?"

"For myself and my son and daughter. But I'm afraid—"

She broke off. She wanted it so dreadfully—so dreadfully.

She felt instinctively that the butler understood. He did not look at her, as he said in a detached, impersonal way:

"I happen to be aware, madam, that the owner requires above all suitable tenants. The rent is of no importance to him. He wants the house to be tenanted by someone who will really care for and appreciate it."

"I should appreciate it," said Mrs. St. Vincent in a low voice.

She turned to go.

"Thank you for showing me over," she said courteously.

"Not at all, madam."

He stood in the doorway, very correct and upright as she walked away down the street. She thought to herself: "He knows. He's sorry for me. He's one of the old lot too. He'd like *me* to have it—not a labor member, or a button manufacturer! We're dying out, our sort, but we hang together."

In the end she decided not to go back to the agents. What was the good? She could afford the rent—but there were servants to be considered. There would have to be servants in a house like that.

The next morning a letter lay by her plate. It was from the house agents. It offered her the tenancy of 7 Cheviot Place for six months at two guineas a week, and went on: "You have, I presume, taken into consideration the fact that the servants are remaining at the landlord's expense? It is really a unique offer."

It was. So startled was she by it, that she read the letter out. A fire of questions followed and she described her visit of yesterday.

"Secretive little Mums!" cried Barbara. "Is it really so lovely?"

Rupert cleared his throat and began a judicial cross-questioning.

"There's something behind all this. It's fishy, if you ask me. Decidedly fishy."

"So's my egg," said Barbara, wrinkling her nose. "Ugh! Why should there be something behind it? That's just like you, Rupert, always making mysteries out of nothing. It's those dreadful detective stories you're always reading."

"The rent's a joke," said Rupert. "In the city," he added importantly, "one gets wise to all sorts of queer things. I tell you, there's something very fishy about this business."

"Nonsense," said Barbara. "House belongs to a man with lots of money, he's fond of it, and he wants it lived in by decent people while he's away. Something of that kind. Money's probably no object to him."

"What did you say the address was?" asked Rupert of his mother.

"Seven Cheviot Place."

"Whew!" He pushed back his chair. "I say, this is exciting. That's the house Lord Listerdale disappeared from."

"Are you sure?" asked Mrs. St. Vincent doubtfully.

"Positive. He's got a lot of other houses all over London, but this is the one he lived in. He walked out of it one evening saying he was going to his club, and nobody ever saw him again. Supposed to have done a bunk to East Africa or somewhere like that, but nobody knows why. Depend upon it, he was murdered in that house. You say there's a lot of paneling?"

"Ye-es," said Mrs. St. Vincent faintly; "but—"

Rupert gave her no time. He went on with immense enthusiasm.

"Paneling! There you are. Sure to be a secret recess somewhere. Body's been stuffed in there and has been there ever since. Perhaps it was embalmed first."

"Rupert, dear, don't talk nonsense," said his mother.

"Don't be a double-dyed idiot," said Barbara. "You've been taking that peroxide blonde to the pictures too much."

Rupert rose with dignity—such dignity as his lanky and awkward age allowed, and delivered a final ultimatum.

"You take that house, Mums. *I'll* ferret out the mystery. You see if I don't."

Rupert departed hurriedly, in fear of being late at the office.

The eyes of the two women met.

"Could we, Mother?" murmured Barbara tremulously. "Oh! If we could."

"The servants," said Mrs. St. Vincent pathetically, "would *eat*, you know. I mean, of course, one would want them to—but that's the drawback. One can so easily—just do without things—when it's only oneself."

She looked piteously at Barbara, and the girl nodded.

"We must think it over," said the mother.

But in reality her mind was made up. She had seen the sparkle in the girl's eyes. She thought to herself: "Jim Masterton *must* see her in proper surroundings. This is a chance—a wonderful chance. I must take it."

She sat down and wrote to the agents accepting their offer.

II

"Quentin, where did the lilies come from? I really can't buy expensive flowers."

"They were sent up from King's Cheviot, madam. It has always been the custom here."

The butler withdrew. Mrs. St. Vincent heaved a sigh of relief. What would she do without Quentin? He made everything so *easy*. She thought to herself: "It's too good to last. I shall wake up soon, I know I shall, and find it's been all a dream. I'm so *happy* here—two months already, and it's passed like a flash."

Life indeed had been astonishingly pleasant. Quentin, the butler, had displayed himself the autocrat of 7 Cheviot Place. "If you will leave everything to me, madam," he had said respectfully. "You will find it the best way."

Each week, he brought her the housekeeping books, their totals astonishingly low. There were only two other servants, a cook and a housemaid. They were pleasant in manner, and efficient in their duties, but it was Quentin who ran the house. Game and poultry appeared on the table sometimes, causing Mrs. St. Vincent solicitude. Quentin reassured her. Sent up from Lord Listerdale's country seat, King's Cheviot, or from his Yorkshire moor. "It has always been the custom, madam."

Privately Mrs. St. Vincent doubted whether the absent Lord Listerdale would agree with those words. She was inclined to suspect Quentin of usurping his master's authority. It was clear that he had taken a fancy to them, and that in his eyes nothing was too good for them.

Her curiosity aroused by Rupert's declaration, Mrs. St. Vincent had made a tentative reference to Lord Listerdale when she next interviewed the house agents. The white-haired old gentleman had responded immediately.

Yes, Lord Listerdale was in East Africa, had been there for the last eighteen months.

"Our client is rather an eccentric man," he had said, smiling broadly. "He left London in a most unconventional manner, as you may perhaps remember? Not a word to anyone. The newspapers got hold of it. There were actually inquiries on foot at Scotland Yard. Luckily, news was received from Lord Listerdale himself from East Africa. He invested his cousin, Colonel Carfax, with power of attorney. It is the latter who conducts all Lord Listerdale's affairs. Yes, rather eccentric, I fear. He has always been a great traveler in the wilds—it is quite on the cards that he may not return for years to England, though he is getting on in years."

"Surely he is not so very old," said Mrs. St. Vincent, with a sudden memory of a bluff, bearded face, rather like an Elizabethan sailor, which she had once noticed in an illustrated magazine.

"Middle-aged," said the white-haired gentleman. "Fifty-three, according to Debrett."

This conversation Mrs. St. Vincent had retailed to Rupert with the intention of rebuking that young gentleman.

Rupert, however, was undismayed.

"It looks fishier than ever to me," he had declared. "Who's this Colonel Carfax? Probably comes into the title if anything happens to Listerdale. The letter from East Africa was probably forged. In three years, or whatever it is, this Carfax will presume death, and take the title. Meantime, he's got all the handling of the estate. Very fishy, I call it."

He had condescended graciously to approve the house. In his leisure moments he was inclined to tap the paneling and make elaborate measurements for the possible location of a secret room, but little by little his interest in the mystery of Lord Listerdale abated. He was also less enthusiastic on the subject of the tobacconist's daughter. Atmosphere tells.

To Barbara the house had brought great satisfaction. Jim Masterton had come home, and was a frequent visitor. He and Mrs. St. Vincent got on splendidly together, and he said something to Barbara one day that startled her.

"This house is a wonderful setting for your mother, you know."

"For *Mother?*"

"Yes. It was made for her! She belongs to it in an extraordinary way. You know there's something queer about this house altogether, something uncanny and haunting."

"Don't get like Rupert," Barbara implored him. "He is convinced that the wicked Colonel Carfax murdered Lord Listerdale and hid his body under the floor."

Masterton laughed.

"I admire Rupert's detective zeal. No, I didn't mean anything of *that* kind. But there's something in the air, some atmosphere that one doesn't quite understand."

They had been three months in Cheviot Place when Barbara came to her mother with a radiant face.

"Jim and I—we're engaged. Yes—last night. Oh, Mother! It all seems like a fairy tale come true."

"Oh, my dear! I'm so glad—so glad."

Mother and daughter clasped each other close.

"You know Jim's almost as much in love with you as he is with me," said Barbara at last, with a mischievous laugh.

Mrs. St. Vincent blushed very prettily.

"He is," persisted the girl. "You thought this house would make such a beautiful setting for me, and all the time it's really a setting for *you*. Rupert and I don't quite belong here. You do."

"Don't talk nonsense, darling."

"It's not nonsense. There's a flavor of enchanted castle about it, with you as an enchanted princess and Quentin as—as—oh!—a benevolent magician."

Mrs. St. Vincent laughed and admitted the last item.

Rupert received the news of his sister's engagement very calmly.

"I thought there was something of the kind in the wind," he observed sapiently.

He and his mother were dining alone together. Barbara was out with Jim.

Quentin placed the port in front of him and withdrew noiselessly.

"That's a rum old bird," said Rupert, nodding toward the closed door. "There's something odd about him, you know, something—"

"Not fishy?" interrupted Mrs. St. Vincent, with a faint smile.

"Why, Mother, how did you know what I was going to say?" demanded Rupert in all seriousness.

"It's rather a word of yours, darling. You think everything is fishy. I suppose you have an idea that it was Quentin who did away with Lord Listerdale and put him under the floor?"

"Behind the paneling," corrected Rupert. "You always get things a little bit wrong, Mother. No, I've inquired about that. Quentin was down at King's Cheviot at the time."

Mrs. St. Vincent smiled at him, as she rose from the table and went up to the drawing room. In some ways Rupert was a long time growing up.

Yet a sudden wonder swept over her for the first time as to Lord Listerdale's reasons for leaving England so abruptly. There must be something behind it, to account for that sudden decision. She was still thinking the matter over when Quentin came in with the coffee tray, and she spoke out impulsively.

"You have been with Lord Listerdale a long time, haven't you, Quentin?"

"Yes, madam; since I was a lad of twenty-one. That was in the late lord's time. I started as third footman."

"You must know Lord Listerdale very well. What kind of a man is he?"

The butler turned the tray a little, so that she could help herself to sugar more conveniently, as he replied in even unemotional tones:

"Lord Listerdale was a very selfish gentleman, madam; with no consideration for others."

He removed the tray and bore it from the room. Mrs. St. Vincent sat with her coffee cup in her hand and a puzzled frown on her face. Something struck her as odd in the speech apart from the views it expressed. In another minute it flashed home to her.

Quentin had used the word *"was,"* not "is." But then, he must think—must believe—She pulled herself up. She was as bad as Rupert! But a very definite uneasiness assailed her. Afterward she dated her first suspicions from that moment.

With Barbara's happiness and future assured, she had time to think her own thoughts, and against her will, they began to center round the mystery of Lord Listerdale. What was the real story? Whatever it was, Quentin knew something about it. Those had been odd words of his—"a very selfish gentleman—no consideration for others." What lay behind them? He had spoken as a judge might speak, detachedly and impartially.

Was Quentin involved in Lord Listerdale's disappearance? Had he taken an active part in any tragedy there might have been? After all, ridiculous as Rupert's assumption had seemed at the time, that single letter with its power of attorney coming from East Africa was—well, open to suspicion.

But try as she would, she could not believe any real evil of Quentin. Quentin, she told herself over and over again, was *good*—she used the word as simply as a child might have done. Quentin was *good*. But he knew something!

She never spoke with him again of his master. The subject was apparently forgotten. Rupert and Barbara had other things to think of, and there were no further discussions.

It was toward the end of August that her vague surmises crystallized into realities. Rupert had gone for a fortnight's holiday with a friend who had a motorcycle and trailer. It was some ten days after his departure that Mrs. St. Vincent was startled to see him rush into the room where she sat writing.

"Rupert!" she exclaimed.

"I know, Mother. You didn't expect to see me for another three days. But something's happened. Anderson—my pal, you know—didn't much care where he went, so I suggested having a look in at King's Cheviot—"

"King's Cheviot? But why—?"

"You know perfectly well, Mother, that I've always scented something fishy about things here. Well, I had a look at the old place—it's let, you know—nothing there. Not that I actually expected to find anything—I was just nosing round, so to speak."

Yes, she thought, Rupert was very like a dog at this moment. Hunting in circles for something vague and undefined, led by instinct, busy and happy.

"It was when we were passing through a village about eight or nine miles away that it happened—that I saw him, I mean."

"Saw whom?"

"Quentin—just going into a little cottage. Something fishy here, I said to myself, and we stopped the bus, and I went back. I rapped on the door and he himself opened it."

"But I don't understand. Quentin hasn't been away—"

"I'm coming to that, Mother. If you'd only listen and not interrupt. It was Quentin, and it wasn't Quentin, if you know what I mean."

Mrs. St. Vincent clearly did not know, so he elucidated matters further.

"It was Quentin all right, but it wasn't *our* Quentin. It was the real man."

"Rupert!"

"You listen. It was taken in myself at first, and said: 'It is Quentin, isn't it?' And the old johnny said: 'Quite right, sir, that is my name. What can I do for you?' And then I saw that it wasn't our man, though it was precious like him, voice and all. I asked a few questions, and it all came out. The old chap hadn't an idea of anything fishy being on. He'd been butler to Lord Listerdale, all right, and was retired on a pension and given this cottage just about the time that Lord Listerdale was supposed to have gone off to Africa. You see where that leads us. This man's an impostor—he's playing the part of Quentin for purposes of his own. My theory is that he came up to town that evening, pretending to be the butler from King's Cheviot, got an interview with Lord Listerdale, killed him and hid his body behind the paneling. It's an old house, there's sure to be a secret recess—"

"Oh, don't let's go into all that again," interrupted Mrs. St. Vincent wildly. "I can't bear it. Why should he—that's what I want to know—why? *If* he did such a thing—which I don't believe for one minute, mind you—what was the *reason* for it all?"

"You're right," said Rupert. "Motive—that's important. Now I've made inquiries. Lord Listerdale had a lot of house property. In the last two days I've discovered that practically every one of these houses of his have been let in the last eighteen months to people like ourselves for a merely nominal rent—*and with the proviso that the servants should remain.* And in every case Quentin himself—the man calling himself Quentin, I mean—has been there for part of the time as butler. That looks as though there were something—jewels, or papers—secreted in one of Lord Listerdale's houses, and the gang doesn't know which. I'm assuming a gang, but of course this fellow Quentin may be in it single-handed. There's a—"

Mrs. St. Vincent interrupted him with a certain amount of determination:

"Rupert! Do stop talking for one minute. You're making my head spin. Anyway, what you are saying is nonsense—about gangs and hidden papers."

"There's another theory," admitted Rupert. "This Quentin may be someone that Lord Listerdale has injured. The real butler told me a long story about a man called Samuel Lowe—an undergardener he was, and about the same height and build as Quentin himself. He'd got a grudge against Listerdale—"

Mrs. St. Vincent started.

"With no consideration for others." The words came back to her mind in their passionless, measured accents. Inadequate words, but what might they not stand for?

In her absorption she hardly listened to Rupert. He made a rapid explanation of something that she did not take in, and went hurriedly from the room.

Then she woke up. Where had Rupert gone? What was he going to do? She had not caught his last words. Perhaps he was going for the police. In that case—

She rose abruptly and rang the bell. With his usual promptness, Quentin answered it.

"You rang, madam?"

"Yes. Come in, please, and shut the door."

The butler obeyed, and Mrs. St. Vincent was silent a moment while she studied him with earnest eyes.

She thought: "He's been kind to me—nobody knows how kind. The children wouldn't understand. This wild story of Rupert's may be all nonsense—On the other hand, there may—yes, there may—be something in it. Why should one judge? One can't *know*. The rights and wrongs of it, I mean. . . . And I'd stake my life—yes, I would!—on his being a good man."

Flushed and tremulous, she spoke.

"Quentin, Mr. Rupert has just got back. He has been down to King's Cheviot—to a village near there—"

She stopped, noticing the quick start he was not able to conceal.

"He has—seen someone," she went on in measured accents.

She thought to herself: "There—he's warned. At any rate, he's warned."

After that first quick start, Quentin had resumed his unruffled demeanor, but his eyes were fixed on her face, watchful and keen, with something in them she had not seen there before. They were, for the first time, the eyes of a man and not of a servant.

He hesitated for a minute, then said in a voice which also had subtly changed:

"Why do you tell me this, Mrs. St. Vincent?"

Before she could answer, the door flew open and Rupert strode into the room. With him was a dignified middle-aged man with little side whiskers and the air of a benevolent archbishop. *Quentin!*

"Here he is," said Rupert. "The real Quentin. I had him outside in the taxi. Now, Quentin, look at this man and tell me—is he Samuel Lowe?"

It was for Rupert a triumphant moment. But it was short-lived; almost at once he scented something wrong. For while the real Quentin was looking abashed and highly uncomfortable, the second Quentin was smiling a broad smile of undisguised enjoyment.

He slapped his embarrassed duplicate on the back.

"It's all right, Quentin. Got to let the cat out of the bag sometime, I suppose. You can tell 'em who I am."

The dignified stranger drew himself up.

"This, sir," he announced in a reproachful tone, "is my master, Lord Listerdale, sir."

THE NEXT MINUTE beheld many things. First, the complete collapse of the cocksure Rupert. Before he knew what was happening, his mouth still open from the shock of the discovery, he found himself being gently maneuvered toward the door, a friendly voice that was, and yet was not, familiar in his ear.

"It's quite all right, my boy. No bones broken. But I want a word with your mother. Very good work of yours, to ferret me out like this."

He was outside on the landing gazing at the shut door. The real Quentin was standing by his side, a gentle stream of explanation flowing from his lips. Inside the room Lord Listerdale was fronting Mrs. St. Vincent.

"Let me explain—if I can! I've been a selfish devil all my life—the fact came home to me one day. I thought I'd try a little altruism for a change, and being a fantastic kind of fool, I started my career fantastically. I'd sent subscriptions to odd things, but I felt the need of doing something—well, something *personal.* I've been sorry always for the class that can't beg, that must suffer in silence—poor gentlefolk. I have a lot of house property. I conceived the idea of leasing these houses to people who—well, needed and appreciated them. Young couples with their way to make, widows with sons and daughters starting in the world. Quentin has been more than butler to me; he's a friend. With his consent and assistance I borrowed his personality. I've always had a talent for acting. The idea came to me on my way to the club one night, and I went straight off to talk it over with Quentin. When I found they were making a fuss about my disappearance, I arranged that a letter should come from me in East Africa. In it, I gave full instructions to my cousin, Maurice Carfax. And—well, that's the long and short of it."

He broke off rather lamely, with an appealing glance at Mrs. St. Vincent. She stood very straight, and her eyes met his steadily.

"It was a kind plan," she said. "A very unusual one, and one that does you credit. I am—most grateful. But—of course, you understand that we cannot stay?"

"I expected that," he said. "Your pride won't let you accept what you'd probably style 'charity.'"

"Isn't that what it is?" she asked steadily.

"No," he answered. "Because I ask something in exchange."

"Something?"

"Everything." His voice rang out, the voice of one accustomed to dominate.

"When I was twenty-three," he went on, "I married the girl I loved. She died a year later. Since then I have been very lonely. I have wished very much I could find a certain lady—the lady of my dreams. . . ."

"Am I that?" she asked, very low. "I am so old—so faded."

He laughed.

"Old? You are younger than either of your children. Now I am old, if you like."

But her laugh rang out in turn, a soft ripple of amusement.

"You? You are a boy still. A boy who loves to dress up!"

She held out her hands and he caught them in his.

THE GIRL IN THE TRAIN

"And that's that!" observed George Rowland ruefully, as he gazed up at the imposing smoke-grimed façade of the building he had just quitted.

It might be said to represent very aptly the power of Money—and Money, in the person of William Rowland, uncle to the aforementioned George, had just spoken its mind very freely. In the course of a brief ten minutes, from being the apple of his uncle's eye, the heir to his wealth, and a young man with a promising business career in front of him, George had suddenly become one of the vast army of the unemployed.

"And in these clothes they won't even give me the dole," reflected Mr. Rowland gloomily, "and as for writing poems and selling them at the door at twopence (or 'what you care to give, lydy') I simply haven't got the brains."

It was true that George embodied a veritable triumph of the tailor's art. He was exquisitely and beautifully arrayed. Solomon and the lilies of the field were simply not in it with George. But man cannot live by clothes alone—unless he has had some considerable training in the art—and Mr. Rowland was painfully aware of the fact.

"And all because of that rotten show last night," he reflected sadly.

The rotten show last night had been a Covent Garden Ball. Mr. Rowland had returned from it at a somewhat late—or rather early—hour—as a matter of fact, he could not strictly say that he remembered returning at all. Rogers, his uncle's butler, was a helpful fellow, and could doubtless give more details on the matter. A splitting head, a cup of strong tea, and an arrival at the office at five minutes to twelve instead of half-past nine had precipitated the catastrophe. Mr. Rowland, senior, who for twenty-four years had condoned and paid up as a tactful relative should, had suddenly abandoned these tactics and revealed himself in a totally new light. The inconsequence of George's replies (the young man's head was still opening and shutting like some mediæval instrument of the Inquisition) had displeased him still further. William Rowland was nothing if not thorough. He cast his nephew adrift upon the world in a few short succinct words, and then settled down to his interrupted survey of some oil fields in Peru.

George Rowland shook the dust of his uncle's office from off his feet, and stepped out into the City of London. George was a practical fellow. A good lunch, he considered, was essential to a review of the situation. He had it. Then he retraced his steps to the family mansion. Rogers opened the door. His well-trained face expressed no surprise at seeing George at this unusual hour.

"Good afternoon, Rogers. Just pack up my things for me, will you? I'm leaving here."

"Yes, sir. Just for a short visit, sir?"

"For good, Rogers. I am going to the colonies this afternoon."

"Indeed, sir?"

"Yes. That is, if there is a suitable boat. Do you know anything about the boats, Rogers?"

"Which colony were you thinking of visiting, sir?"

"I'm not particular. Any of 'em will do. Let's say Australia. What do you think of the idea, Rogers?"

Rogers coughed discreetly.

"Well, sir, I've certainly heard it said that there's room out there for anyone who really wants to work."

Mr. Rowland gazed at him with interest and admiration.

"Very neatly put, Rogers. Just what I was thinking myself. I shan't go to Australia—not today, at any rate. Fetch me an *ABC*, will you? We will select something nearer at hand."

Rogers brought the required volume. George opened it at random and turned the pages with a rapid hand.

"Perth—too far away—Putney Bridge—too near at hand. Ramsgate? I think not. Reigate also leaves me cold. Why—what an extraordinary thing! There's actually a place called Rowland's Castle. Ever heard of it, Rogers?"

"I fancy, sir, that you go there from Waterloo."

"What an extraordinary fellow you are, Rogers. You know everything. Well, well, Rowland's Castle! I wonder what sort of a place it is."

"Not much of a place, I should say, sir."

"All the better; there'll be less competition. These quiet little country hamlets have a lot of the old feudal spirit knocking about. The last of the original Rowlands ought to meet with instant appreciation. I shouldn't wonder if they elected me mayor in a week."

He shut up the *ABC* with a bang.

"The die is cast. Pack me a small suitcase, will you, Rogers? Also my compliments to the cook, and will she oblige me with a loan of the cat. Dick Whittington, you know. When you set out to become a Lord Mayor, a cat is essential."

"I'm sorry, sir, but the cat is not available at the present moment."

"How is that?"

"A family of eight, sir. Arrived this morning."

"You don't say so. I thought its name was Peter."

"So it is, sir. A great surprise to all of us."

"A case of careless christening and the deceitful sex, eh? Well, well, I shall have to go catless. Pack up those things at once, will you?"

"Very good, sir."

Rogers withdrew, to reappear ten minutes later.

"Shall I call a taxi, sir?"

"Yes, please."

Rogers hesitated, then advanced a little farther into the room.

"You'll excuse the liberty, sir, but if I was you, I shouldn't take too much notice of anything Mr. Rowland said this morning. He was at one of those city dinners last night and—"

"Say no more," said George. "I understand."

"And being inclined to gout—"

"I know, I know. Rather a strenuous evening for you, Rogers, with two of us, eh? But I've set my heart on distinguishing myself at Rowland's Castle—the cradle of my historic race—that would go well in a speech, wouldn't it? A wire to me there, or a discreet advertisement in the morning papers, will recall me at any time if a fricassee of veal is in preparation. And now—to Waterloo!—as Wellington said on the eve of the historic battle."

Waterloo Station was not at its brightest and best that afternoon. Mr. Rowland eventually discovered a train that would take him to his destination, but it was an undistinguished train, an unimposing train—a train that nobody seemed anxious to travel by. Mr. Rowland had a first-class carriage to himself, up in the front of the train. A fog was descending in an indeterminate way over the metropolis, now it lifted, now it descended. The platform was deserted, and only the asthmatic breathing of the engine broke the silence.

And then, all of a sudden, things began to happen with bewildering rapidity.

A girl happened first. She wrenched open the door and jumped in, rousing Mr. Rowland from something perilously near a nap, exclaiming as she did so: "Oh! Hide me—oh! Please hide me."

George was essentially a man of action—his not to reason why, his but to do and die, etc. There is only one place to hide in a railway carriage—under the seat. In seven seconds the girl was bestowed there, and George's suitcase, negligently standing on end, covered her retreat. None too soon. An infuriated face appeared at the carriage window.

"My niece! You have her here. I want my niece."

George, a little breathless, was reclining in the corner, deep in the sporting column of the evening paper, one-thirty edition. He laid it aside with the air of a man recalling himself from far away.

"I beg your pardon, sir?" he said politely.

"My niece—what have you done with her?"

Acting on the policy that attack is always better than defense, George leaped into action.

"What the devil do you mean?" he cried, with a very creditable imitation of his own uncle's manner.

The other paused a minute, taken aback by this sudden fierceness. He was a fat man, still panting a little as though he had run some way. His hair was cut *en brosse,* and he had a mustache of the Hohenzollern persuasion. His accents were decidedly guttural, and the stiffness of his carriage denoted that he was more at home in uniform than out of it. George had the trueborn Briton's prejudice against foreigners—and an especial distaste for German-looking foreigners.

"What the devil do you mean, sir?" he repeated angrily.

"She came in here," said the other. "I saw her. What have you done with her?"

George flung aside the paper and thrust his head and shoulders through the window.

"So that's it, is it?" he roared. "Blackmail. But you've tried it on the wrong person. I read all about you in the *Daily Mail* this morning. Here, guard, guard!"

Already attracted from afar by the altercation, that functionary came hurrying up.

"Here, guard," said Mr. Rowland, with that air of authority which the lower classes so adore. "This fellow is annoying me. I'll give him in charge for attempted blackmail if necessary. Pretends I've got his niece hidden in here. There's a regular gang of these foreigners trying this sort of thing on. It ought to be stopped. Take him away, will you? Here's my care if you want it."

The guard looked from one to the other. His mind was soon made up. His training led him to despise foreigners and to respect and admire well-dressed gentlemen who traveled first-class.

He laid his hand on the shoulder of the intruder.

"Here," he said, "you come out of this."

At this crisis the stranger's English failed him, and he plunged into passionate profanity in his native tongue.

"That's enough of that," said the guard. "Stand away, will you? She's due out."

Flags were waved and whistles were blown. With an unwilling jerk the train drew out of the station.

George remained at his observation post until they were clear of the platform. Then he drew in his head, and picking up the suitcase tossed it into the rack.

"It's quite all right. You can come out," he said reassuringly.

The girl crawled out.

"Oh!" she gasped. "How can I thank you?"

"That's quite all right. It's been a pleasure, I assure you," returned George nonchalantly.

He smiled at her reassuringly. There was a slightly puzzled look in her eyes. She seemed to be missing something to which she was accustomed. At that moment, she caught sight of herself in the narrow glass opposite, and gave a heartfelt gasp.

Whether the carriage cleaners do, or do not, sweep under the seats every day is doubtful. Appearances were against their doing so, but it may be that every particle of dirt and smoke finds its way there like a homing bird. George had hardly had time to take in the girl's appearance, so sudden had been her arrival, and so brief the space of time before she crawled into hiding, but it was certainly a trim and well-dressed young woman who had disappeared under the seat. Now her little red hat was crushed and dented, and her face was disfigured with long streaks of dirt.

"Oh!" said the girl.

She fumbled for her bag. George, with the tact of a true gentleman, looked fixedly out of the window and admired the streets of London south of the Thames.

"How can I thank you?" said the girl again.

Taking this as a hint that conversation might now be resumed, George withdrew his gaze and made another polite disclaimer, but this time with a good deal of added warmth in his manner.

The girl was absolutely lovely! Never before, George told himself, had he seen such a lovely girl. The *empressement* of his manner became even more marked.

"I think it was simply splendid of you," said the girl with enthusiasm.

"Not at all. Easiest thing in the world. Only too pleased been of use," mumbled George.

"Splendid," she reiterated emphatically.

It is undoubtedly pleasant to have the loveliest girl you have ever seen gazing into your eyes and telling you how splendid you are. George enjoyed it as much as anyone would.

Then there came a rather difficult silence. It seemed to dawn upon the girl that further explanation might be expected. She flushed a little.

"The awkward part of it is," she said nervously, "that I'm afraid I can't explain."

She looked at him with a piteous air of uncertainty.

"You can't explain?"

"No."

"How perfectly splendid!" said Mr. Rowland with enthusiasm.

"I beg your pardon?"

"I said, 'How perfectly splendid.' Just like one of those books that keep you up all night. The heroine always says, 'I can't explain' in the first chapter. She explains in the last, of course, and there's never any real reason why she shouldn't have done so in the beginning—except that it would spoil the story. I can't tell you how pleased I am to be mixed up in a real mystery—I didn't know there were such things. I hope it's got something to do with secret documents of immense importance, and the Balkan express. I dote upon the Balkan express."

The girl stared at him with wide, suspicious eyes.

"What makes you say the Balkan express?" she asked sharply.

"I hope I haven't been indiscreet," George hastened to put in. "Your uncle traveled by it, perhaps."

"My uncle—" She paused, then began again, "My uncle—"

"Quite so," said George sympathetically. "I've got an uncle myself. Nobody should be held responsible for their uncles. Nature's little throwbacks—that's how I look at it."

The girl began to laugh suddenly. When she spoke, George was aware of the slight foreign inflection in her voice. At first he had taken her to be English.

"What a refreshing and unusual person you are, Mr.—"

"Rowland. George to my friends."

"My name is Elizabeth—"

She stopped abruptly.

"I like the name of Elizabeth," said George, to cover her momentary confusion. "They don't call you Bessie or anything horrible like that, I hope?"

She shook her head.

"Well," said George, "now that we know each other, we'd better get down to business. If you'll stand up, Elizabeth, I'll brush down the back of your coat."

She stood up obediently, and George was as good as his word.

"Thank you, Mr. Rowland."

"George. George to my friends, remember. And you can't come into my nice empty carriage, roll under the seat, induce me to tell lies to your uncle, and then refuse to be friends, can you?"

"Thank you, George."

"That's better."

"Do I look quite all right now?" asked Elizabeth, trying to see over her left shoulder.

"You look—oh! you look—you look all right," said George, curbing himself sternly.

"It was all so sudden, you see," explained the girl.

"It must have been."

"He saw us in the taxi, and then at the station I just bolted in here knowing he was close behind me. Where is this train going to, by the way?"

"Rowland's Castle," said George firmly.

The girl looked puzzled.

"Rowland's Castle?"

"Not at once, of course. Only after a good deal of stopping and slow going. But I confidently expect to be there before midnight. The old South-Western was a very reliable line—slow but sure—and I'm sure the Southern Railway is keeping up the old traditions."

"I don't know that I want to go to Rowland's Castle," said Elizabeth doubtfully.

"You hurt me. It's a delightful spot."

"Have you ever been there?"

"Not exactly. But there are lots of other places you can go to, if you don't fancy Rowland's Castle. There's Woking, and Weybridge, and Wimbledon. The train is sure to stop at one or other of them."

"I see," said the girl. "Yes, I can get out there, and perhaps motor back to London. That would be the best plan, I think."

Even as she spoke, the train began to slow up. Mr. Rowland gazed at her with appealing eyes.

"If I can do anything—"

"No, indeed. You've done a lot already."

There was a pause, then the girl broke out suddenly:

"I—I wish I could explain. I—"

"For heaven's sake, don't do that! It would spoil everything. But look here, isn't there anything that I could do? Carry the secret papers to Vienna—or something of that kind? There always are secret papers. Do give me a chance."

The train had stopped. Elizabeth jumped quickly out onto the platform. She turned and spoke to him through the window.

"Are you in earnest? Would you really do something for us—for me?"

"I'd do anything in the world for you, Elizabeth."

"Even if I could give you no reasons?"

"Rotten things, reasons!"

"Even if it were—dangerous?"

"The more danger, the better."

She hesitated a minute, then seemed to make up her mind.

"Lean out of the window. Look down the platform as though you weren't really looking." Mr. Rowland endeavored to comply with this somewhat difficult recommendation. "Do you see that man getting in—with a small dark beard—light overcoat? Follow him, see what he does and where he goes."

"Is that all?" asked Mr. Rowland. "What do I—"

She interrupted him.

"Further instructions will be sent to you. Watch him—and guard this." She thrust a small sealed packet into his hand. "Guard it with your life. It's the key to everything."

The train went on. Mr. Rowland remained staring out of the window, watching Elizabeth's tall, graceful figure threading its way down the platform. In his hand he clutched the small sealed packet.

The rest of his journey was both monotonous and uneventful. The train was a slow one. It stopped everywhere. At every station, George's head shot out of the window, in case his quarry should alight. Occasionally he strolled up and down the platform when the wait promised to be a long one, and reassured himself that the man was still there.

The eventual destination of the train was Portsmouth, and it was there that the black-bearded traveler alighted. He made his way to a small second-class hotel where he booked a room. Mr. Rowland also booked a room.

The rooms were in the same corridor, two doors from each other. The arrangement seemed satisfactory to George. He was a complete novice in the art of shadowing, but was anxious to acquit himself well, and justify Elizabeth's trust in him.

At dinner George was given a table not far from that of his quarry. The room was not full, and the majority of the diners George put down as commercial travelers, quiet respectable men who ate their food with appetite. Only one man attracted his special notice, a small man with ginger hair and mustache and a suggestion of horsiness in his apparel. He seemed to be interested in George also, and suggested a drink and a game of billiards when the meal had come to a close. But George had just espied the black-bearded man putting on his hat and overcoat, and declined politely. In another minute he was out in the street, gaining fresh insight into the difficult art of shadowing. The chase was a long and a weary one—and in the end it seemed to lead nowhere. After twisting and turning through the streets of Portsmouth for about four miles, the man returned to the hotel, George hard upon his heels. A faint doubt assailed the latter. Was it possible that the man was aware of his presence? As he debated this point, standing in the hall, the outer door was pushed open, and the little ginger man entered. Evidently he, too, had been out for a stroll.

George was suddenly aware that the beauteous damsel in the office was addressing him.

"Mr. Rowland, isn't it? Two gentlemen have called to see you. Two foreign gentlemen. They are in the little room at the end of the passage."

Somewhat astonished, George sought the room in question. Two men who were sitting there rose to their feet and bowed punctiliously.

"Mr. Rowland? I have no doubt, sir, that you can guess our identity."

George gazed from one to the other of them. The spokesman was the elder of the two, a gray-haired, pompous gentlemen who spoke excellent English. The other was a tall, somewhat pimply young man, with a blond Teutonic cast of countenance which was not rendered more attractive by the fierce scowl which he wore at the present moment.

Somewhat relieved to find that neither of his visitors was the old gentleman he had encountered at Waterloo, George assumed his most debonair manner.

"Pray sit down, gentlemen. I'm delighted to make your acquaintance. How about a drink?"

The elder man held up a protesting hand.

"Thank you, Lord Rowland—not for us. We have but a few brief moments—just time for you to answer one question."

"It's very kind of you to elect me to the peerage," said George. "I'm sorry you won't have a drink. And what is this momentous question?"

"Lord Rowland, you left London in company with a certain lady. You arrived here alone. Where is the lady?"

George rose to his feet.

"I fail to understand the question," he said coldly, speaking as much like the hero of a novel as he could. "I have the honor to wish you good evening, gentlemen."

"But you do understand it. You understand it perfectly," cried the younger man, breaking out suddenly. "What have you done with Alexa?"

"Be calm, sir," murmured the other. "I beg of you to be calm."

"I can assure you," said George, "that I know no lady of that name. There is some mistake."

The older man was eyeing him keenly.

"That can hardly be," he said dryly. "I took the liberty of examining the hotel register. You entered yourself as Mr. G. Rowland of Rowland's Castle."

George was forced to blush.

"A—a little joke of mine," he explained feebly.

"A somewhat poor subterfuge. Come, let us not beat about the bush. Where is Her Highness?"

"If you mean Elizabeth—"

With a howl of rage the young man flung himself forward again.

"Insolent pig-dog! To speak of her thus."

"I am referring," said the other slowly, "as you very well know, to the Grand Duchess Anastasia Sophia Alexandra Marie Helena Olga Elizabeth of Catonia."

"Oh!" said Mr. Rowland helplessly.

He tried to recall all that he had ever known of Catonia. It was, as far as he remembered, a small Balkan kingdom, and he seemed to remember something about a revolution having occurred there. He rallied himself with an effort.

"Evidently we mean the same person," he said cheerfully, "only *I* call her Elizabeth."

"You will give me satisfaction for that," snarled the younger man. "We will fight."

"Fight?"

"A duel."

"I never fight duels," said Mr. Rowland firmly.

"Why not?" demanded the other unpleasantly.

"I'm too afraid of getting hurt."

"Aha! Is that so? Then I will at least pull your nose for you."

The young man advanced fiercely. Exactly what happened was difficult to see, but he described a sudden semicircle in the air and fell to the ground with a heavy thud. He picked himself up in a dazed manner. Mr. Rowland was smiling pleasantly.

"As I was saying," he remarked, "I'm always afraid of getting hurt. That's why I thought it well to learn ju-jitsu."

There was a pause. The two foreigners looked doubtfully at this amiable-looking young man, as though they suddenly realized that some dangerous quality lurked behind the pleasant nonchalance of his manner. The young Teuton was white with passion.

"You will repent this," he hissed.

The older man retained his dignity.

"That is your last word, Lord Rowland? You refuse to tell us Her Highness's whereabouts?"

"I am unaware of them myself."

"You can hardly expect me to believe that."

"I am afraid you are of an unbelieving nature, sir."

The other merely shook his head, and murmuring: "This is not the end; you will hear from us again." The two men took their leave.

George passed his hand over his brow. Events were proceeding at a bewildering rate. He was evidently mixed up in a first-class European scandal.

"It might even mean another war," said George hopefully, as he hunted round to see what had become of the man with the black beard.

To his great relief, he discovered him sitting in a corner of the commercial room. George sat down in another corner. In about three minutes the black-bearded man got up and went up to bed. George followed and saw him go into his room and close the door. George heaved a sigh of relief.

"I need a night's rest," he murmured. "Need it badly."

Then a dire thought struck him. Supposing the black-bearded man had realized that George was on his trail? Supposing that he should slip away during the night while George himself was sleeping the sleep of the just? A few minutes' reflection suggested to Mr.

Rowland a way of dealing with this difficulty. He unravelled one of his socks till he got a good length of neutral-colored wool, then creeping quietly out of his room, he pasted one end of the wool to the farther side of the stranger's door with stamp paper, carrying the wool across it and along to his own room. There he hung the end with a small silver bell—a relic of last night's entertainment. He surveyed these arrangements with a good deal of satisfaction. Should the black-bearded man attempt to leave his room, George would be instantly warned by the ringing of the bell.

This matter disposed of, George lost no time in seeking his couch. The small packet he placed carefully under his pillow. As he did so, he fell into a momentary brown study. His thoughts could have been translated thus:

"Anastasia Sophia Marie Alexandra Olga Elizabeth. Hang it all, I've missed out one. I wonder now—"

He was unable to go to sleep immediately, being tantalized with his failure to grasp the situation. What was it all about? What was the connection between the escaping Grand Duchess, the sealed packet and the black-bearded man? What was the Grand Duchess escaping from? Were the two foreigners aware that the sealed packet was in his possession? What was it likely to contain?

Pondering these matters, with an irritated sense that he was no nearer their solution, Mr. Rowland fell asleep.

He was awakened by the faint jangle of a bell. Not one of those men who awake to instant action, it took him just a minute and a half to realize the situation. Then he jumped up, thrust on some slippers, and, opening the door with the utmost caution, slipped out into the corridor. A faint moving patch of shadow at the far end of the passage showed him the direction taken by his quarry. Moving as noiselessly as possible, Mr. Rowland followed the trail. He was just in time to see the black-bearded man disappear into a bathroom. That was puzzling, particularly so as there was a bathroom just opposite his own room. Moving up close to the door, which was ajar, George peered through the crack. The man was on his knees by the side of the bath, doing something to the skirting board immediately behind it. He remained there for about five minutes, then he rose to his feet, and

George beat a prudent retreat. Safe in the shadow of his own door, he watched the other pass and regain his own room.

"Good," said George to himself. "The mystery of the bathroom will be investigated tomorrow morning."

He got into bed and slipped his hand under the pillow to assure himself that the precious packet was still there. In another minute, he was scattering the bedclothes in a panic. The packet was gone!

It was a sadly chastened George who sat consuming eggs and bacon the following morning. He had failed Elizabeth. He had allowed the precious packet she had entrusted to his charge to be taken from him, and the "Mystery of the Bathroom" was miserably inadequate. Yes, undoubtedly George had made a mutt of himself.

After breakfast he strolled upstairs again. A chambermaid was standing in the passage looking perplexed.

"Anything wrong, my dear?" said George kindly.

"It's the gentleman here, sir. He asked to be called at half-past eight, and I can't get any answer and the door's locked."

"You don't say so," said George.

An uneasy feeling arose in his own breast. He hurried into his room. Whatever plans he was forming were instantly brushed aside by a most unexpected sight. There on the dressing table was the little packet which had been stolen from him the night before!

George picked it up and examined it. Yes, it was undoubtedly the same. But the seals had been broken. After a minute's hesitation, he unwrapped it. If other people had seen its contents, there was no reason why he should not see them also. Besides, it was possible that the contents had been abstracted. The unwound paper revealed a small cardboard box, such as jewelers use. George opened it. Inside, nestling on a bed of cotton wool, was a plain gold wedding ring.

He picked it up and examined it. There was no inscription inside—nothing whatever to mark it out from any other wedding ring. George dropped his head into his hands with a groan.

"Lunacy," he murmured. "That's what it is. Stark, staring lunacy. There's no sense anywhere."

Suddenly he remembered the chambermaid's statement, and at the same time he observed that there was a broad parapet outside the window. It was not a feat he would ordinarily have attempted, but he was so aflame with curiosity and anger that he was in the mood to make light of difficulties. He sprang upon the window sill. A few seconds later he was peering in at the window of the room occupied by the black-bearded man. The window was open and the room was empty. A little farther along was a fire escape. It was clear how the quarry had taken his departure.

George jumped in through the window. The missing man's effects were still scattered about. There might be some clue among them to shed light on George's perplexities. He began to hunt about, starting with the contents of a battered kit bag.

It was a sound that arrested his search—a very slight sound, but a sound indubitably in the room. George's glance leaped to the big wardrobe. He sprang up and wrenched open the door. As he did so, a man jumped out from it and went rolling over the floor locked in George's embrace. He was no mean antagonist. All George's special tricks availed very little. They fell apart at length in sheer exhaustion, and for the first time George saw who his adversary was. It was the little man with the ginger mustache!

"Who the devil are you?" demanded George.

For answer the other drew out a card and handed it to him. George read it aloud.

"Detective-Inspector Jarrold, Scotland Yard."

"That's right, sir. And you'd do well to tell me all you know about this business."

"I would, would I?" said George thoughtfully. "Do you know, inspector, I believe you're right. Shall we adjourn to a more cheerful spot?"

In a quiet corner of the bar George unfolded his soul. Inspector Jarrold listened sympathetically.

"Very puzzling, as you say, sir," he remarked when George had finished. "There's a lot as I can't make head or tail of myself, but there's one or two points I can clear up for you. I was here after Mardenberg (your black-bearded friend) and your turning up and watching him the way you did made me suspicious. I couldn't place you. I slipped into your room last night when you were out of it, and it was

I who sneaked the little packet from under your pillow. When I opened it and found it wasn't what I was after, I took the first opportunity of returning it to your room."

"That makes things a little clearer certainly," said George thoughtfully. "I seem to have made rather an ass of myself all through."

"I wouldn't say that, sir. You did uncommon well for a beginner. You say you visited the bathroom this morning and took away what was concealed behind the skirting board?"

"Yes. But it's only a rotten love letter," said George gloomily. "Dash it all, I didn't mean to go nosing out the poor fellow's private life."

"Would you mind letting me see it, sir?"

George took a folded letter from his pocket and passed it to the inspector. The latter unfolded it.

"As you say, sir. But I rather fancy that if you drew lines from one dotted *i* to another, you'd get a different result. Why, bless you, sir, this is a plan of the Portsmouth harbor defenses."

"What?"

"Yes. We've had our eye on the gentleman for some time. But he was too sharp for us. Got a woman to do most of the dirty work."

"A woman?" said George in a faint voice. "What was her name?"

"She goes by a good many, sir. Most usually known as Betty Brighteyes. A remarkably good-looking young woman she is."

"Betty—Brighteyes," said George. "Thank you, inspector."

"Excuse me, sir, but you're not looking well."

"I'm not well. I'm very ill. In fact, I think I'd better take the first train back to town."

The inspector looked at his watch.

"That will be a slow train, I'm afraid, sir. Better wait for the express."

"It doesn't matter," said George gloomily. "No train could be slower than the one I came down by yesterday."

Seated once more in a first-class carriage, George leisurely perused the day's news. Suddenly he sat bolt upright and stared at the sheet in front of him.

"A romantic wedding took place yesterday in London when Lord Roland Gaigh, second son of the Marquis of Axminster, was married to the Grand Duchess Anastasia of Catonia. The ceremony was kept a profound secret. The Grand Duchess has been living in Paris with her uncle since the upheaval in Catonia. She met Lord Roland when he was secretary to the British Embassy in Catonia and their attachment dates from that time."

"Well, I'm—"

Mr. Rowland could not think of anything strong enough to express his feelings. He continued to stare into space. The train stopped at a small station and a lady got in. She sat down opposite him.

"Good morning, George," she said sweetly.

"Good heavens!" cried George. "Elizabeth!"

She smiled at him. She was, if possible, lovelier than ever.

"Look here," cried George, clutching his head. "For God's sake tell me. Are you the Grand Duchess Anastasia, or are you Betty Brighteyes?"

She stared at him.

"I'm not either. I'm Elizabeth Gaigh. I can tell you all about it now. And I've got to apologize too. You see, Roland (that's my brother) has always been in love with Alexa—"

"Meaning the Grand Duchess?"

"Yes, that's what the family call her. Well, as I say, Roland was always in love with her, and she with him. And then the revolution came, and Alexa was in Paris, and they were just going to fix it up when old Stürm, the chancellor, came along and insisted on carrying off Alexa and forcing her to marry Prince Karl, her cousin, a horrid pimply person—"

"I fancy I've met him," said George.

"Whom she simply hates. And old Prince Osric, her uncle, forbade her to see Roland again. So she ran away to England, and I came up to town and met her, and we wired to Roland, who was in Scotland. And just at the very last minute, when we were driving to the Registry Office in a taxi, whom should we meet in another taxi face to face, but old Prince Osric. Of course he followed us, and we were at our wits' end what to do because he'd have made the most fearful scene, and, anyway, he is her guardian. Then I had the brilliant idea of changing places. You can practically see nothing of a girl nowadays but the tip of her nose. I put on Alexa's red hat and brown wrap coat, and she put on my gray. Then we told the taxi to go to Waterloo, and I skipped out there and hurried into the station. Old Osric followed the red hat all right, without a thought for the other occupant of the taxi sitting huddled up inside, but of course it wouldn't do for him to see my face. So I just bolted into your carriage and threw myself on your mercy."

"I've got that all right," said George. "It's the rest of it."

"I know. That's what I've got to apologize about. I hope you won't be awfully cross. You see, you looked so keen on its being a real mystery—like in books, that I really couldn't resist the temptation. I picked out a rather sinister-looking man on the platform and told you to follow him. And then I thrust the parcel on you."

"Containing a wedding ring."

"Yes. Alexa and I bought that, because Roland wasn't due to arrive from Scotland until just before the wedding. And of course I knew that by the time I got to London, they wouldn't want it—they would have had to use a curtain ring or something."

"I see," said George. "It's like all these things—so simple when you know! Allow me, Elizabeth."

He stripped off her left glove and uttered a sigh of relief at the sight of the bare third finger.

"That's all right," he remarked. "That ring won't be wasted after all."

"Oh!" cried Elizabeth. "But I don't know anything about you."

"You know how nice I am," said George. "By the way, it has just occurred to me, you are the Lady Elizabeth Gaigh, of course."

"Oh! George, are you a snob?"

"As a matter of fact, I am, rather. My best dream was one where King George borrowed half a crown from me to see him over the weekend. But I was thinking of my uncle—the one from whom I am estranged. He's a frightful snob. When he knows I'm going to marry you, and that we'll have a title in the family, he'll make me a partner at once!"

"Oh! George, is he very rich?"

"Elizabeth, are you mercenary?"

"Very. I adore spending money. But I was thinking of Father. Five daughters, full of beauty and blue blood. He's just yearning for a rich son-in-law."

"H'm," said George. "It will be one of those marriages made in heaven and approved on earth. Shall we live at Rowland's Castle? They'd be sure to make me Lord Mayor with you for a wife. Oh! Elizabeth, darling, it's probably contravening the company's bylaws, but I simply must kiss you!"

THE MANHOOD OF EDWARD ROBINSON

"With a swing of his mighty arms, Bill lifted her right off her feet, crushing her to his breast. With a deep sigh she yielded her lips in such a kiss as he had never dreamed of—"

With a sigh, Mr. Edward Robinson put down *When Love Is King* and stared out of the window of the underground train. They were running through Stamford Brook. Edward Robinson was thinking about Bill. Bill was the real hundred percent he-man beloved of lady novelists. Edward envied him his muscles, his rugged good looks, and his terrific passions. He picked up the book again and read the description of the proud Marchesa Bianca (she who had yielded her lips). So ravishing was her beauty, the intoxication of her was so great, that strong men went down before her like ninepins, faint and helpless with love.

"Of course," said Edward to himself, "it's all bosh, this sort of stuff. All bosh, it is. And yet, I wonder—"

His eyes looked wistful. Was there such a thing as a world of romance and adventure somewhere? Where there women whose beauty intoxicated? Was there such a thing as love that devoured one like a flame?

"This is real life, this is," said Edward. "I've got to go on the same just like all the other chaps."

On the whole, he supposed, he ought to consider himself a lucky young man. He had an excellent berth—a clerkship in a flourishing concern. He had good health, no one dependent upon him, and he was engaged to Maud.

But the mere thought of Maud brought a shadow over his face. Though he would never have admitted it, he was afraid of Maud. He loved her—yes—he still remembered the thrill with which he had admired the back of her white neck rising out of the cheap four and elevenpenny blouse on the first occasion they had met. He had sat behind her at the cinema, and the friend he was with had known her and had introduced them. No doubt about it, Maud was very superior. She was good-looking and clever and very ladylike, and she was always right about everything. The kind of girl, everyone said, who would make such an excellent wife.

Edward wondered whether the Marchesa Bianca would have made an excellent wife. Somehow, he doubted it. He couldn't picture the voluptuous Bianca, with her red lips and her swaying form, tamely sewing on buttons, say, for the virile Bill. No, Bianca was Romance, and this was real life. He and Maud would be very happy together. She had so much common sense . . .

But all the same, he wished that she wasn't quite so—well, sharp in manner. So prone to "jump upon him."

It was, of course, her prudence and her common sense which made her do so. Maud was very sensible. And, as a rule, Edward was very sensible too, but sometimes—He had wanted to get married this Christmas, for instance. Maud had pointed out how much more prudent it would be to wait a while—a year or two, perhaps. His salary was not large. He had wanted to give her an expensive ring—she had been horror-stricken, and had forced him to take it back and exchange it for a cheaper one. Her qualitites were all excellent qualitites, but sometimes Edward wished that she had more faults and less virtues. It was her virtues that drove him to desperate deeds.

For instance—

A blush of guilt overspread his face. He had got to tell her—and tell her soon. His secret guilt was already making him behave strangely. Tomorrow was the first of three days' holiday, Christmas Eve, Christmas Day and Boxing Day. She had suggested that he should come around and spend the day with her people, and in a clumsy, foolish manner, a manner that could not fail to arouse her suspicions, he had managed to get out of it—had told a long, lying story about a pal of his in the country with whom he had promised to spend the day.

And there was no pal in the country. There was only his guilty secret.

Three months ago, Edward Robinson, in company with a few hundred thousand other young men, had gone in for a competition in one of the weekly papers. Twelve girls' names had to be arranged in order of popularity. Edward had had a brilliant idea. His own preference was sure to be wrong—he had noticed that in several similar competitions. He wrote down the twelve names arranged in his own order of merit, then he wrote them down again, this time placing one from the top and one from the bottom of the list alternately.

When the result was announced, Edward had got eight right out of the twelve, and was awarded the first prize of £500. This result, which might easily be ascribed to luck, Edward persisted in regarding as the direct outcome of his "system." He was inordinately proud of himself.

The next thing was, what to do with the £500? He knew very well what Maud would say. Invest it. A nice little nest egg for the future. And, of course, Maud would be quite right, he knew that. But to win money as the result of a competition is an entirely different feeling from anything else in the world.

Had the money been left to him as a legacy, Edward would have invested it religiously in Conversion Loan or Savings Certificates as a matter of course. But money that one has achieved by a mere stroke of the pen, by a lucky and unbelievable chance, comes under the same heading as a child's sixpence—"for your very own—to spend as you like."

And in a certain rich shop which he passed daily on his way to the office, was the unbelievable dream, a small two-seater car, with a long shining nose, and the price clearly displayed on it—£465.

"If I were rich," Edward had said to it, day after day. "If I were rich, I'd have you."

And now he was—if not rich—at least possessed of a lump sum of money sufficient to realize his dream. That car, that shining, alluring piece of loveliness, was his if he cared to pay the price.

He had meant to tell Maud about the money. Once he had told her, he would have secured himself against temptation. In face of Maud's horror and disapproval, he would never have the courage to persist in his madness. But, as it chanced, it was Maud herself who clinched the matter. He had taken her to the cinema—and to the best seats in the house. She had pointed out to him, kindly but firmly, the criminal folly of his behavior—wasting good money—three and sixpence against two and four-pence, when one saw just as well from the latter places.

Edward took her reproaches in sullen silence. Maud felt contentedly that she was making an impression. Edward could not be allowed to continue in these extravagant ways. She loved Edward, but she realized that he was weak—hers the task of being ever at hand to influence him in the way he should go. She observed his wormlike demeanor with satisfaction.

Edward was indeed wormlike. Like worms, he turned. He remained crushed by her words, but it was at that precise minute that he made up his mind to buy the car.

"Damn it," said Edward to himself. "For once in my life, I'll do what I like. Maud can go hang!"

And the very next morning he had walked into that palace of plate glass, with its lordly inmates in their glory of gleaming enamel and shimmering metal, and with an insouciance that surprised himself, he bought the car. It was the easiest thing in the world, buying a car!

It had been his for four days now. He had gone about, outwardly calm, but inwardly bathed in ecstasy. And to Maud he had as yet breathed no word. For four days, in his luncheon hour, he had received instruction in the handling of the lovely creature. He was an apt pupil.

Tomorrow, Christmas Eve, he was to take her out into the country. He had lied to Maud, and he would lie again if need be. He was enslaved body and soul by his new possession. It stood to him for Romance, for Adventure, for all the things that he had longed for and had never had. Tomorrow, he and his mistress would take the road together. They would rush through the keen cold air, leaving the throb and fret of London far behind them—out into the wide, clear spaces . . .

At this moment, Edward, though he did not know it, was very near to being a poet.

Tomorrow—

He looked down at the book in his hand—*When Love Is King*. He laughed and stuffed it into his pocket. The car, and the red lips of the Marchesa Bianca, and the amazing prowess of Bill seemed all mixed up together. Tomorrow—

The weather, usually a sorry jade to those who count upon her, was kindly disposed toward Edward. She gave him the day of his dreams, a day of glittering frost, and pale-blue sky, and a primrose-yellow sun.

So, in a mood of high adventure, of daredevil wickedness, Edward drove out of London. There was trouble at Hyde Park Corner, and a sad *contretemps* at Putney Bridge, there was much protesting of gears, and a frequent jarring of brakes, and much abuse was freely showered upon Edward by the drivers of other vehicles. But for a novice he did not acquit himself so badly, and presently he came out onto one of those fair, wide roads that are the joy of the motorist. There was little congestion on this particular road today. Edward drove on and on, drunk with his mastery over this creature of the gleaming sides, speeding through the cold white world with the elation of a god.

It was a delirious day. He stopped for lunch at an old-fashioned inn, and again later for tea. Then reluctantly he turned homewards—back again to London, to Maud, to the inevitable explanation, recriminations . . .

He shook off the thought with a sigh. Let tomorrow look after itself. He still had today. And what could be more fascinating than this? Rushing through the darkness with the headlights searching out the way in front. Why, this was the best of all!

He judged that he had no time to stop anywhere for dinner. This driving through the darkness was a ticklish business. It was going to take longer to get back to London than he had thought. It was just eight o'clock when he passed through Hindhead and came out upon the rim of the Devil's Punch Bowl. There was moonlight, and the snow that had fallen two days ago was still unmelted.

He stopped the car and stood staring. What did it matter if he didn't get back to London until midnight? What did it matter if he never got back? He wasn't going to tear himself away from this all at once.

He got out of the car and approached the edge. There was a path winding down temptingly near him. Edward yielded to the spell. For the next half-hour he wandered deliriously in a snowbound world. Never had he imagined anything quite like this. And it was his, his very own, given to him by his shining mistress who waited for him faithfully on the road above.

He climbed up again, got into the car and drove off, still a little dizzy from that discovery of sheer beauty which comes to the most prosaic men once in a while.

Then, with a sigh, he came to himself, and thrust his hand into the pocket of the car where he had stuffed an additional muffler earlier in the day.

But the muffler was no longer there. The pocket was empty. No, not completely empty—there was something scratchy and hard—like pebbles.

Edward thrust his hand deep down. In another minute he was staring like a man bereft of his senses. The object that he held in his hand, dangling from his fingers, with the moonlight striking a hundred fires from it, was a diamond necklace.

Edward stared and stared. But there was no doubting possible. A diamond necklace worth probably thousands of pounds (for the stones were large ones) had been casually reposing in the side pocket of the car.

But who had put it there? It had certainly not been there when he started from town. Someone must have come along when he was walking about in the snow and deliberately thrust it in. But why? Why choose *his* car? Had the owner of the necklace made a mistake? Or was it—could it possibly be—a *stolen* necklace?

And then, as all these thoughts went whirling through his brain, Edward suddenly stiffened and went cold all over. *This was not his car.*

It was very like it, yes. It was the same brilliant shade of scarlet—red as the Marchesa Bianca's lips—it had the same long and gleaming nose, but by a thousand small signs, Edward realized that it was not his car. Its shining newness was scarred here and there, it bore signs, faint but unmistakable, of wear and tear. In that case . . .

Edward, without more ado, made haste to turn the car. Turning was not his strong point. With the gear in reverse, he invariably lost his head and twisted the wheel the wrong way. Also, he frequently became entangled between the accelerator and the foot brake with disastrous results. In the end, however, he succeeded, and straightaway the car began purring up the hill again.

Edward remembered that there had been another car standing some little distance away. He had not noticed it particularly at the time. He had returned from his walk by a different path from that by which he had gone down into the hollow. This second path had brought him out on the road immediately behind, as he had thought, his own car. It must really have been the other one.

In about ten minutes he was once more at the spot where he had halted. But there was now no car at all by the roadside. Whoever had owned this car must now have gone off in Edward's—he also, perhaps, misled by the resemblance.

Edward took out the diamond necklace from his pocket and let it run through his fingers perplexedly.

What to do next? Run on to the nearest police station? Explain the circumstances, hand over the necklace, and give the number of his own car.

By the by, what was the number of his car? Edward thought and thought, but for the life of him he couldn't remember. He felt a cold sinking sensation. He was going to look the most utter fool at the police station. There was an eight in it, that was all that he could remember. Of course, it didn't really matter—at least . . . He looked uncomfortably at the diamonds. Supposing they should think—oh, but they wouldn't—and yet again they might—that he had stolen the car and the diamonds? Because, after all, when one came to think of it, would anyone in their senses thrust a valuable diamond necklace carelessly into the open pocket of a car?

Edward got out and went round to the back of the motor. Its number was XRI0061. Beyond the fact that that was certainly not the number of his car, it conveyed nothing to him. Then he set to work systematically to search all the pockets. In the one where he had found the diamonds he made a discovery—a small scrap of paper with some words pencilled on it. By the light of the headlights, Edward read them easily enough.

"Meet me, Greane, corner of Salter's Lance, ten o'clock."

He remembered the name Greane. He had seen it on a signpost earlier in the day. In a minute, his mind was made up. He would go to this village, Greane, find Salter's Lane, meet the person who had written the note, and explain the circumstances. That would be much better than looking a fool in the local police station.

He started off almost happily. After all, this was an adventure. This was the sort of thing that didn't happen every day. The diamond necklace made it exciting and mysterious.

He had some little difficulty in finding Greane, and still more difficulty in finding Salter's Lane, but after calling at two cottages, he succeeded.

Still, it was a few minutes after the appointed hour when he drove cautiously along a narrow road, keeping a sharp lookout on the left-hand side, where he had been told Salter's Lane branched off.

He came upon it quite suddenly round a bend, and even as he drew up, a figure came forward out of the darkness.

"At last!" a girl's voice cried. "What an age you've been, Gerald!"

As she spoke, the girl stepped right into the glare of the headlights, and Edward caught his breath. She was the most glorious creature he had ever seen.

She was quite young, with hair black as night, and wonderful scarlet lips. The heavy cloak that she wore swung open, and Edward saw that she was in full evening dress—a kind of flame-colored sheath, outlining her perfect body. Round her neck was a row of exquisite pearls.

Suddenly the girl started.

"Why," she cried; "it isn't Gerald."

"No," said Edward hastily. "I must explain." He took the diamond necklace from his pocket and held it out to her. "My name is Edward—"

He got no further, for the girl clapped her hands and broke in:

"Edward, of course! I am so glad. But that idiot Jimmy told me over the phone that he was sending Gerald along with the car. It's awfully sporting of you to come. I've been dying to meet you. Remember I haven't seen you since I was six years old. I see you've got the necklace all right. Shove it in your pocket again. The village policeman might come along and see it. Brrr, it's cold as ice waiting here! Let me get in."

As though in a dream Edward opened the door, and she sprang lightly in beside him. Her furs swept his cheek, and an elusive scent, like that of violets after rain, assailed his nostrils.

He had no plan, no definite thought even. In a minute, without conscious volition, he had yielded himself to the adventure. She had called him Edward—what matter if he were the wrong Edward? She would find him out soon enough. In the meantime, let the game go on. He let in the clutch and they glided off.

Presently the girl laughed. Her laugh was just as wonderful as the rest of her.

"It's easy to see you don't know much about cars. I suppose they don't have them out there?"

"I wonder where 'out there' is?" thought Edward. Aloud he said, "Not much."

"Better let me drive," said the girl. "It's tricky work finding your way round these lanes until we get on the main road again."

He relinquished his place to her gladly. Presently they were humming through the night at a pace and with a recklessness that secretly appalled Edward. She turned her head toward him.

"I like pace. Do you? You know—you're not a bit like Gerald. No one would ever take you to be brothers. You're not a bit like what I imagined, either."

"I suppose," said Edward, "that I'm so completely ordinary. Is that it?"

"Not ordinary—different. I can't make you out. How's poor old Jimmy? Very fed-up, I suppose?"

"Oh, Jimmy's all right," said Edward.

"It's easy enough to say that—but it's rough luck on him having a sprained ankle. Did he tell you the whole story?"

"Not a word. I'm completely in the dark. I wish you'd enlighten me."

"Oh, the thing worked like a dream. Jimmy went in at the front door, togged up in his girl's clothes. I gave him a minute or two, and then skinned up to the window. Agnes Larella's maid was there laying out Agnes's dress and jewels, and all the rest. Then there was a great yell downstairs, and the squib went off, and everyone shouted fire. The maid dashed out, and I hopped in, helped myself to the necklace, and was out and down in a flash, and out of the place the back way across the Punch Bowl. I shoved the necklace and the notice where to pick me up in the pocket of the car in passing. Then I joined Louise at the hotel, having shed my snow boots, of course. Perfect alibi for me. She'd no idea I'd been out at all."

"And what about Jimmy?"

"Well, you know more about that than I do."

"Well, in the general rag, he caught his foot in his skirt and managed to sprain it. They had to carry him to the car, and the Larellas' chauffeur drove him home. Just fancy if the chauffeur had happened to put his hand in the pocket!"

Edward laughed with her, but his mind was busy. He understood the position more or less now. The name of Larella was vaguely familiar to him—it was a name that spelled wealth. This girl, and an unknown man called Jimmy, had conspired together to steal the necklace, and had succeeded. Owing to his sprained ankle and the presence of the Larellas' chauffeur, Jimmy had not been able to look in the pocket of the car before telephoning to the girl—probably had had no wish to do so. But it was almost certain that the other unknown "Gerald" would do so at any early opportunity. And in it, he would find Edward's muffler!

"Good going," said the girl.

A tram flashed past them, they were on the outskirts of London. They flashed in and out of the traffic. Edward's heart stood in his mouth. She was a wonderful driver, this girl, but she took risks!

Quarter of an hour later they drew up before an imposing house in a frigid square.

"We can shed some of our clothing here," said the girl, "before we go on to Ritson's."

"Ritson's?" queried Edward. He mentioned the famous nightclub almost reverently.

"Yes, didn't Gerald tell you?"

"He did not," said Edward grimly. "What about my clothes?"

She frowned.

"Didn't they tell you *anything*? We'll rig you up somehow. We've got to carry this through."

A stately butler opened the door and stood aside to let them enter.

"Mr. Gerald Champneys rang up, your ladyship. He was very anxious to speak to you, but he wouldn't leave a message."

"I bet he was anxious to speak to her," said Edward to himself. "At any rate, I know my full name now. Edward Champneys. But who is she? Your ladyship, they called her. What does she want to steal a necklace for? Bridge debts?"

In the magazine stories which he occasionally read, the beautiful and titled heroine was always driven desperate by bridge debts.

Edward was led away by the stately butler and delivered over to a smooth-mannered valet. A quarter of an hour later he rejoined his hostess in the hall, exquisitely attired in evening clothes made in Savile Row which fitted him to a nicety.

Heavens! What a night!

They drove in the car to the famous Ritson's. It common with everyone else, Edward had read scandalous paragraphs concerning Ritson's. Anyone who was anyone turned up at Ritson's sooner or later. Edward's only fear was that someone who knew the real Edward Champneys might turn up. He consoled himself by the reflection that the real man had evidently been out of England for some years.

Sitting at a little table against the wall, they sipped cocktails. Cocktails! To the simple Edward they represented the quintessence of the fast life. The girl, wrapped in a wonderful embroidered shawl, sipped nonchalantly. Suddenly she dropped the shawl from her shoulders and rose.

"Let's dance."

Now the one thing that Edward could do to perfection was to dance. When he and Maud took the floor together at the Palais de Danse, lesser lights stood still and watched in admiration.

"I nearly forgot," said the girl suddenly. "The necklace?"

She held out her hand. Edward, completely bewildered, drew it from his pocket and gave it to her. To his utter amazement, she coolly clasped it round her neck. Then she smiled up at him intoxicatingly.

"Now," she said softly, "we'll dance."

They danced. And in all Ritson's nothing more perfect could be seen.

Then, as at length they returned to their table, an old gentleman with a would-be rakish air accosted Edward's companion.

"Ah! Lady Noreen, always dancing! Yes, yes. Is Captain Folliot here tonight?"

"Jimmy's taken a toss—racked his ankle."

"You don't say so? How did that happen?"

"No details as yet."

She laughed and passed on.

Edward followed, his brain in a whirl. He knew now. Lady Noreen Elliot, the famous Lady Noreen herself, perhaps the most talked-of girl in England. Celebrated for her beauty, for her daring—the leader of that set known as the Bright Young People. Her engagement to Captain James Folliot, V.C., of the Household Cavalry, had been recently announced.

But the necklace? He still couldn't understand the necklace. He must risk giving himself away, but know he must.

As they sat down again, he pointed to it.

"Why that, Noreen?" he said. "Tell me why?"

She smiled dreamily, her eyes far away, the spell of the dance still holding her.

"It's difficult for you to understand, I suppose. One gets so tired to the same thing—always the same thing. Treasure hunts were all very well for a while, but one gets used to everything. 'Burglaries' were my idea. Fifty pounds' entrance fee, and lots to be drawn. This is the third. Jimmy and I drew Agnes Larella. You know the rules? Burglary to be carried out within three days and the loot to be worn for at least an hour in a public place, or you forfeit your stake and a hundred-pound fine. It's rough luck on Jimmy spraining his ankle, but we'll scoop the pool all right."

"I see," said Edward, drawing a deep breath. "I see."

Noreen rose suddenly, pulling her shawl round her.

"Drive me somewhere in the car. Down to the docks. Somewhere horrible and exciting. Wait a minute—" She reached up and unclasped the diamonds from her neck. "You'd better take these again. I don't want to be murdered for them."

They went out of Ritson's together. The car stood in a small by-street, narrow and dark. As they turned the corner toward it, another car drew up to the curb, and a young man sprang out.

"Thank the Lord, Noreen, I've got hold of you at last," he cried. "There's the devil to pay. That ass Jimmy got off with the wrong car. God knows where those diamonds are at this minute. We're in the devil of a mess."

Lady Noreen stared at him.

"What do you mean? We've got the diamonds—at least Edward has."

"Edward?"

"Yes." She might a slight gesture to indicate the figure by her side.

"It's I who am in the devil of a mess," thought Edward. "Ten to one this is brother Gerald."

The young man stared at him.

"What do you mean?" he said slowly. "Edward's in Scotland."

"Oh!" cried the girl. She stared at Edward. "Oh!"

Her color came and went.

"So you," she said in a low voice, "are the real thing?"

It took Edward just one minute to grasp the situation. There was awe in the girl's eyes—was it, could it be—admiration? Should he explain? Nothing so tame! He would play up to the end.

He bowed ceremoniously.

"I have to thank you, Lady Noreen," he said in the best highwayman manner, "for a most delightful evening."

One quick look he cast at the car from which the other had just alighted. A scarlet car with a shining bonnet. His car!

"And I will wish you good evening."

One quick spring and he was inside, his foot on the clutch. The car started forward. Gerald stood paralyzed, but the girl was quicker. As the car slid past, she leaped for it, alighting on the running board.

The car swerved, shot blindly round the corner and pulled up. Noreen, still panting from her spring, laid her hand on Edward's arm.

"You must give it me—oh, you must give it me. I've got to return it to Agnes Larella. Be a sport—we've had a good evening together—we've danced—we've been—pals. Won't you give it to me? To *me?*"

A woman who intoxicated you with her beauty. There were such women then . . .

Also, Edward was only too anxious to get rid of the necklace. It was a heaven-sent opportunity for a *beau geste*.

He took it from his pocket and dropped it into her outstretched hand.

"We've been—pals," he said.

"Ah!" Her eyes smoldered—lit up.

Then surprisingly she bent her head to him. For a moment he held her, her lips against his . . .

Then she jumped off. The scarlet car sped forward with a great leap.

Romance!

Adventure!

* * *

AT TWELVE O'CLOCK on Christmas Day, Edward Robinson strode into the tiny drawing room of a house in Clapham, with the customary greeting of "Merry Christmas."

Maud, who was rearranging a piece of holly, greeted him coldly.

"Have a good day in the country with that friend of yours?" she inquired.

"Look here," said Edward. "That was a lie I told you. I won a competition—£500, and I bought a car with it. I didn't tell you because I knew you'd kick up a row about it. That's the first thing. I've bought the car and there's nothing more to be said about it. The second thing is this—I'm not going to hang about for years. My prospects are quite good enough and I mean to marry you next month. See?"

"Oh!" said Maud faintly.

Was this—could this be—*Edward* speaking in this masterful fashion?

"Will you?" said Edward. "Yes or no?"

She gazed at him, fascinated. There was awe and admiration in her eyes, and the sight of that look was intoxicating to Edward. Gone was that patient motherliness which had roused him to exasperation.

So had the Lady Noreen looked at him last night. But the Lady Noreen had receded far away, right into the region of Romance, side by side with the Marchesa Bianca. This was the Real Thing. This was his woman.

"Yes or no?" he repeated, and drew a step nearer.

"Ye—ye-es," faltered Maud. "But, oh, Edward, what has happened to you? You're quite different today."

"Yes," said Edward. "For twenty-four hours I've been a man instead of a worm—and, by God, it pays!"

He caught her in his arms almost as Bill the superman might have done.

"Do you love me, Maud? Tell me, do you love me?"

"Oh, Edward!" breathed Maud. "I adore you. . . ."

JANE IN SEARCH OF A JOB

Jane Cleveland rustled the pages of the *Daily Leader* and sighed—a deep sigh that came from the innermost recesses of her being. She looked with distaste at the marble-topped table, the poached egg on toast which reposed on it, and the small pot of tea. Not because she was not hungry. That was far from being the case. Jane was extremely hungry. At that moment she felt like consuming a pound and a half of well-cooked beefsteak, with chip potatoes, and possibly French beans. The whole washed down with some more exciting vintage than tea.

But young women whose exchequers are in a parlous condition cannot be choosers. Jane was lucky to be able to order a poached egg and a pot of tea. It seemed unlikely that she would be able to do so tomorrow. That is unless—

She turned once more to the advertisement columns of the *Daily Leader*. To put it plainly, Jane was out of a job, and the position was becoming acute. Already the genteel lady who presided over the shabby boarding house was looking askance at this particular young woman.

"And yet," said Jane to herself, throwing up her chin indignantly, which was a habit of hers, "and yet I'm intelligent and good-looking and well-educated. What more does anyone want?"

According to the *Daily Leader,* they seemed to want shorthand-typists of vast experience, managers for business houses with a little capital to invest, ladies to share in the profits of poultry farming (here again a little capital was required), and innumerable cooks, house-maids and parlormaids—particularly parlormaids.

"I wouldn't mind being a parlormaid," said Jane to herself. "But there again, no one would take me without experience. I could go somewhere, I dare say, as a Willing Young Girl—but they don't pay willing young girls anything to speak of."

She sighed again, propped the paper up in front of her, and attacked the poached egg with all the vigor of healthy youth.

When the last mouthful had been despatched, she turned the paper and studied the Agony and Personal column while she drank her tea. The Agony column was always the last hope.

Had she but possessed a couple of thousand pounds, the thing would have been easy enough. There were at least seven unique opportunities—all yielding not less than three thousand a year. Jane's lip curled a little.

"If I had two thousand pounds," she murmured, "it wouldn't be easy to separate from it."

She cast her eyes rapidly down to the bottom of the column and ascended with the ease born of long practice.

There was the lady who gave such wonderful prices for castoff clothing. "Ladies' wardrobes inspected at their own dwellings." There were the gentlemen who bought ANYTHING—but principally TEETH. There were ladies of title going abroad who would dispose of their furs at a ridiculous figure. There was the distressed clergyman and the hardworking widow, and the disabled officer, all needing sums varying from fifty pounds to two thousand. And then suddenly Jane came to an abrupt halt. She put down her teacup and read the advertisement through again.

"There's a catch in it, of course," she murmured. "There always is a catch in these sort of things. I shall have to be careful. But still—"

The advertisement which so intrigued Jane Cleveland ran as follows:

> If a young lady of twenty-five to thirty years of age, eyes dark blue, very fair hair, black lashes and brows, straight nose, slim figure, height five feet seven inches, good mimic and able to speak French, will call at 7 Endersleigh Street, between 5 and 6 P.M., she will hear of something to her advantage.

"Guileless Gwendolen, or why girls go wrong," murmured Jane. "I shall certainly have to be careful. But there are too many specifications, really, for that sort of thing. I wonder now . . . Let us overhaul the catalog."

She proceeded to do so.

"Twenty-five to thirty—I'm twenty-six. Eyes dark blue, that's right. Hair very fair—black lashes and brows—all O.K. Straight nose? Ye-es—straight enough, anyway. It doesn't hook or turn up. And I've got a slim figure—slim even for nowadays. I'm only five feet six inches—but I could wear high heels. I am a good mimic—nothing wonderful, but I can copy people's voices, and I speak French like an angel or a Frenchwoman. In fact, I'm absolutely the goods. They ought to tumble over themselves with delight when I turn up. Jane Cleveland, go in and win."

Resolutely Jane tore out the advertisement and placed it in her handbag. Then she demanded her bill, with a new briskness in her voice.

At ten minutes to five Jane was reconnoitering in the neighborhood of Endersleigh Street. Endersleigh Street itself is a small street sandwiched between two larger streets in the neighborhood of Oxford Circus. It is drab, but respectable.

No. 7 seemed in no way different from the neighboring houses. It was composed like they were of offices. But looking up at it, it dawned upon Jane for the first time that she was not the only blue-eyed, fair-haired, straight-nosed, slim-figured girl of between twenty-five and thirty years of age. London was evidently full of such girls, and forty or fifty of them at least were grouped outside No. 7 Endersleigh Street.

"Competition," said Jane. "I'd better join the queue quickly."

She did so, just as three more girls turned the corner of the street. Others followed them. Jane amused herself by taking stock of her immediate neighbors. In each case she managed to find something wrong—fair eyelashes instead of dark, eyes more gray than blue, fair hair that owed its fairness to art and not to nature, interesting variations in noses, and figures that only an all-embracing charity could have described as slim. Jane's spirits rose.

"I believe I've got as good an all-around chance as anyone," she murmured to herself. "I wonder what it's all about? A beauty chorus, I hope."

The queue was moving slowly but steadily forward. Presently a second stream of girls began, issuing from inside the house. Some of them tossed their heads, some of them smirked.

"Rejected," said Jane with glee. "I hope to goodness they won't be full up before I get in."

And still the queue of girls moved forward. There were anxious glances in tiny mirrors, and a frenzied powdering of noses. Lipsticks were brandished freely.

"I wish I had a smarter hat," said Jane to herself sadly.

At last it was her turn. Inside the door of the house was a glass door at one side, with the legend Messrs. Cuthbertsons inscribed on it. It was through this glass door that the applicants were passing one by one. Jane's turn came. She drew a deep breath and entered.

Inside was an outer office, obviously intended for clerks. At the end was another glass door. Jane was directed to pass through this, and did so. She found herself in a smaller room. There was a big desk in it, and behind the desk was a keen-eyed man of middle age with a thick, rather foreign-looking mustache. His glance swept over Jane, then he pointed to a door on the left.

"Wait in there, please," he said crisply.

Jane obeyed. The apartment she entered was already occupied. Five girls sat there, all very upright and all glaring at each other. It was clear to Jane that she had been included among the likely candidates, and her spirits rose. Nevertheless, she was forced to admit that these five girls were equally eligible with herself as far as the terms of the advertisement went.

The time passed. Streams of girls were evidently passing through the inner office. Most of them were dismissed through another door giving on the corridor, but every now and then a recruit arrived to swell the select assembly. At half past six there were fourteen girls assembled there.

Jane heard a murmur of voices from the inner office, and then the foreign-looking gentleman, whom she had nicknamed in her mind "the Colonel" owing to the military character of his mustaches, appeared in the doorway.

"I will see you ladies one at a time, if you please," he announced. "In the order in which you arrived, please."

Jane was, of course, the sixth on the list. Twenty minutes elapsed before she was called in. "The Colonel" was standing with his hands behind his back. He put her through a rapid catechism, tested her knowledge of French, and measured her height.

"It is possible, mademoiselle," he said in French, "that you may suit. I do not know. But it is possible."

"What is this post, may I ask?" said Jane bluntly.

He shrugged his shoulders.

"That I cannot tell you as yet. If you are chosen—then you shall know."

"This seems very mysterious," objected Jane. "I couldn't possibly take up anything without knowing all about it. Is it connected with the stage, may I ask?"

"The stage? Indeed, no."

"Oh!" said Jane, rather taken aback.

He was looking at her keenly.

"You have intelligence, yes? And discretion?"

"I've quantities of intelligence and discretion," said Jane calmly. "What about the pay?"

"The pay will amount to two thousand pounds—for a fortnight's work."

"Oh!" said Jane faintly.

She was too taken aback by the munificence of the sum named to recover all at once.

The Colonel resumed speaking.

"One other young lady I have already selected. You and she are equally suitable. There may be others I have not yet seen. I will give you instructions as to your further proceedings. You know Harridge's Hotel?"

Jane gasped. Who in England did not know Harridge's Hotel, that famous hostelry situated modestly in a bystreet of Mayfair, where notabilities and royalties arrived and departed as a matter of course? Only this morning Jane had read of the arrival of the Grand Duchess Pauline of Ostrova. She had come over to open a big bazaar in aid of Russian refugees, and was, of course, staying at Harridge's.

"Yes," said Jane, in answer to the Colonel's question.

"Very good. Go there. Ask for Count Streptitch. Send up your card—you have a card?"

Jane produced one. The Colonel took it from her and inscribed in the corner a minute P. He handed the card back to her.

"That ensures that the count will see you. He will understand that you come from me. The final decision lies with him—and another. If he considers you suitable, he will explain matters to you, and you can accept or decline his proposal. Is that satisfactory?"

"Perfectly satisfactory," said Jane.

"So far," she murmured to herself as she emerged into the street, "I can't see the catch. And yet, there must be one. There's no such thing as money for nothing. It must be crime! There's nothing else left."

Her spirits rose. In moderation Jane did not object to crime. The papers had been full lately of the exploits of various girl bandits. Jane had seriously thought of becoming one if all else failed.

She entered the exclusive portals of Harridge's with slight trepidation. More than ever, she wished that she had a new hat.

But she walked bravely up to the bureau and produced her card and asked for Count Streptitch without a shade of hesitation in her manner. She fancied that the clerk looked at her rather curiously. He took the card, however, and gave it to a small page boy with some low-voiced instructions which Jane did not catch. Presently the page returned, and Jane was invited to accompany him. They went up in the lift and along a corridor to some big double doors where the page knocked. A moment later Jane found herself in a big room, facing a tall thin man with a fair beard, who was holding her card in a languid white hand.

"Miss Jane Cleveland," he read slowly. "I am Count Streptitch."

His lips parted suddenly in what was presumably intended to be a smile, disclosing two rows of white even teeth. But no effect of merriment was obtained.

"I understand that you applied in answer to our advertisement," continued the count. "The good Colonel Kranin sent you on here."

"He *was* a colonel," thought Jane, pleased with her perspicacity, but she merely bowed her head.

"You will pardon me if I ask you a few questions?"

He did not wait for a reply, but proceeded to put Jane through a catechism very similar to that of Colonel Kranin. Her replies seemed to satisfy him. He nodded his head once or twice.

"I will ask you now, mademoiselle, to walk to the door and back again slowly."

"Perhaps they want me to be a mannequin," thought Jane, as she complied. "But they wouldn't pay two thousand pounds to a mannequin. Still, I suppose I'd better not ask questions yet awhile."

Count Streptitch was frowning. He tapped on the table with his white fingers. Suddenly he rose, and opening the door of an adjoining room, he spoke to someone inside.

He returned to his seat, and a short middle-aged lady came through the door, closing it behind her. She was plump and extremely ugly, but had nevertheless the air of being a person of importance.

"Well, Anna Michaelovna," said the count. "What do you think of her?"

The lady looked Jane up and down much as though the girl had been a waxwork at a show. She made no pretense of any greeting.

"She might do," she said at length. "Of actual likeness in the real sense of the word, there is very little. But the figure and the coloring are very good, better than any of the others. What do you think of it, Feodor Alexandrovitch?"

"I agree with you, Anna Michaelovna."

"Does she speak French?"

"Her French is excellent."

Jane felt more and more of a dummy. Neither of these strange people appeared to remember that she was a human being.

"But will she be discreet?" asked the lady, frowning heavily at the girl.

"This is the Princess Poporensky," said Count Streptitch to Jane in French. "She asks whether you can be discreet?"

Jane addressed her reply to the princess.

"Until I have had the position explained to me, I can hardly make promises."

"It is just what she says there, the little one," remarked the lady. "I think she is intelligent, Feodor Alexandrovitch—more intelligent than the others. Tell me, little one, have you also courage?"

"I don't know," said Jane, puzzled. "I don't particularly like being hurt, but I can bear it."

"Ah! That is not what I mean. You do not mind danger, no?"

"Oh!" said Jane. "Danger! That's all right. I like danger."

"And you are poor? You would like to earn much money?"

"Try me," said Jane with something approaching enthusiasm.

Count Streptitch and Princess Poporensky exchanged glances. Then, simultaneously, they nodded.

"Shall I explain matters, Anna Michaelovna?" the former asked.

The princess shook her head.

"Her Highness wishes to do that herself."

"It is unnecessary—and unwise."

"Nevertheless those are her commands. I was to bring the girl in as soon as you had done with her."

Streptitch shrugged his shoulders. Clearly he was not pleased. Equally clearly he had no intention of disobeying the edict. He turned to Jane.

"The Princess Poporensky will present you to Her Highness the Grand Duchess Pauline. Do not be alarmed."

Jane was not in the least alarmed. She was delighted at the idea of being presented to a real live grand duchess. There was nothing of the Socialist about Jane. For the moment she had even ceased to worry about her hat.

The Princess Poporensky led the way, waddling along with a gait that she managed to invest with a certain dignity in spite of adverse circumstances. They passed through the adjoining room, which was a kind of antechamber, and the princess knocked upon a door in the farther wall. A voice from inside replied and the princess opened the door and passed in, Jane close upon her heels.

"Let me present to you, madame," said the princess in a solemn voice, "Miss Jane Cleveland."

A young woman who had been sitting in a big armchair at the other end of the room jumped up and ran forward. She stared fixedly at Jane for a minute or two, and then laughed merrily.

"But this is splendid, Anna," she cried. "I never imagined we should succeed so well. Come, let us see ourselves side by side."

Taking Jane's arm, she drew the girl across the room, pausing before a full-length mirror which hung on the wall.

"You see?" she cried delightedly. "It is a perfect match!"

Already, with her first glance at the Grand Duchess Pauline, Jane had begun to understand. The Grand Duchess was a young woman perhaps a year or two older than Jane. She had the same shade of fair hair, and the same slim figure. She was, perhaps, a shade taller. Now that they stood side by side, the likeness was very apparent. Detail for detail, the coloring was almost exactly the same.

The Grand Duchess clapped her hands. She seemed an extremely cheerful young woman.

"Nothing could be better," she declared. "You must congratulate Feodor Alexandrovitch for me, Anna. He has indeed done well."

"As yet, madame," murmured the princess in a low voice, "this young woman does not know what is required of her."

"True," said the Grand Duchess, becoming somewhat calmer in manner. "I forgot. Well, I will enlighten her. Leave us together, Anna Michaelovna."

"But, madame—"

"Leave us alone, I say."

She stamped her foot angrily. With considerable reluctance Anna Michaelovna left the room. The Grand Duchess sat down and motioned to Jane to do the same.

"They are tiresome, these old women," remarked Pauline. "But one has to have them. Anna Michaelovna is better than most. Now, then, Miss—ah, yes, Miss Jane Cleveland. I like the name. I like you too. You are sympathetic. I can tell at once if people are sympathetic."

"That's very clever of you, ma'am," said Jane, speaking for the first time.

"I am clever," said Pauline calmly. "Come now, I will explain things to you. Not that there is much to explain. You know the history of Ostrova. Practically all of my family are dead—massacred by the Communists. I am, perhaps, the last of my line. I am a woman, I cannot sit upon the throne. You think they would let me be. But no, wherever I go, attempts are made to assassinate me. Absurd, is it not? These vodka-soaked brutes never have any sense of proportion."

"I see," said Jane, feeling that something was required of her.

"For the most part I live in retirement—where I can take precautions, but now and then I have to take part in public ceremonies. While I am here, for instance, I have to attend several semi-public functions. Also in Paris on my way back. I have an estate in Hungary, you know. The sport there is magnificent."

"Is it really?" said Jane.

"Superb. I adore sport. Also—I ought not to tell you this, but I shall because your face is so sympathetic—there are plans being made there—very quietly, you understand. Altogether it is very important that I should not be assassinated during the next two weeks."

"But surely the police—" began Jane.

"The police? Oh, yes, they are very good, I believe. And we too—we have our spies. It is possible that I shall be forewarned when the attempt is to take place. But then, again, I might not."

She shrugged her shoulders.

"I begin to understand," said Jane slowly. "You want me to take your place?"

"Only on certain occasions," said the Grand Duchess eagerly.

"You must be somewhere at hand, you understand? I may require you twice, three times, four times in the next fortnight. Each time it will be upon the occasion of some public function. Naturally in intimacy of any kind, you could not represent me."

"Of course not," agreed Jane.

"You will do very well indeed. It was clever of Feodor Alexandrovitch to think of an advertisement, was it not?"

"Supposing," said Jane, "that I get assassinated?"

The Grand Duchess shrugged her shoulders.

"There is the risk, of course, but according to our own secret information, they want to kidnap me, not kill me outright. But I will be quite honest—it is always possible that they might throw a bomb."

"I see," said Jane.

She tried to imitate the lighthearted manner of Pauline. She wanted very much to come to the question of money, but did not quite see how best to introduce the subject. But Pauline saved her the trouble.

"We will pay you well, of course," she said carelessly. "I cannot remember now exactly how much Feodor Alexandrovitch suggested. We were speaking in francs or kronen."

"Colonel Kranin," said Jane, "said something about two thousand pounds."

"That was it," said Pauline, brightening. "I remember now. It is enough, I hope? Or would you rather have three thousand?"

"Well," said Jane, "if it's all the same to you, I'd rather have three thousand."

"You are businesslike, I see," said the Grand Duchess kindly. "I wish I was. But I have no idea of money at all. What I want I have to have, that is all."

It seemed to Jane a simple but admirable attitude of mind.

"And of course, as you say, there is danger," Pauline continued thoughtfully. "Although you do not look to me as though you minded danger. I do not myself. I hope you do not think that it is because I am a coward that I want you to take my place? You see, it is most important for Ostrova that I should marry and have at least two sons. After that, it does not matter what happens to me."

"I see," said Jane.

"And you accept?"

"Yes," said Jane resolutely. "I accept."

Pauline clapped her hands vehemently several times. Princess Poporensky appeared immediately.

"I have told her all, Anna," announced the Grand Duchess. "She will do what we want, and she is to have three thousand pounds. Tell Feodor to make a note of it. She is really very like me, is she not? I think she is better-looking, though."

The princess waddled out of the room, and returned with Count Streptitch.

"We have arranged everything, Feodor Alexandrovitch," the Grand Duchess said.

He bowed.

"Can she play her part, I wonder?" he queried, eyeing Jane doubtfully.

"I'll show you," said the girl suddenly. "You permit, ma'am?" she said to the Grand Duchess.

The latter nodded delightedly.

Jane stood up.

"But this is splendid, Anna," she said. "I never imagined. We should succeed so well. Come, let us see ourselves side by side."

And, as Pauline had done, she drew the other girl to the glass.

"You see? A perfect match!"

Words, manner and gesture, it was an excellent imitation of Pauline's greeting. The princess nodded her head and uttered a grunt of approbation.

"It is good, that," she declared. "It would deceive most people."

"You are very clever," said Pauline appreciatively. "I could not imitate anyone else to save my life."

Jane believed her. It had already struck her that Pauline was a young woman who was very much herself.

"Anna will arrange details with you," said the Grand Duchess. "Take her into my bedroom, Anna, and try some of my clothes on her."

She nodded a gracious farewell, and Jane was convoyed away by the Princess Poporensky.

"This is what Her Highness will wear to open the bazaar," explained the old lady, holding up a daring creation of white and black. "That is in three days' time. It may be necessary for you to take her place there. We do not know. We have not yet received information."

At Anna's bidding, Jane slipped off her own shabby garments and tried on the frock. It fitted her perfectly. The other nodded approvingly.

"It is almost perfect—just a shade long on you, because you are an inch or so shorter than Her Highness."

"That is easily remedied," said Jane quickly. "The Grand Duchess wears low-heeled shoes, I noticed. If I wear the same kind of shoes, but with high heels, it will adjust things nicely."

Anna Michaelovna showed her the shoes that the Grand Duchess usually wore with the dress—lizard skin with a strap across. Jane memorized them, and arranged to get a pair just like them, but with different heels.

"It would be well," said Anna Michaelovna, "for you to have a dress of distinctive color and material quite unlike Her Highness's. Then in case it becomes necessary for you to change places at a moment's notice, the substitution is less likely to be noticed."

Jane thought a minute.

"What about flame-red marocain? And I might, perhaps, have plain glass pince-nez. That alters the appearance very much."

Both suggestions were approved, and they went into further details.

Jane left the hotel with banknotes for a hundred pounds in her purse and instructions to purchase the necessary outfit and engage rooms at the Blitz Hotel as Miss Montresor of New York.

On the second day after this, Count Streptitch called upon her there.

"A transformation indeed," he said as he bowed.

Jane made him a mock bow in return. She was enjoying the new clothes and the luxury of her life very much.

"All this is very nice," she sighed. "But I suppose that your visit means I must get busy and earn my money."

"That is so. We have received information. It seems possible that an attempt will be made to kidnap Her Highness on the way home from the bazaar. That is to take place, as you know, at Orion House, which is about ten miles out of London. Her Highness will be forced to attend the bazaar in person, as the Countess of Anchester, who is promoting it, knows her personally. But the following is the plan I have concocted."

Jane listened attentively as he outlined it to her.

She asked a few questions and finally declared that she understood perfectly the part that she had to play.

The next day dawned bright and clear—a perfect day for one of the great events of the London Season, the bazaar at Orion House, promoted by the Countess of Anchester in aid of Ostrovian refugees in this country.

Having regard to the uncertainty of the English climate, the bazaar itself took place within the spacious rooms of Orion House, which has been for five hundred years in the possession of the Earls of Anchester. Various collections had been loaned, and a charming idea was the gift by a hundred society women of one pearl each taken from their own necklaces, each pearl to be sold by auction on the second day. There were also numerous side shows and attractions in the grounds.

Jane was there early in the rôle of Miss Montresor. She wore a dress of flame-colored marocain, and a small red cloche hat. On her feet were high-heeled lizard-skin shoes.

The arrival of the Grand Duchess Pauline was a great event. She was escorted to the platform and duly presented with a bouquet of roses by a small child. She made a short but charming speech and declared the bazaar open. Count Streptitch and Princess Poporensky were in attendance upon her.

She wore the dress that Jane had seen, white with a bold design of black, and her hat was a small cloche of black with a profusion of white ospreys hanging over the brim and a tiny lace veil coming halfway down the face. Jane smiled to herself.

The Grand Duchess went round the bazaar, visiting every stall, making a few purchases, and being uniformly gracious. Then she prepared to depart.

Jane was prompt to take up her cue. She requested a word with the Princess Poporensky and asked to be presented to the Grand Duchess.

"Ah, yes!" said Pauline in a clear voice. "Miss Montresor, I remember the name. She is an American journalist, I believe. She has done much for our cause. I should be glad to give her a short interview for her paper. Is there anywhere where we could be undisturbed?"

A small anteroom was immediately placed at the Grand Duchess's disposal, and Count Streptitch was despatched to bring in Miss Montresor. As soon as he had done so, and withdrawn again, the Princess Poporensky remaining in attendance, a rapid exchange of garments took place.

Three minutes later, the door opened and the Grand Duchess emerged, her bouquet of roses held up to her face.

Bowing graciously, and uttering a few words of farewell to Lady Anchester in French, she passed out and entered her car, which was waiting. Princess Poporensky took her place beside her, and the car drove off.

"Well," said Jane, "that's done. I wonder how Miss Montresor's getting on."

"No one will notice her. She can slip out quietly."

"That's true," said Jane. "I did it nicely, didn't I?"

"You acted your part with great discretion."

"Why isn't the Count with us?"

"He was forced to remain. Someone must watch over the safety of Her Highness."

"I hope nobody's going to throw bombs," said Jane apprehensively. "Hi! We're turning off the main road. Why's that?"

Gathering speed, the car was shooting down a side road.

Jane jumped up and put her head out of the window, remonstrating with the driver. He only laughed and increased his speed. Jane sank back into her seat again.

"Your spies were right," she said with a laugh. "We're for it, all right. I suppose the longer I keep it up, the safer it is for the Grand Duchess. At all events we must give her time to return to London safely."

At the prospect of danger, Jane's spirits rose. She had not relished the prospect of a bomb, but this type of adventure appealed to her sporting instincts.

Suddenly, with a grinding of brakes, the car pulled up in its own length. A man jumped on the step. In his hand was a revolver.

"Put your hands up," he snarled.

The Princess Poporensky's hands rose swiftly, but Jane merely looked at him disdainfully and kept her hands on her lap.

"Ask him the meaning of this outrage," she said in French to her companion.

But before the latter had time to say a word, the man broke in. He poured out a torrent of words in some foreign language.

Not understanding a single thing, Jane merely shrugged her shoulders and said nothing. The chauffeur had got down from his seat and joined the other man.

"Will the illustrious lady be pleased to descend?" he asked with a grin.

Raising the flowers to her face again, Jane stepped out of the car. The Princess Poporensky followed her.

"Will the illustrious lady come this way?"

Jane took no notice of the man's mock insolent manner, but of her own accord she walked toward a low-built rambling house which stood about a hundred yards away from where the car had stopped. The road had been a cul-de-sac ending in the gateway and drive which led to this apparently untenanted building.

The man, still brandishing his pistol, came close behind the two women. As they passed up the steps, he brushed past them and flung open a door on the left. It was an empty room, into which a table and two chairs had evidently been brought.

Jane passed in and sat down. Anna Michaelovna followed her. The man banged the door and turned the key.

Jane walked to the window and looked out.

"I could jump out, of course," she remarked. "But I shouldn't get far. No, we'll just have to stay here for the present and make the best of it. I wonder if they'll bring us anything to eat?"

About half an hour later her question was answered.

A big bowl of steaming soup was brought in and placed on the table in front of her. Also two pieces of dry bread.

"No luxury for aristocrats evidently," remarked Jane cheerily as the door was shut and locked again. "Will you start, or shall I?"

The Princess Poporensky waved the mere idea of food aside with horror.

"How could I eat? Who knows what danger my mistress might not be in?"

"She's all right," said Jane. "It's myself I'm worrying about. You know these people won't be at all pleased when they find they have got hold of the wrong person. In fact, they may be very unpleasant. I shall keep up the haughty Grand Duchess stunt as long as I can, and do a bunk if the opportunity offers."

The Princess Poporensky offered no reply.

Jane, who was hungry, drank up all the soup. It had a curious taste, but was hot and savory.

Afterward she felt rather sleepy. The Princess Poporensky seemed to be weeping quietly. Jane arranged herself on her uncomfortable chair in the least uncomfortable way, and allowed her head to droop.

She slept.

JANE AWOKE WITH A start. She had an idea that she had been a very long time asleep. Her head felt heavy and uncomfortable.

And then suddenly she saw something that jerked her faculties wide awake again.

She was wearing the flame-colored marocain frock.

She sat up and looked around her. Yes, she was still in the room in the empty house. Everything was exactly as it had been when she went to sleep, except for two facts. The first fact was that the Princess Poporensky was no longer sitting on the other chair. The second was her own inexplicable change of costume.

"I can't have dreamed it," said Jane. "Because if I'd dreamed it, I shouldn't be here."

She looked across at the window and registered a second significant fact. When she had gone to sleep, the sun had been pouring through the window. Now the house threw a sharp shadow on the sunlit drive.

"The house faces west," she reflected. "It was afternoon when I went to sleep. Therefore it must be tomorrow morning now. Therefore that soup was drugged. Therefore—oh, I don't know. It all seems mad."

She got up and went to the door. It was unlocked. She explored the house. It was silent and empty.

Jane put her hand to her aching head and tried to think.

And then she caught sight of a torn newspaper lying by the front door. It had glaring headlines which caught her eye.

"American Girl Bandit in England," she read. "The Girl in the Red Dress. Sensational Holdup at Orion House Bazaar."

Jane staggered out into the sunlight. Sitting on the steps, she read, her eyes growing bigger and bigger. The facts were short and succinct.

Just after the departure of the Grand Duchess Pauline, three men and a girl in a red dress had produced revolvers and successfully held up the crowd. They had annexed the hundred pearls and made a getaway in a fast racing car. Up to now, they had not been traced.

In the stop press (it was a late evening paper) were a few words to the effect that the "girl bandit in the red dress" had been staying at the Blitz as a Miss Montresor of New York.

"I'm dished," said Jane. "Absolutely dished. I always knew there was a catch in it."

And then she started. A strange sound had smote the air. The voice of a man, uttering one word at frequent intervals.

"Damn," it said. "Damn." And yet again, "Damn!"

Jane thrilled to the sound. It expressed so exactly her own feelings. She ran down the steps. By the corner of them lay a young man. He was endeavoring to raise his head from the ground. His face struck Jane as one of the nicest faces she had ever seen. It was freckled and slightly quizzical in expression.

"Damn my head," said the young man. "Damn it. I—"

He broke off and stared at Jane.

"I must be dreaming," he said faintly.

"That's what I said," said Jane. "But we're not. What's the matter with your head?"

"Somebody hit me on it. Fortunately it's a thick one."

He pulled himself into a sitting position, and made a wry face.

"My brain will begin to function shortly, I expect. I'm still in the same old spot, I see."

"How did you get here?" asked Jane curiously.

"That's a long story. By the way, you're not the Grand Duchess What's-her-name, are you?"

"I'm not. I'm plain Jane Cleveland."

"You're not plain, anyway," said the young man, looking at her with frank admiration.

Jane blushed.

"I ought to get you some water or something, oughtn't I?" she asked uncertainly.

"I believe it is customary," agreed the young man. "All the same, I'd rather have whiskey if you can find it."

Jane was unable to find any whiskey. The young man took a deep draft of water, and announced himself better.

"Shall I relate my adventures, or will you relate yours?" he asked.

"You first."

"There's nothing much to mine. I happened to notice that the Grand Duchess went into that room with low-heeled shoes on and came out with high-heeled ones. It struck me as rather odd. I don't like things to be odd.

"I followed the car on my motor bicycle. I saw you taken into the house. About ten minutes later a big racing car came tearing up. A girl in red got out and three men. She had low-heeled shoes on, all right. They went into the house. Presently low heels came out dressed in black and white, and went off in the first car, with an old pussy and a tall man with a fair beard. The others went off in the racing car. I thought they'd all gone, and was just trying to get in at that window and rescue you when someone hit me on the head from behind. That's all. Now for your turn."

Jane related her adventures.

"And it's awfully lucky for me that you did follow," she ended. "Do you see what an awful hole I should have been in otherwise? The Grand Duchess would have had a perfect alibi. She left the bazaar before the holdup began, and arrived in London in her car. Would anybody ever have believed my fantastic, improbable story?"

"Not on your life," said the young man with conviction.

They had been so absorbed in their respective narratives that they had been quite oblivious of their surroundings. They looked up now with a slight start to see a tall sad-faced man leaning against the house. He nodded at them.

"Very interesting," he commented.

"Who are you?" demanded Jane.

The sad-faced man's eyes twinkled a little.

"Detective-Inspector Farrell," he said gently. "I've been very interested in hearing your story and this young lady's. We might have found a little difficulty in believing hers, but for one or two things."

"For instance?"

"Well, you see, we heard this morning that the real Grand Duchess had eloped with a chauffeur in Paris."

Jane gasped.

"And then we knew that this American 'girl bandit' had come to this country, and we expected a coup of some kind. We'll have laid hands on them very soon, I can promise you that. Excuse me a minute, will you?"

He ran up the steps into the house.

"*Well!*" said Jane. She put a lot of force into the expression.

"I think it was awfully clever of you to notice those shoes," she said suddenly.

"Not at all," said the young man. "I was brought up in the boot trade. My father's a sort of boot king. He wanted me to go into the trade—marry and settle down. All that sort of thing. Nobody in particular—just the principle of the thing. But I wanted to be an artist." He sighed.

"I'm so sorry," said Jane kindly.

"I've been trying for six years. There's no blinking it. I'm a rotten painter. I've a good mind to chuck it and go home like the prodigal son. There's a good billet waiting for me."

"A job is the great thing," agreed Jane wistfully. "Do you think you could get me one trying on boots somewhere?"

"I could give you a better one than that—if you'd take it."

"Oh, what?"

"Never mind now. I'll tell you later. You know, until yesterday I never saw a girl I felt I could marry."

"Yesterday?"

"At the bazaar. And then I saw her—the one and only Her!"

He looked very hard at Jane.

"How beautiful the delphiniums are," said Jane hurriedly, with very pink cheeks.

"They're lupins," said the young man.

"It doesn't matter," said Jane.

"Not a bit," he agreed. And he drew a little nearer.

A FRUITFUL SUNDAY

"Well, really, I call this too delightful," said Miss Dorothy Pratt for the fourth time. "How I wish the old cat could see me now. She and her Janes!"

The "old cat" thus scathingly alluded to was Miss Pratt's highly estimable employer, Mrs. Mackenzie Jones, who had strong views upon the Christian names suitable for parlormaids and had repudiated Dorothy in favor of Miss Pratt's despised second name of Jane.

Miss Pratt's companion did not reply at once—for the best of reasons. When you have just purchased a Baby Austin, fourth hand, for the sum of twenty pounds, and are taking it out for the second time only, your whole attention is necessarily focused on the difficult task of using both hands and feet as the emergencies of the moment dictate.

"Er—ah!" said Mr. Edward Palgrove, and negotiated a crisis with a horrible grinding sound that would have set a true motorist's teeth on edge.

"Well, you don't talk to a girl much," complained Dorothy.

Mr. Palgrove was saved from having to respond as at that moment he was roundly and soundly cursed by the driver of a motor omnibus.

"Well, of all the impudence," said Miss Pratt, tossing her head.

"I only wish *he* had this foot brake," said her swain bitterly.

"Is there anything wrong with it?"

"You can put your foot on it till kingdom comes," said Mr. Palgrove. "But nothing happens."

"Oh, well, Ted, you can't expect everything for twenty pounds. After all, here we are, in a real car, on Sunday afternoon going out of town the same as everybody else."

More grinding and crashing sounds.

"Ah," said Ted, flushed with triumph. "That was a better change."

"You do drive something beautiful," said Dorothy admiringly.

Emboldened by feminine appreciation, Mr. Palgrove attempted a dash across Hammersmith Broadway, and was severely spoken to by a policeman.

"Well, I never," said Dorothy as they proceeded toward Hammersmith Bridge in a chastened fashion. "I don't know what the police are coming to. You'd think they'd be a bit more civil-spoken, seeing the way they've been shown up lately."

"Anyway, I didn't want to go along this road," said Edward sadly. "I wanted to go down the Great West Road and do a bust."

"And be caught in a trap as likely as not," said Dorothy. "That's what happened to the master the other day. Five pounds and costs."

"The police aren't so dusty after all," said Edward generously. "They pitch into the rich, all right. No favor. It makes me mad to think of these swells who can walk into a place and buy a couple of Rolls-Royces without turning a hair. There's no sense in it. I'm as good as they are."

"And the jewelry," said Dorothy, sighing. "Those shops in Bond Street. Diamonds and pearls and I don't know what! And me with a string of Woolworth pearls."

She brooded sadly upon the subject. Edward was able once more to give full attention to his driving. They managed to get through Richmond without mishap. The altercation with the policeman had shaken Edward's nerve. He now took the line of least resistance, following blindly behind any car in front whenever a choice of thoroughfares presented itself.

In this way he presently found himself following a shady country lane which many an experienced motorist would have given his soul to find.

"Rather clever turning off the way I did," said Edward, taking all the credit to himself.

"Sweetly pretty, I call it," said Miss Pratt. "And I do declare, there's a man with fruit to sell."

Sure enough, at a convenient corner was a small wicker table with baskets of fruit on it, and the legend EAT MORE FRUIT displayed on a banner.

"How much?" said Edward apprehensively, when frenzied pulling of the hand brake had produced the desired result.

"Lovely strawberries," said the man in charge.

He was an unprepossessing-looking individual with a leer.

"Just the thing for the lady. Ripe fruit, fresh-picked. Cherries, too. Genuine English. Have a basket of cherries, lady?"

"They do look nice ones," said Dorothy.

"Lovely, that's what they are," said the man hoarsely. "Bring you luck, lady, that basket will." He at last condescended to reply to Edward. "Two shillings, sir, and dirt-cheap. You'd say so if you knew what was inside the basket."

"They look awfully nice," said Dorothy.

Edward sighed and paid over two shillings. His mind was obsessed by calculation. Tea later, petrol—this Sunday motoring business wasn't what you'd call *cheap*. That was the worst of taking girls out! They always wanted everything they saw.

"Thank you, sir," said the unprepossessing-looking one. "You've got more than your money's worth in that basket of cherries."

Edward shoved his foot savagely down and the Baby Austin leaped at the cherry vendor after the manner of an infuriated Alsatian.

"Sorry," said Edward. "I forgot she was in gear."

"You ought to be careful, dear," said Dorothy. "You might have hurt him."

Edward did not reply. Another half-mile brought them to an ideal spot by the banks of a stream. The Austin was left by the side of the road and Edward and Dorothy sat affectionately upon the river bank and munched cherries. A Sunday paper lay unheeded at their feet.

"What's the news?" said Edward at last, stretching himself flat on his back and tilting his hat to shade his eyes.

Dorothy glanced over the headlines.

"The Woeful Wife. Extraordinary Story. Twenty-eight People Drowned Last Week. Reported Death of Airman. Startling Jewel Robbery. Ruby Necklace Worth Fifty Thousand Pounds Missing. Oh, Ted! Fifty thousand pounds. Just fancy!" She went on reading. "The necklace is composed of twenty-one stones set in platinum and was sent by registered post from Paris. On arrival, the packet was found to contain a few pebbles and the jewels were missing."

"Pinched in the post," said Edward. "The posts in France are awful, I believe."

"I'd like to see a necklace like that," said Dorothy. "All glowing like blood—pigeon's blood, that's what they call the color. I wonder what it would feel like to have a thing like that hanging round your neck."

"Well, you're never likely to know, my girl," said Edward facetiously.

Dorothy tossed her head.

"Why not, I should like to know. It's amazing the way girls can get on in the world. I might go on the stage."

"Girls that behave themselves don't get anywhere," said Edward discouragingly.

Dorothy opened her mouth to reply, checked herself, and murmured, "Pass me the cherries."

"I've been eating more than you have," she remarked. "I'll divide up what's left and—why, whatever's this at the bottom of the basket?"

She drew it out as she spoke—a long glittering chain of blood-red stones.

They both stared at it in amazement.

"In the basket, did you say?" said Edward at last.

Dorothy nodded.

"Right at the bottom—under the fruit."

Again they stared at each other.

"How did it get there, do you think?"

"I can't imagine. It's odd, Ted, just after reading that bit in the paper—about the rubies."

Edward laughed.

"You don't imagine you're holding fifty thousand pounds in your hand, do you?"

"I just said it was odd. Rubies set in platinum. Platinum is that sort of dull silvery stuff—like this. Don't they sparkle and aren't they a lovely color? I wonder how many of them there are?" She counted. "I say, Ted, there are twenty-one exactly."

"No!"

"Yes. The same number as the paper said. Oh, Ted, you don't think—"

"It couldn't be." But he spoke irresolutely. "There's some sort of way you can tell—scratching them on glass."

"That's diamonds. But you know, Ted, that was a very odd-looking man—the man with the fruit—a nasty-looking man. And he was funny about it—said we'd got more than our money's worth in the basket."

"Yes, but look here, Dorothy. What would he want to hand us over fifty thousand pounds for?"

Miss Pratt shook her head, discouraged.

"It doesn't seem to make sense," she admitted. "Unless the police were after him."

"The police?" Edward paled slightly.

"Yes. It goes on to say in the paper—'the police have a clue.'"

Cold shivers ran down Edward's spine.

"I don't like this, Dorothy. Supposing the police get after us."

Dorothy stared at him with her mouth open.

"But we haven't done anything, Ted. We found it in the basket."

"And that'll sound a silly sort of story to tell! It isn't likely."

"It isn't very," admitted Dorothy. "Oh, Ted, do you really think it is IT? It's like a fairy story!"

"I don't think it sounds like a fairy story," said Edward. "It sounds to me more like the kind of story where the hero goes to Dartmoor unjustly accused for fourteen years."

But Dorothy was not listening. She had clasped the necklace round her neck and was judging the effect in a small mirror taken from her handbag.

"The same as a duchess might wear," she murmured ecstatically.

"I won't believe it," said Edward violently. "They're imitation. They must be imitation."

"Yes, dear," said Dorothy, still intent on her reflection in the mirror. "Very likely."

"Anything else would be too much of a—a coincidence."

"Pigeon's blood," murmured Dorothy.

"It's absurd. That's what I say. Absurd. Look here, Dorothy, are you listening to what I say, or are you not?"

Dorothy put away the mirror. She turned to him, one hand on the rubies round her neck.

"How do I look?" she asked.

Edward stared at her, his grievance forgotten. He had never seen Dorothy quite like this. There was a triumph about her, a kind of regal beauty that was completely new to him. The belief that she had jewels round her neck worth fifty thousand pounds had made of Dorothy Pratt a new woman. She looked insolently serene a kind of Cleopatra and Semiramis and Zenobia rolled into one.

"You look—you look—stunning," said Edward humbly.

Dorothy laughed, and her laugh, too, was entirely different.

"Look here," said Edward. "We've got to do something. We must take them to a police station or something."

"Nonsense," said Dorothy. "You said yourself just now that they wouldn't believe you. You'll probably be sent to prison for stealing them."

"But—but what else can we do?"

"Keep them," said the new Dorothy Pratt.

Edward stared at her.

"Keep them? You're mad."

"We found them, didn't we? Why should we think they're valuable? We'll keep them and I shall wear them."

"And the police will pinch you."

Dorothy considered this for a minute or two.

"All right," she said. "We'll sell them. And you can buy a Rolls-Royce, or two Rolls-Royces, and I'll buy a diamond headthing and some rings."

Still Edward stared. Dorothy showed impatience.

"You've got your chance now—it's up to you to take it. We didn't steal the thing—I wouldn't hold with that. It's come to us and it's probably the only chance we'll ever have of getting all the things we want. Haven't you got any spunk at all, Edward Palgrove?"

Edward found his voice.

"Sell it, you say? That wouldn't be so jolly easy. Any jeweler would want to know where I got the blooming thing."

"You don't take it to a jeweler. Don't you ever read detective stories, Ted? You take it to a 'fence,' of course."

"And how should I know any fences? I've been brought up respectable."

"Men ought to know everything," said Dorothy. "That's what they're for."

He looked at her. She was serene and unyielding.

"I wouldn't have believed it of you," he said weakly.

"I thought you had more spirit."

There was a pause. Then Dorothy rose to her feet.

"Well," she said lightly. "We'd best be getting home."

"Wearing that thing round your neck?"

Dorothy removed the necklace, looked at it reverently and dropped it into her handbag.

"Look here," said Edward. "You give that to me."

"No."

"Yes, you do. I've been brought up honest, my girl."

"Well, you can go on being honest. You need have nothing to do with it."

"Oh, hand it over," said Edward recklessly. "I'll do it. I'll find a fence. As you say, it's the only chance we shall ever have. We came by it honest—bought it for two shillings. It's no more than what gentlemen do in antique shops every day of their life and are proud of it."

"That's it!" said Dorothy. "Oh, Edward, you're splendid!"

She handed over the necklace and he dropped it into his pocket. He felt worked up, exalted, the very devil of a fellow! In this mood, he started the Austin. They were both too excited to remember tea. They drove back to London in silence. Once at a crossroads, a policeman stepped toward the car, and Edward's heart missed a beat. By a miracle, they reached home without mishap.

Edward's last words to Dorothy were imbued with the adventurous spirit.

"We'll go through with this. Fifty thousand pounds! It's worth it!"

He dreamed that night of broad arrows and Dartmoor, and rose early, haggard, and unrefreshed. He had to set about finding a fence—and how to do it he had not the remotest idea!

His work at the office was slovenly and brought down upon him two sharp rebukes before lunch.

How did one find a "fence"? Whitechapel, he fancied, was the correct neighborhood—or was it Stepney?

On his return to the office a call came though for him on the telephone. Dorothy's voice spoke—tragic and tearful.

"Is that you, Ted? I'm using the telephone, but she may come in any minute, and I'll have to stop. Ted, you haven't done anything, have you?"

Edward replied in the negative.

"Well, look here, Ted, you mustn't. I've been lying awake all night. It's been awful. Thinking of how it says in the Bible you mustn't steal. I must have been mad yesterday—I really must. You won't do anything, will you, Ted, dear?"

Did a feeling of relief steal over Mr. Palgrove? Possibly it did—but he wasn't going to admit any such thing.

"When I say I'm going through with a thing, I go through with it," he said in a voice such as might belong to a strong superman with eyes of steel.

"Oh, but, Ted, dear, you mustn't. Oh, Lord, she's coming. Look here, Ted, she's going out to dinner tonight. I can slip out and meet you. Don't do anything till you've seen me. Eight o'clock. Wait for me round the corner." Her voice changed to a seraphic murmur. "Yes, ma'am, I think it was a wrong number. It was Bloomsbury 0243 they wanted."

As Edward left the office at six o'clock, a huge headline caught his eye.

JEWEL ROBBERY.
LATEST DEVELOPMENTS

Hurriedly he extended a penny. Safely ensconced in the tube, having dexterously managed to gain a seat, he eagerly perused the printed sheet. He found what he sought easily enough.

A suppressed whistle escaped him.

"Well—I'm—"

And then another adjacent paragraph caught his eye. He read it through and let the paper slip to the floor unheeded.

Precisely at eight o'clock, he was waiting at the rendezvous. A breathless Dorothy, looking pale but pretty, came hurrying along to join him.

"You haven't done anything, Ted?"

"I haven't done anything." He took the ruby chain from his pocket. "You can put it on."

"But, Ted—"

"The police have got the rubies all right—and the man who pinched them. And now read this!"

He thrust a newspaper paragraph under her nose Dorothy read:

NEW ADVERTISING STUNT

A clever new advertising dodge is being adopted by the All-English Fivepenny Fair who intend to challenge the famous Woolworths. Baskets of fruit were sold yesterday and will be on sale every Sunday. Out of every fifty baskets, one will contain an imitation necklace in different colored stones. These necklaces are really wonderful value for the money. Great excitement and merriment was caused by them yesterday and EAT MORE FRUIT will have a great vogue next Sunday. We congratulate the Fivepenny Fair on their resource and wish them all good luck in their campaign of Buy British Goods.

"Well—" said Dorothy.

And after a pause: "Well!"

"Yes," said Edward. "I felt the same."

A passing man thrust a paper into his hand.

"Take one, brother," he said.

"The price of a virtuous woman is far above rubies."

"There!" said Edward. "I hope that cheers you up."

"I don't know," said Dorothy doubtfully. "I don't exactly want to *look* like a good woman."

"You don't," said Edward. "That's why the man gave me that paper. With those rubies round your neck you don't look one little bit like a good woman."

Dorothy laughed.

"You're rather a dear, Ted," she said. "Come on, let's go to the pictures."

THE GOLDEN BALL

George Dundas stood in the City of London meditating.

All about him toilers and moneymakers surged and flowed like an enveloping tide. But George, beautifully dressed, his trousers exquisitely creased, took no heed of them. He was busy thinking what to do next.

Something had occurred! Between George and his rich uncle (Ephraim Leadbetter of the firm of Leadbetter and Gilling) there had been what is called in a lower walk of life "words." To be strictly accurate, the words had been almost entirely on Mr. Leadbetter's side. They had flowed from his lips in a steady stream of bitter indignation, and the fact that they consisted almost entirely of repetition did not seem to have worried him. To say a thing once beautifully and then let it alone was not one of Mr. Leadbetter's mottoes.

The theme was a simple one—the criminal folly and wickedness of a young man, who has his way to make, taking a day off in the middle of the week without even asking leave. Mr. Leadbetter, when he had said everything he could think of and several things twice, paused for breath and asked George what he meant by it.

George replied simply that he had felt he wanted a day off. A holiday, in fact.

And what, Mr. Leadbetter wanted to know, were Saturday afternoon and Sunday? To say nothing of Whitsuntide, not long past, and August Bank Holiday to come?

George said he didn't care for Saturday afternoons, Sundays or Bank Holidays. He meant a real day, when it might be possible to find some spot where half London was not assembled already.

Mr. Leadbetter then said that he had done his best by his dead sister's son—nobody could say he hadn't given him a chance. But it was plain that it was no use. And in future George could have five real days with Saturday and Sunday added to do with as he liked.

"The golden ball of opportunity has been thrown up for you, my boy," said Mr. Leadbetter in a last touch of poetical fancy. "And you have failed to grasp it."

George said it seemed to him that that was just what he *had* done, and Mr. Leadbetter dropped poetry for wrath and told him to get out.

Hence George—meditating. Would his uncle relent or would he not? Had he any secret affection for George, or merely a cold distaste?

It was just at that moment that a voice—a most unlikely voice—said, "Hallo!"

A scarlet touring car with an immense long hood had drawn up to the curb beside him. At the wheel was that beautiful and popular society girl, Mary Montresor. (The description is that of the illustrated papers who produced a portrait of her at least four times a month.) She was smiling at George in an accomplished manner.

"I never knew a man could look so like an island," said Mary Montresor. "Would you like to get in?"

"I should love it above all things," said George with no hesitation, and stepped in beside her.

They proceeded slowly because the traffic forbade anything else.

"I'm tired of the city," said Mary Montresor. "I came to see what it was like. I shall go back to London."

Without presuming to correct her geography, George said it was a splendid idea. They proceeded sometimes slowly, sometimes with wild bursts of speed when Mary Montresor saw a chance of cutting in. It seemed to George that she was somewhat optimistic in the latter view, but he reflected that one could only die once. He thought it best, however, to essay no conversation. He preferred his fair driver to keep strictly to the job in hand.

It was she who reopened the conversation, choosing the moment when they were doing a wild sweep round Hyde Park Corner.

"How would you like to marry me?" she inquired casually.

George gave a gasp, but that may have been due to a large bus that seemed to spell certain destruction. He prided himself on his quickness in response.

"I should love it," he replied easily.

"Well," said Mary Montresor vaguely. "Perhaps you may someday."

They turned into the straight without accident, and at that moment George perceived large new bills at Hyde Park Corner tube station. Sandwiched between GRAVE POLITICAL SITUATION and COLONEL IN DOCK, one said SOCIETY GIRL TO MARRY DUKE, and the other DUKE OF EDGEHILL AND MISS MONTRESOR.

"What's this about the Duke of Edgehill?" demanded George sternly.

"Me and Bingo? We're engaged."

"But then—what you said just now—"

"Oh, *that,*" said Mary Montresor. "You see, I haven't made up my mind who I shall actually marry."

"Then why did you get engaged to him?"

"Just to see if I could. Everybody seemed to think it would be frightfully difficult, and it wasn't a bit!"

"Very rough luck on—er—Bingo," said George, mastering his embarrassment at calling a real live duke by a nickname.

"Not at all," said Mary Montresor. "It will be good for Bingo, if anything *could* do him good—which I doubt."

George made another discovery—again aided by a convenient poster.

"Why, of course, it's cup day at Ascot. I should have thought that was the one place you were simply bound to be today."

Mary Montresor sighed.

"I wanted a holiday," she said plaintively.

"Why, so did I," said George, delighted. "And as a result my uncle has kicked me out to starve."

"Then in case we marry," said Mary, "my twenty thousand a year may come in useful?"

"It will certainly provide us with a few home comforts," said George.

"Talking of homes," said Mary, "let's go in the country and find a home we would like to live in."

It seemed a simple and charming plan. They negotiated Putney Bridge, reached the Kingston by-pass and with a sigh of satisfaction Mary pressed her foot down on the accelerator. They got into the country very quickly. It was half an hour later that with a sudden exclamation Mary shot out a dramatic hand and pointed.

On the brow of a hill in front of them there nestled a house of what house agents describe (but seldom truthfully) as "old-world charm." Imagine the description of most houses in the country really come true for once, and you get an idea of this house.

Mary drew up outside a white gate.

"We'll leave the car and go up and look at it. It's our house!"

"Decidedly, it's our house," agreed George. "But just for the moment other people seem to be living in it."

Mary dismissed the other people with a wave of her hand. They walked up the winding drive together. The house appeared even more desirable at close quarters.

"We'll go and peep in at all the windows," said Mary.

George demurred.

"Do you think the other people—"

"I shan't consider them. It's our house—they're only living in it by a sort of accident. Besides, it's a lovely day and they're sure to be out. And if anyone does catch us, I shall say—I shall say—that I thought it was Mrs.—Mrs. Pardonstenger's house, and that I am so sorry I made a mistake."

"Well, that ought to be safe enough," said George reflectively.

They looked in through windows. The house was delightfully furnished. They had just got to the study when footsteps crunched on the gravel behind them and they turned to face a most irreproachable butler.

"Oh!" said Mary. And then putting on her most enchanting smile, she said, "Is Mrs. Pardonstenger in? I was looking to see if she was in the study."

"Mrs. Pardonstenger is at home, madam," said the butler. "Will you come this way, please."

They did the only thing they could. They followed him. George was calculating what the odds against this happening could possibly be. With a name like Pardonstenger he came to the conclusion it was about one in twenty thousand. His companion whispered, "Leave it to me. It will be all right."

George was only too pleased to leave it to her. The situation, he considered, called for feminine finesse.

They were shown into a drawing room. No sooner had the butler left the room than the door almost immediately reopened and a big florid lady with peroxide hair came in expectantly.

Mary Montresor made a movement toward her, then paused in well-stimulated surprise.

"Why!" she exclaimed. "It isn't Amy! What an extraordinary thing!"

"It *is* an extraordinary thing," said a grim voice.

A man had entered behind Mrs. Pardonstenger, an enormous man with a bulldog face and a sinister frown. George thought he had never seen such an unpleasant brute. The man closed the door and stood with his back against it.

"A very extraordinary thing," he repeated sneeringly. "But I fancy we understand your little game!" He suddenly produced what seemed an outsize in revolvers. "Hands up. Hands up, I say. Frisk 'em, Bella."

George in reading detective stories had often wondered what it meant to be frisked. Now he knew. Bella (alias Mrs. P.) satisfied herself that neither he nor Mary concealed any lethal weapons on their persons.

"Thought you were mighty clever, didn't you?" sneered the man. "Coming here like this and playing the innocents. You've made a mistake this time—a bad mistake. In fact, I very much doubt whether your friends and relations will ever see you again. Ah! You would, would you?" as George made a movement. "None of your games. I'd shoot you as soon as look at you."

"Be careful, George," quavered Mary.

"I shall," said George with feeling. "Very careful."

"And now march," said the man. "Open the door, Bella. Keep your hands above your heads, you two. The lady first—that's right. I'll come behind you both. Across the hall. Upstairs . . ."

They obeyed. What else could they do? Mary mounted the stairs, her hands held high. George followed. Behind them came the huge ruffian, revolver in hand.

Mary reached the top of the staircase and turned the corner. At the same moment, without the least warning, George lunged out a fierce backward kick. He caught the man full in the middle and he capsized backward down the stairs. In a moment George had turned and leaped down after him, kneeling on his chest. With his right hand, he picked up the revolver which had fallen from the other's hand as he fell.

Bella gave a scream and retreated through a baize door. Mary came running down the stairs, her face as white as paper.

"George, you haven't killed him?"

The man was lying absolutely still. George bent over him.

"I don't think I've killed him," he said regretfully. "But he's certainly taken the count all right."

"Thank God." She was breathing rapidly.

"Pretty neat," said George with permissible self-admiration. "Many a lesson to be learned from a jolly old mule. Eh, what?"

Mary pulled at his hand.

"Come away," she cried feverishly. "Come away quick."

"If we had something to tie this fellow up with," said George, intent on his own plans. "I suppose you couldn't find a bit of rope or cord anywhere?"

"No, I couldn't," said Mary. "And come away, please—please—I'm so frightened."

"You needn't be frightened," said George with manly arrogance. "*I'm* here."

"Darling George, please—for my sake. I don't want to be mixed up in this. Please let's go."

The exquisite way in which she breathed the words "for my sake" shook George's resolution. He allowed himself to be led forth from the house and hurried down the drive to the waiting car. Mary said faintly: "You drive. I don't feel I can." George took command of the wheel.

"But we've got to see this thing through," he said. "Heaven knows what blackguardism that nasty-looking fellow is up to. I won't bring the police into it if you don't want me to—but I'll have a try on my own. I ought to be able to get on their track all right."

"No, George, I don't want you to."

"We have a first-class adventure like this, and you want me to back out of it? Not on my life."

"I'd no idea you were so bloodthirsty," said Mary tearfully.

"I'm not bloodthirsty. I didn't begin it. The damned cheek of the fellow—threatening us with an outsize revolver. By the way—why on earth didn't that revolver go off when I kicked him downstairs?"

He stopped the car and fished the revolver out of the side pocket of the car where he had placed it. After examining it, he whistled.

"Well, I'm damned! The thing isn't loaded. If I'd known that—" He paused, wrapped in thought. "Mary, this is a very curious business."

"I know it is. That's why I'm begging you to leave it alone."

"Never," said George firmly.

Mary uttered a heart-rending sigh.

"I see," she said, "that I shall have to tell you. And the worst of it is that I haven't the least idea how you'll take it."

"What do you mean—tell me?"

"You see, it's like this." She paused. "I feel girls should stick together nowadays—they should insist on knowing something about the men they meet."

"Well?" said George, utterly fogged.

"And the most important thing to a girl is how a man will behave in an emergency—has he got presence of mind—courage—quick-wittedness? That's the kind of thing you can hardly ever know—until it's too late. An emergency mightn't arise until you'd been married for years. All you do know about a man is how he dances and if he's good at getting taxis on a wet night."

"Both very useful accomplishments," George pointed out.

"Yes, but one wants to feel a man is a man."

"The great wide-open spaces where men are men," George quoted absently.

"Exactly. But we have no wide-open spaces in England. So one has to create a situation artificially. That's what I did."

"Do you mean—"

"I do mean. That house, as it happens, actually *is* my house. We came to it by design—not by chance. And the man—that man that you nearly killed—"

"Yes?"

"He's Rube Wallace—the film actor. He does prize fighters, you know. The dearest and gentlest of men. I engaged him. Bella's his wife. That's why I was so terrified that you'd killed him. Of course the revolver wasn't loaded. It's a stage property. Oh, George, are you very angry?"

"Am I the first person you have—er—tried this test on?"

"Oh, no. There have been—let me see—nine and a half!"

"Who was the half?" inquired George with curiosity.

"Bingo," replied Mary coldly.

"Did any of them think of kicking like a mule?"

"No—they didn't. Some tried to bluster and some gave in at once, but they all allowed themselves to be marched upstairs and tied up, and gagged. Then, of course, I managed to work myself loose from my bonds—like in books—and I freed them and we got away—finding the house empty."

"And nobody thought of the mule trick or anything like it?"

"No."

"In that case," said George graciously, "I forgive you."

"Thank you, George," said Mary meekly.

"In fact," said George, "the only question that arises is: Where do we go now? I'm not sure if it's Lambeth Palace or Doctor's Commons, wherever that is."

"What *are* you talking about?"

"The license. A special license, I think, is indicated. You're too fond of getting engaged to one man and then immediately asking another one to marry you."

"I didn't ask you to marry me!"

"You did. At Hyde Park Corner. Not a place I should choose for a proposal myself, but everyone has their idiosyncrasies in these matters."

"I did nothing of the kind. I just asked, as a joke, whether you would care to marry me? It wasn't intended seriously."

"If I were to take counsel's opinion, I am sure that he would say it constituted a genuine proposal. Besides, you know you want to marry me."

"I don't."

"Not after nine and a half failures? Fancy what a feeling of security it will give you to go through life with a man who can extricate you from any dangerous situation."

Mary appeared to weaken slightly at this telling argument. But she said firmly: "I wouldn't marry any man unless he went on his knees to me."

George looked at her. She was adorable. But George had other characteristics of the mule besides its kick. He said with equal firmness:

"To go on one's knees to any woman is degrading. I will not do it."

Mary said with enchanting wistfulness: "What a pity."

They drove back to London. George was stern and silent. Mary's face was hidden by the brim of her hat. As they passed Hyde Park Corner, she murmured softly: "Couldn't you go on your knees to me?"

George said firmly: "No."

He felt he was being a superman. She admired him for his attitude. But unluckily he suspected her of mulish tendencies herself. He drew up suddenly.

"Excuse me," he said.

He jumped out of the car, retraced his steps to a fruit barrow they had passed and returned so quickly that the policeman who was bearing down upon them to ask what they meant by it, had not had time to arrive.

George drove on, lightly tossing an apple into Mary's lap.

"Eat more fruit," he said. "Also symbolical."

"Symbolical?"

"Yes, originally Eve gave Adam an apple. Nowadays Adam gives Eve one. See?"

"Yes," said Mary rather doubtfully.

"Where shall I drive you?" inquired George formally.

"Home, please."

He drove to Grosvenor Square. His face was absolutely impassive. He jumped out and came round to help her out. She made a last appeal.

"Darling George—couldn't you? Just to please me?"

"Never," said George.

And at that moment it happened. He slipped, tried to recover his balance and failed. He was kneeling in the mud before her. Mary gave a squeal of joy and clapped her hands.

"Darling George! Now I will marry you. You can go straight to Lambeth Palace and fix up with the Archbishop of Canterbury about it."

"I didn't mean to," said George hotly. "It was a bl—er—a banana skin." He held the offender up reproachfully.

"Never mind," said Mary. "It happened. When we quarrel and you throw it in my teeth that I proposed to you, I can retort that you had to go on your knees to me before I would marry you. And all because of that blessed banana skin! It *was* a blessed banana skin you were going to say?"

"Something of the sort," said George.

AT FIVE-THIRTY THAT afternoon, Mr. Leadbetter was informed that his nephew had called and would like to see him.

"Called to eat humble pie," said Mr. Leadbetter to himself. "I dare say I was rather hard on the lad, but it was for his own good."

And he gave orders that George should be admitted.

George came in airily.

"I want a few words with you, Uncle," he said. "You did me a grave injustice this morning. I should like to know whether, at my age, you could have gone out into the street, disowned by your relatives, and between the hours of eleven-fifteen and five-thirty acquire an income of twenty thousand a year. That is what I have done!"

"You're mad, boy."

"Not mad; resourceful! I am going to marry a young, rich, beautiful society girl. One, moreover, who is throwing over a duke for my sake."

"Marrying a girl for her money? I'd not have thought it of you."

"And you'd have been right. I would never have dared to ask her if she hadn't—very fortunately—asked me. She retracted afterward, but I made her change her mind. And do you know, Uncle, how all this was done? By a judicious expenditure of twopence and a grasping of the golden ball of opportunity."

"Why the tuppence?" asked Mr. Leadbetter, financially interested.

"One banana—off a barrow. Not everyone would have thought of that banana. Where do you get a marriage license? Is it Doctor's Commons or Lambeth Palace?"

THE RAJAH'S EMERALD

With a serious effort James Bond bent his attention once more on the little yellow book in his hand. On its outside the book bore the simple but pleasing legend, "Do you want your salary increased by £300 per annum?" Its price was one shilling. James had just finished reading two pages of crisp paragraphs instructing him to look his boss in the face, to cultivate a dynamic personality, and to radiate an atmosphere of efficiency. He had now arrived at subtler matter, "There is a time for frankness, there is a time for discretion," the little yellow book informed him. "A strong man does not always blurt out all he knows." James let the little book close and, raising his head, gazed out over a blue expanse of ocean. A horrible suspicion assailed him, that he was not a strong man. A strong man would have been in command of the present situation, not a victim to it. For the sixtieth time that morning James rehearsed his wrongs.

This was his holiday. His holiday! Ha, ha! Sardonic laughter. Who had persuaded him to come to that fashionable seaside resort, Kimpton-on-Sea? Grace. Who had urged him into an expenditure of more than he could afford? Grace. And he had fallen in with the plan eagerly. She had got him here, and what was the result? While he was staying in an obscure boarding house about a mile and a half from the sea front, Grace, who should have been in a similar boarding house (not the same one—the proprieties of James's circle were very strict), had flagrantly deserted him and was staying at no less than the Esplanade Hotel upon the sea front.

It seemed that she had friends there. Friends! Again James laughed sardonically. His mind went back over the last three years of his leisurely courtship of Grace. Extremely pleased she had been when he first singled her out for notice. That was before she had risen to heights of glory in the millinery salons at Messrs. Bartles in the High Street. In those early days it had been James who gave himself airs; now, alas! the boot was on the other leg. Grace was what is technically known as "earning good money." It had made her uppish. Yes, that was it, thoroughly uppish. A confused fragment out of a poetry book came back to James's mind, something about "thanking heaven fasting, for a good man's love." But there was nothing of that kind of thing observable about Grace. Well-fed on an Esplanade Hotel breakfast, she was ignoring the good man's love utterly. She was indeed accepting the attentions of a poisonous idiot called Claud Sopworth, a man, James felt convinced, of no moral worth whatsoever.

James ground a heel into the earth and scowled darkly at the horizon. Kimpton-on-Sea. What had possessed him to come to such a place? It was preeminently a resort of the rich and fashionable, it possessed two large hotels, and several miles of picturesque bungalows belonging to fashionable actresses, rich merchants and those members of the English aristocracy who had married wealthy wives. The rent, furnished, of the smallest bungalow was twenty-five guineas a week. Imagination boggled at what the rent of the large ones might amount to. There was one of these palaces immediately behind James's seat. It belonged to that famous sportsman Lord Edward Campion, and there were staying there at the moment a houseful of distinguished guests including the Rajah of Maraputna, whose wealth was fabulous. James had read all about him in the local weekly newspaper that morning: the extent of his Indian possessions, his palaces, his wonderful collection of jewels, with a special mention of one famous emerald which the papers declared enthusiastically was the size of a pigeon's egg. James, being town-bred, was somewhat hazy about the size of a pigeon's egg, but the impression left on his mind was good.

"If I had an emerald like that," said James, scowling at the horizon again, "I'd show Grace."

The sentiment was vague, but the enunciation of it made James feel better. Laughing voices hailed him from behind, and he turned abruptly to confront Grace. With her was Clara Sopworth, Alice Sopworth, Dorothy Sopworth and—alas! Claud Sopworth. The girls were arm-in-arm and giggling.

"Why, you are quite a stranger," cried Grace archly.

"Yes," said James.

He could, he felt, have found a more telling retort. You cannot convey the impression of a dynamic personality by the use of the one word "yes." He looked with intense loathing at Claud Sopworth. Claud Sopworth was almost as beautifully dressed as the hero of a musical comedy. James longed passionately for the moment when an enthusiastic beach dog should plant wet, sandy forefeet on the unsullied whiteness of Claud's flannel trousers. He himself wore a serviceable pair of dark-gray flannel trousers which had seen better days.

"Isn't the air beautiful?" said Clara, sniffing it appreciatively. "Quite sets you up, doesn't it?"

She giggled.

"It's ozone," said Alice Sopworth. "It's as good as a tonic, you know." And she giggled also.

James thought: "I should like to knock their silly heads together. What is the sense of laughing all the time? They are not saying anything funny."

The immaculate Claud murmured languidly: "Shall we have a bathe, or is it too much of a fag?"

The idea of bathing was accepted shrilly. James fell into line with them. He even managed, with a certain amount of cunning, to draw Grace a little behind the others.

"Look here!" he complained. "I am hardly seeing anything of you."

"Well, I am sure we are all together now," said Grace, "and you can come and lunch with us at the hotel, at least—"

She looked dubiously at James's legs.

"What is the matter?" demanded James ferociously. "Not smart enough for you, I suppose?"

"I do think, dear, you might take a little more pains," said Grace. "Everyone is so fearfully smart here. Look at Claud Sopworth!"

"I have looked at him," said James grimly. "I have never seen a man who looked a more complete ass than he does."

Grace drew herself up.

"There is no need to criticize my friends, James; it's not manners. He's dressed just like any other gentleman at the hotel is dressed."

"Bah!" said James. "Do you know what I read the other day in 'Society Snippets'? Why, that the Duke of—the Duke of, I can't remember, but one duke, anyway, was the worst-dressed man in England, there!"

"I dare say," said Grace, "but then, you see, he is a duke."

"Well?" demanded James. "What is wrong with my being a duke someday? At least, well, not perhaps a duke, but a peer."

He slapped the yellow book in his pocket and recited to her a long list of peers of the realm who had started life much more obscurely than James Bond. Grace merely giggled.

"Don't be so soft, James," she said. "Fancy you Earl of Kimpton-on-Sea!"

James gazed at her in mingled rage and despair. The air of Kimpton-on-Sea had certainly gone to Grace's head.

The beach at Kimpton is a long, straight stretch of sand. A row of bathing huts and boxes stretches evenly along it for about a mile and a half. The party had just stopped before a row of six huts all labeled imposingly, "For visitors to the Esplanade Hotel only."

"Here we are," said Grace brightly; "but I'm afraid you can't come in with us, James; you'll have to go along to the public tents over there; we'll meet you in the sea. So long!"

"So long!" said James, and he strode off in the direction indicated.

Twelve dilapidated tents stood solemnly confronting the ocean. An aged mariner guarded them, a roll of blue paper in his hand. He accepted a coin of the realm from James, tore him off a blue ticket from his roll, threw him over a towel, and jerked one thumb over his shoulder.

"Take your turn," he said huskily.

It was then that James awoke to the fact of competition. Others besides himself had conceived the idea of entering the sea. Not only was each tent occupied, but outside each tent was a determined-looking crowd of people glaring at each other. James attached himself to the smallest group and waited. The strings of the tent parted, and a beautiful young woman, sparsely clad, emerged on the scene settling her bathing cap with the air of one who had the whole morning to waste. She strolled down to the water's edge and sat down dreamily on the sands.

"That's no good," said James to himself, and attached himself forthwith to another group.

After waiting five minutes, sounds of activity were apparent in the second tent. With heavings and strainings, the flaps parted asunder and four children and a father and mother emerged. The tent being so small, it had something of the appearance of a conjuring trick. On the instant two women sprang forward, each grasping one flap of the tent.

"Excuse me," said the first young woman, panting a little.

"Excuse *me,*" said the other young woman, glaring.

"I would have you know I was here quite ten minutes before you were," said the first young woman rapidly.

"I have been here a good quarter of an hour, as anyone will tell you," said the second young woman defiantly.

"Now then, now then," said the aged mariner, drawing near.

Both young women spoke to him shrilly. When they had finished, he jerked his thumb at the second young woman and said briefly: "It's yours."

Then he departed, deaf to remonstrances. He neither knew nor cared which had been there first, but his decision, as they say in newspaper competitions, was final. The despairing James caught at his arm.

"Look here! I say!"

"Well, mister?"

"How long is it going to be before I get a tent?"

The aged mariner threw a dispassionate glance over the waiting throng.

"Might be an hour, might be an hour and a half; I can't say."

At that moment James espied Grace and the Sopworth girls running lightly down the sands toward the sea.

"Damn!" said James to himself. "Oh, damn!"

He plucked once more at the aged mariner.

"Can't I get a tent anywhere else? What about one of these huts along here? They all seem empty."

"The huts," said the ancient mariner with dignity, "are *private.*"

Having uttered this rebuke, he passed on. With a bitter feeling of having been tricked, James detached himself from the waiting groups and strode savagely down the beach. It was the limit! It was the absolute, complete limit! He glared savagely at the trim bathing huts he passed. In that moment from being an Independent Liberal, he became a red-hot Socialist. Why should the rich have bathing huts and be able to bathe any minute they chose without waiting in a crowd? "This system of ours," said James vaguely, "is all wrong."

From the sea came the coquettish screams of the splashed. Grace's voice! And above her squeaks, the inane "Ha, ha, ha" of Claud Sopworth.

"Damn!" said James, grinding his teeth, a thing which he had never before attempted, only read about in works of fiction.

He came to a stop, twirling his stick savagely, and turning his back firmly on the sea. Instead, he gazed with concentrated hatred upon Eagle's Nest, Buena Vista, and Mon Desir. It was the custom of the inhabitants of Kimpton-on-Sea to label their bathing huts with fancy names. Eagle's Nest merely struck James as being silly, and Buena Vista was beyond his linguistic accomplishments. But his knowledge of French was sufficient to make him realize the appositeness of the third name.

"Mon Desir," said James. "I should jolly well think it was."

And on that moment he saw that while the doors of the other bathing huts were tightly closed, that of Mon Desir was ajar. James looked thoughtfully up and down the beach; this particular spot was mainly occupied by mothers of large families, busily engaged in superintending their offspring. It was only ten o'clock, too early as yet for the aristocracy of Kimpton-on-Sea to have come down to bathe.

"Eating quails and mushrooms in their beds as likely as not, brought to them on trays by powdered footmen, pah! Not one of them will be down here before twelve o'clock," thought James.

He looked again toward the sea. With the obedience of a well-trained "leit motif," the shrill scream of Grace rose upon the air. It was followed by the "Ha, ha, ha" of Claud Sopworth.

"I will," said James between his teeth.

He pushed open the door of Mon Desir and entered. For the moment he had a fright, as he caught sight of sundry garments hanging from pegs, but he was quickly reassured. The hut was partitioned into two; on the right-hand side, a girl's yellow sweater, a battered panama hat and a pair of beach shoes were depending from a peg. On the left-hand side an old pair of gray flannel trousers, a pullover, and a sou'wester proclaimed the fact that the sexes were segregated. James hastily transferred himself to the gentlemen's part of the hut, and undressed rapidly. Three minutes later, he was in the sea puffing and snorting importantly, doing extremely short bursts of professional-looking swimming—head under the water, arms lashing the sea—that style.

"Oh, there you are!" cried Grace. "I was afraid you wouldn't be in for ages with all that crowd of people waiting there."

"Really?" said James.

He thought with affectionate loyalty of the yellow book. "The strong man can on occasions be discreet." For the moment his temper was quite restored. He was able to say pleasantly but firmly to Claud Sopworth, who was teaching Grace the overarm stroke:

"No, no old man; you have got it all wrong. *I'll* show her."

And such was the assurance of his tone, that Claud withdrew discomfited. The only pity of it was that his triumph was short-lived. The temperature of our English waters is not such as to induce bathers to remain in them for any length of time. Grace and the Sopworth girls were already displaying blue chins and chattering teeth.

They raced up the beach, and James pursued his solitary way back to Mon Desir. As he toweled himself vigorously and slipped his shirt over his head, he was pleased with himself. He had, he felt, displayed a dynamic personality.

And then suddenly he stood still, frozen with terror. Girlish voices sounded from outside, and voices quite different from those of Grace and her friends. A moment later he had realized the truth; the rightful owners of Mon Desir were arriving. It is possible that if James had been fully dressed, he would have waited their advent in a dignified manner and attempted an explanation. As it was, he acted on panic. The windows of Mon Desir were modestly screened by dark green curtains. James flung himself on the door and held the knob in a desperate clutch. Hands tried ineffectually to turn it from outside.

"It's locked after all," said a girl's voice. "I thought Pug said it was open."

"No, Woggle said so."

"Woggle is the limit," said the other girl. "How perfectly foul; we shall have to go back for the key."

James heard their footsteps retreating. He drew a long, deep breath. In desperate haste he huddled on the rest of his garments. Two minutes later saw him strolling negligently down the beach with an almost aggressive air of innocence. Grace and the Sopworth girls joined him on the beach a quarter of an hour later. The rest of the morning passed agreeably in stone throwing, writing in the sand and light badinage. Then Claud glanced at his watch.

"Lunchtime," he observed. "We'd better be strolling back."

"I'm terribly hungry," said Alice Sopworth.

All the other girls said that they were terribly hungry too.

"Are you coming, James?" asked Grace.

Doubtless James was unduly touchy. He chose to take offense at her tone.

"Not if my clothes are not good enough for you," he said bitterly. "Perhaps, as you are so particular, I'd better not come."

That was Grace's cue for murmured protestations, but the seaside air had affected Grace unfavorably. She merely replied: "Very well. Just as you like; see you this afternoon then."

James was left dumbfounded.

"Well!" he said, staring after the retreating group. "Well, of all the—"

He strolled moodily into the town. There are two cafés in Kimpton-on-Sea; they are both hot, noisy and overcrowded. It was the affair of the bathing huts once more. James had to wait his turn. He had to wait longer than his turn, an unscrupulous matron who had just arrived forestalling him when a vacant seat did present itself. At last he was seated at a small table. Close to his left ear three raggedly bobbed maidens were making a determined hash of Italian opera. Fortunately James was not musical. He studied the bill of fare dispassionately, his hands thrust deep into his pockets. He thought to himself:

"Whatever I ask for, it's sure to be 'off.' That's the kind of fellow I am."

His right hand, groping in the recesses of his pocket, touched an unfamiliar object. It felt like a pebble, a large round pebble.

"What on earth did I want to put a stone in my pocket for?" thought James.

His fingers closed round it. A waitress drifted up to him.

"Fried plaice and chipped potatoes, please," said James.

"Fried plaice is 'off,'" murmured the waitress, her eyes fixed dreamily on the ceiling.

"Then I'll have curried beef," said James.

"Curried beef is 'off.'"

"Is there anything on this beastly menu that isn't 'off?'" demanded James.

The waitress looked pained and placed a pale-gray forefinger against haricot mutton. James resigned himself to the inevitable and ordered haricot mutton. His mind still seething with resentment against the ways of cafés, he drew his hand out of his pocket, the stone still in it. Unclosing his fingers, he looked absent-mindedly at the object in his palm. Then with a shock all lesser matters passed from his mind, and he stared with all his eyes. The thing he held was not a pebble, it was—he could hardly doubt it—an emerald, an enormous green emerald. James stared at it horror-stricken. No, it couldn't be an emerald; it must be colored glass. There couldn't be an emerald of that size, unless—printed words danced before James's eyes, "The Rajah of Maraputna—famous emerald the size of a pigeon's egg." Was it—could it be—*that* emerald at which he was looking now? The waitress returned with the haricot mutton, and James closed his fingers spasmodically. Hot and cold shivers chased themselves up and down his spine. He had the sense of being caught in a terrible dilemma. If this was the emerald—but was it? Could it be? He unclosed his fingers and peeped anxiously. James was no expert on precious stones, but the depth and the glow of the jewel convinced him this was the real thing. He put both elbows on the table and leaned forward staring with unseeing eyes at the haricot mutton slowly congealing on the dish in front of him. He had got to think this out. If this was the Rajah's emerald, what was he going to do about it? The world "police" flashed into his mind. If you found anything of value, you took it to the police station. Upon this axiom had James been brought up.

Yes, but—how on earth had the emerald got into his trouser pocket? That was doubtless the question the police would ask. It was an awkward question, and it was moreover a question to which he had at the moment no answer. How had the emerald got into his trouser pocket? He looked despairingly down at his legs, and as he did so, a misgiving shot through him. He looked more closely. One pair of old gray flannel trousers is very much like another pair of old gray flannel trousers, but all the same, James had an instinctive feeling that these were not his trousers after all. He sat back in his chair stunned with the force of the discovery. He saw now what had happened; in the hurry of getting out of the bathing hut, he had taken the wrong trousers. He had hung his own, he remembered, on an adjacent peg to the old pair hanging there. Yes, that explained matters so far; he had taken the wrong trousers. But all the same, what on earth was an emerald worth hundreds and thousands of pounds doing there? The more he thought about it, the more curious it seemed. He could, of course, explain to the police—

It was awkward, no doubt about it, it was decidedly awkward. One would have to mention the fact that one had deliberately entered someone else's bathing hut. It was not, of course, a serious offense, but it started him off wrong.

"Can I bring you anything else, sir?"

It was the waitress again. She was looking pointedly at the untouched haricot mutton. James hastily dumped some of it on his plate and asked for his bill. Having obtained it, he paid and went out. As he stood undecidedly in the street, a poster opposite caught his eye. The adjacent town of Harchester possessed an evening paper, and it was the contents bill of this paper that James was looking at. It announced a simple, sensational fact: "THE RAJAH'S EMERALD STOLEN." "My God," said James faintly, and leaned against a pillar. Pulling himself together, he fished out a penny and purchased a copy of the paper. He was not long in finding what he sought. Sensational items of local news were few and far between. Large headlines adorned the front page. "Sensational Burglary at Lord Edward Campion's. Theft of Famous Historical Emerald. Rajah of Maraputna's Terrible Loss." The facts were few and simple. Lord Edward Campion had entertained several friends the evening before. Wishing to show the stone to one of the ladies present, the Rajah had gone to fetch it and had found it missing. The police had been called in. So far no clue had been obtained. James let the paper fall to the ground. It was still not clear to him how the emerald had come to be reposing in the pocket of an old pair of flannel trousers in a bathing hut, but it was borne in upon him every minute that the police would certainly regard his own story as suspicious. What on earth was he to do? Here he was, standing in the principal street of Kimpton-on-Sea with stolen booty worth a king's ransom reposing idly in his pocket, while the entire police force of the district were busily searching for just that same booty. There were two courses open to him. Course number one, to go straight to the police station and tell his story—but it must be admitted that James funked that course badly. Course number two, somehow or other to get rid of the emerald. It occurred to him to do it up in a neat little parcel and post it back to the Rajah. Then he shook his head. He had read too many detective stories for that sort of thing. He knew how your super-sleuth could get busy with a magnifying glass and every kind of patent device. Any detective worth his salt would get busy on James's parcel and would in half an hour or so have discovered the sender's profession, age, habits, and personal appearance. After that it would be a mere matter of hours before he was tracked down.

It was then that a scheme of dazzling simplicity suggested itself to James. It was the luncheon hour, the beach would be comparatively deserted. He would return to Mon Desir, hang up the trousers where he had found them, and regain his own garments. He started briskly toward the beach.

Nevertheless, his conscience pricked him slightly. The emerald ought to be returned to the Rajah. He conceived the idea that he might perhaps do a little detective work—once, that is, that he had regained his own trousers and replaced the others. In pursuance of this idea, he directed his steps toward the aged mariner, whom he rightly regarded as being an inexhaustible source of Kimpton information.

"Excuse me!" said James politely; "but I believe a friend of mine has a hut on this beach, Mr. Charles Lampton. It is called Mon Desir, I fancy?"

The aged mariner was sitting very squarely in a chair, a pipe in his mouth, gazing out to sea. He shifted his pipe a little and replied without removing his gaze from the horizon:

"Mon Desir belongs to his lordship, Lord Edward Campion; everyone knows that. I never heard of Mr. Charles Lampton; he must be a newcomer."

"Thank you," said James, and withdrew.

The information staggered him. Surely the Rajah could not himself have slipped the stone into the pocket and forgotten it. James shook his head. The theory did not satisfy him, but evidently some member of the house party must be the thief. The situation reminded James of some of his favorite works of fiction.

Nevertheless, his own purpose remained unaltered. All fell out easily enough. The beach was, as he hoped it would be, practically deserted. More fortunate still, the door of Mon Desir remained ajar. To slip in was the work of a moment, Edward was just lifting his own trousers from the hook, when a voice behind him made him spin round suddenly.

"So I have caught you, my man!" said the voice.

James stared open-mouthed. In the doorway of Mon Desir stood a stranger—a well-dressed man of about forty years of age, his face keen and hawklike.

"So I have caught you!" the stranger repeated.

"Who—who are you?" stammered James.

"Detective-Inspector Merrilees from the Yard," said the other crisply. "And I will trouble you to hand over that emerald."

"The—the emerald?"

James was seeking to gain time.

"That's what I said, didn't I?" said Inspector Merrilees.

He had a crisp, businesslike enunciation. James tried to pull himself together.

"I don't know what you are talking about," he said with an assumption of dignity.

"Oh, yes, my lad, I think you do."

"The whole thing," said James, "is a mistake. I can explain it quite easily—" He paused.

A look of weariness had settled on the face of the other.

"They always say that," murmured the Scotland Yard man dryly. "I suppose you picked it up as you were strolling along the beach, eh? That is the sort of explanation."

It did indeed bear a resemblance to it. James recognized the fact, but still he tried to gain time.

"How do I know you are what you say you are?" he demanded weakly.

Merrilees flapped back his coat for a moment, showing a badge. Edward stared at him with eyes that popped out of his head.

"And now," said the other almost genially, "you see what you are up against! You are a novice—I can tell that. Your first job, isn't it?"

James nodded.

"I thought as much. Now, my boy, are you going to hand over that emerald, or have I got to search you?"

James found his voice.

"I—I haven't got it on me," he declared.

He was thinking desperately.

"Left it at your lodgings?" queried Merrilees.

James nodded.

"Very well, then," said the detective, "we will go there together."

He slipped his arm through James's.

"I am taking no chances of your getting away from me," he said gently. "We will go to your lodgings, and you will hand that stone over to me."

James spoke unsteadily.

"If I do, will you let me go?" he asked tremulously.

Merrilees appeared embarrassed.

"We know just how that stone was taken," he explained, "and about the lady involved, and, of course, as far as that goes—well, the Rajah wants it hushed up. You know what these native rulers are?"

James, who knew nothing whatsoever about native rulers, except for one *cause célèbre,* nodded his head with an appearance of eager comprehension.

"It will be most irregular, of course," said the detective, "but you *may* get off scot-free."

Again James nodded. They had walked the length of the Esplanade, and were now turning into the town. James intimated the direction, but the other man never relinquished his sharp grip on James's arm.

Suddenly James hesitated and half spoke. Merrilees looked up sharply, and then laughed. They were just passing the police station, and he noticed James's agonized glances at it.

"I am giving you a chance first," he said good-humoredly.

It was at that moment that things began to happen. A loud bellow broke from James; he clutched the other's arm, and yelled at the top of his voice:

"Help! Thief. Help! Thief."

A crowd surrounded them in less than a minute. Merrilees was trying to wrench his arm from James's grasp.

"I charge this man," cried James. "I charge this man; he picked my pocket."

"What are you talking about, you fool?" cried the other.

A constable took charge of matters. Mr. Merrilees and James were escorted into the police station. James reiterated his complaint.

"This man has just picked my pocket," he declared excitedly. "He has got my notecase in his right-hand pocket, there!"

"The man is mad," grumbled the other. "You can look for yourself, inspector, and see if he is telling the truth."

At a sign from the inspector, the constable slipped his hand deferentially into Merrilees's pocket. He drew something up and held it out with a gasp of astonishment.

"My God!" said the inspector, startled out of professional decorum. "It must be the Rajah's emerald."

Merrilees looked more incredulous than anyone else.

"This is monstrous," he spluttered; "monstrous. The man must have put it into my pocket himself as we were walking along together. It's a plant."

The forceful personality of Merrilees caused the inspector to waver. His suspicions swung round to James. He whispered something to the constable, and the latter went out.

"Now then, gentlemen," said the inspector, "let me have your statements please, one at a time."

"Certainly," said James. "I was walking along the beach when I met this gentleman, and he pretended he was acquainted with me. I could not remember having met him before, but I was too polite to say so. We walked along together. I had my suspicions of him, and just when we got opposite the police station, I found his hand in my pocket. I held on to him and shouted for help."

The inspector transferred his glance to Merrilees.

"And now you, sir."

Merrilees seemed a little embarrassed.

"The story is very nearly right," he said slowly, "but not quite. It was not I who scraped acquaintance with him, but he who scraped acquaintance with me. Doubtless he was trying to get rid of the emerald, and slipped it into my pocket while we were talking."

The inspector stopped writing.

"Ah!" he said impartially. "Well, there will be a gentleman here in a minute who will help us to get to the bottom of the case."

Merrilees frowned.

"It is really impossible for me to wait," he murmured, pulling out his watch. "I have an appointment. Surely, inspector, you can't be so ridiculous as to suppose I'd steal the emerald and walk along with it in my pocket?"

"It is not likely, sir, I agree," the inspector replied. "But you will have to wait just a matter of five or ten minutes till we get this thing cleared up. Ah! Here is his lordship."

A tall man of forty strode into the room. He was wearing a pair of dilapidated trousers and an old sweater.

"Now then, inspector, what is all this?" he said. "You have got hold of the emerald, you say? That's splendid; very smart work. Who are these people you have got here?"

His eye ranged over James and came to rest on Merrilees. The forceful personality of the latter seemed to dwindle and shrink.

"Why—Jones!" exclaimed Lord Edward Campion.

"You recognize this man, Lord Edward?" asked the inspector sharply.

"Certainly I do," said Lord Edward dryly. "He is my valet, came to me a month ago. The fellow they sent down from London was on to him at once, but there was not a trace of the emerald anywhere among his belongings."

"He was carrying it in his coat pocket," the inspector declared. "This gentleman put us on to him." He indicated James.

In another minute James was being warmly congratulated and shaken by the hand.

"My dear fellow," said Lord Edward Campion. "So you suspected him all along, you say?"

"Yes," said James. "I had to trump up the story about my pocket being picked to get him into the police station."

"Well, it is splendid," said Lord Edward, "absolutely splendid. You must come back and lunch with us; that is, if you haven't lunched? It is late, I know, getting on for two o'clock."

"No," said James; "I haven't lunched—but—"

"Not a word, not a word," said Lord Edward. "The Rajah, you know, will want to thank you for getting back his emerald for him. Not that I have quite got the hang of the story yet."

They were out of the police station by now, standing on the steps.

"As a matter of fact," said James, "I think I should like to tell you the true story."

He did so. His lordship was very much entertained.

"Best thing I ever heard in my life," he declared. "I see it all now. Jones must have hurried down to the bathing hut as soon as he had pinched the thing, knowing that the police would make a thorough search of the house. That old pair of trousers I sometimes put on for going out fishing; nobody was likely to touch them, and he could recover the jewel at his leisure. Must have been a shock to him when he came today to find it gone. As soon as you appeared, he realized that you were the person who had removed the stone. I still don't quite see how you managed to see through that detective pose of his, though!"

"A strong man," thought James to himself, "knows when to be frank and when to be discreet."

He smiled deprecatingly while his fingers passed gently over the inside of his coat lapel feeling the small silver badge of that little-known club, the Merton Park Super Cycling Club. An astonishing coincidence that the man Jones should also be a member, but there it was!

"Hallo, James!"

He turned. Grace and the Sopworth girls were calling to him from the other side of the road. He turned to Lord Edward.

"Excuse me a moment?"

He crossed the road to them.

"We are going to the pictures," said Grace. "Thought you might like to come."

"I am sorry," said James. "I am just going back to lunch with Lord Edward Campion. Yes, that man over there in the comfortable old clothes. He wants me to meet the Rajah of Maraputna."

He raised his hat politely and rejoined Lord Edward.

SWAN SONG

It was eleven o'clock on a May morning in London. Mr. Cowan was looking out of the window; behind him was the somewhat ornate splendor of a sitting room in a suite at the Ritz Hotel. The suite in question had been reserved for Mme. Paula Nazorkoff, the famous operatic star, who had just arrived in London. Mr. Cowan, who was Madame's principal man of business, was awaiting an interview with the lady. He turned his head suddenly as the door opened, but it was only Miss Read, Mme. Nazorkoff's secretary, a pale girl with an efficient manner.

"Oh, so it's you, my dear," said Mr. Cowan. "Madame not up yet, eh?"

Miss Read shook her head.

"She told me to come round at ten o'clock," Mr. Cowan said. "I have been waiting an hour."

He displayed neither resentment nor surprise. Mr. Cowan was indeed accustomed to the vagaries of the artistic temperament. He was a tall man, clean-shaven, with a frame rather too well covered, and clothes that were rather too faultless. His hair was very black and shining, and his teeth were aggressively white. When he spoke, he had a way of slurring his "s's" which was not quite a lisp, but came perilously near to it. At that minute a door at the other side of the room opened, and a trim French girl hurried through.

"Madame getting up?" inquired Cowan hopefully. "Tell us the news, Elise."

Elise immediately elevated both hands to heaven.

"Madame she is like seventeen devils this morning; nothing pleases her! The beautiful yellow roses which monsieur sent to her last night, she says they are all very well for New York, but that it is *imbécile* to send them to her in London. In London, she says, red roses are the only things possible, and straightaway she opens the door and precipitates the yellow roses into the passage, where they descend upon a monsieur, *très comme il faut,* a military gentleman, I think, and he is justly indignant, that one!"

Cowan raised his eyebrows, but displayed no other signs of emotion. Then he took from his pocket a small memorandum book and pencilled in it the words "red roses."

Elise hurried out through the other door, and Cowan turned once more to the window. Vera Read sat down at the desk and began opening letters and sorting them. Ten minutes passed in silence, and then the door of the bedroom burst open, and Paula Nazorkoff flamed into the room. Her immediate effect upon it was to make it seem smaller; Vera Read appeared more colorless, and Cowan retreated into a mere figure in the background.

"Ah, ha! My children," said the prima donna. "Am I not punctual?"

She was a tall woman, and for a singer not unduly fat. Her arms and legs were still slender, and her neck was a beautiful column. Her hair, which was coiled in a great roll halfway down her neck, was of a dark, glowing red. If it owed some at least of its color to henna, the result was none the less effective. She was not a young woman, forty at least, but the lines of her face were still lovely, though the skin was loosened and wrinkled round the flashing, dark eyes. She had the laugh of a child, the digestion of an ostrich, and the temper of a fiend, and she was acknowledged to be the greatest dramatic soprano of her day. She turned directly upon Cowan.

"Have you done as I asked you? Have you taken that abominable English piano away and thrown it into the Thames?"

"I have got another for you," said Cowan, and gestured toward where it stood in the corner.

Nazorkoff rushed across to it and lifted the lid.

"An Erard," she said; "that is better. Now let us see."

The beautiful soprano voice rang out in an arpeggio, then it ran lightly up and down the scale twice, then took a soft little run up to a high note, held it, its volume swelling louder and louder, then softened again till it died away in nothingness.

"Ah!" said Paula Nazorkoff in naïve satisfaction. "What a beautiful voice I have! Even in London I have a beautiful voice."

"That is so," agreed Cowan in hearty congratulation. "And you bet London is going to fall for you all right, just as New York did."

"You think so?" queried the singer.

There was a slight smile on her lips, and it was evident that for her the question was a mere commonplace.

"Sure thing," said Cowan.

Paula Nazorkoff closed the piano lid down and walked across to the table with that slow undulating walk that proved so effective on the stage.

"Well, well," she said, "let us get to business. You have all the arrangements there, my friend?"

Cowan took some papers out of the portfolio he had laid on a chair.

"Nothing has been altered much," he remarked. "You will sing five times at Covent Garden, three times in *Tosca,* twice in *Aïda.*"

"*Aïda!* Pah," said the prima donna, "it will be unutterable boredom. *Tosca,* that is different."

"Ah, yes," said Cowan. "*Tosca* is *your* part."

Paula Nazorkoff drew herself up.

"I am the greatest Tosca in the world," she said simply.

"That is so," agreed Cowan. "No one can touch you."

"Roscari will sing 'Scarpia,' I suppose?"

Cowan nodded.

"And Emile Lippi."

"What?" shrieked Nazorkoff. "Lippi—that hideous little barking frog, croak—croak—croak. I will not sing with him. I will bite him. I will scratch his face."

"Now, now," said Cowan soothingly.

"He does not sing, I tell you, he is a mongrel dog who barks."

"Well, we'll see; we'll see," said Cowan.

He was too wise ever to argue with temperamental singers.

"The Cavaradossi?" demanded Nazorkoff.

"The American tenor, Hensdale."

The other nodded.

"He is a nice little boy; he sings prettily."

"And Barrère is to sing it once, I believe."

"He is an artist," said Madame generously. "But to let that croaking frog Lippi be Scarpia! Bah—I'll not sing with him."

"You leave it to me," said Cowan soothingly.

He cleared his throat and took up a fresh set of papers.

"I am arranging for a special concert at the Albert Hall."

Nazorkoff made a grimace.

"I know, I know," said Cowan; "but everybody does it."

"I will be good," said Nazorkoff, "and it will be filled to the ceiling, and I shall have much money. *Ecco!*"

Again Cowan shuffled papers.

"Now here is quite a different proposition," he said, "from Lady Rustonbury. She wants you to go down and sing."

"Rustonbury?"

The prima donna's brow contracted as if in the effort to recollect something.

"I have read the name lately, very lately. It is a town—or a village, isn't it?"

"That's right, pretty little place in Hertfordshire. As for Lord Rustonbury's place, Rustonbury Castle, it's a real dandy old feudal seat, ghosts and family pictures, and secret staircases, and a slap-up private theater. Rolling in money they are, and always giving some private show. She suggests that we give a complete opera, preferably *Butterfly*."

"*Butterfly*?"

Cowan nodded.

"And they are prepared to pay. We'll have to square Covent Garden, of course, but even after that it will be well worth your while financially. In all probability, royalty will be present. It will be a slap-up advertisement."

Madame raised her still beautiful chin.

"Do I need advertisement?" she demanded proudly.

"You can't have too much of a good thing," said Cowan, unabashed.

"Rustonbury," murmured the singer; "where did I see—"

She sprang up suddenly and, running to the center table, began turning over the pages of an illustrated paper which lay there. There was a sudden pause as her hand stopped, hovering over one of the pages, then she let the periodical slip to the floor and returned slowly to her seat. With one of her swift changes of mood, she seemed now an entirely different personality. Her manner was very quiet, almost austere.

"Make all arrangements for Rustonbury. I would like to sing there, but there is one condition—the opera must be *Tosca*."

Cowan looked doubtful.

"That will be rather difficult—for a private show, you know, scenery and all that."

"*Tosca* or nothing."

Cowan looked at her very closely. What he saw seemed to convince him; he gave a brief nod and rose to his feet.

"I will see what I can arrange," he said quietly.

Nazorkoff rose too. She seemed more anxious than was usual, with her, to explain her decision.

"It is my greatest role, Cowan. I can sing that part as no other woman has ever sung it."

"It is a fine part," said Cowan. "Jeritza made a great hit in it last year."

"Jeritza?" cried the other, a flush mounting in her cheeks. She proceeded to give him at great length her opinion of Jeritza.

Cowan, who was used to listening to singers' opinions of other singers, abstracted his attention till the tirade was over; he then said obstinately:

"Anyway, she sings 'Vissi D'Arte' lying on her stomach."

"And why not?" demanded Nazorkoff. "What is there to prevent her? I will sing it on my back with my legs waving in the air."

Cowan shook his head with perfect seriousness.

"I don't believe that would go down any," he informed her. "All the same, that sort of thing takes on, you know."

"No one can sing 'Vissi D'Arte' as I can," said Nazorkoff confidently. "I sing it in the voice of the convent—as the good nuns taught me to sing years and years ago. In the voice of a choir boy or an angel, without feeling, without passion."

"I know," said Cowan heartily. "I have heard you; you are wonderful."

"That is art," said the prima donna, "to pay the price, to suffer, to endure, and in the end not only to have all knowledge, but also the power to go back, right back to the beginning and recapture the lost beauty of the heart of a child."

Cowan looked at her curiously. She was staring past him with a strange, blank look in her eyes, and something about that look of hers gave him a creepy feeling. Her lips just parted, and she whispered a few words softly to herself. He only just caught them.

"At last," she murmured. "At last—after all these years."

II

Lady Rustonbury was both an ambitious and an artistic woman; she ran the two qualities in harness with complete success. She had the good fortune to have a husband who cared for neither ambition nor art and who therefore did not hamper her in any way. The Earl of Rustonbury was a large, square man, with an interest in horseflesh and in nothing else. He admired his wife, and was proud of her, and was glad that his great wealth enabled her to indulge all her schemes. The private theater had been built less than a hundred years ago by his grandfather. It was Lady Rustonbury's chief toy—

she had already given an Ibsen drama in it, and a play of the ultra new school, all divorce and drugs, also a poetical fantasy with Cubist scenery. The forthcoming performance of *Tosca* had created widespread interest. Lady Rustonbury was entertaining a very distinguished house party for it, and all London that counted was motoring down to attend.

Mme. Nazorkoff and her company had arrived just before luncheon. The new young American tenor, Hensdale, was to sing "Cavaradossi," and Roscari, the famous Italian baritone, was to be Scarpia. The expense of the production had been enormous, but nobody cared about that. Paula Nazorkoff was in the best of humors; she was charming, gracious, her most delightful and cosmopolitan self. Cowan was agreeably surprised, and prayed that this state of things might continue.

After luncheon the company went out to the theater and inspected the scenery and various appointments. The orchestra was under the direction of Mr. Samuel Ridge, one of England's most famous conductors. Everything seemed to be going without a hitch, and strangely enough, that fact worried Mr. Cowan. He was more at home in an atmosphere of trouble; this unusual peace disturbed him.

"Everything is going a darned sight too smoothly," murmured Mr. Cowan to himself. "Madame is like a cat that has been fed on cream. It's too good to last; something is bound to happen."

Perhaps as the result of his long contact with the operatic world, Mr. Cowan had developed the sixth sense, certainly his prognostications were justified. It was just before seven o'clock that evening when the French maid, Elise, came running to him in great distress.

"Ah, Mr. Cowan, come quickly; I beg of you come quickly."

"What's the matter?" demanded Cowan anxiously. "Madame got her back up about anything—ructions, eh, is that it?"

"No, no, it is not Madame; it is Signor Roscari. He is ill; he is dying!"

"Dying? Oh, come now."

Cowan hurried after her as she led the way to the stricken Italian's bedroom. The little man was lying on his bed, or rather jerking himself all over it in a series of contortions that would have been humorous had they been less grave. Paula Nazorkoff was bending over him; she greeted Cowan imperiously.

"Ah! There you are. Our poor Roscari, he suffers horribly. Doubtless he has eaten something."

"I am dying," groaned the little man. "The pain—it is terrible. Ow!"

He contorted himself again, clasping both hands to his stomach, and rolling about on the bed.

"We must send for a doctor," said Cowan.

Paula arrested him as he was about to move to the door.

"The doctor is already on his way; he will do all that can be done for the poor suffering one, that is arranged for, but never, never will Roscari be able to sing tonight."

"I shall never sing again; I am dying," groaned the Italian.

"No, no, you are not dying," said Paula. "It is but an indigestion, but all the same, impossible that you should sing."

"I have been poisoned."

"Yes, it is the ptomaine without doubt," said Paula. "Stay with him, Elise, till the doctor comes."

The singer swept Cowan with her from the room.

"What are we to do?" she demanded.

Cowan shook his head hopelessly. The hour was so far advanced that it would not be possible to get anyone from London to take Roscari's place. Lady Rustonbury, who had just been informed of her guest's illness, came hurrying along the corridor to join them. Her principal concern, like Paula Nazorkoff's, was the success of *Tosca*.

"If there were only someone near at hand," groaned the prima donna.

"Ah!" Lady Rustonbury gave a sudden cry. "Of course! Bréon."

"Bréon?"

"Yes, Edouard Bréon, you know, the famous French baritone. He lives near here. There was a picture of his house in this week's *Country Homes*. He is the very man."

"It is an answer from heaven," cried Nazorkoff. "Bréon as Scarpia, I remember him well, it was one of his greatest rôles. But he has retired, has he not?"

"I will get him," said Lady Rustonbury. "Leave it to me."

And being a woman of decision, she straightway ordered out the Hispano Suiza. Ten minutes later, M. Edouard Bréon's country retreat was invaded by an agitated countess. Lady Rustonbury, once she had made her mind up, was a very determined woman, and doubtless M. Bréon realized that there was nothing for it but to submit. Also, it must be confessed, he had a weakness for countesses. Himself a man of very humble origin, he had climbed to the top of his profession, and had consorted on equal terms with dukes and princes, and the fact never failed to gratify him. Yet, since his retirement to this old-world English spot, he had known discontent. He missed the life of adulation and applause, and the English county had not been as prompt to recognize him as he thought they should have been. So he was greatly flattered and charmed by Lady Rustonbury's request.

"I will do my poor best," he said, smiling. "As you know, I have not sung in public for a long time now. I do not even take pupils, only one or two as a great favor. But there—since Signor Roscari is unfortunately indisposed—"

"It was a terrible blow," said Lady Rustonbury.

"Not that he is really a singer," said Bréon.

He told her at some length why this was so. There had been, it seemed, no baritone of distinction since Edouard Bréon retired.

"Mme. Nazorkoff is singing 'Tosca,'" said Lady Rustonbury. "You know her, I dare say?"

"I have never met her," said Bréon. "I heard her sing once in New York. A great artist—she has a sense of drama."

Lady Rustonbury felt relieved—one never knew with these singers—they had such queer jealousies and antipathies.

She reentered the hall at the castle some twenty minutes later waving a triumphant hand.

"I have got him," she cried, laughing. "Dear M. Bréon has really been too kind. I shall never forget it."

Everyone crowded round the Frenchman, and their gratitude and appreciation were as incense to him. Edouard Bréon, though now close on sixty, was still a fine-looking man, big and dark, with a magnetic personality.

"Let me see," said Lady Rustonbury. "Where is Madame—? Oh! There she is."

Paula Nazorkoff had taken no part in the general welcoming of the Frenchman. She had remained quietly sitting in a high oak chair in the shadow of the fireplace. There was, of course, no fire, for the evening was a warm one and the singer was slowly fanning herself with an immense palm-leaf fan. So aloof and detached was she, that Lady Rustonbury feared she had taken offense.

"M. Bréon." She led him up to the singer. "You have never yet met Madame Nazorkoff, you say."

With a last wave, almost a flourish, of the palm leaf, Paula Nazorkoff laid it down and stretched out her hand to the Frenchman. He took it and bowed low over it, and a faint sigh escaped from the prima donna's lips.

"Madame," said Bréon, "we have never sung together. That is the penalty of my age! But Fate has been kind to me, and come to my rescue."

Paula laughed softly.

"You are too kind, M. Bréon. When I was still but a poor little unknown singer, I have sat at your feet. Your 'Rigoletto'—what art, what perfection! No one could touch you."

"Alas!" said Bréon, pretending to sigh. "My day is over. Scarpia, Rigoletto, Radamès, Sharpless, how many times have I not sung them, and now—no more!"

"Yes—tonight."

"True, madame—I forgot. Tonight."

"You have sung with many 'Tosca's,'" said Nazorkoff arrogantly, "but never with *me!*"

The Frenchman bowed.

"It will be an honor," he said softly. "It is a great part, madame."

"It needs not only a singer, but an actress," put in Lady Rustonbury.

"That is true," Bréon agreed. "I remember when I was a young man in Italy, going to a little out-of-the-way theater in Milan. My seat cost me only a couple of lira, but I heard as good singing that night as I have heard in the Metropolitan Opera House in New York. Quite a young girl sang 'Tosca'; she sang it like an angel. Never shall I forget her voice in 'Vissi D'Arte,' the clearness of it, the purity. But the dramatic force, that was lacking."

Nazorkoff nodded.

"That comes later," she said quietly.

"True. This young girl—Bianca Capelli her name was—I interested myself in her career. Through me she had the chance of big engagements, but she was foolish—regrettably foolish."

He shrugged his shoulders.

"How was she foolish?"

It was Lady Rustonbury's twenty-four-year-old daughter, Blanche Amery, who spoke—a slender girl with wide blue eyes.

The Frenchman turned to her at once politely.

"Alas! Mademoiselle, she had embroiled herself with some low fellow, a ruffian, a member of the Camorra. He got into trouble with the police, was condemned to death; she came to me begging me to do something to save her lover."

Blanche Amery was staring at him.

"And did you?" she asked breathlessly.

"Me, mademoiselle, what could I do? A stranger in the country."

"You might have had influence?" suggested Nazorkoff in her low, vibrant voice.

"If I had, I doubt whether I should have exerted it. The man was not worth it. I did what I could for the girl."

He smiled a little, and his smile suddenly struck the English girl as having something peculiarly disagreeable about it. She felt that, at that moment, his words fell far short of representing his thoughts.

"You did what you could," said Nazorkoff. "That was kind of you, and she was grateful, eh?"

The Frenchman shrugged his shoulders.

"The man was executed," he said, "and the girl entered a convent. Eh, *voilà!* The world has lost a singer."

Nazorkoff gave a low laugh.

"We Russians are more fickle," she said lightly.

Blanche Amery happened to be watching Cowan just as the singer spoke, and she saw his quick look of astonishment, and his lips that half opened and then shut tight in obedience to some warning glance from Paula.

The butler appeared in the doorway.

"Dinner," said Lady Rustonbury, rising. "You poor things, I am so sorry for you. It must be dreadful always to have to starve yourself before singing. But there will be a very good supper afterward."

"We shall look forward to it," said Paula Nazorkoff. She laughed softly. "Afterward!"

III

Inside the theater, the first act of *Tosca* had just drawn to a close. The audience stirred, spoke to each other. The royalties, charming and gracious, sat in the three velvet chairs in the front row. Everyone was whispering and murmuring to each other; there was a general feeling that in the first act Nazorkoff had hardly lived up to her great reputation. Most of the audience did not realize that in this the singer showed her art; in the first act she was saving her voice and herself. She made of La Tosca a light, frivolous figure, toying with love, coquettishly jealous and exacting. Bréon, though the glory of his voice was past its prime, still struck a magnificent figure as the cynical Scarpia. There was no hint of the decrepit roué in his conception of the part. He made of Scarpia a handsome, almost benign figure, with just a hint of the subtle malevolence that underlay the outward seeming. In the last passage, with the organ and the procession, when Scarpia stands lost in thought, gloating over his plan to secure Tosca, Bréon had displayed a wonderful art. Now the curtain rose upon the second act, the scene in Scarpia's apartments.

This time, when Tosca entered, the art of Nazorkoff at once became apparent. Here was a woman in deadly terror playing her part with the assurance of a fine actress. Her easy greeting of Scarpia, her nonchalance, her smiling replies to him! In this scene, Paula Nazorkoff acted with her eyes; she carried herself with deadly quietness, with an impassive, smiling face. Only her eyes that kept darting glances at Scarpia betrayed her true feelings. And so the story went on, the torture scene, the breaking down of Tosca's composure, and her utter abandonment when she fell at Scarpia's feet imploring him vainly for mercy. Old Lord Leconmere, a connoisseur of music, moved appreciatively, and a foreign ambassador sitting next to him murmured:

"She surpasses herself, Nazorkoff, tonight. There is no other woman on the stage who can let herself go as she does."

Leconmere nodded.

And now Scarpia has named his price, and Tosca, horrified, flies from him to the window. Then comes the beat of drums from afar, and Tosca flings herself wearily down on the sofa. Scarpia, standing over her, recites how his people are raising up the gallows—and then silence, and again the far-off beat of drums. Nazorkoff lay prone on the sofa, her head hanging downward almost touching the floor, masked by her hair. Then, in exquisite contrast to the passion and stress of the last twenty minutes, her voice rang out, high and clear, the voice, as she had told Cowan, of a choir boy or an angel.

"Vissi d'arte, vissi d'amore, no feci mai male ad anima vival.
Con man furtiva quante miserie conobbi, aiu-tai."

It was the voice of a wondering, puzzled child. Then she is once more kneeling and imploring, till the instant when Spoletta enters. Tosca, exhausted, gives in, and Scarpia utters his fateful words of double-edged meaning. Spoletta departs once more. Then comes the dramatic moment when Tosca, raising a glass of wine in her trembling hand, catches sight of the knife on the table and slips it behind her.

Bréon rose up, handsome, saturnine, inflamed with passion. *"Tosca, finalmente mia!"* The lightning stab with the knife, and Tosca's hiss of vengeance:

"Questo e il baccio di Tosca!" ("It is thus that Tosca kisses.")

Never had Nazorkoff shown such an appreciation of Tosca's act of vengeance. That last fierce whispered *"Muori dannato,"* and then in a strange, quiet voice that filled the theater:

"Or gli perdono!" ("Now I forgive him!")

The soft death tune began as Tosca set about her ceremonial, placing the candles each side of his head, the crucifix on his breast, her last pause in the doorway looking back, the roll of distant drums, and the curtain fell.

This time real enthusiasm broke out in the audience, but it was short-lived. Someone hurried out from behind the wings and spoke to Lord Rustonbury. He rose, and after a minute or two's consultation, turned and beckoned to Sir Donald Calthorp, who was an eminent physician. Almost immediately the truth spread through the audience. Something had happened; an accident; someone was badly hurt. One of the singers appeared before the curtain and explained that M. Bréon had unfortunately met with an accident—the opera could not proceed. Again the rumor went round, Bréon had been stabbed, Nazorkoff had lost her head, she had lived in her part so completely that she had actually stabbed the man who was acting with her. Lord Leconmere, talking to his ambassador friend, felt a touch on his arm, and turned to look into Blanche Amery's eyes.

"It was not an accident," the girl was saying. "I am sure it was not an accident. Didn't you hear, just before dinner, that story he was telling about the girl in Italy? That girl was Paula Nazorkoff. Just after, she said something about being Russian, and I saw Mr. Cowan look amazed. She may have taken a Russian name, but he knows well enough that she is Italian."

"My dear Blanche," said Lord Leconmere.

"I tell you I am sure of it. She had a picture paper in her bedroom opened at the page showing M. Bréon in his English country home. She knew before she came down here. I believe she gave something to that poor little Italian man to make him ill."

"But why?" cried Lord Leconmere. "Why?"

"Don't you see? It's the story of Tosca all over again. He wanted her in Italy, but she was faithful to her lover, and she went to him to try to get him to save her lover, and he pretended he would. Instead he let him die. And now at last her revenge has come. Didn't you hear the way she hissed *'I am Tosca'*? And I saw Bréon's face when she said it, he knew then—he recognized her!"

In her dressing room, Paula Nazorkoff sat motionless, a white ermine cloak held round her. There was a knock at the door.

"Come in," said the prima donna.

Elise entered. She was sobbing.

"Madame, madame, he is dead! And—"

"Yes?"

"Madame, how can I tell you? There are two gentlemen of the police there; they want to speak to you."

Paula Nazorkoff rose to her full height.

"I will go to them," she said quietly.

She untwisted a collar of pearls from her neck and put them into the French girl's hands.

"Those are for you, Elise; you have been a good girl. I shall not need them now where I am going. You understand, Elise? I shall not sing 'Tosca' again."

She stood a moment by the door, her eyes sweeping over the dressing room, as though she looked back over the past thirty years of her career.

Then softly between her teeth, she murmured the last line of another opera:

"La commedia e finita!"

THE HOUND OF DEATH

It was from William P. Ryan, American newspaper correspondent, that I first heard of the affair. I was dining with him in London on the eve of his return to New York and happened to mention that on the morrow I was going down to Folbridge.

He looked up and said sharply: "Folbridge, Cornwall?"

Now only about one person in a thousand knows that there is a Folbridge in Cornwall. They always take it for granted that the Folbridge, Hampshire, is meant. So Ryan's knowledge aroused my curiosity.

"Yes," I said. "Do you know it?"

He merely replied that he was darned. He then asked if I happened to know a house called Trearne down there.

My interest increased.

"Very well indeed. In fact, it's to Trearne I'm going. It's my sister's house."

"Well," said William P. Ryan. "If that doesn't beat the band!"

I suggested that he should cease making cryptic remarks and explain himself.

"Well," he said. "To do that I shall have to go back to an experience of mine at the beginning of the war."

I sighed. The events which I am relating took place in 1921. To be reminded of the war was the last thing any man wanted. We were, thank God, beginning to forget. . . . Besides, William P. Ryan on his war experiences was apt, as I knew, to be unbelievably long-winded.

But there was no stopping him now.

"At the start of the war, as I dare say you know, I was in Belgium for my paper—moving about some. Well, there's a little village—I'll call it X. A one-horse place if there ever was one, but there's quite a big convent there, Nuns in white what do you call 'em—I don't know the name of the order. Anyway, it doesn't matter. Well, this little burg was right in the way of the German advance. The Uhlans arrived—"

I shifted uneasily. William P. Ryan lifted a hand reasuringly.

"It's all right," he said. "This isn't a German atrocity story. It might have been, perhaps, but it isn't. As a matter of fact, the boot's on the other leg. The Huns made for that convent—they got there and the whole thing blew up."

"Oh!" I said, rather startled.

"Odd business, wasn't it? Of course, offhand, I should say the Huns had been celebrating and had monkeyed round with their own explosives. But it seems they hadn't anything of that kind with them. They weren't the high explosive johnnies. Well, then, I ask you, what should a pack of nuns know about high explosive? Some nuns, I should say!"

"It is odd," I agreed.

"I was interested in hearing the peasants' account of the matter. They'd got it all cut and dried. According to them it was a slap-up, one hundred percent efficient first-class modern miracle. It seems one of the nuns had got something of a reputation—a budding saint—went into trances and saw visions. And according to them she worked the stunt. She called down the lightning to blast the impious Hun—and it blasted him, all right—and everything else within range. A pretty efficient miracle, that!

"I never really got at the truth of the matter—hadn't time. But miracles were all the rage just then—angels at Mons and all that. I wrote up the thing, put in a bit of sob stuff, and pulled the religious stop out well, and sent it to my paper. It went down very well in the States. They were liking that kind of thing just then.

"But (I don't know if you'll understand this) in writing, I got kind of interested. I felt I'd like to know what really had happened. There was nothing to see at the spot itself. Two walls still left standing, and on one of them was a black powder mark that was the exact shape of a great hound. The peasants round about were scared to death of that mark. They called it the Hound of Death and they wouldn't pass that way after dark.

"Superstition's always interesting. I felt I'd like to see the lady who worked the stunt. She hadn't perished, it seemed. She'd gone to England with a batch of other refugees. I took the trouble to trace her. I found she'd been sent to Trearne, Folbridge, Cornwall."

I nodded.

"My sister took in a lot of Belgian refugees the beginning of the war. About twenty."

"Well, I always meant, if I had time, to look up the lady. I wanted to hear her own account of the disaster. Then, what with being busy and one thing and another, it slipped my memory. Cornwall's a bit out of the way anyhow. In fact, I'd forgotten the whole thing till your mentioning Folbridge just now brought it back."

"I must ask my sister," I said. "She may have heard something about it. Of course, the Belgians have all been repatriated long ago."

"Naturally. All the same, in case your sister does know anything, I'll be glad if you'd pass it on to me."

"Of course I will," I said heartily.

And that was that.

II

It was the second day after my arrival at Trearne that the story recurred to me. My sister and I were having tea on the terrace.

"Kitty," I said. "Didn't you have a nun among your Belgians?"

"You don't mean Sister Marie Angelique, do you?"

"Possibly I do," I said cautiously. "Tell me about her."

"Oh, my dear! She was the most uncanny creature. She's still here, you know."

"What? In the house?"

"No, no in the village. Dr. Rose—you remember Dr. Rose?"

I shook my head.

"I remember an old man of about eighty-three."

"Dr. Laird. Oh! He died. Dr. Rose has only been here a few years. He's quite young and very keen on new ideas. He took the most enormous interest in Sister Marie Angelique. She has hallucinations and things, you know, and apparently is most frightfully interesting from a medical point of view. Poor thing, she'd nowhere to go—and really was in my opinion quite potty—only impressive, if you know what I mean—well, as I say, she'd nowhere to go, and Dr. Rose very kindly fixed her up in the village. I believe he's writing a monograph or whatever it is that doctors write, about her."

She paused and then said: "But what do you know about her?"

"I heard a rather curious story."

I passed on the story as I had received it from Ryan. Kitty was very much interested.

"She looks the sort of person who could blast you—if you know what I mean," she said.

"I really think," I said, my curiosity heightened, "that I must see this young woman."

"Do. I'd like to know what you think of her. Go and see Dr. Rose first. Why not walk down to the village after tea?"

I accepted the suggestion.

I found Dr. Rose at home and introduced myself. He seemed a pleasant young man, yet there was something about his personality that rather repelled me. It was too forceful to be altogether agreeable.

The moment I mentioned Sister Marie Angelique he stiffened to attention. He was evidently keenly interested. I gave him Ryan's account of the matter.

"Ah!" he said thoughtfully. "That explains a great deal."

He looked up quickly at me and went on.

"The case is really an extraordinarily interesting one. The woman arrived here having evidently suffered some severe mental shock. She was in a state of great mental excitement also. She was given to hallucinations of a most startling character. Her personality is most unusual. Perhaps you would like to come with me and call upon her. She is really well worth seeing."

I agreed readily.

We set out together. Our objective was a small cottage on the outskirts of the village. Folbridge is a most picturesque place. It lies in the mouth of the river Fol mostly on the east bank; the west bank is too precipitous for building, though a few cottages do cling to the cliff-side there. The doctor's own cottage was perched on the extreme edge of the cliff on the west side. From it you looked down on the big waves lashing against the black rocks.

The little cottage to which we were now proceeding lay inland out of sight of the sea.

"The district nurse lives here," explained Dr. Rose. "I have arranged for Sister Marie Angelique to board with her. It is just as well that she should be under skilled supervision."

"Is she quite normal in her manner?" I asked curiously.

"You can judge for yourself in a minute," he replied, smiling.

The district nurse, a dumpy, pleasant little body, was just setting out on her bicycle when we arrived.

"Good evening, nurse; how's your patient?" called out the doctor.

"She's much as usual, doctor. Just sitting there with her hands folded and her mind far away. Often enough she'll not answer when I speak to her, though for the matter of that it's little enough English she understands even now."

Rose nodded, and as the nurse bicycled away, he went up to the cottage door, rapped sharply and entered.

Sister Marie Angelique was lying in a long chair near the window. She turned her head as we entered.

It was a strange face—pale, transparent-looking, with enormous eyes. There seemed to be an infinitude of tragedy in those eyes.

"Good evening, my sister," said the doctor in French.

"Good evening, M. le docteur."

"Permit me to introduce a friend, Mr. Anstruther."

I bowed and she inclined her head with a faint smile.

"And how are you today?" inquired the doctor, sitting down beside her.

"I am much the same as usual." She paused and then went on. "Nothing seems real to me. Are they days that pass—or months—or years? I hardly know. Only my dreams seem real to me."

"You still dream a lot, then?"

"Always—always—and, you understand?—the dreams seem more real than life."

"You dream of your own country—of Belgium?"

She shook her head.

"No. I dream of a country that never existed—never. But you know this, M. le docteur. I have told you many times." She stopped and then said abruptly: "But perhaps this gentleman is also a doctor—a doctor perhaps for the diseases of the brain?"

"No, no." Rose was reassuring, but as he smiled, I noticed how extraordinarily pointed his canine teeth were, and it occurred to me that there was something wolflike about the man. He went on:

"I thought you might be interested to meet Mr. Anstruther. He knows something of Belgium. He has lately been hearing news of your convent."

Her eyes turned to me. A faint flush crept into her cheeks.

"It's nothing, really," I hastened to explain. "But I was dining the other evening with a friend who was describing the ruined walls of the convent to me."

"So it was ruined!"

It was a soft exclamation, uttered more to herself than to us. Then looking at me once more, she asked hesitatingly: "Tell me, monsieur, did your friend say how—in what way—it was ruined?"

"It was blown up," I said, and added: "The peasants are afraid to pass that way at night."

"Why are they afraid?"

"Because of a black mark on a ruined wall. They have a superstitious fear of it."

She leaned forward.

"Tell me, monsieur—quick—quick—tell me! What is that mark like?"

"It has the shape of a huge hound," I answered. "The peasants call it the Hound of Death."

"Ah!"

A shrill cry burst from her lips.

"It is true then—it is true. All that I remember is true. It is not some black nightmare. It happened! It happened!"

"What happened, my sister?" asked the doctor in a low voice.

She turned to him eagerly.

"*I remembered.* There on the steps, I remembered. I remembered the way of it. I used the power as we used to use it. I stood on the altar steps and I bade them to come no farther. I told them to depart in peace. They would not listen, they came on although I warned them. And so—" She leaned forward and made a curious gesture. "And so I loosed the Hound of Death on them. . . ."

She lay back on her chair shivering all over, her eyes closed.

The doctor rose, fetched a glass from a cupboard, half filled it with water, added a drop or two from a little bottle which he produced from his pocket, then took the glass to her.

"Drink this," he said authoritatively.

She obeyed—mechanically as it seemed. Her eyes looked far away as though they contemplated some inner vision of her own.

"But then it is all true," she said. "Everything. The City of the Circles, the People of the Crystal—everything. It is all true."

"It would seem so," said Rose.

His voice was low and soothing, clearly designed to encourage and not to disturb her train of thought.

"Tell me about the City," he said. "The City of Circles, I think you said?"

She answered absently and mechanically.

"Yes—there were three circles. The first circle for the chosen, the second for the priestesses, and the outer circle for the priests."

"And in the center?"

She drew her breath sharply and her voice sank to a tone of indescribable awe.

"The House of the Crystal. . . ."

As she breathed the words, her right hand went to her forehead and her finger traced some figure there.

Her figure seemed to grow more rigid, her eyes closed, she swayed a little—then suddenly she sat upright with a jerk, as though she had suddenly awakened.

"What is it?" she said confusedly. "What have I been saying?"

"It is nothing," said Rose. "You are tired. You want to rest. We will leave you."

She seemed a little dazed as we took our departure.

"Well," said Rose when we were outside. "What do you think of it?"

He shot a sharp glance sideways at me.

"I suppose her mind must be totally unhinged," I said slowly.

"It struck you like that?"

"No—as a matter of fact, she was—well, curiously convincing. When listening to her I had the impression that she actually had done what she claimed to do—worked a kind of gigantic miracle. Her belief that she did so seems genuine enough. That is why—"

"That is why you say her mind must be unhinged. Quite so. But now approach the matter from another angle. Supposing that she did actually work that miracle—supposing that she did, personally, destroy a building and several hundred human beings."

"By the mere exercise of will?" I said with a smile.

"I should not put it quite like that. You will agree that one person could destroy a multitude by touching a switch which controlled a system of mines."

"Yes, but that is mechanical."

"True, that is mechanical, but it is, in essence, the harnessing and controlling of natural forces. The thunderstorm and the powerhouse are, fundamentally, the same thing."

"Yes, but to control the thunderstorm we have to use mechanical means."

Rose smiled.

"I am going off at a tangent now. There is a substance called wintergreen. It occurs in nature in vegetable form. It can also be built up by man synthetically and chemically in the laboratory."

"Well?"

"My point is that there are often two ways of arriving at the same result. Ours is, admittedly, the synthetic way. There might be another. The extraordinary results arrived at by Indian fakirs, for instance, cannot be explained away in any easy fashion. The things we call supernatural are not necessarily supernatural at all. An electric flashlight would be supernatural to a savage. The supernatural is only the natural of which the laws are not yet understood."

"You mean?" I asked, fascinated.

"That I cannot entirely dismiss the possibility that a human being *might* be able to tap some vast destructive force and use it to further his or her ends. The means by which this was accomplished might seem to us supernatural—but would not be so in reality."

I stared at him.

He laughed.

"It's a speculation, that's all," he said lightly. "Tell me. Did you notice a gesture she made when she mentioned the House of the Crystal?"

"She put her hand to her forehead."

"Exactly. And traced a circle there. Very much as a Catholic makes the sign of the cross. Now, I will tell you something rather interesting, Mr. Anstruther. The word crystal having occurred so often in my patient's rambling, I tried an experiment. I borrowed a crystal from someone and produced it unexpectedly one day to test my patient's reaction to it."

"Well?"

"Well, the result was very curious and suggestive. Her whole body stiffened. She stared at it as though unable to believe her eyes. Then she slid to her knees in front of it, murmured a few words—and fainted."

"What were the few words?"

"Very curious ones. She said: *'The Crystal! Then the Faith still lives!'*"

"Extraordinary!"

"Suggestive, is it not? Now the next curious thing. When she came round from her faint, she had forgotten the whole thing. I showed her the crystal and asked her if she knew what it was. She replied that she supposed it was a crystal such as fortunetellers used. I asked her if she had ever seen one before? She replied: 'Never, M. le docteur.' But I saw a puzzled look in her eyes. 'What troubles you, my sister?' I asked. She replied: 'Because it is so strange. I have never seen a crystal before and yet—it seems to me that I know it well. There is something—if only I could remember. . . .' The effort at memory was obviously so distressing to her that I forbade her to think any more. That was two weeks ago. I have purposely been biding my time. Tomorrow I shall proceed to a further experiment."

"With the crystal?"

"With the crystal. I shall get her to gaze into it. I think the result ought to be interesting."

"What do you expect to get hold of?" I asked curiously.

The words were idle ones but they had an unlooked-for result. Rose stiffened, flushed, and his manner when he spoke had changed insensibly. It was more formal, more professional.

"Light on certain mental disorders imperfectly understood. Sister Marie Angelique is a most interesting study."

So Rose's interest was purely professional? I wondered.

"Do you mind if I come along, too?" I asked.

It may have been my fancy, but I thought he hesitated before he replied. I had a sudden intuition that he did not want me.

"Certainly. I can see no objection."

He added:

"I suppose you're not going to be down here very long?"

"Only till the day after tomorrow."

I fancied that the answer pleased him. His brow cleared and he began talking of some recent experiments carried out on guinea pigs.

III

I met the doctor by appointment the following afternoon, and we went together to Sister Marie Angelique. Today the doctor was all geniality. He was anxious, I thought, to efface the impression he had made the day before.

"You must not take what I said too seriously," he observed, laughing. "I shouldn't like you to believe me a dabbler in occult sciences. The worst of me is I have an infernal weakness for making out a case."

"Really?"

"Yes, and the more fantastic it is, the better I like it."

He laughed as a man laughs at an amusing weakness.

When we arrived at the cottage, the district nurse had something she wanted to consult Rose about, so I was left with Sister Marie Angelique.

I saw her scrutinizing me closely. Presently she spoke.

"The good nurse here, she tells me that you are the brother of the kind lady at the big house where I was brought when I came from Belgium?"

"Yes," I said.

"She was very kind to me. She is good."

She was silent, as though following out some train of thought. Then she said:

"M. le docteur, he, too, is a good man?"

I was a little embarrassed.

"Why, yes. I mean—I think so."

"Ah!" She paused and then said: "Certainly he has been very kind to me."

"I'm sure he has."

She looked up at me sharply.

"Monsieur—you—you who speak to me now—do you believe that I am mad?"

"Why, my sister, such an idea never—"

She shook her head slowly—interrupting my protest.

"Am I mad? I do not know—the things I remember—the things I forget . . ."

She sighed, and at that moment Rose entered the room.

He greeted her cheerily and explained what he wanted her to do.

"Certain people, you see, have a gift for seeing things in a crystal. I fancy you might have such a gift, my sister."

She looked distressed.

"No, no, I cannot do that. To try to read the future—that is sinful."

Rose was taken aback. It was the nun's point of view for which he had not allowed. He changed his ground cleverly.

"One should not look into the future. You are quite right. But to look into the past—that is different."

"The past?"

"Yes—there are many strange things in the past. Flashes come back to one—they are seen for a moment—then gone again. Do not seek to see anything in the crystal, since that is not allowed you. Just take it in your hands—so. Look into it—look deep. Yes—deeper—deeper still. You remember, do you not? You remember. You hear me speaking to you. You can answer my questions. Can you not hear me?"

Sister Marie Angelique had taken the crystal as bidden, handling it with a curious reverence. Then, as she gazed into it, her eyes became blank and unseeing, her head dropped. She seemed to sleep.

Gently the doctor took the crystal from her and put it on the table. He raised the corner of her eyelid. Then he came and sat by me.

"We must wait till she wakes. It won't be long, I fancy."

He was right. At the end of five minutes, Sister Marie Angelique stirred. Her eyes opened dreamily.

"Where am I?"

"You are here—at home. You have had a little sleep. You have dreamed, have you not?"

She nodded.

"Yes, I have dreamed."

"You have dreamed of the Crystal?"

"Yes."

"Tell us about it."

"You will think me mad, M. le docteur. For see you, in my dream, the Crystal was a holy emblem. I even figured to myself a second Christ, a Teacher of the Crystal who died for his faith, his followers hunted down—persecuted. . . . But the faith endured."

"The faith endured?"

"Yes—for fifteen thousand full moons—I mean, for fifteen thousand years."

"How long was a full moon?"

"Thirteen ordinary moons. Yes, it was in the fifteenth thousandth full moon—of course, I was a Priestess of the Fifth Sign in the House of the Crystal. It was in the first days of the coming of the Sixth Sign . . ."

Her brows drew together, a look of fear passed over her head.

"Too soon," she murmured. "Too soon. A mistake. . . . Ah, yes! I remember! The Sixth Sign!"

She half sprang to her feet, then dropped back, passing her hand over her face and murmuring:

"But what am I saying? I am raving. These things never happened."

"Now don't distress yourself."

But she was looking at him in anguished perplexity.

"M. le docteur, I do not understand. Why should I have these dreams—these fancies? I was only sixteen when I entered the religious life. I have never traveled. Yet I dream of cities, of strange people, of strange customs. Why?" She pressed both hands to her head.

"Have you ever been hypnotized, my sister? Or been in a state of trance?"

"I have never been hypnotized, M. le docteur. For the other, when at prayer in the chapel, my spirit has often been caught up from my body, and I have been as one dead for many hours. It was undoubtedly a blessed state, the Reverend Mother said—a state of grace. Ah, yes!" She caught her breath. *"I remember; we, too, called it a state of grace."*

"I would like to try an experiment, my sister." Rose spoke in a matter-of-fact voice. "It may dispel those painful half-recollections. I will ask you to gaze once more in the crystal. I will then say a certain word to you. You will answer with another. We will continue in this way until you become tired. Concentrate your thoughts on the crystal, not upon the words."

As I once more unwrapped the crystal and gave it into Sister Marie Angelique's hands, I noticed the reverent way her hands touched it. Reposing on the black velvet, it lay between her slim palms. Her wonderful deep eyes gazed into it. There was a short silence, then the doctor said: *"Hound."*

Immediately Sister Marie Angelique answered: *"Death."*

IV

I do not propose to give a full account of the experiment. Many unimportant and meaningless words were purposely introduced by the doctor. Other words he repeated several times, sometimes getting the same answer to them, sometimes a different one.

That evening in the doctor's little cottage on the cliffs we discussed the result of the experiment.

He cleared his throat and drew his notebook closer to him.

"These results are very interesting—very curious. In answer to the words 'Sixth Sign,' we get variously *Destruction, Purple, Hound, Power,* then again *Destruction,* and finally *Power.* Later, as you may have noticed, I reversed the method, with the following results. In answer to *Destruction,* I get *Hound;* to *Purple, Power;* to *Hound, Death* again, and to *Power, Hound.* That all holds together, but on a second repetition of *Destruction,* I get *Sea,* which appears utterly irrelevant. To the words 'Fifth Sign,' I get *Blue, Thoughts, Bird, Blue* again, and finally the rather suggestive phrase *Opening of mind to mind.* From the fact that 'Fourth Sign' elicits the word *Yellow,* and later *Light,* and that 'First Sign' is answered by *Blood,* I deduce that each Sign had a particular color, and possibly a particular symbol, that of the Fifth Sign being a *bird,* and that of the Sixth a *hound.* However, I surmise that the Fifth Sign represented what is familiarly known as telepathy—the opening of mind to mind. The Sixth Sign undoubtedly stands for the Power of Destruction."

"What is the meaning of *Sea*?"

"That I confess I cannot explain. I introduced the word later and got the ordinary answer of *Boat*. To Seventh Sign I got first *Life,* the second time *Love*. To Eighth Sign, I got the answer *None*. I take it therefore that Seven was the sum and number of the signs."

"But the Seventh was not achieved," I said on a sudden inspiration. "Since through the Sixth came *Destruction*!"

"Ah! You think so? But we are taking these—mad ramblings very seriously. They are really only interesting from a medical point of view."

"Surely they will attract the attention of psychic investigators."

The doctor's eyes narrowed. "My dear sir, I have no intention of making them public."

"Then your interest?"

"Is purely personal. I shall make notes on the case, of course."

"I see." But for the first time I felt, like the blind man, that I didn't see at all. I rose to my feet.

"Well, I'll wish you good night, doctor. I'm off to town again tomorrow."

"Ah!" I fancied there was satisfaction, relief perhaps, behind the exclamation.

"I wish you good luck with your investigations," I continued lightly. "Don't loose the Hound of Death on me next time we meet!"

His hand was in mine as I spoke, and I felt the start it gave. He recovered himself quickly. His lips drew back from his long pointed teeth in a smile.

"For a man who loved power, what a power that would be!" he said. "To hold every human being's life in the hollow of your hand!"

And his smile broadened.

V

That was the end of my direct connection with the affair.

Later, the doctor's notebook and diary came into my hands. I will reproduce the few scanty entries in it here, though you will understand that it did not really come into my possession until sometime afterward.

Aug. 5th. Have discovered that by "the Chosen," Sister M.A. means those who reproduced the race. Apparently they were held in the highest honor, and exalted above the Priesthood. Contrast this with early Christians.

Aug. 7th. Persuaded Sister M.A. to let me hypnotize her. Succeeded in inducing hypnotic sleep and trance, but no *rapport* established.

Aug. 9th. Have there been civilizations in the past to which ours is as nothing? Strange if it should be so, and I the only man with the clue to it. . . .

Aug. 12th. Sister M.A. not at all amenable to suggestion when hypnotized. Yet state of trance easily induced. Cannot understand it.

Aug. 13th. Sister M.A. mentioned today that in "state of grace" the "gate must be closed, lest another should command the body." Interesting—but baffling.

Aug. 18th. So the First Sign is none other than . . . *(words erased here)* . . . then how many centuries will it take to reach the Sixth? But if there should be a shortcut to Power . . .

Aug. 20th, Have arranged for M.A. to come here with Nurse. Have told her it is necessary to keep patient under morphia. Am I mad? Or shall I be the Superman, with the Power of Death in my hands?

(Here the entries cease.)

VI

It was, I think, on August 29 that I received the letter. It was directed to me, care of my sister-in-law, in a sloping foreign handwriting. I opened it with some curiosity. It ran as follows:

Cher Monsieur,—I have seen you but twice, but I have felt that I could trust you. Whether my dreams are real or not, they have grown clearer of late. . . . And, monsieur, one thing at all events, the Hound of Death is no dream. . . . In the days I told you of (whether they are real or not, I do not know) He Who was Guardian of the Crystal revealed the Sixth Sign to the People too soon. . . . Evil entered into their hearts. They had the power to slay at will—and they slew without justice—in anger. They were drunk with the lust of Power. When we saw this, we who were yet pure, we knew that once again we should not complete the Circle and come to the Sign of Everlasting Life. He who would have been the next Guardian of the Crystal was bidden to act. That the old might die, and the new, after endless ages, might come again, he loosed the Hound of Death upon the sea (being careful not to close the Circle), and the sea rose up in the shape of a Hound and swallowed the land utterly. . . .

Once before I remembered this—on the altar steps in Belgium. . . .

The Dr. Rose, he is of the Brotherhood. He knows the First Sign, and the form of the Second, though its meaning is hidden to all save a chosen few. He would learn of me the Sixth. I have withstood him so far—but I grow weak. Monsieur, it is not well that a man should come to power before his time. Many centuries must go by ere the world is ready to have the power of death delivered into its hand. . . . I beseech of you, monsieur, you who love goodness and truth, to help me . . . before it is too late.

YOUR SISTER IN CHRIST,
MARIE ANGELIQUE.

I let the paper fall. The solid earth beneath me seemed a little less solid than usual. Then I began to rally. The poor woman's belief, genuine enough, had almost affected me! One thing was clear. Dr.

Rose, in his zeal for a case, was grossly abusing his professional standing. I would run down and—

Suddenly I noticed a letter from Kitty among my other correspondence. I tore it open. I read:

> Such an awful thing has happened. You remember Dr. Rose's little cottage on the cliff? It was swept away by a landslide last night, and the doctor and that poor nun, Sister Marie Angelique, were killed. The débris on the beach is too awful—all piled up in a fantastic mass—fron a distance it looks like a great *hound*. . . .

The letter dropped from my hand.

The other facts may be coincidence. A Mr. Rose, whom I discovered to be a wealthy relative of the doctor's, died suddenly that same night—it was said struck by lightning. As far as was known, no thunderstorm had occurred in the neighborhood, but one or two people declared they had heard one peal of thunder. He had an electric burn on him "of a curious shape." His will left everything to his nephew, Dr. Rose.

Now, supposing that Dr. Rose succeeded in obtaining the secret of the Sixth Sign from Sister Marie Angelique. I had always felt him to be an unscrupulous man—he would not shrink at taking his uncle's life if he were sure it could not be brought home to him. But one sentence of Sister Marie Angelique's letter rings in my brain: ". . . being careful not to close the Circle. . . ." Dr. Rose did not exercise that care—was perhaps unaware of the steps to take, or even of the need for them. So the Force he employed returned, completing its circuit. . . .

But of course it is all nonsense! Everything can be accounted for quite naturally. That the doctor believed in Sister Marie Angelique's hallucinations merely proves that *his* mind, too, was slightly unbalanced.

Yet sometimes I dream of a continent under the seas where men once lived and attained to a degree of civilization far ahead of ours. . . .

Or did Sister Marie Angelique remember *backward*—as some say is possible—and is this City of the Circles in the future and not the past?

Nonsense—of course the whole thing was mere hallucination!

THE GIPSY

Macfarlane had often noticed that his friend, Dickie Carpenter,had a strange aversion to gipsies. He had never known the reason for it. But when Dickie's engagement to Esther Lawes was broken off, there was a momentary tearing down of reserves between the two men.

Macfarlane had been engaged to the younger sister, Rachel, for about a year. He had known both the Lawes girls since they were children. Slow and cautious in all things, he had been unwilling to admit to himself the growing attraction that Rachel's childlike face and honest brown eyes had for him. Not a beauty like Esther, no! But unutterably truer and sweeter. With Dickie's engagement to the elder sister, the bond between the two men seemed to be drawn closer.

And now, after a few brief weeks, the engagement was off again, and Dickie, simple Dickie, hard-hit. So far in his young life all had gone so smoothly. His career in the navy had been well chosen. His craving for the sea was inborn. There was something of the Viking about him, primitive and direct, a nature on which subtleties of thought were wasted. He belonged to that inarticulate order of young

Englishmen who dislike any form of emotion, and who find it peculiarly hard to explain their mental processes in words. . . .

Macfarlane, that dour Scot, with a Celtic imagination hidden away somewhere, listened and smoked while his friend floundered along in a sea of words. He had known an unburdening was coming. But he had expected the subject matter to be different. To begin with, anyway, there was no mention of Esther Lawes. Only, it seemed, the story of a childish terror.

"It all started with a dream I had when I was a kid. Not a nightmare exactly. She—the gipsy, you know—would just come into any old dream—even a good dream (or a kid's idea of what's good—a party and crackers and things). I'd be enjoying myself no end, and then I'd feel, I'd *know,* that if I looked up, *she*'d be there, standing as she always stood, watching me. . . . With sad eyes, you know, as though she understood something that I didn't. . . . Can't explain why it rattled me so—but it did! Every time! I used to wake up howling with terror, and my old nurse used to say: 'There! Master Dickie's had one of his gipsy dreams again!' "

"Ever been frightened by real gipsies?"

"Never saw one till later. That was queer, too. I was chasing a pup of mine. He'd run away. I got out through the garden door, and along one of the forest paths. We lived in the New Forest then, you know. I came to a sort of clearing at the end, with a wooden bridge over a stream. And just beside it a gipsy was standing—with a red handkerchief over her head—just the same as in my dream. And at once I was frightened! She looked at me, you know. . . . Just the same look—as though she knew something I didn't, and was sorry about it. . . . And then she said quite quietly, nodding her head at me: '*I shouldn't go that way, if I were you.*' I can't tell you why, but it frightened me to death. I dashed past her onto the bridge. I suppose it was rotten. Anyway, it gave way, and I was chucked into the stream. It was running pretty fast, and I was nearly drowned. Beastly to be nearly drowned. I've never forgotten it. And I felt it had all to do with the gipsy. . . ."

"Actually, though, she warned you against it?"

"I suppose you could put it like that." Dickie paused, then went on: "I've told you about this dream of mine, not because it has anything to do with what happened after (at least, I suppose it hasn't), but because it's the jumping-off point, as it were. You'll understand now what I mean by the 'gipsy feeling.' So I'll go on to that first night at the Lawes.' I'd just come back from the west coast then. It was awfully rum to be in England again. The Lawes were old friends of my people's. I hadn't seen the girls since I was about seven, but young Arthur was a great pal of mine, and after he died, Esther used to write to me, and send me out papers. Awfully jolly letters, she wrote! Cheered me up no end. I always wished I was a better hand at writing back. I was awfully keen to see her. It seemed odd to know a girl quite well from her letters, and not otherwise. Well, I went down to the Lawes' place first thing. Esther was away when I arrived, but was expected back that evening. I sat next to Rachel at dinner, and as I looked up and down the long table, a queer feeling came over me. I felt someone was watching me, and it made me uncomfortable. Then I saw her—"

"Saw who?"

"Mrs. Haworth—what I'm telling you about."

It was on the tip of Macfarlane's tongue to say: "I thought you were telling me about Esther Lawes." But he remained silent, and Dickie went on.

"There was something about her quite different from all the rest. She was sitting next to old Lawes—listening to him very gravely with her head bent down. She had some of that red tulle stuff round her neck. It had got torn, I think; anyway, it stood up behind her head like little tongues of flame. . . . I said to Rachel: 'Who's that woman over there? Dark—with a red scarf!' "

"Do you mean Alistair Haworth? She's got a red scarf. But she's fair. Very fair."

"So she was, you know. Her hair was a lovely pale shining yellow. Yet I could have sworn positively she was dark. Queer what tricks one's eyes play on one. . . . After dinner, Rachel introduced us, and we walked up and down in the garden. We talked about reincarnation. . . ."

"Rather out of your line, Dickie!"

"I suppose it is. I remember saying that it seemed to be a jolly sensible way of accounting for how one seems to know some people right off—as if you'd met them before. She said: 'You mean lovers . . .' There was something queer about the way she said it—something soft and eager. It reminded me of something—but I couldn't remember what. We went on jawing a bit, and then old Lawes called us from the terrace—said Esther had come and wanted to see me. Mrs. Haworth put her hand on my arm and said: 'You're going in?' 'Yes,' I said. 'I suppose we'd better,' and then—then—"

"Well?"

"It sounds such rot. Mrs. Haworth said: *'I shouldn't go in if I were you. . . .'*" He paused. "It frightened me, you know. It frightened me badly. That's why I told you about the dream. . . . Because, you see, she said it just the same way—quietly, as though she knew something I didn't. It wasn't just a pretty woman who wanted to keep me out in the garden with her. Her voice was just kind—and very sorry. Almost as though she knew what was to come. . . . I suppose it was rude, but I turned and left her—almost ran to the house. It seemed like safety. I knew then that I'd been afraid of her from the first. It was a relief to see old Lawes. Esther was there beside him. . . ." He hesitated a minute, and then muttered rather obscurely: "There was no question—the moment I saw her, I knew I'd got it in the neck."

Macfarlane's mind flew swiftly to Esther Lawes. He had once heard her summed up as "Six foot one of Jewish perfection." A shrewd portrait, he thought, as he remembered her unusual height and the long slenderness of her, the marble whiteness of her face with its delicate down-drooping nose, and the black splendor of hair and eyes. Yes, he did not wonder that the boyish simplicity of Dickie had capitulated. Esther could never have made his own pulses beat one jot faster, but he admitted her magnificence.

"And then," continued Dickie, "we got engaged."

"At once?"

"Well, after about a week. It took her about a fortnight after that to find out that she didn't care after all. . . ." He gave a short bitter laugh.

"It was the last evening before I went back to the old ship. I was coming back from the village through the woods—and then I saw *her*—Mrs. Haworth, I mean. She had on a red tam-o'-shanter, and—just for a minute, you know—it made me jump! I've told you about my dream, so you'll understand. . . . Then we walked along a bit. Not that there was a word Esther couldn't have heard, you know. . . ."

"No?" Macfarlane looked at his friend curiously. Strange how people told you things of which they themselves were unconscious!

"And then, when I was turning to go back to the house, she stopped me. She said: 'You'll be home soon enough. *I shouldn't go back too soon if I were you. . . .*' And then I *knew*—that there was something beastly waiting for me . . . and . . . as soon as I got back, Esther met me and told me—that she'd found out she didn't really care. . . ."

Macfarlane grunted sympathetically. "And Mrs. Haworth?" he asked.

"I never saw her again—until tonight."

"Tonight?"

"Yes. At that doctor Johnny's nursing home. They had a look at my leg, the one that got messed up in that torpedo business. It's worried me a bit lately. The old chap advised an operation—it'll be quite a simple thing. Then as I left the place, I ran into a girl in a red jumper over her nurse's things, and she said: *'I wouldn't have that operation, if I were you. . . .'* Then I saw it was Mrs. Haworth. She passed on so quickly I couldn't stop her. I met another nurse, and asked about her. But she said there wasn't anyone of that name in the home. . . . Queer. . . ."

"Sure it was her?"

"Oh! Yes, you see—she's very beautiful. . . ." He paused, and then added: "I shall have the old op. of course—but—but in case my number *should* be up—"

"Rot!"

"Of course it's rot. But all the same I'm glad I told you about this gipsy business. . . . You know, there's more of it if only I could remember. . . ."

II

Macfarlane walked up the steep moorland road. He turned in at the gate of a house near the crest of the hill. Setting his jaw squarely, he pulled the bell.

"Is Mrs. Haworth in?"

"Yes, sir. I'll tell her." The maid left him in a low long room, with windows that gave on the wildness of the moorland. He frowned a little. Was he making a colossal ass of himself?

Then he started. A low voice was singing overhead:

"The gipsy woman
Lives on the moor—"

The voice broke off. Macfarlane's heartbeat a shade faster. The door opened.

The bewildering, almost Scandinavian fairness of her came as a shock. In spite of Dickie's description, he had imagined her gipsy-dark. . . . And he suddenly remembered Dickie's words, and the peculiar tone of them. *"You see, she's very beautiful. . . ."* Perfect unquestionable beauty is rare, and perfect unquestionable beauty was what Alistair Haworth possessed.

He caught himself up, and advanced toward her. "I'm afraid you don't know me from Adam. I got your address from the Lawes. But—I'm a friend of Dickie Carpenter's."

She looked at him closely for a minute or two. Then she said: "I was going out. Up on the moor. Will you come too?"

She pushed open the window and stepped out on the hillside. He followed her. A heavy, rather foolish-looking man was sitting in a basket chair smoking.

"My husband! We're going out on the moor, Maurice. And then Mr. Macfarlane will come back to lunch with us. You will, won't you?"

"Thanks very much." He followed her easy stride up the hill, and thought to himself: "Why? Why, on God's earth, marry *that?*"

Alistair made her way to some rocks. "We'll sit here. And you shall tell me—what you came to tell me."

"You knew?"

"I always know when bad things are coming. It is bad, isn't it? About Dickie?"

"He underwent a slight operation—quite successfully. But his heart must have been weak. He died under the anesthetic."

What he expected to see on her face, he scarcely knew—hardly that look of utter eternal weariness. . . . He heard her murmur: "Again—to wait—so long—so long. . . ." She looked up: "Yes, what were you going to say?"

"Only this. Someone warned him against this operation. A nurse. He thought it was you. Was it?"

She shook her head. "No, it wasn't me. But I've got a cousin who is a nurse. She's rather like me in a dim light. I dare say that was it." She looked up at him again. "It doesn't matter, does it?" And then suddenly her eyes widened. She drew in her breath. "Oh!" she said. "Oh! How funny! You don't understand. . . ."

Macfarlane was puzzled. She was still staring at him.

"I thought you did. . . . You should. You look as though you'd got it, too. . . ."

"Got what?"

"The gift—curse—call it what you like. I believe you have. Look hard at that hollow in the rocks. Don't think of anything, just look. . . . Ah!" she marked his slight start. "Well—you saw something?"

"It must have been imagination. Just for a second I saw it full of—blood!"

She nodded. "I knew you had it. That's the place where the old sun-worshippers sacrificed victims. I knew that before anyone told me. And there are times when I know just how they felt about it—almost as though I'd been there myself. . . . And there's something about the moor that makes me feel as though I were coming back home. . . . Of course it's natural that I should have the gift. I'm a Ferguesson. There's second sight in the family. And my mother was a medium until my father married her. Cristine was her name. She was rather celebrated."

"Do you mean by 'the gift' the power of being able to see things before they happen?"

"Yes, forward or backward—it's all the same. For instance, I saw you wondering why I married Maurice—oh! yes, you did! It's simply because I've always known that there's something dreadful hanging over him. . . . I wanted to save him from it. . . . Women are like that. With my gift, I ought to be able to prevent it happening . . . if one ever can. . . . I couldn't help Dickie. And Dickie wouldn't understand. . . . He was afraid. He was very young."

"Twenty-two."

"And I'm thirty. But I didn't mean that. There are so many ways of being divided, length and height and breadth . . . but to be divided by time is the worst way of all. . . ." She fell into a long brooding silence.

The low peal of a gong from the house below roused them.

At lunch, Macfarlane watched Maurice Haworth. He was undoubtedly madly in love with his wife. There was the unquestioning happy fondness of a dog in his eyes. Macfarlane marked also the tenderness of her response, with its hint of maternity. After lunch he took his leave.

"I'm staying down at the inn for a day or so. May I come and see you again? Tomorrow, perhaps?"

"Of course. But—"

"But what—"

She brushed her hand quickly across her eyes. "I don't know. I—I fancied that we shouldn't meet again—that's all. . . . Good-bye."

He went down the road slowly. In spite of himself, a cold hand seemed tightening round his heart. Nothing in her words, of course, but—

A motor swept round the corner. He flattened himself against the hedge . . . only just in time. A curious grayish pallor crept across his face. . . .

III

"Good Lord, my nerves are in a rotten state," muttered Macfarlane, as he awoke the following morning. He reviewed the events of the afternoon before dispassionately. The motor, the shortcut to the inn and the sudden mist that had made him lose his way with the knowledge that a dangerous bog was no distance off. Then the chimney pot that had fallen off the inn, and the smell of burning in the night which he had traced to a cinder on his hearth rug. Nothing in it all! Nothing at all—but for her words, and that deep unacknowledged certainty in his heart that she *knew*. . . .

He flung off the bedclothes with sudden energy. He must go up and see her first thing. That would break the spell. That is, if he got there safely. . . . Lord, what a fool he was!

He could eat little breakfast. Ten o'clock saw him starting up the road. At ten-thirty his hand was on the bell. Then, and not till then, he permitted himself to draw a long breath of relief.

"Is Mrs. Haworth in?"

It was the same elderly woman who had opened the door before. But her face was different—ravaged with grief.

"Oh! sir. Oh! sir. You haven't heard, then?"

"Heard what?"

"Miss Alistair, the pretty lamb. It was her tonic. She took it every night. The poor captain is beside himself; he's nearly mad. He took the wrong bottle off the shelf in the dark. . . . They sent for the doctor, but he was too late—"

And swiftly there recurred to Macfarlane the words: *"I've always known there was something dreadful hanging over him. I ought to be able to prevent it happening—if one ever can—"* Ah! but one couldn't cheat Fate. . . . Strange fatality of vision that had destroyed where it sought to save. . . .

The old servant went on: "My pretty lamb! So sweet and gentle she was, and so sorry for anything in trouble. Couldn't bear anyone to be hurt." She hesitated, then added: "Would you like to go up and see her, sir? I think, from what she said, that you must have known her long ago. A *very* long time ago, she said. . . ."

Macfarlane followed the old woman up the stairs into the room over the drawing room where he had heard the voice singing the day before. There was stained glass at the top of the windows. It threw a red light on the head of the bed. . . . *A gipsy with a red handkerchief over her head.* . . . Nonsense, his nerves were playing tricks again. He took a long last look at Alistair Haworth.

IV

"There's a lady to see you, sir."

"Eh?" Macfarlane looked at the landlady abstractedly. "Oh! I beg your pardon, Mrs. Rowse, I've been seeing ghosts."

"Not really, sir? There's queer things to be seen on the moor after nightfall, I know. There's the white lady, and the Devil's blacksmith, and the sailor and the gipsy—"

"What's that? A sailor and a gipsy?"

"So they say, sir. It was quite a tale in my young days. Crossed in love they were, a while back. . . . But they've not walked for many a long day now."

"No? I wonder if—perhaps—they will again now. . . ."

"Lor'! sir, what things you do say! About that young lady—"

"What young lady?"

"The one that's waiting to see you. She's in the parlor. Miss Lawes, she said her name was."

"Oh!"

Rachel! He felt a curious feeling of contraction, a shifting of perspective. He had been peeping through at another world. He had forgotten Rachel, for Rachel belonged to this life only. . . . Again that curious shifting of perspective, that slipping back to a world of three dimensions only.

He opened the parlor door. Rachel—with her honest brown eyes.

And suddenly, like a man awakening from a dream, a warm rush of glad reality swept over him. He was alive—alive! He thought: "There's only one life one can be sure about! This one!"

"Rachel!" he said, and, lifting her chin, he kissed her lips.

THE LAMP

It was undoubtedly an old house. The whole square was old, with that disapproving dignified old age often met with in a cathedral town. But No. 19 gave the impression of an elder among elders; it had a veritable patriarchal solemnity; it towered grayest of the gray, haughtiest of the haughty, chillest of the chill. Austere, forbidding, and stamped with that particular desolation attaching to all houses that have been long untenanted, it reigned above the other dwellings.

In any other town it would have been freely labeled "haunted," but Weyminster was averse from ghosts and considered them hardly respectable except as the appanage of a "county family." So No. 19 was never alluded to as a haunted house; but nevertheless it remained, year after year, "To Be Let or Sold."

MRS. LANCASTER LOOKED AT the house with approval as she drove up with the talkative house agent, who was in an unusually hilarious mood at the idea of getting No. 19 off his books. He inserted the key in the door without ceasing his appreciative comments.

"How long has the house been empty?" inquired Mrs. Lancaster, cutting short his flow of language rather brusquely.

Mr. Raddish (of Raddish and Foplow) became slightly confused. "Er—er—some time," he remarked blandly.

"So I should think," said Mrs. Lancaster dryly.

The dimly lighted hall was chill with a sinister chill. A more imaginative woman might have shivered, but this woman happened to be eminently practical. She was tall, with much dark brown hair just tinged with gray and rather cold blue eyes.

She went over the house from attic to cellar, asking a pertinent question from time to time. The inspection over, she came back into one of the front rooms looking out on the square and faced the agent with a resolute mien.

"What is the matter with the house?"

Mr. Raddish was taken by surprise.

"Of course, an unfurnished house is always a little gloomy," he parried feebly.

"Nonsense," said Mrs. Lancaster. "The rent is ridiculously low for such a house—purely nominal. There must be some reason for it. I suppose the house is haunted?"

Mr. Raddish gave a nervous little start but said nothing.

Mrs. Lancaster eyed him keenly. After a few moments she spoke again.

"Of course that is all nonsense. I don't believe in ghosts or anything of that sort, and personally it is no deterrent to my taking the house; but servants, unfortunately, are very credulous and easily frightened. It would be kind of you to tell me exactly what—what thing *is* supposed to haunt this place."

"I—er—really don't know," stammered the house agent.

"I am sure you must," said the lady quietly. "I cannot take the house without knowing. What was it? A murder?"

"Oh, no!" cried Mr. Raddish, shocked by the idea of anything so alien to the respectability of the square. "It's—it's—only a child."

"A child?"

"Yes."

"I don't know the story exactly," he continued reluctantly. "Of course, there are all kinds of different versions, but I believe that about thirty years ago a man going by the name of Williams took Number Nineteen. Nothing was known of him; he kept no servants; he had no friends; he seldom went out in the daytime. He had one child, a little boy. After he had been there about two months, he went up to London, and had barely set foot in the metropolis before he was recognized as being a man 'wanted' by the police on some charge—exactly what, I do not know. But it must have been a grave one, because, sooner than give himself up, he shot himself. Meanwhile, the child lived on here, alone in the house. He had food for a little time, and he waited day after day for his father's return. Unfortunately, it had been impressed upon him that he was never under any circumstances to go out of the house or to speak to anyone. He was a weak, ailing, little creature, and did not dream of disobeying this command. In the night, the neighbors, not knowing that his father had gone away, often heard him sobbing in the awful loneliness and desolation of the empty house."

Mr. Raddish paused.

"And—er—the child starved to death," he concluded in the same tones as he might have announced that it had just begun to rain.

"And it is the child's ghost that is supposed to haunt the place?" asked Mrs. Lancaster.

"It is nothing of consequence really," Mr. Raddish hastened to assure her. "There's nothing *seen,* not *seen,* only people say, ridiculous, of course, but they do say they hear—the child—crying, you know."

Mrs. Lancaster moved toward the front door.

"I like the house very much," she said. "I shall get nothing as good for the price. I will think it over and let you know."

"IT REALLY LOOKS VERY cheerful, doesn't it, Papa?"

Mrs. Lancaster surveyed her new domain with approval. Gay rugs, well-polished furniture, and many knickknacks, had quite transformed the gloomy aspect of No. 19.

She spoke to a thin, bent old man with stooping shoulders and a delicate mystical face. Mr. Winburn did not resemble his daughter; indeed no greater contrast could be imagined than that presented by her resolute practicalness and his dreamy abstraction.

"Yes," he answered with a smile, "no one would dream the house was haunted."

"Papa, don't talk nonsense! On our first day, too."

Mr. Winburn smiled.

"Very well, my dear, we will agree that there are no such things as ghosts."

"And please," continued Mrs. Lancaster, "don't say a word before Geoff. He's so imaginative."

Geoff was Mrs. Lancaster's little boy. The family consisted of Mr. Winburn, his widowed daughter, and Geoffrey.

Rain had begun to beat against the window—pitter-patter, pitter-patter.

"Listen," said Mr. Winburn. "Is it not like little footsteps?"

"It's more like rain," said Mrs. Lancaster, with a smile.

"But *that, that* is a footstep," cried her father, bending forward to listen.

Mrs. Lancaster laughed outright.

"That's Geoff coming downstairs."

Mr. Winburn was obliged to laugh, too. They were having tea in the hall, and he had been sitting with his back to the staircase. He now turned his chair round to face it.

Little Geoffrey was coming down, rather slowly and sedately, with a child's awe of a strange place. The stairs were of polished oak, uncarpeted. He came across and stood by his mother. Mr. Winburn gave a slight start. As the child was crossing the floor, he distinctly heard another pair of footsteps on the stairs, as of someone following Geoffrey. Dragging footsteps, curiously painful they were. Then he shrugged his shoulders incredulously. "The rain, no doubt," he thought.

"I'm looking at the sponge cakes," remarked Geoff with the admirably detached air of one who points out an interesting fact.

His mother hastened to comply with the hint.

"Well, Sonny, how do you like your new home?" she asked.

"Lots," replied Geoffrey with his mouth generously filled. "Pounds and pounds and pounds." After this last assertion, which was evidently expressive of the deepest contentment, he relapsed into silence, only anxious to remove the sponge cake from the sight of man in the least time possible.

Having bolted the last mouthful, he burst forth into speech.

"Oh! Mummy, there's attics here, Jane says; and can I go at once and *eggz*plore them? And there might be a secret door. Jane says there isn't, but I think there must be, and, anyhow, I know there'll be pipes, water pipes (with a face full of ecstasy), and can I play with them, and, oh! can I go and see tie boi-i-ler?" He spun out the last word with such evident rapture that his grandfather felt ashamed to reflect that this peerless delight of childhood only conjured up to his imagination the picture of hot water that wasn't hot, and heavy and numerous plumber's bills.

"We'll see about the attics tomorrow, darling," said Mrs. Lancaster. "Suppose you fetch your bricks and build a nice house, or an engine."

"Don't want to build an 'ouse."

"*H*ouse."

"House, or h'engine h'either."

"Build a boiler," suggested his grandfather.

Geoffrey brightened.

"With pipes?"

"Yes, lots of pipes."

Geoffrey ran away happily to fetch his bricks.

The rain was still falling. Mr. Winburn listened. Yes, it must have been the rain he had heard; but it did sound like footsteps.

He had a queer dream that night.

He dreamed that he was walking through a town, a great city it seemed to him. But it was a children's city; there were no grown-up people there, nothing but children, crowds of them. In his dream they all rushed to the stranger crying: "Have you brought him?" It seemed that he understood what they meant and shook his head sadly. When they saw this, the children turned away and began to cry, sobbing bitterly.

The city and the children faded away and he awoke to find himself in bed, but the sobbing was still in his ears. Though wide awake, he heard it distinctly; and he remembered that Geoffrey slept on the floor below, while this sound of a child's sorrow descended from above. He sat up and struck a match. Instantly the sobbing ceased.

MR. WINBURN DID NOT tell his daughter of the dream or its sequel. That it was no trick of his imagination, he was convinced; indeed soon afterward he heard it again in the daytime. The wind was howling in the chimney but *this* was a separate sound—distinct, unmistakable: pitiful little heartbroken sobs.

He found out, too, that he was not the only one to hear them. He overheard the housemaid saying to the parlormaid that she "didn't think as that there nurse was kind to Master Geoffrey, she'd 'eard 'im crying 'is little 'eart out only that very morning." Geoffrey had come down to breakfast and lunch beaming with health and happiness; and Mr. Winburn knew that it was not Geoff who had been crying, but that other child whose dragging footsteps had startled him more than once.

Mrs. Lancaster alone never heard anything. Her ears were not perhaps attuned to catch sounds from another world.

Yet one day she also received a shock.

"Mummy," said Geoff plaintively. "I wish you'd let me play with that little boy."

Mrs. Lancaster looked up from her writing table with a smile.

"What little boy, dear?"

"I don't know his name. He was in a attic, sitting on the floor crying, but he ran away when he saw me. I suppose he was shy (with slight contempt), not like a big boy, and then, when I was in the nursery building, I saw him standing in the door watching me build, and he looked so awful lonely and as though he wanted to play wiv me. I said: 'Come and build a h'engine,' but he didn't say nothing, just looked as—as though he saw a lot of chocolates, and his mummy had told him not to touch them." Geoff sighed, sad personal reminiscences evidently recurring to him. "But when I asked Jane who he was and told her I wanted to play wiv him, she said there wasn't no little boy in the 'ouse and not to tell naughty stories. I don't love Jane at all."

Mrs. Lancaster got up.

"Jane was right. There was no little boy."

"But I saw him. Oh! Mummy, do let me play wiv him, he did look so awful lonely and unhappy. I do want to do something to 'make him better.'"

Mrs. Lancaster was about to speak again, but her father shook his head.

"Geoff," he said very gently, "that poor little boy *is* lonely, and perhaps you may do something to comfort him; but you must find out how by yourself—like a puzzle—do you see?"

"Is it because I am getting big I must do it all my lone?"

"Yes, because you are getting big."

As the boy left the room, Mrs. Lancaster turned to her father impatiently.

"Papa, this is absurd. To encourage the boy to believe the servants' idle tales!"

"No servant has told the child anything," said the old man gently. "He's seen—what I hear, what I could see perhaps if I were his age."

"But it's such nonsense! Why don't I see it or hear it?"

Mr. Winburn smiled, a curiously tired smile, but did not reply.

"Why?" repeated his daughter. "And why did you tell him he could help the—the—thing. It's—it's all so impossible."

The old man looked at her with his thoughtful glance.

"Why not?" he said. "Do you remember these words:

"What Lamp has Destiny to guide
Her little Children stumbling in the Dark?"
"A Blind Understanding," Heaven replied.

"Geoffrey has that—a blind understanding. All children possess it. It is only as we grow older that we lose it, that we cast it away from us. Sometimes, when we are quite old, a faint gleam comes back to us, but the Lamp burns brightest in childhood. That is why I think Geoffrey may help."

"I don't understand," murmured Mrs. Lancaster feebly.

"No more do I. That—that child is in trouble and wants—to be set free. But how? I do not know, but—it's awful to think of it—sobbing its heart out—a *child.*"

A MONTH AFTER THIS conversation Geoffrey fell very ill. The east wind had been severe, and he was not a strong child. The doctor shook his head and said that it was a grave case. To Mr. Winburn he divulged more and confessed that the case was quite hopeless. "The child would never have lived to grow up, under any circumstances," he added. "There has been serious lung trouble for a long time."

It was when nursing Geoff that Mrs. Lancaster became aware of that—other child. At first the sobs were an indistinguishable part of the wind, but gradually they became more distinct, more unmistakable. Finally she heard them in moments of dead calm: a child's sobs—dull, hopeless, heartbroken.

Geoff grew steadily worse and in his delirium he spoke of the "little boy" again and again. "I do want to help him get away, I do!" he cried.

Succeeding the delirium there came a state of lethargy. Geoffrey lay very still, hardly breathing, sunk in oblivion. There was nothing to do but wait and watch. Then there came a still night, clear and calm, without one breath of wind.

Suddenly the child stirred. His eyes opened. He looked past his mother toward the open door. He tried to speak and she bent down to catch the half-breathed words.

"All right, I'm comin'," he whispered; then he sank back.

The mother felt suddenly terrified; she crossed the room to her father. Somewhere near them the other child was laughing. Joyful, contented, triumphant, the silvery laughter echoed through the room.

"I'm frightened; I'm frightened," she moaned.

He put his arm round her protectingly. A sudden gust of wind made them both start, but it passed swiftly and left the air quiet as before.

The laughter had ceased and there crept to them a faint sound, so faint as hardly to be heard, but growing louder till they could distinguish it. Footsteps—light footsteps, swiftly departing.

Pitter-patter, pitter-patter, they ran—those well-known halting little feet. Yet—surely—now *other* footsteps suddenly mingled with them, moving with a quicker and a lighter tread.

With one accord they hastened to the door.

Down, down, down, past the door, close to them, pitter-patter, pitter-patter, went the unseen feet of the little children together.

Mrs. Lancaster looked up wildly.

"There are *two* of them—*two!*"

Gray with sudden fear, she turned toward the cot in the corner, but her father restrained her gently and pointed away.

"There," he said simply.

Pitter-patter, pitter-patter—fainter and fainter.

And then—silence.

THE STRANGE CASE OF SIR ARTHUR CARMICHAEL

(Taken from the notes of the late Dr. Edward Carstairs, M.D., the eminent psychologist.)

I am perfectly aware that there are two distinct ways of looking at the strange and tragic events which I have set down here. My own opinion has never wavered. I have been persuaded to write the story out in full, and indeed I believe it to be due to science that such strange and inexplicable facts should not be buried in oblivion.

It was a wire from my friend, Dr. Settle, that first introduced me to the matter. Beyond mentioning the name Carmichael, the wire was not explicit, but in obedience to it I took the 12:20 train from Paddington to Wolden, in Herefordshire.

The name of Carmichael was not unfamiliar to me. I had been slightly acquainted with the late Sir William Carmichael of Wolden, though I had seen nothing of him for the last eleven years. He had, I knew, one son, the present baronet, who must now be a young man of about twenty-three. I remembered vaguely having heard some rumors about Sir William's second marriage, but could recall nothing definite unless it were a vague impression detrimental to the second Lady Carmichael.

Settle met me at the station.

"Good of you to come," he said as he wrung my hand.

"Not at all. I understand this is something in my line?"

"Very much so."

"A mental case, then?" I hazarded. "Possessing some unusual features?"

We had collected my luggage by this time and were seated in a dogcart driving away from the station in the direction of Wolden, which lay about three miles away. Settle did not answer for a minute or two. Then he burst out suddenly.

"The whole thing's incomprehensible! Here is a young man, twenty-three years of age, thoroughly normal in every respect. A pleasant amiable boy, with no more than his fair share of conceit, not brilliant intellectually perhaps, but an excellent type of the ordinary upper-class young Englishman. Goes to bed in his usual health one evening, and is found the next morning wandering about the village in a semi-idiotic condition, incapable of recognizing his nearest and dearest."

"Ah!" I said, stimulated. This case promised to be interesting. "Complete loss of memory? And this occurred—?"

"Yesterday morning. The ninth of August."

"And there has been nothing—no shock that you know of—to account for this state?"

"Nothing."

I had a sudden suspicion.

"Are you keeping anything back?"

"N-no."

His hesitation confirmed my suspicion.

"I must know everything."

"It's nothing to do with Arthur. It's to do with—with the house."

"With the house," I repeated, astonished.

"You've had a great deal to do with that sort of thing, haven't you, Carstairs? You've 'tested' so-called haunted houses. What's your opinion of the whole thing?"

"In nine cases out of ten, fraud," I replied. "But the tenth—well,

I have come across phenomena that is absolutely unexplainable from the ordinary materialistic standpoint. I am a believer in the occult."

Settle nodded. We were just turning in at the Park gates. He pointed with his whip at a low-lying white mansion on the side of a hill.

"That's the house," he said. "And—there's *something* in that house, something uncanny—horrible. We all feel it. . . . And I'm not a superstitious man. . . ."

"What form does it take?" I asked.

He looked straight in front of him. "I'd rather you knew nothing. You see, if you—coming here unbiased—knowing nothing about it—see it too—well—"

"Yes," I said, "it's better so. But I should be glad if you will tell me a little more about the family."

"Sir William," said Settle, "was twice married. Arthur is the child of his first wife. Nine years ago he married again, and the present Lady Carmichael is something of a mystery. She is only half English, and, I suspect, has Asiatic blood in her veins."

He paused.

"Settle," I said, "you don't like Lady Carmichael."

He admitted it frankly. "No, I don't. There has always seemed to me to be something sinister about her. Well, to continue, by his second wife Sir William had another child, also a boy, who is now eight years old. Sir William died three years ago, and Arthur came into the title and place. His stepmother and half-brother continued to live with him at Wolden. The estate, I must tell you, is very much impoverished. Nearly the whole of Sir Arthur's income goes to keeping it up. A few hundreds a year was all Sir William could leave his wife, but fortunately Arthur has always got on splendidly with his stepmother, and has been only too delighted to have her live with him. Now—"

"Yes?"

"Two months ago Arthur became engaged to a charming girl, a Miss Phyllis Patterson." He added, lowering his voice with a touch of emotion: "They were to have been married next month. She is staying here now. You can imagine her distress—"

I bowed my head silently.

We were driving up close to the house now. On our right the green lawn sloped gently away. And suddenly I saw a most charming picture. A young girl was coming slowly across the lawn to the house. She wore no hat, and the sunlight enhanced the gleam of her glorious golden hair. She carried a great basket of roses, and a beautiful gray Persian cat twined itself lovingly round her feet as she walked.

I looked at Settle interrogatively.

"That is Miss Patterson," he said.

"Poor girl," I said, "poor girl. What a picture she makes with her roses and her gray cat."

I heard a faint sound and looked quickly round at my friend. The reins had slipped out of his fingers, and his face was quite white.

"What's the matter?" I exclaimed.

He recovered himself with an effort.

"Nothing," he said, "nothing."

In a few moments more we had arrived, and I was following him into the green drawing room, where tea was laid out.

A middle-aged but still beautiful woman rose as we entered and came forward with an outstretched hand.

"This is my friend, Dr. Carstairs, Lady Carmichael."

I cannot explain the instinctive wave of repulsion that swept over me as I took the proffered hand of this charming and stately woman who moved with the dark and languorous grace that recalled Settle's surmise of Oriental blood.

"It is very good of you to come, Dr. Carstairs," she said in a low musical voice, "and to try and help us in our great trouble."

I made some trivial reply and she handed me my tea.

In a few minutes the girl I had seen on the lawn outside entered the room. The cat was no longer with her, but she still carried the basket of roses in her hand. Settle introduced me and she came forward impulsively.

"Oh! Dr. Carstairs, Dr. Settle has told us so much about you. I have a feeling that you will be able to do something for poor Arthur."

Miss Patterson was certainly a very lovely girl, though her cheeks were pale, and her frank eyes were outlined with dark circles.

"My dear young lady," I said reassuringly, "indeed you must not despair. These cases of lost memory, or secondary personality, are often of very short duration. At any minute the patient may return to his full powers."

She shook her head. "I can't believe in this being a second personality," she said. "This isn't Arthur at all. It is no personality of his. It isn't him. I—"

"Phyllis, dear," said Lady Carmichael's soft voice, "here is your tea."

And something in the expression of her eyes as they rested on the girl told me that Lady Carmichael had little love for her prospective daughter-in-law.

Miss Patterson declined the tea, and I said, to ease the conversation: "Isn't the pussycat going to have a saucer of milk?"

She looked at me rather strangely.

"The—pussycat?"

"Yes, your companion of a few moments ago in the garden—"

I was interrupted by a crash. Lady Carmichael had upset the tea kettle, and the hot water was pouring all over the floor. I remedied the matter, and Phyllis Patterson looked questioningly at Settle. He rose.

"Would you like to see your patient now, Carstairs?"

I followed him at once. Miss Patterson came with us. We went upstairs and Settle took a key from his pocket.

"He sometimes has a fit of wandering," he explained. "So I usually lock the door when I'm away from the house."

He turned the key in the lock and we went in.

A young man was sitting on the window seat where the last rays of the westerly sun struck broad and yellow. He sat curiously still, rather hunched together, with every muscle relaxed. I thought at first that he was quite unaware of our presence until I suddenly saw that, under immovable lids, he was watching us closely. His eyes dropped as they met mine, and he blinked. But he did not move.

"Come, Arthur," said Settle cheerfully. "Miss Patterson and a friend of mine have come to see you."

But the young fellow on the window seat only blinked. Yet a moment or two later I saw him watching us again—furtively and secretly.

"Want your tea?" asked Settle, still loudly and cheerfully, as though talking to a child.

He set on the table a cup full of milk. I lifted my eyebrows in surprise, and Settle smiled.

"Funny thing," he said, "the only drink he'll touch is milk."

In a moment or two, without undue haste, Sir Arthur uncoiled himself, limb by limb, from his huddled position and walked slowly over to the table. I recognized suddenly that his movements were absolutely silent, his feet made no sound as they trod. Just as he reached the table, he gave a tremendous stretch, poised on one leg forward, the other stretching out behind him. He prolonged this exercise to its utmost extent, and then yawned. Never have I seen such a yawn! It seemed to swallow up his entire face.

He now turned his attention to the milk, bending down to the table until his lips touched the fluid.

Settle answered my inquiring look.

"Won't make use of his hands at all. Seems to have returned to a primitive state. Odd, isn't it?"

I felt Phyllis Patterson shrink against me a little, and I laid my hand soothingly on her arm.

The milk was finished at last, and Arthur Carmichael stretched himself once more, and then with the same quiet noiseless footsteps he regained the window seat, where he sat, huddled up as before, blinking at us.

Miss Patterson drew us out into the corridor. She was trembling all over.

"Oh! Dr. Carstairs," she cried. "It isn't him—that thing in there isn't Arthur! I should feel—I should know—"

I shook my head sadly.

"The brain can play strange tricks, Miss Patterson."

I confess that I was puzzled by the case. It presented unusual features. Though I had never seen young Carmichael before, there was something about his peculiar manner of walking, and the way he blinked, that reminded me of someone or something that I could not quite place.

Our dinner that night was a quiet affair, the burden of conversation being sustained by Lady Carmichael and myself. When the ladies had withdrawn, Settle asked me my impression of my hostess.

"I must confess," I said, "that for no cause or reason I dislike her intensely. You were quite right, she has Eastern blood, and, I should say, possesses marked occult powers. She is a woman of extraordinary magnetic force."

Settle seemed on the point of saying something, but checked himself and merely remarked after a minute or two: "She is absolutely devoted to her little son."

We sat in the green drawing room again after dinner. We had just finished coffee and were conversing rather stiffly on the topics of the day when the cat began to miaw piteously for admission outside the door. No one took any notice, and, as I am fond of animals, after a moment or two I rose.

"May I let the poor thing in?" I asked Lady Carmichael.

Her face seemed very white, I thought, but she made a faint gesture of the head which I took as assent and, going to the door, I opened it. But the corridor outside was quite empty.

"Strange," I said; "I could have sworn I heard a cat."

As I came back to my chair, I noticed they were all watching me intently. It somehow made me feel a little uncomfortable.

We retired to bed early. Settle accompanied me to my room.

"Got everything you want?" he asked, looking round.

"Yes, thanks."

He still lingered rather awkwardly as though there was something he wanted to say but could not quite get out.

"By the way," I remarked, "you said there was something uncanny about this house? As yet it seems most normal."

"You call it a cheerful house?"

"Hardly that, under the circumstances. It is obviously under the shadow of a great sorrow. But as regards any abnormal influence, I should give it a clean bill of health."

"Good night," said Settle abruptly. "And pleasant dreams."

Dream I certainly did. Miss Patterson's gray cat seemed to have impressed itself upon my brain. All night long, it seemed to me, I dreamed of the wretched animal.

Awaking with a start, I suddenly realized what had brought the cat so forcibly into my thoughts. The creature was miawing persistently outside my door. Impossible to sleep with that racket going on. I lit my candle and went to the door. But the passage outside my room was empty, though the miawing still continued. A new idea struck me. The unfortunate animal was shut up somewhere, unable to get out. To the left was the end of the passage, where Lady Carmichael's room was situated. I turned therefore to the right, but had taken but a few paces when the noise broke out again from behind me. I turned sharply and the sound came again, this time distinctly on the right of me.

Something, probably a draft in the corridor, made me shiver, and I went sharply back to my room. Everything was silent now, and I was soon asleep once more—to wake to another glorious summer's day.

As I was dressing, I saw from my window the disturber of my night's rest. The gray cat was creeping slowly and stealthily across the lawn. I judged its object of attack to be a small flock of birds who were busy chirruping and preening themselves not far away.

And then a very curious thing happened. The cat came straight on and passed through the midst of the birds, its fur almost brushing against them—and the birds did not fly away. I could not understand it—the thing seemed incomprehensible.

So vividly did it impress me that I could not refrain from mentioning it at breakfast.

"Do you know," I said to Lady Carmichael, "that you have a very unusual cat?"

I heard the quick rattle of a cup on a saucer, and I saw Phyllis Patterson, her lips parted and her breath coming quickly, gazing earnestly at me.

There was a moment's silence, and then Lady Carmichael said in a distinctly disagreeable manner: "I think you must have made a mistake. There is no cat here. I have never had a cat."

It was evident that I had managed to put my foot in it badly, so I hastily changed the subject.

But the matter puzzled me. Why had Lady Carmichael declared there was no cat in the house? Was it perhaps Miss Patterson's, and its presence concealed from the mistress of the house? Lady Carmichael might have one of those strange antipathies to cats which are so often met with nowadays. It hardly seemed a plausible explanation, but I was forced to rest content with it for the moment.

Our patient was still in the same condition. This time I made a thorough examination and was able to study him more closely than the night before. At my suggestion it was arranged that he should spend as much time with the family as possible. I hoped not only to have a better opportunity of observing him when he was off his guard, but that the ordinary everyday routine might awaken some gleam of intelligence. His demeanor, however, remained unchanged. He was quiet and docile, seemed vacant, but was, in point of fact, intensely and rather slyly watchful. One thing certainly came as a surprise to me—the intense affection he displayed toward his stepmother. Miss Patterson he ignored completely, but he always managed to sit as near Lady Carmichael as possible, and once I saw him rub his head against her shoulder in a dumb expression of love.

I was worried about the case. I could not but feel that there was some clue to the whole matter which had so far escaped me.

"This is a very strange case," I said to Settle.

"Yes," said he, "it's very—suggestive."

He looked at me—rather furtively, I thought.

"Tell me," he said. "He doesn't—remind you of anything?"

The words struck me disagreeably, reminding me of my impression of the day before.

"Remind me of what?" I asked.

He shook his head.

"Perhaps it's my fancy," he muttered. "Just my fancy."

And he would say no more on the matter.

Altogether there was mystery shrouding the affair. I was still obsessed with that baffling feeling of having missed the clue that should elucidate it to me. And concerning a lesser matter there was also mystery. I mean that trifling affair of the gray cat. For some reason or other the thing was getting on my nerves. I dreamed of cats—I continually fancied I heard them. Now and then in the distance I caught a glimpse of the beautiful animal. And the fact that there was some mystery connected with it fretted me unbearably. On a sudden impulse I applied one afternoon to the footman for information.

"Can you tell me anything," I said, "about the cat I see?"

"The cat, sir?" He appeared politely surprised.

"Wasn't there—isn't there—a cat?"

"Her ladyship *had* a cat sir. A great pet. Had to be put away though. A great pity, as it was a beautiful animal."

"A gray cat?" I asked slowly.

"Yes, sir. A Persian."

"And you say it was destroyed?"

"Yes, sir."

"You're quite sure it was destroyed?"

"Oh, quite sure, sir! Her ladyship wouldn't have him sent to the vet—but did it herself. A little less than a week ago now. He's buried out there under the copper beech, sir." And he went out of the room, leaving me to my meditations.

Why had Lady Carmichael affirmed so positively that she had never had a cat?

I felt an intuition that this trifling affair of the cat was in some way significant. I found Settle and took him aside.

"Settle," I said, "I want to ask you a question. Have you, or have you not, both seen and heard a cat in this house?"

He did not seem surprised at the question. Rather did he seem to have been expecting it.

"I've heard it," he said. "I've not seen it."

"But that first day," I cried. "On the lawn with Miss Patterson!"

He looked at me very steadily.

"I saw Miss Patterson walking across the lawn. Nothing else."

I began to understand. "Then," I said, "the cat—?"

He nodded.

"I wanted to see if you—unprejudiced—would hear what we all hear . . . ?"

"You all hear it then?"

He nodded again.

"It's strange," I murmured thoughtfully. "I never heard of a cat haunting a place before."

I told him what I had learned from the footman, and he expressed surprise.

"That's news to me. I didn't know that."

"But what does it mean?" I asked helplessly.

He shook his head. "Heaven only knows! But I'll tell you, Carstairs—I'm afraid. The—thing's voice sounds—menacing."

"Menacing?" I said sharply. "To whom?"

He spread out his hands. "I can't say."

It was not till that evening after dinner that I realized the meaning of his words. We were sitting in the green drawing room, as on the night of my arrival, when it came—the loud insistent miawing of a cat outside the door. But this time it was unmistakably angry in its tone—a fierce cat yowl, long-drawn and menacing. And then as it ceased, the brass hook outside the door was rattled violently as by a cat's paw.

Settle started up.

"I swear that's real," he cried.

He rushed to the door and flung it open.

There was nothing there.

He came back mopping his brow. Phyllis was pale and trembling, Lady Carmichael deathly white. Only Arthur, squatting contentedly like a child, his head against his stepmother's knee, was calm and undisturbed.

Miss Patterson laid her hand on my arm as we went upstairs.

"Oh! Dr. Carstairs," she cried. "What is it? What does it all mean?"

"We don't know yet, my dear young lady," I said. "But I mean to find out. But you mustn't be afraid. I am convinced there is no danger to you personally."

She looked at me doubtfully. "You think that?"

"I am sure of it," I answered firmly. I remembered the loving way the gray cat had twined itself round her feet, and I had no misgivings. The menace was not for her.

I was some time dropping off to sleep, but at length I fell into an uneasy slumber from which I awoke with a sense of shock. I heard a scratching, sputtering noise as of something being violently ripped or torn. I sprang out of bed and rushed out into the passage. At the same moment Settle burst out of his room opposite. The sound came from our left.

"You hear it, Carstairs?" he cried. "You hear it?"

We came swiftly up to Lady Carmichael's door. Nothing had passed us, but the noise had ceased. Our candles glittered blankly on the shiny panels of Lady Carmichael's door. We stared at one another.

"You know what it was?" he half whispered.

I nodded. "A cat's claws ripping and tearing something." I shivered a little. Suddenly I gave an exclamation and lowered the candle I held.

"Look here, Settle."

"Here" was a chair that rested against the wall—and the seat of it was ripped and torn in long strips. . . .

We examined it closely. He looked at me and I nodded.

"Cat's claws," he said, drawing in his breath sharply. "Unmistakable." His eyes went from the chair to the closed door. "That's the person who is menaced. Lady Carmichael!"

I slept no more that night. Things had come to a pass where something must be done. As far as I knew, there was only one person who had the key to the situation. I suspected Lady Carmichael of knowing more than she chose to tell.

She was deathly pale when she came down the next morning, and only toyed with the food on her plate. I was sure that only an iron determination kept her from breaking down. After breakfast I requested a few words with her. I went straight to the point.

"Lady Carmichael," I said. "I have reason to believe that you are in very grave danger."

"Indeed?" She braved it out with wonderful unconcern.

"There is in this house," I continued, "a Thing—a Presence—that is obviously hostile to you."

"What nonsense," she murmured scornfully. "As if I believed in any rubbish of that kind."

"The chair outside your door," I remarked dryly, "was ripped to ribbons last night."

"Indeed?" With raised eyebrows she pretended surprise, but I saw that I had told her nothing she did not know. "Some stupid practical joke, I suppose."

"It was not that," I replied with some feeling. "And I want you to tell me—for your own sake—" I paused.

"Tell you what?" she queried.

"Anything that can throw light on the matter," I said gravely.

She laughed.

"I know nothing," she said. "Absolutely nothing."

And no warnings of danger could induce her to relax the statement. Yet I was convinced that she did know a great deal more than any of us, and held some clue to the affair of which we were absolutely ignorant. But I saw that it was quite impossible to make her speak.

I determined, however, to take every precaution that I could, convinced as I was that she was menaced by a very real and immediate danger. Before she went to her room the following night, Settle and I made a thorough examination of it. We had agreed that we would take it in turns to watch in the passage.

I took the first watch, which passed without incident, and at three o'clock Settle relieved me. I was tired after my sleepless night the day before, and dropped off at once. And I had a very curious dream.

I dreamed that the gray cat was sitting at the foot of my bed and that its eyes were fixed on mine with a curious pleading. Then, with the ease of dreams, I knew that the creature wanted me to follow it. I did so, and it led me down the great staircase and right to the opposite wing of the house to a room which was obviously the library. It paused there at one side of the room and raised its front paws till they rested on one of the lower shelves of books, while it gazed at me once more with that same moving look of appeal.

Then—cat and library faded, and I awoke to find that morning had come.

Settle's watch had passed without incident, but he was keenly interested to hear of my dream. At my request he took me to the library, which coincided in every particular with my vision of it. I could even point out the exact spot where the animal had given me that last sad look.

We both stood there in silent perplexity. Suddenly an idea occurred to me, and I stooped to read the titles of the books in that exact place. I noticed that there was a gap in the line.

"Some book had been taken out of here," I said to Settle.

He stooped also to the shelf.

"Hallo," he said. "There's a nail at the back here that has torn off a fragment of the missing volume."

He detached the little scrap of paper with care. It was not more than an inch square—but on it were printed two significant words: "The cat. . . ."

We looked at each other.

"This thing gives me the creeps," said Settle. "It's simply horribly uncanny."

"I'd give anything to know," I said, "what book it is that is missing from here. Do you think there is any way of finding out?"

"May be a catalog somewhere. Perhaps Lady Carmichael—"

I shook my head.

"Lady Carmichael will tell you nothing."

"You think so?"

"I am sure of it. While we are guessing and feeling about in the dark, Lady Carmichael *knows*. And for reasons of her own she will say nothing. She prefers to run a most horrible risk sooner than break silence."

The day passed with an uneventfulness that reminded me of the calm before a storm. And I had a strange feeling that the problem was near solution. I was groping about in the dark, but soon I should see. The facts were all there, ready, waiting for the little flash of illumination that should weld them together and show out their significance.

And come it did! In the strangest way!

It was when we were all sitting together in the green drawing room as usual after dinner. We had been very silent. So noiseless indeed was the room that a little mouse ran across the floor—and in an instant the thing happened.

With one long spring Arthur Carmichael leaped from his chair. His quivering body was swift as an arrow on the mouse's track. It had disappeared behind the wainscoting, and there he crouched—watchful—his body still trembling with eagerness.

It was horrible! I have never known such a paralyzing moment. I was no longer puzzled as to that something that Arthur Carmichael reminded me of with his stealthy feet and watching eyes. And in a flash an explanation, wild, incredible, unbelievable, swept into my mind. I rejected it as impossible—unthinkable! But I could not dismiss it from my thoughts.

I hardly remember what happened next. The whole thing seemed blurred and unreal. I know that somehow we got upstairs and said our good nights briefly, almost with a dread of meeting each other's eyes, lest we should see there some confirmation of our own fears.

Settle established himself outside Lady Carmichael's door to take the first watch, arranging to call me at 3 A.M. I had no special fears for Lady Carmichael; I was too taken up with my fantastic impossible theory. I told myself it was impossible—but my mind returned to it, fascinated.

And then suddenly the stillness of the night was disturbed. Settle's voice rose in a shout, calling me. I rushed out into the corridor.

He was hammering and pounding with all his might on Lady Carmichael's door.

"Devil take the woman!" he cried. "She's locked it!"

"But—"

"*It's* in there, man! Can't you hear it?"

From behind the locked door a long-drawn cat yowl sounded fiercely. And then following it a horrible scream—and another. . . . I recognized Lady Carmichael's voice.

"The door!" I yelled. "We must break it in. In another minute we shall be too late."

We set our shoulders against it, and heaved with all our might. It gave with a crash—and we almost fell into the room.

Lady Carmichael lay on the bed bathed in blood. I have seldom seen a more horrible sight. Her heart was still beating, but her injuries were terrible, for the skin of the throat was all ripped and torn. . . . Shuddering, I whispered: "The Claws . . ." A thrill of superstitious horror ran over me.

I dressed and bandaged the wounds carefully and suggested to Settle that the exact nature of the injuries had better be kept secret, especially from Miss Patterson. I wrote out a telegram for a hospital nurse to be despatched as soon as the telegraph office was open.

The dawn was now stealing in at the window. I looked out on the lawn below.

"Get dressed and come out," I said abruptly to Settle. "Lady Carmichael will be all right now."

He was soon ready, and we went out into the garden together.

"What are you going to do?"

"Dig up the cat's body," I said briefly. "I must be sure—"

I found a spade in a tool shed and we set to work beneath the large copper beech tree. At last our digging was rewarded. It was not a pleasant job. The animal had been dead a week. But I saw what I wanted to see.

"That's the cat," I said. "The identical cat I saw the first day I came here."

Settle sniffed. An odor of bitter almonds was still perceptible.

"Prussic acid," he said.

I nodded.

"What are you thinking?" he asked curiously.

"What you think, too!"

My surmise was no new one to him—it had passed through his brain also, I could see.

"It's impossible," he murmured. "Impossible! It's against all science—all nature. . . ." His voice tailed off in a shudder. "That mouse last night," he said. "But—oh, it couldn't be!"

"Lady Carmichael," I said, "is a very strange woman. She has occult powers—hypnotic powers. Her forebears came from the East. Can we know what use she might have made of these powers over a weak lovable nature such as Arthur Carmichael's? And remember, Settle, if Arthur Carmichael remains a hopeless imbecile, devoted to her, the whole property is practically hers and her son's—whom you have told me she adores. And Arthur was going to be married!"

"But what are we going to do, Carstairs?"

"There's nothing to be done," I said. "We'll do our best, though, to stand between Lady Carmichael and vengeance."

Lady Carmichael improved slowly. Her injuries healed themselves as well as could be expected—the scars of that terrible assault she would probably bear to the end of her life.

I had never felt more helpless. The power that defeated us was still at large, undefeated, and though quiescent for the minute we could hardly regard as doing otherwise than biding its time. I was determined upon one thing. As soon as Lady Carmichael was well enough to be moved, she must be taken away from Wolden. There was just a chance that the terrible manifestation might be unable to follow her. So the days went on.

I had fixed September 18 as the date of Lady Carmichael's removal. It was on the morning of the 14th when the unexpected crisis arose.

I was in the library discussing details of Lady Carmichael's case with Settle when an agitated housemaid rushed into the room.

"Oh, sir!" she cried. "Be quick! Mr. Arthur—he's fallen into the pond. He stepped on the punt and it pushed off with him, and he overbalanced and fell in! I saw it from the window."

I waited for no more, but ran straight out of the room followed by Settle. Phyllis was just outside and had heard the maid's story. She ran with us.

"But you needn't be afraid," she cried. "Arthur is a magnificent swimmer."

I felt forebodings, however, and redoubled my pace. The surface of the pond was unruffled. The empty punt floated lazily about—but of Arthur there was no sign.

Settle pulled off his coat and his boots. "I'm going in," he said. "You take me boat hook and fish about from the other punt. It's not very deep."

Very long the time seemed as we searched vainly. Minute followed minute. And then, just as we were despairing, we found him, and bore the apparently lifeless body of Arthur Carmichael to shore.

As long as I live I shall never forget the hopeless agony of Phyllis's face.

"Not—not—" Her lips refused to frame the dreadful word.

"No, no, my dear," I cried. "We'll bring him round, never fear."

But inwardly I had little hope. He had been under water for half an hour. I sent off Settle to the house for hot blankets and other necessaries, and began myself to apply artificial respiration.

We worked vigorously with him for over an hour, but there was no sign of life. I motioned to Settle to take my place again, and I approached Phyllis.

"I'm afraid," I said gently, "that it is no good. Arthur is beyond our help."

She stayed quite still for a moment and then suddenly flung herself down on the lifeless body.

"Arthur!" she cried desperately. "Arthur! Come back to me! Arthur—come back—come back!"

Her voice echoed away into silence. Suddenly I touched Settle's arm. "Look!" I said.

A faint tinge of color had crept into the drowned man's face. I felt his heart.

"Go on with the respiration," I cried. "He's coming round!"

The moments seemed to fly now. In a marvelously short time his eyes opened.

Then suddenly I realized a difference. These were intelligent eyes, human eyes. . . .

They rested on Phyllis.

"Hallo! Phil," he said weakly. "Is it you? I thought you weren't coming until tomorrow."

She could not yet trust herself to speak, but she smiled at him. He looked around with increasing bewilderment.

"But, I say, where am I? And—how rotten I feel! What's the matter with me? Hallo, Dr. Settle!"

"You've been nearly drowned—that's what's the matter," returned Settle grimly.

Sir Arthur made a grimace.

"I've always heard it was beastly coming back afterward! But how did it happen? Was I walking in my sleep?"

Settle shook his head.

"We must get him to the house," I said, stepping forward.

He stared at me, and Phyllis introduced me. "Dr. Carstairs, who is staying here."

We supported him between us and started for the house. He looked up suddenly as though struck by an idea.

"I say, doctor, this won't knock me up for the twelfth, will it?"

"The twelfth?" I said slowly, "you mean the twelfth of August?"

"Yes—next Friday."

"Today is the fourteenth of September," said Settle abruptly.

His bewilderment was evident.

"But—but I thought it was the eighth of August? I must have been ill then?"

Phyllis interposed rather quickly in her gentle voice.

"Yes," she said, "you've been very ill."

He frowned. "I can't understand it. I was perfectly all right when I went to bed last night—at least of course it wasn't really last night. I had dreams, though. I remember, dreams. . . ." His brow furrowed itself still more as he strove to remember. "Something—what was it?—something dreadful—someone had done it to me—and I was angry—desperate. . . . And then I dreamed I was a cat—yes, a cat! Funny, wasn't it? But it wasn't a funny dream. It was more—horrible! But I can't remember. It all goes when I think."

I laid my hand on his shoulder. "Don't try to think, Sir Arthur," I said gravely. "Be content—to forget."

He looked at me in a puzzled way and nodded. I heard Phyllis draw a breath of relief. We had reached the house.

"By the way," said Sir Arthur suddenly, "where's the mater?"

"She has been—ill," said Phyllis after a momentary pause.

"Oh! Poor old mater!" His voice rang with genuine concern. "Where is she? In her room?"

"Yes," I said, "but you had better not disturb—"

The words froze on my lips. The door of the drawing room

opened and Lady Carmichael, wrapped in a dressing gown, came out into the hall.

Her eyes were fixed on Arthur, and if ever I have seen a look of absolute guilt-stricken terror, I saw it then. Her face was hardly human in its frenzied terror. Her hand went to her throat.

Arthur advanced toward her with boyish affection.

"Hallo, mater! So you've been ill too? I say, I'm awfully sorry."

She shrank back before him, her eyes dilating. Then suddenly, with the shriek of a doomed soul, she fell backward through the open door.

I rushed and bent over her, then beckoned to Settle.

"Hush," I said. "Take him upstairs quietly and then come down again. Lady Carmichael is dead."

He returned in a few minutes.

"What was it?" he asked. "What caused it?"

"Shock," I said grimly. "The shock of seeing Arthur Carmichael, the *real*Arthur Carmichael, restored to life! Or you may call it, as I prefer to, the judgment of God!"

"You mean—" He hesitated.

I looked at him in the eyes so that he understood.

"A life for a life," I said significantly.

"But—"

"Oh! I know that a strange and unforeseen accident permitted the spirit of Arthur Carmichael to return to his body. But, nevertheless, Arthur Carmichael was murdered."

He looked at me half fearfully. "With prussic acid?" he asked in a low tone.

"Yes," I answered. "With prussic acid."

Settle and I have never spoken of our belief. It is not one likely to be credited. According to the orthodox point of view Arthur Carmichael merely suffered from loss of memory, Lady Carmichael lacerated her own throat in a temporary fit of mania, and the apparition of the Gray Cat was mere imagination.

But there are two facts that to my mind are unmistakable. One is the ripped chair in the corridor. The other is even more significant. A catalog of the library was found, and after exhaustive search it was proved that the missing volume was an ancient and curious work on the possibilities of the metamorphosis of human beings into animals!

One thing more. I am thankful to say that Arthur knows nothing. Phyllis has locked the secret of those weeks in her own heart, and she will never, I am sure, reveal them to the husband she loves so dearly, and who came back across the barrier of the grave at the call of her voice.

THE CALL OF WINGS

Silas Hamer heard it first on a wintry night in February. He and Dick Borrow had walked from a dinner given by Bernard Seldon, the nerve specialist. Borrow had been unusually silent, and Silas Hamer asked him with some curiosity what he was thinking about. Borrow's answer was unexpected.

"I was thinking that of all these men tonight, only two among them could lay claim to happiness. And that these two, strangely enough, were you and I!"

The word "strangely" was apposite, for no two men could be more dissimilar than Richard Borrow, the hardworking east-end parson, and Silas Hamer, the sleek, complacent man whose millions were a matter of household knowledge.

"It's odd, you know," mused Borrow. "I believe you're the only contented millionaire I've ever met."

Hamer was silent a moment. When he spoke, his tone had altered.

"I used to be a wretched shivering little newspaper boy. I wanted then—what I've got now!—the comfort and the luxury of money, not its power. I wanted money, not to wield as a force, but to spend lavishly—on myself! I'm frank about it, you see. Money can't buy everything, they say. Very true. But it can buy everything I want—therefore I'm satisfied. I'm a materialist, Borrow, out and out a materialist!"

The broad glare of the lighted thoroughfare confirmed this confession of faith. The sleek lines of Silas Hamer's body were amplified by the heavy fur-lined coat, and the white light emphasized the thick rolls of flesh beneath his chin. In contrast to him walked Dick Borrow, with the thin ascetic face and the star-gazing fanatical eyes.

"It's *you,*" said Hamer with emphasis, "that I can't understand."

Borrow smiled.

"I live in the midst of misery, want, starvation—all the ills of the flesh! And a predominant Vision upholds me. It's not easy to understand unless you believe in Visions, which I gather you don't."

"I don't believe," said Silas Hamer stolidly, "in any thing I can't see and hear and touch."

"Quite so. That's the difference between us. Well, good-bye, the earth now swallows me up!"

They had reached the doorway of a lighted tube station, which was Borrow's route home.

Hamer proceeded alone. He was glad he had sent away the car tonight and elected to walk home. The air was keen and frosty, his senses were delightfully conscious of the enveloping warmth of the fur-lined coat.

He paused for an instant on the curbstone before crossing the road. A great motor 'bus was heavily plowing its way toward him. Hamer, with the feeling of infinite leisure, waited for it to pass. If he were to cross in front of it, he would have to hurry—and hurry was distasteful to him.

By his side a battered derelict of the human race rolled drunkenly off the pavement. Hamer was aware of a shout, an ineffectual swerve of the motor 'bus, and then—he was looking stupidly, with a gradually awakening horror, at a limp inert heap of rags in the middle of the road.

A crowd gathered magically, with a couple of policemen and the 'bus driver as its nucleus. But Hamer's eyes were riveted in horrified fascination on that lifeless bundle that had once been a man—a man like himself! He shuddered as at some menace.

"Dahn't yer blime yerself, guv'nor," remarked a rough-looking man at his side. "Yer couldn't 'a done nothin'. 'E was done for anyways."

Hamer stared at him. The idea that it was possible in any way to save the man had quite honestly never occurred to him. He scouted the notion now as an absurdity. Why, if he had been so foolish, he might at this moment . . . His thoughts broke off abruptly, and he walked away from the crowd. He felt himself shaking with a nameless unquenchable dread. He was forced to admit to himself that he was afraid—horribly afraid—of Death—Death that came with dreadful swiftness and remorseless certainty to rich and poor alike. . . .

He walked faster, but the new fear was still with him, enveloping him in its cold and chilling grasp.

He wondered at himself, for he knew that by nature he was no coward. Five years ago, he reflected, this fear would not have attacked nun. For then Life had not been so sweet. . . . Yes, that was it; love of Life was the key to the mystery. The zest of living was at its height for him; it knew but one menace—Death, the destroyer!

He turned out of the lighted thoroughfare. A narrow passageway, between high walls, offered a short cut to the Square where his house, famous for its art treasures, was situated.

The noise of the streets behind him lessened and faded, the soft thud of his own footsteps was the only sound to be heard.

And then out of the gloom in front of him came another sound. Sitting against the wall was a man playing the flute. One of the enormous tribe of street musicians, of course, but why had he chosen such a peculiar spot? Surely at this time of night the police—Hamer's reflections were interrupted suddenly as he realized with a shock that the man had no legs. A pair of crutches rested against the wall beside him. Hamer saw now that it was not a flute he was playing but a strange instrument whose notes were much higher and clearer than those of a flute.

The man played on. He took no notice of Hamer's approach. His head was flung far back on his shoulders, as though uplifted in the joy of his own music, and the notes poured out clearly and joyously, rising higher and higher. . . .

It was a strange tune—strictly speaking, it was not a tune at all, but a single phrase, not unlike the slow turn given out by the violins of *Rienzi,* repeated again and again, passing from key to key, from harmony to harmony, but always rising and attaining each time to a greater and more boundless freedom.

It was unlike anything Hamer had ever heard. There was something strange about it, something inspiring—and uplifting . . . it . . . He caught frantically with both hands to a projection in the wall beside him. He was conscious of one thing only—that he must keep down—at all costs he must *keep down*. . . .

He suddenly realized that the music had stopped. The legless man was reaching out for his crutches. And here was he, Silas Hamer, clutching like a lunatic at a stone buttress, for the simple reason that he had had the utterly preposterous notion—absurd on the face of it!—that he was rising from the ground—that the music was carrying him upward. . . .

He laughed. What a wholly mad idea! Of course his feet had never left the earth for a moment, but what a strange hallucination! The quick tap-tapping of wood on the pavement told him that the cripple was moving away. He looked after him until the man's figure was swallowed up in the gloom. An odd fellow!

He proceeded on his way more slowly; he could not efface from his mind the memory of that strange, impossible sensation when the ground had failed beneath his feet. . . .

And then on an impulse he turned and followed hurriedly in the direction the other had taken. The man could not have gone far—he would soon overtake him.

He shouted as soon as he caught sight of the maimed figure swinging itself slowly along.

"Hi! One minute."

The man stopped and stood motionless until Hamer came abreast of him. A lamp burned just over his head and revealed every feature. Silas Hamer caught his breath in involuntary surprise. The man possessed the most singularly beautiful head he had ever seen. He might have been any age; assuredly he was not a boy, yet youth was the most predominant characteristic—youth and vigor in passionate intensity!

Hamer found an odd difficulty in beginning his conversation.

"Look here," he said awkwardly, "I want to know—what was that thing you were playing just now?"

The man smiled. . . . With his smile the world seemed suddenly to leap into joyousness. . . .

"It was an old tune—a very old tune. . . . Years old—centuries old."

He spoke with an odd purity and distinctness of enunciation, giving equal value to each syllable. He was clearly not an Englishman, yet Hamer was puzzled as to his nationality.

"You're not English? Where do you come from?"

Again the broad joyful smile.

"From over the sea, sir. I came—a long time ago—a very long time ago."

"You must have had a bad accident. Was it lately?"

"Some time now, sir."

"Rough luck to lose both legs."

"It was well," said the man very calmly. He turned his eyes with a strange solemnity on his interlocutor. "They were evil."

Hamer dropped a shilling in his hand and turned away. He was puzzled and vaguely disquieted. "They were evil!" What a strange thing to say! Evidently an operation for some form of disease, but—how odd it had sounded.

Hamer went home thoughtful. He tried in vain to dismiss the incident from his mind. Lying in bed, with the first incipient sensation of drowsiness stealing over him, he heard a neighboring clock strike one. One clear stroke and then silence—silence that was broken by a faint familiar sound. . . . Recognition came leaping. Hamer felt his heart beating quickly. It was the man in the passageway playing, somewhere not far distant. . . .

The notes came gladly, the slow turn with its joyful call, the same haunting little phrase. . . . "It's uncanny," murmured Hamer; "it's uncanny. It's got wings to it. . . ."

Clearer and clearer, higher and higher—each wave rising above the last, and catching him up with it. This time he did not struggle;

he let himself go. . . . Up—up. . . . The waves of sound were carrying him higher and higher. . . . Triumphant and free, they swept on.

Higher and higher. . . . They had passed the limits of human sound now, but they still continued—rising, ever rising. . . . Would they reach the final goal, the full perfection of height?

Rising . . .

Something was pulling—pulling him downward. Something big and heavy and insistent. It pulled remorselessly—pulled him back, and down . . . down. . . .

He lay in bed gazing at the window opposite. Then, breathing heavily and painfully, he stretched an arm out of bed. The movement seemed curiously cumbrous to him. The softness of the bed was oppressive; oppressive, too, were the heavy curtains over the window that blocked out light and air. The ceiling seemed to press down upon him. He felt stifled and choked. He moved slightly under the bedclothes, and the weight of his body seemed to him the most oppressive of all. . . .

II

"I want your advice, Seldon."

Seldon pushed back his chair an inch or so from the table. He had been wondering what was the object of this tête-à-tête dinner. He had seen little of Hamer since the winter, and he was aware tonight of some indefinable change in his friend.

"It's just this," said the millionaire. "I'm worried about myself."

Seldon smiled as he looked across the table.

"You're looking in the pink of condition."

"It's not that." Hamer paused a minute, then added quietly, "I'm afraid I'm going mad."

The nerve specialist glanced up with a sudden keen interest. He poured himself out a glass of port with a rather slow movement, and then said quietly, but with a sharp glance at the other man: "What makes you think that?"

"Something that's happened to me. Something inexplicable, unbelievable. It can't be true, so I must be going mad."

"Take your time," said Seldon, "and tell me about it."

"I don't believe in the supernatural," began Hamer. "I never have. But this thing . . . Well, I'd better tell you the whole story from the beginning. It began last winter one evening after I had dined with you."

Then briefly and concisely he narrated the events of his walk home and the strange sequel.

"That was the beginning of it all. I can't explain it to you properly—the feeling, I mean—but it was wonderful! Unlike anything I've ever felt or dreamed. Well, it's gone on ever since. Not every night, just now and then. The music, the feeling of being uplifted, the soaring flight . . . and then the terrible drag, the pull back to earth, and afterward the pain, the actual physical pain of the awakening. It's like coming down from a high mountain—you know the pains in the ears one gets? Well, this is the same thing, but intensified—and with it goes the awful sense of *weight*—of being hemmed in, stifled. . . ."

He broke off and there was a pause.

"Already the servants think I'm mad. I couldn't bear the roof and the walls—I've had a place arranged up at the top of the house, open to the sky, with no furniture or carpets, or any stifling things. . . . But even then the houses all round are nearly as bad. It's open country I want, somewhere where one can breathe. . . ." He looked across at Seldon. "Well, what do you say? Can you explain it?"

"H'm," said Seldon. "Plenty of explanations. You've been hypnotized, or you've hypnotized yourself. Your nerves have gone wrong. Or it may be merely a dream."

Hamer shook his head. "None of those explanations will do."

"And there are others," said Seldon slowly, "but they're not generally admitted."

"You are prepared to admit them?"

"On the whole, yes! There's a great deal we can't understand which can't possibly be explained normally. We've any amount to find out still, and I for one believe in keeping an open mind."

"What do you advise me to do?" asked Hamer after a silence.

Seldon leaned forward briskly. "One of several things. Go away from London, seek out your 'open country.' The dreams may cease."

"I can't do that," said Hamer quickly. "It's come to this that I can't do without them. I don't want to do without them."

"Ah! I guessed as much. Another alternative, find this fellow, this cripple. You're endowing him now with all sorts of supernatural attributes. Talk to him. Break the spell."

Hamer shook his head again.

"Why not?"

"I'm afraid," said Hamer simply.

Seldon made a gesture of impatience. "Don't believe in it all so blindly! This tune now, the medium that starts it all, what is it like?"

Hamer hummed it, and Seldon listened with a puzzled frown.

"Rather like a bit out of the overture to *Rienzi.* There *is* something uplifting about it—it had wings. But I'm not carried off the earth! Now, these flights of yours, are they all exactly the same?"

"No, no." Hamer leaned forward eagerly. "They develop. Each time I see a little more. It's difficult to explain. You see, I'm always conscious of reaching a certain point—the music carried me there—not direct, but by a succession of *waves,* each reaching higher than the last, until the highest point where one can go no further. I stay there until I'm dragged back. It isn't a place, it's more a state. Well, not just at first, but after a little while, I began to understand that there were other things all round me waiting until I was able to perceive them. Think of a kitten. It has eyes, but at first it can't see with them. It's blind and had to learn to see. Well, that was what it was to me. Mortal eyes and ears were no good to me, but there was something corresponding to them that hadn't yet been developed—something that wasn't bodily at all. And little by little that grew . . . there were sensations of light . . . then of sound . . . then of color. . . . All very vague and unformulated. It was more the knowledge of things than seeing or hearing them. First it was light, a light that grew stronger and clearer . . . then sand, great stretches of reddish sand . . . and here and there straight, long lines of water like canals—"

Seldon drew in his breath sharply. "*Canals!* That's interesting. Go on."

"But these things didn't matter—they didn't count any longer. The real things were the things I couldn't see yet—but I heard them. . . . It was a sound like the rushing of wings . . . Somehow, I can't explain why, it was glorious! There's nothing like it here. And then came another glory—*I saw them*—the Wings! Oh, Seldon, the Wings!"

"But what were they? Men—angels—birds?"

"I don't know. I couldn't see—not yet. But the color of them! Wing color—we haven't got it here—it's a wonderful color."

"Wing color?" repeated Seldon. "What's it like?"

Hamer flung up his hand impatiently. "How can I tell you? Explain the color blue to a blind person! It's a color you've never seen—Wing color!"

"Well?"

"Well? That's all. That's as far as I've got. But each time the coming back has been worse—more painful. I can't understand that. I'm convinced my body never leaves the bed. In this place I get to I'm convinced I've got no *physical* presence. Why should it hurt so confoundedly then?"

Seldon shook his head in silence.

"It's something awful—the coming back. The pull of it—then the pain, pain in every limb and every nerve, and my ears feel as though they were bursting. Then everything presses so, the weight of it all, the dreadful sense of imprisonment. I want light, air, space—above all space to breathe in! And I want freedom."

"And what," asked Seldon, "of all the other things that used to mean so much to you?"

"That's the worst of it. I care for them still as much as, if not more than, ever. And these things, comfort, luxury, pleasure, seem to pull opposite ways to the Wings. It's a perpetual struggle between them—and I can't see how it's going to end."

Seldon sat silent. The strange tale he had been listening to was fantastic enough in all truth. Was it all a delusion, a wild hallucination—or could it by any possibility be true? And if so, why Hamer, of all men . . . ? Surely the materialist, the man who loved the flesh and denied the spirit, was the last man to see the sights of another world.

Across the table Hamer watched him anxiously.

"I suppose," said Seldon slowly, "that you can only wait. Wait and see what happens."

"I can't! I tell you I can't! Your saying that shows you don't understand. It's tearing me in two, this awful struggle—this killing, long-drawn-out fight between—between—" He hesitated.

"The flesh and the spirit?" suggested Seldon.

Hamer stared heavily in front of him. "I suppose one might call it that. Anyway, it's unbearable. . . . I can't get free. . . ."

Again Bernard Seldon shook his head. He was caught up in the grip of the inexplicable. He made one more suggestion.

"If I were you," he advised, "I would get hold of that cripple."

But as he went home, he muttered to himself: "*Canals*—I wonder."

III

Silas Hamer went out of the house the following morning with a new determination in his step. He had decided to take Seldon's advice and find the legless man. Yet inwardly he was convinced that his search would be in vain and that the man would have vanished as completely as though the earth had swallowed him up.

The dark buildings on either side of the passageway shut out the sunlight and left it dark and mysterious. Only in one place, halfway up it, there was a break in the wall, and through it there fell a shaft of golden light that illuminated with radiance a figure sitting on the ground. A figure—yes, it was the man!

The instrument of pipes leaned against the wall beside his crutches, and he was covering the paving stones with designs in colored chalk. Two were completed, sylvan scenes of marvelous beauty and delicacy, swaying trees and a leaping brook that seemed alive.

And again Hamer doubted. Was this man a mere street musician, a pavement artist? Or was he something more . . . ?

Suddenly the millionaire's self-control broke down, and he cried fiercely and angrily: "Who are you? For God's sake, who are you?"

The man's eyes met his, smiling.

"Why don't you answer? Speak, man, speak!"

Then he noticed that the man was drawing with incredible rapidity on a bare slab of stone. Hamer followed the movement with his eyes. . . . A few bold strokes, and giant trees took form. Then, seated on a boulder . . . a man . . . playing an instrument of pipes. A man with a strangely beautiful face—*and goat's legs*. . . .

The cripple's hand made a swift movement. The man still sat on the rock, but the goat's legs were gone. Again his eyes met Hamer's.

"They were evil," he said.

Hamer stared, fascinated. For the face before him was the face of the picture, but strangely and incredibly beautified. . . . Purified from all but an intense and exquisite joy of living.

Hamer turned and almost fled down the passageway into the bright sunlight, repeating to himself incessantly: "It's impossible. Impossible. . . . I'm mad—dreaming!" But the face haunted him—the face of Pan. . . .

He went into the park and sat on a bench. It was a deserted hour. A few nursemaids with their charges sat in the shade of the trees, and dotted here and there in the stretches of green, like islands in a sea, lay the recumbent forms of men. . . .

The words "a wretched tramp" were to Hamer an epitome of misery. But suddenly, today, he envied them. . . .

They seemed to him of all created beings the only free ones. The earth beneath them, the sky above them, the world to wander in . . . they were not hemmed in or chained.

Like a flash it came to him that that which bound him so remorselessly was the thing he had worshipped and prized above all others—wealth! He had thought it the strongest thing on earth, and now, wrapped round by its golden strength, he saw the truth of his words. It was his money that held him in bondage. . . .

But was it? Was that really it? Was there a deeper and more pointed truth that he had not seen? Was it the money or was it his own love of the money? He was bound in fetters of his own making; not wealth itself, but love of wealth was the chain.

He knew now clearly the two forces that were tearing at him, the warm composite strength of materialism that enclosed and surrounded him, and, opposed to it, the clear imperative call—he named it to himself the Call of the Wings.

And while the one fought and clung, the other scorned war and would not stoop to struggle. It only called—called unceasingly. . . . He heard it so clearly that it almost spoke in words.

"You cannot make terms with Me," it seemed to say. "For I am above all other things. If you follow my call, you must give up all else and cut away the forces that hold you. For only the Free shall follow where I lead. . . ."

"I can't," cried Hamer. "I can't. . . ."

A few people turned to look at the big man who sat talking to himself.

So sacrifice was being asked of him, the sacrifice of that which was most dear to him, that which was part of himself.

Part of himself—he remembered the man without legs. . . .

IV

"What in the name of Fortune brings you here?" asked Borrow.

Indeed the east-end mission was an unfamiliar background to Hamer.

"I've listened to a good many sermons," said the millionaire, "all saying what could be done if you people had funds. I've just come to tell you this: you can have the funds."

"Very good of you," answered Borrow, with some surprise. "A big subscription, eh?"

Hamer smiled dryly. "I should say so. Just every penny I've got"

"What?"

Hamer rapped out details in a brisk, businesslike manner. Borrow's head was whirling.

"You—you mean to say that you're making over your entire fortune to be devoted to the relief of the poor in the East End, with myself appointed as trustee?"

"That's it."

"But why—*why?*"

"I can't explain," said Hamer slowly. "Remember our talk about visions last February? Well, a vision has got hold of me."

"It's splendid!" Borrow leaned forward, his eyes gleaming.

"There's nothing particularly splendid about it," said Hamer grimly. "I don't care a button about poverty in the East End. All they want is grit! *I* was poor enough—and I got out of it. But I've got to get rid of the money, and these tom-fool societies shan't get hold of it. You're a man I can trust Feed bodies or souls with it—preferably the former. I've been hungry, but you can do as you like."

"There's never been such a thing known," stammered Borrow.

"The whole thing's done and finished with," continued Hamer. "The lawyers have fixed it up at last, and I've signed everything. I can tell you I've been busy this last fortnight. It's almost as difficult getting rid of a fortune as making one."

"But you—you've kept something?"

"Not a penny," said Hamer cheerfully. "At least—that's not quite true. I've just twopence in my pocket." He laughed.

He said good-bye to his bewildered friend and walked out of the mission into the narrow evil-smelling streets. The words he had said so gaily just now came back to him with an aching sense of loss. "Not a penny!" Of all his vast wealth he had kept nothing. He was afraid now—afraid of poverty and hunger and cold. Sacrifice had no sweetness for him.

Yet behind it all he was conscious that the weight and menace of things had lifted; he was no longer oppressed and bound down. The severing of the chain had seared and torn him, but the vision of freedom was there to strengthen him. His material needs might dim the Call, but they could not deaden it, for he knew it to be a thing of immortality that could not die.

There was a touch of autumn in the air, and the wind blew chill. He felt the cold and shivered, and then, too, he was hungry—he had forgotten to have any lunch. It brought the future very near to him. It was incredible that he should have given it all up; the ease, the comfort, the warmth! His body cried out impotently. . . . And then once again there came to him a glad and uplifting sense of freedom.

Hamer hesitated. He was near a tube station. He had twopence in his pocket. The idea came to him to journey by it to the park where he had watched the recumbent idlers a fortnight ago. Beyond this whim he did not plan for the future. He believed honestly enough now that he was mad—sane people did not act as he had done. Yet, if so, madness was a wonderful and amazing thing.

Yes, he would go now to the open country of the park, and there was a special significance to him in reaching it by tube. For the tube represented to him all the horrors of buried, shut-in life. . . . He would ascend from its imprisonment free to the wide green and the trees that concealed the menace of the pressing houses.

The lift bore him swiftly and relentlessly downward. The air was heavy and lifeless. He stood at the extreme end of the platform, away from the mass of people. On his left was the opening of the tunnel from which the train, snakelike, would presently emerge. He felt the whole place to be subtly evil. There was no one near him but a hunched-up lad sitting on a seat, sunk, it seemed, in a drunken stupor.

In the distance came the faint menacing roar of the train. The lad rose from his seat and shuffled unsteadily to Hamer's side, where he stood on the edge of the platform peering into the tunnel.

Then—it happened so quickly as to be almost incredible—he lost his balance and fell. . . .

A hundred thoughts rushed simultaneously to Hamer's brain. He saw a huddled heap run over by a motor 'bus, and heard a hoarse voice saying: "Dahn't yer blime yerself, guv'nor. Yer couldn't 'a done nothin'." And with that came the knowledge that *this* life could only be saved, if it were saved, by himself. There was no one else near, and the train was close. . . . It all passed through his mind with lightning rapidity. He experienced a curious calm lucidity of thought.

He had one short second in which to decide, and he knew in that moment that his fear of Death was unabated. He was horribly afraid.

And then—was it not a forlorn hope? A useless throwing away of two lives?

To the terrified spectators at the other end of the platform there seemed no gap between the boy's fall and the man's jump after him—and then the train, rushing round the curve of the tunnel, powerless to pull up in time.

Swiftly Hamer caught up the lad in his arms. No natural gallant impulse swayed him, his shivering flesh was but obeying the command of the alien spirit that called for sacrifice. With a last effort he flung the lad forward onto the platform, falling himself. . . .

Then suddenly his fear died. The material world held him down no longer. He was free of his shackles. He fancied for a moment that he heard the joyous piping of Pan. Then—nearer and louder—swallowing up all else—came the glad rushing of innumerable Wings . . . enveloping and encircling him. . . .

MAGNOLIA BLOSSOM

Vincent Easton was waiting under the clock at Victoria Station.

Now and then he glanced up at it uneasily. He thought to himself: "How many other men have waited here for a woman who didn't come?"

A sharp pang shot through him. Supposing that Theo didn't come, that she had changed her mind? Women did that sort of thing. Was he sure of her—had he ever been sure of her? Did he really know anything at all about her? Hadn't she puzzled him from the first? There had seemed to be two women—the lovely, laughing creature who was Richard Darrell's wife, and the other—silent, mysterious, who had walked by his side in the garden of Haymer's Close. Like a magnolia flower—that was how he thought of her—perhaps because it was under the magnolia tree that they had tasted their first rapturous, incredulous kiss. The air had been sweet with the scent of magnolia bloom, and one or two petals, velvety-soft and fragrant, had floated down, resting on that upturned face that was as creamy and as soft and as silent as they. Magnolia blossom—exotic, fragrant, mysterious.

That had been a fortnight ago—the second day he had met her. And now he was waiting for her to come to him forever. Again incredulity shot through him. She wouldn't come. How could he ever have believed it? It would be giving up so much. The beautiful Mrs. Darrell couldn't do this sort of thing quietly. It was bound to be a nine days' wonder, a far-reaching scandal that would never quite be forgotten. There were better, more expedient ways of doing these things—a discreet divorce, for instance.

But they had never thought of that for a moment—at least he had not. Had she, he wondered? He had never known anything of her thoughts. He had asked her to come away with him almost timorously—for after all, what was he? Nobody in particular—one of a thousand orange-growers in the Transvaal. What a life to take her to—after the brilliance of London! And yet, since he wanted her so desperately, he must needs ask.

She had consented very quietly, with no hesitations or protests, as though it were the simplest thing in the world that he was asking her.

"Tomorrow?" he had said, amazed, almost unbelieving.

And she had promised in that soft, broken voice that was so different from the laughing brilliance of her social manner. He had compared her to a diamond when he first saw her—a thing of flashing fire, reflecting light from a hundred facets. But at that first touch, that first kiss, she had changed miraculously to the clouded softness of a pearl—a pearl like a magnolia blossom, creamy-pink.

She had promised. And now he was waiting for her to fulfill that promise.

He looked again at the clock. If she did not come soon, they would miss the train.

Sharply a wave of reaction set in. She wouldn't come! Of course she wouldn't come. Fool that he had been ever to expect it! What were promises? He would find a letter when he got back to his rooms—explaining, protesting, saying all the things that women do when they are excusing themselves for lack of courage.

He felt anger—anger and the bitterness of frustration.

Then he saw her coming toward him down the platform, a faint smile on her face. She walked slowly, without haste or fluster, as one who had all eternity before her. She was in black—soft black that clung, with a little black hat that framed the wonderful creamy pallor of her face.

He found himself grasping her hand, muttering stupidly:

"So you've come—you have come. After all!"

"Of course."

How calm her voice sounded! How calm!

"I thought you wouldn't," he said, releasing her hand and breathing hard.

Her eyes opened—wide, beautiful eyes. There was wonder in them, the simple wonder of a child.

"Why?"

He didn't answer. Instead he turned aside and requisitioned a passing porter. They had not much time. The next few minutes were all bustle and confusion. Then they were sitting in their reserved compartment and the drab houses of southern London were drifting by them.

II

Theodora Darrell was sitting opposite him. At last she was his. And he knew now how incredulous, up to the very last minute, he had been. He had not dared to let himself believe. That magical, elusive quality about her had frightened him. It had seemed impossible that she should ever belong to him.

Now the suspense was over. The irrevocable step was taken. He looked across at her. She lay back in the corner, quite still. The faint smile lingered on her lips, her eyes were cast down, the long, black lashes swept the creamy curve of her cheek.

He thought: "What's in her mind now? What is she thinking of? Me? Her husband? What does she think about him anyway? Did she care for him once? Or did she never care? Does she hate him, or is she indifferent to him?" And with a pang the thought swept through him: "I don't know. I never shall know. I love her, and I don't know anything about her—what she thinks or what she feels."

His mind circled round the thought of Theodora Darrell's husband. He had known plenty of married women who were only too ready to talk about their husbands—of how they were misunderstood by them, of how their finer feelings were ignored. Vincent Easton reflected cynically that it was one of the best-known opening gambits.

But except casually, Theo had never spoken of Richard Darrell. Easton knew of him what everybody knew. He was a popular man, handsome, with an engaging, carefree manner. Everybody liked Darrell. His wife always seemed on excellent terms with him. But that proved nothing, Vincent reflected. Theo was well-bred—she would not air her grievances in public.

And between them, no word had passed. From that second evening of their meeting, when they had walked together in the garden, silent, their shoulders touching, and he had felt the faint tremor that shook her at his touch, there had been no explainings, no defining of the position. She had returned his kisses, a dumb, trembling creature, shorn of all that hard brilliance which, together with her cream-and-rose beauty, had made her famous. Never once had she spoken of her husband. Vincent had been thankful for that at the time. He had been glad to be spared the arguments of a woman who wished to assure herself and her lover that they were justified in yielding to their love.

Yet now the tacit conspiracy of silence worried him. He had again that panic-stricken sense of knowing nothing about this strange creature who was willingly linking her life to his. He was afraid.

In the impulse to reassure himself, he bent forward and laid a hand on the black-clad knee opposite him. He felt once again the faint tremor that shook her, and he reached up for her hand. Bending forward, he kissed the palm, a long, lingering kiss. He felt the response of her fingers on his and, looking up, met her eyes, and was content.

He leaned back in his seat. For the moment, he wanted no more. They were together. She was his. And presently he said in a light, almost bantering tone:

"You're very silent?"

"Am I?"

"Yes." He waited a minute, then said in a graver tone: "You're sure you don't—regret?"

Her eyes opened wide at that. "Oh, no!"

He did not doubt the reply. There was an assurance of sincerity behind it.

"What are you thinking about? I want to know."

In a low voice she answered: "I think I'm afraid."

"Afraid?"

"Of happiness."

He moved over beside her then, held her to him and kissed the softness of her face and neck.

"I love you," he said. "I love you—love you."

Her answer was in the clinging of her body, the abandon of her lips.

Then he moved back to his own corner. He picked up a magazine and so did she. Every now and then, over the top of the magazines, their eyes met. Then they smiled.

They arrived at Dover just after five. They were to spend the night there, and cross to the Continent on the following day. Theo entered their sitting room in the hotel with Vincent close behind her. He had a couple of evening papers in his hand which he threw down on the table. Two of the hotel servants brought in the luggage and withdrew.

Theo turned from the window where she had been standing looking out. In another minute they were in each other's arms.

There was a discreet tap on the door and they drew apart again.

"Damn it all," said Vincent, "it doesn't seem as though we were ever going to be alone."

Theo smiled. "It doesn't look like it," she said softly. Sitting down on the sofa, she picked up one of the papers.

The knock proved to be a waiter bearing tea. He laid it on the table, drawing the latter up to the sofa on which Theo was sitting, cast a deft glance round, inquired if there were anything further, and withdrew.

Vincent, who had gone into the adjoining room, came back into the sitting room.

"Now for tea," he said cheerily, but stopped suddenly in the middle of the room. "Anything wrong?" he asked.

Theo was sitting bolt upright on the sofa. She was staring in front of her with dazed eyes, and her face had gone deathly white.

Vincent took a quick step toward her.

"What is it, sweetheart?"

For answer she held out the paper to him, her finger pointing to the headline.

Vincent took the paper from her. "FAILURE OF HOBSON, JEKYLL AND LUCAS," he read. The name of the big city firm conveyed nothing to him at the moment, though he had an irritating conviction in the back of his mind that it ought to do so. He looked inquiringly at Theo.

"Richard is Hobson, Jekyll and Lucas," she explained.

"Your husband?"

"Yes."

Vincent returned to the paper and read the bald information it conveyed carefully. Phrases such as "sudden crash," "serious revelations to follow," "other houses affected" struck him disagreeably.

Roused by a movement, he looked up. Theo was adjusting her little black hat in front of the mirror. She turned at the movement he made. Her eyes looked steadily into his.

"Vincent—I must go to Richard."

He sprang up.

"Theo—don't be absurd."

She repeated mechanically:

"I must go to Richard."

"But, my dear—"

She made a gesture toward the paper on the floor.

"That means ruin—bankruptcy. I can't choose this day of all others to leave him."

"You had left him before you heard of this. Be reasonable!"

She shook her head mournfully.

"You don't understand. I must go to Richard."

And from that he could not move her. Strange that a creature so soft, so pliant, could be so unyielding. After the first, she did not argue. She let him say what he had to say unhindered. He held her in his arms, seeking to break her will by enslaving her senses, but though her soft mouth returned his kisses, he felt in her something aloof and invincible that withstood all his pleadings.

He let her go at last, sick and weary of the vain endeavor. From pleading he had turned to bitterness, reproaching her with never having loved him. That, too, she took in silence, without protest, her face, dumb and pitiful, giving the lie to his words. Rage mastered him in the end; he hurled at her every cruel word he could think of, seeking only to bruise and batter her to her knees.

At last the words gave out; there was nothing more to say. He sat, his head in his hands, staring down at the red pile carpet. By the door, Theodora stood, a black shadow with a white face.

It was all over.

She said quietly: "Good-bye, Vincent."

He did not answer.

The door opened—and shut again.

III

The Darrells lived in a house in Chelsea—an intriguing, old-world house, standing in a little garden of its own. Up the front of the house grew a magnolia tree, smutty, dirty, begrimed, but still a magnolia.

Theo looked up at it, as she stood on the doorstep some three hours later. A sudden smile twisted her mouth in pain.

She went straight to the study at the back of the house. A man was pacing up and down in the room—a young man, with a handsome face and a haggard expression.

He gave an ejaculation of relief as she came in.

"Thank God you've turned up, Theo. They said you'd taken your luggage with you and gone off out of town somewhere."

"I heard the news and came back."

Richard Darrell put an arm about her and drew her to the couch. They sat down upon it side by side. Theo drew herself free of the encircling arm in what seemed a perfectly natural manner.

"How bad is it, Richard?" she asked quietly.

"Just as bad as it can be—and that's saying a lot."

"Tell me!"

He began to walk up and down again as he talked. Theo sat and watched him. He was not to know that every now and then the room went dim, and his voice faded from her hearing, while another room in a hotel at Dover came clearly before her eyes.

Nevertheless she managed to listen intelligently enough. He came back and sat down on the couch by her.

"Fortunately," he ended, "they can't touch your marriage settlement. The house is yours also."

Theo nodded thoughtfully.

"We shall have that at any rate," she said. "Then things will not be too bad? It means a fresh start, that is all."

"Oh! Quite so. Yes."

But his voice did not ring true, and Theo thought suddenly: "There's something else. He hasn't told me everything."

"There's nothing more, Richard?" she said gently. "Nothing worse?"

He hesitated for just half a second, then: "Worse? What should there be?"

"I don't know," said Theo.

"It'll be all right," said Richard, speaking more as though to reassure himself than Theo. "Of course, it'll be all right."

He flung an arm about her suddenly.

"I'm glad you're here," he said. "It'll be all right now that you're here. Whatever else happens, I've got you, haven't I?"

She said gently: "Yes, you've got me." And this time she left his arm round her.

He kissed her and held her close to him, as though in some strange way he derived comfort from her nearness.

"I've got you, Theo," he said again presently, and she answered as before: "Yes, Richard."

He slipped from the couch to the floor at her feet.

"I'm tired out," he said fretfully. "My God, it's been a day. Awful!

I don't know what I should do if you weren't here. After all, one's wife is one's wife, isn't she?"

She did not speak, only bowed her head in assent.

He laid his head on her lap. The sigh he gave was like that of a tired child.

Theo thought again: "There's something he hasn't told me. What is it?"

Mechanically her hand dropped to his smooth, dark head, and she stroked it gently, as a mother might comfort a child.

Richard murmured vaguely:

"It'll be all right now you're here. You won't let me down."

His breathing grew slow and even. He slept. Her hand still smoothed his head.

But her eyes looked steadily into the darkness in front of her, seeing nothing.

"DON'T YOU THINK, Richard," said Theodora, "that you'd better tell me everything?"

It was three days later. They were in the drawing room before dinner.

Richard started, and flushed.

"I don't know what you mean," he parried.

"Don't you?"

He shot a quick glance at her.

"Of course there are—well—details."

"I ought to know everything, don't you think, if I am to help?"

He looked at her strangely.

"What makes you think I want you to help?"

She was a little astonished.

"My dear Richard, I'm your wife."

He smiled suddenly, the old, attractive, carefree smile.

"So you are, Theo. And a very good-looking wife, too. I never could stand ugly women."

He began walking up and down the room, as was his custom when something was worrying him.

"I won't deny you're right in a way," he said presently. "There is something."

He broke off.

"Yes?"

"It's so damned hard to explain things of this kind to women. They get hold of the wrong end of the stick—fancy a thing is—well, what it isn't."

Theo said nothing.

"You see," went on Richard, "the law's one thing, and right and wrong are quite another. I may do a thing that's perfectly right and honest, but the law wouldn't take the same view of it. Nine times out of ten, everything pans out all right, and the tenth time you—well, hit a snag."

Theo began to understand. She thought to herself: "Why am I not surprised? Did I always know, deep down, that he wasn't straight?"

Richard went on talking. He explained himself at unnecessary lengths. Theo was content for him to cloak the actual details of the affair in this mantle of verbosity. The matter concerned a large tract of South African property. Exactly what Richard had done, she was not concerned to know. Morally, he assured her, everything was fair and aboveboard; legally—well, there it was; no getting away from the fact, he had rendered himself liable to criminal prosecution.

He kept shooting quick glances at his wife as he talked. He was nervous and uncomfortable. And still he excused himself and tried to explain away that which a child might have seen in its naked truth. Then finally in a burst of justification, he broke down. Perhaps Theo's eyes, momentarily scornful, had something to do with it. He sank down in a chair by the fireplace, his head in his hands.

"There it is, Theo," he said brokenly. "What are you going to do about it?"

She came over to him with scarcely a moment's pause and, kneeling down by the chair, put her face against his.

"What can be done, Richard? What can we do?"

He caught her to him.

"You mean it? You'll stick to me?"

"Of course. My dear, of course."

He said, moved to sincerity in spite of himself: "I'm a thief, Theo. That's what it means, shorn of fine language—just a thief."

"Then I'm a thief's wife, Richard. We'll sink or swim together."

They were silent for a little while. Presently Richard recovered something of his jaunty manner.

"You know, Theo, I've got a plan, but we'll talk of that later. It's just on dinnertime. We must go and change. Put on that creamy thingummybob of yours, you know—the Caillot model."

Theo raised her eyebrows quizzically.

"For an evening at home?"

"Yes, yes, I know. But I like it. Put it on, there's a good girl. It cheers me up to see you looking your best."

Theo came down to dinner in the Caillot. It was a creation in creamy brocade, with a faint pattern of gold running through it and an undernote of pale pink to give warmth to the cream. It was cut daringly low in the back, and nothing could have been better-designed to show off the dazzling whiteness of Theo's neck and shoulders. She was truly now a magnolia flower.

Richard's eye rested upon her in warm approval. "Good girl. You know, you look simply stunning in that dress."

They went in to dinner. Throughout the evening Richard was nervous and unlike himself, joking and laughing about nothing at all, as if in a vain attempt to shake off his cares. Several times Theo tried to lead him back to the subject they had been discussing before, but he edged away from it.

Then suddenly, as she rose to go to bed, he came to the point.

"No, don't go yet. I've got something to say. You know, about this miserable business."

She sat down again.

He began talking rapidly. With a bit of luck, the whole thing could be hushed up. He had covered his tracks fairly well. So long as certain papers didn't get into the receiver's hands—

He stopped significantly.

"Papers?" asked Theo perplexedly. "You mean you will destroy them?"

Richard made a grimace.

"I'd destroy them fast enough if I could get hold of them. That's the devil of it all!"

"Who has them, then?"

"A man we both know—Vincent Easton."

A very faint exclamation escaped Theo. She forced it back, but Richard had noticed it.

"I've suspected he knew something of the business all along. That's why I've asked him here a good bit. You may remember that I asked you to be nice to him?"

"I remember," said Theo.

"Somehow I never seem to have got on really friendly terms with him. Don't know why. But he likes you. I should say he likes you a good deal."

Theo said in a very clear voice: "He does."

"Ah!" said Richard appreciatively. "That's good. Now you see what I'm driving at. I'm convinced that if you went to Vincent Easton and asked him to give you those papers, he wouldn't refuse. Pretty woman, you know—all that sort of thing."

"I can't do that," said Theo quickly.

"Nonsense."

"It's out of the question."

The red came slowly out in blotches on Richard's face. She saw that he was angry.

"My dear girl, I don't think you quite realize the position. If this comes out, I'm liable to go to prison. It's ruin—disgrace."

"Vincent Easton will not use those papers against you. I am sure of that."

"That's not quite the point. He mayn't realize that they incriminate me. It's only taken in conjunction with—with my affairs—with the figures they're bound to find. Oh! I can't go into details. He'll ruin me without knowing what he's doing unless somebody puts the position before him."

"You can do that yourself, surely. Write to him."

"A fat lot of good that would be! No, Theo, we've only got one hope. You're the trump card. You're my wife. You must help me. Go to Easton tonight—"

A cry broke from Theo.

"Not tonight. Tomorrow perhaps."

"My God, Theo, can't you realize things? Tomorrow may be too late. If you could go now—at once—to Easton's rooms." He saw her flinch, and tried to reassure her. "I know, my dear girl, I know. It's a beastly thing to do. But it's life or death. Theo, you won't fail me? You said you'd do anything to help me—"

Theo heard herself speaking in a hard, dry voice. "Not this thing. There are reasons."

"It's life or death, Theo. I mean it. See here."

He snapped open a drawer of the desk and took out a revolver. If there was something theatrical about that action, it escaped her notice.

"It's that or shooting myself. I can't face the racket. If you won't do as I ask you, I'll be a dead man before morning. I swear to you solemnly that that's the truth."

Theo gave a low cry. "No, Richard, not that!"

"Then help me."

He flung the revolver down on the table and knelt by her side. "Theo, my darling—if you love me—if you've ever loved me—do this for me. You're my wife, Theo. I've no one else to turn to."

On and on his voice went, murmuring, pleading. And at last Theo heard her own voice saying: "Very well—yes."

Richard took her to the door and put her into a taxi.

IV

"Theo!"

Vincent Easton sprang up in incredulous delight. She stood in the doorway. Her wrap of white ermine was hanging from her shoulders. Never, Easton thought, had she looked so beautiful.

"You've come after all."

She put out a hand to stop him as he came toward her.

"No, Vincent, this isn't what you think."

She spoke in a low, hurried voice.

"I'm here from my husband. He thinks there are some papers which may—do him harm. I have come to ask you to give them to me."

Vincent stood very still, looking at her. Then he gave a short laugh.

"So that's it, is it? I thought Hobson, Jekyll and Lucas sounded familiar the other day, but I couldn't place them at the minute. Didn't know your husband was connected with the firm. Things have been going wrong there for some time. I was commissioned to look into the matter. I suspected some underling. Never thought of the man at the top."

Theo said nothing. Vincent looked at her curiously.

"It makes no difference to you, this?" he asked. "That—well, to put it plainly, that your husband's a swindler?"

She shook her head.

"It beats me," said Vincent. Then he added quietly: "Will you wait a minute or two? I will get the papers."

Theo sat down in a chair. He went into the other room. Presently he returned and delivered a small package into her hand.

"Thank you," said Theo. "Have you a match?"

Taking the matchbox he proffered, she knelt down by the fireplace. When the papers were reduced to a pile of ashes, she stood up.

"Thank you," she said again.

"Not at all," he answered formally. "Let me get you a taxi."

He put her into it, saw her drive away. A strange, formal little interview. After the first, they had not even dared look at each other. Well, that was that, the end. He would go away, abroad, try and forget.

Theo leaned her head out of the window and spoke to the taxi driver. She could not go back at once to the house in Chelsea. She must have a breathing space. Seeing Vincent again had shaken her horribly. If only—if only. But she pulled herself up. Love for her husband she had none—but she owed him loyalty. He was down, she must stick by him. Whatever else he might have done, he loved her; his offense had been committed against society, not against her.

The taxi meandered on through the wide streets of Hampstead. They came out on the heath, and a breath of cool, invigorating air fanned Theo's cheeks. She had herself in hand again now. The taxi sped back toward Chelsea.

Richard came out to meet her in the hall.

"Well," he demanded, "you've been a long time."

"Have I?"

"Yes—a very long time. Is it—all right?"

He followed her, a cunning look in his eyes. His hands were shaking.

"It's—it's all right, eh?" he said again.

"I burned them myself."

"Oh!"

She went on into the study, sinking into a big armchair. Her face was dead white and her whole body drooped with fatigue. She thought to herself: "If only I could go to sleep now and never, never wake up again!"

Richard was watching her. His glance, shy, furtive, kept coming and going. She noticed nothing. She was beyond noticing.

"It went off quite all right, eh?"

"I've told you so."

"You're sure they were the right papers? Did you look?"

"No."

"But then—"

"I'm sure, I tell you. Don't bother me, Richard. I can't bear any more tonight."

Richard shifted nervously.

"No, no. I see."

He fidgeted about the room. Presently he came over to her, laid a hand on her shoulder. She shook it off.

"Don't touch me." She tried to laugh. "I'm sorry, Richard. My nerves are on edge. I feel I can't bear to be touched."

"I know. I understand."

Again he wandered up and down.

"Theo," he burst out suddenly. "I'm damned sorry."

"What?" She looked up, vaguely startled.

"I oughtn't to have let you go there at this time of night. I never dreamed that you'd be subjected to any—unpleasantness."

"Unpleasantness?" She laughed. The word seemed to amuse her. "You don't know! Oh, Richard, you don't know!"

"I don't know what?"

She said very gravely, looking straight in front of her: "What this night has cost me."

"My God! Theo! I never meant—You—you did that, for me? The swine! Theo—Theo—I couldn't have known. I couldn't have guessed. My God!"

He was kneeling by her now stammering, his arms round her, and she turned and looked at him with faint surprise, as though his words had at last really penetrated to her attention.

"I—I never meant—"

"You never meant what, Richard?"

Her voice startled him.

"Tell me. What was it that you never meant?"

"Theo, don't let us speak of it. I don't want to know. I want never to think of it."

She was staring at him, wide awake now, with every faculty alert. Her words came clear and distinct:

"You never meant—What do you think happened?"

"It didn't happen, Theo. Let's say it didn't happen."

And still she stared, till the truth began to come to her.

"You think that—"

"I don't want—"

She interrupted him: "You think that Vincent Easton asked a price for those letters? You think that I—paid him?"

Richard said weakly and unconvincingly: "I—I never dreamed he was that kind of man."

V

"Didn't you?" She looked at him searchingly. His eyes fell before hers. "Why did you ask me to put on this dress this evening? Why did you send me there alone at this time of night? You guessed he—cared for me. You wanted to save your skin—save it at any cost—even at the cost of my honor." She got up.

"I see now. You meant that from the beginning—or at least you saw it as a possibility, and it didn't deter you."

"Theo—"

"You can't deny it. Richard, I thought I knew all there was to know about you years ago. I've known almost from the first that you weren't straight as regards the world. But I thought you were straight with me."

"Theo—"

"Can you deny what I've just been saying?"

He was silent, in spite of himself.

"Listen, Richard. There is something I must tell you. Three days ago when this blow fell on you, the servants told you I was away—gone to the country. That was only partly true. I had gone away with Vincent Easton—"

Richard made an inarticulate sound. She held out a hand to stop him.

"Wait. We were at Dover. I saw a paper—I realized what had happened. Then, as you know, I came back."

She paused.

Richard caught her by the wrist. His eyes burned into hers.

"You came back—in time?"

Theo gave a short, bitter laugh.

"Yes, I came back, as you say, 'in time,' Richard."

Her husband relinquished his hold on her arm. He stood by the mantelpiece, his head thrown back. He looked handsome and rather noble.

"In that case," he said, "I can forgive."

"I cannot."

The two words came crisply. They had the semblance and the effect of a bomb in the quiet room. Richard started forward, staring, his jaw dropped with an almost ludicrous effect.

"You—er—what did you say, Theo?"

"I said I cannot forgive! In leaving you for another man, I

sinned—not technically, perhaps, but in intention, which is the same thing. But if I sinned, I sinned through love. You, too, have not been faithful to me since our marriage. Oh, yes, I know. That I forgave, because I really believed in your love for me. But the thing you have done tonight is different. It is an ugly thing, Richard—a thing no woman should forgive. You sold me, your own wife, to purchase safety!"

She picked up her wrap and turned toward the door.

"Theo," he stammered out, "where are you going?"

She looked back over her shoulder at him.

"We all have to pay in this life, Richard. For my sin I must pay in loneliness. For yours—well, you gambled with the thing you love, and you have lost it!"

"You are going?"

She drew a long breath.

"To freedom. There is nothing to bind me here."

He heard the door shut. Ages passed, or was it a few minutes? Something fluttered down outside the window—the last of the magnolia petals, soft, fragrant.

NEXT TO A DOG

The ladylike woman behind the Registry Office table cleared her throat and peered across at the girl who sat opposite.

"Then you refuse to consider the post? It only came in this morning. A very nice part of Italy, I believe, a widower with a little boy of three and an elderly lady, his mother or aunt."

Joyce Lambert shook her head.

"I can't go out of England," she said in a tired voice; "there are reasons. If only you could find me a daily post?"

Her voice shook slightly—ever so slightly, for she had it well under control. Her dark blue eyes looked appealingly at the woman opposite her.

"It's very difficult, Mrs. Lambert. The only kind of daily governess required is one who has full qualifications. You have none. I have hundreds on my books—literally hundreds." She paused. "You have someone at home you can't leave?"

Joyce nodded.

"A child?"

"No, not a child." And a faint smile flickered across her face.

"Well, it is very unfortunate. I will do my best, of course, but—"

The interview was clearly at an end. Joyce rose. She was biting her lip to keep the tears from springing to her eyes as she emerged from the frowsy office into the street.

"You mustn't," she admonished herself sternly. "Don't be a sniveling little idiot. You're panicking—that's what you're doing—panicking. No good ever came of giving way to panic. It's quite early in the day still and lots of things may happen. Aunt Mary ought to be good for a fortnight anyway. Come on, girl, step out, and don't keep your well-to-do relations waiting."

She walked down Edgware Road, across the park, and then down to Victoria Street, where she turned into the Army and Navy Stores. She went to the lounge and sat down glancing at her watch. It was just half-past one. Five minutes sped by and then an elderly lady with her arms full of parcels bore down upon her.

"Ah! There you are, Joyce. I'm a few minutes late, I'm afraid. The service is not as good as it used to be in the luncheon room. You've had lunch, of course?"

Joyce hesitated a minute or two, then she said quietly: "Yes, thank you."

"I always have mine at half-past twelve," said Aunt Mary, settling herself comfortably with her parcels. "Less rush and a clearer atmosphere. The curried eggs here are excellent."

"Are they?" said Joyce faintly. She felt that she could hardly bear to think of curried eggs—the hot steam rising from them—the delicious smell! She wrenched her thoughts resolutely aside.

"You look peaky, child," said Aunt Mary, who was herself of a comfortable figure. "Don't go in for this modern fad of eating no meat. All fal-de-lal. A good slice off the joint never did anyone any harm."

Joyce stopped herself from saying "It wouldn't do me any harm now." If only Aunt Mary would stop talking about food. To raise your hopes by asking you to meet her at half-past one and then to talk of curried eggs and slices of roast meat—oh! cruel—cruel.

"Well, my dear," said Aunt Mary. "I got your letter—and it was very nice of you to take me at my word. I said I'd be pleased to see you anytime and so I should have been—but as it happens, I've just had an extremely good offer to let the house. Quite too good to be missed, and bringing their own plate and linen. Five months. They come in on Thursday and I go to Harrogate. My rheumatism's been troubling me lately."

"I see," said Joyce. "I'm so sorry."

"So it'll have to be for another time. Always pleased to see you, my dear."

"Thank you, Aunt Mary."

"You know, you do look peaky," said Aunt Mary, considering her attentively. "You're thin, too; no flesh on your bones, and what's happened to your pretty color? You always had a nice healthy color. Mind you take plenty of exercise."

"I'm taking plenty of exercise today," said Joyce grimly. She rose. "Well, Aunt Mary, I must be getting along."

Back again—through St. James's Park this time, and so on through Berkeley Square and across Oxford Street and up Edgware Road, past Praed Street to the point where the Edgware Road begins to think of becoming something else. Then aside, through a series of dirty little streets till one particular dingy house was reached.

Joyce inserted her latchkey and entered a small frowsy hall. She ran up the stairs till she reached the top landing. A door faced her and from the bottom of this door a snuffling noise proceeded succeeded in a second by a series of joyful whines and yelps.

"Yes, Terry darling—it's Missus come home."

As the door opened, a white body precipitated itself upon the girl—an aged wire-haired terrier very shaggy as to coat and suspiciously bleary as to eyes. Joyce gathered him up in her arms and sat down on the floor.

"Terry darling! Darling, darling Terry. Love your Missus, Terry; love your Missus a lot!"

And Terry obeyed, his eager tongue worked busily, he licked her face, her ears, her neck and all the time his stump of a tail wagged furiously.

"Terry darling, what are we going to do? What's going to become of us? Oh! Terry darling, I'm so tired."

"Now then, miss," said a tart voice behind her. "If you'll give over hugging and kissing that dog, here's a cup of nice hot tea for you."

"Oh! Mrs. Barnes, how good of you."

Joyce scrambled to her feet. Mrs. Barnes was a big, formidable-looking woman. Beneath the exterior of a dragon she concealed an unexpectedly warm heart.

"A cup of hot tea never did anyone any harm," enunciated Mrs. Barnes, voicing the universal sentiment of her class.

Joyce sipped gratefully. Her landlady eyed her covertly.

"Any luck, miss—ma'am, I should say?"

Joyce shook her head, her face clouded over.

"Ah!" said Mrs. Barnes with a sigh. "Well, it doesn't seem to be what you might call a lucky day."

Joyce looked up sharply.

"Oh, Mrs. Barnes—you don't mean—"

Mrs. Barnes was nodding gloomily.

"Yes—it's Barnes. Out of work again. What we're going to do, I'm sure I don't know."

"Oh, Mrs. Barnes—I must—I mean you'll want—"

"Now don't you fret, my dear. I'm not denying but that I'd be glad if you'd found something—but if you haven't—you haven't. Have you finished that tea? I'll take the cup."

"Not quite."

"Ah!" said Mrs. Barnes accusingly. "You're going to give what's left to that dratted dog—I know you."

"Oh, please, Mrs. Barnes. Just a little drop. You don't mind really, do you?"

"It wouldn't be any use if I did. You're crazy about that cantankerous brute. Yes, that's what I say—and that's what he is. As near as nothing bit me this morning, he did."

"Oh, no, Mrs. Barnes! Terry wouldn't do such a thing."

"Growled at me—showed his teeth. I was just trying to see if there was anything could be done to those shoes of yours."

"He doesn't like anyone touching my things. He things he ought to guard them."

"Well, what does he want to think for? It isn't a dog's business to think. He'd be well enough in his proper place, tied up in the yard to keep off burglars. All this cuddling! He ought to be put away, miss—that's what I say."

"No, no, no. Never. Never!"

"Please yourself," said Mrs. Barnes. She took the cup from the table, retrieved the saucer from the floor where Terry had just finished his share, and stalked from the room.

"Terry," said Joyce. "Come here and talk to me. What are we going to do, my sweet?"

She settled herself in the rickety armchair, with Terry on her knees. She threw off her hat and leaned back. She put one of Terry's paws on each side of her neck and kissed him lovingly on his nose and between his eyes. Then she began talking to him in a soft low voice, twisting his ears gently between her fingers.

"What are we going to do about Mrs. Barnes, Terry? We owe her four weeks—and she's such a lamb, Terry—such a lamb. She'd never turn us out. But we can't take advantage of her being a lamb, Terry. We can't do that. Why does Barnes want to be out of work? I hate Barnes. He's always getting drunk. And if you're always getting drunk, you are usually out of work. But I don't get drunk, Terry, and yet I'm out of work.

"I can't leave you, darling. I can't leave you. There's not even anyone I could leave you with—nobody who'd be good to you. You're getting old, Terry—twelve years old—and nobody wants an old dog who's rather blind and a little deaf and a little—yes, just a little—bad-tempered. You're sweet to me, darling, but you're not sweet to everyone, are you? You growl. It's because you know the world's turning against you. We've just got each other, haven't we, darling?"

Terry licked her cheek delicately.

"Talk to me, darling."

Terry gave a long lingering groan—almost a sigh, then he nuzzled his nose in behind Joyce's ear.

"You trust me, don't you, angel? You know I'd never leave you. But what are we going to do? We're right down to it now, Terry."

She settled back further in the chair, her eyes half closed.

"Do you remember, Terry, all the happy times we used to have? You and I and Michael and Daddy. Oh, Michael—Michael! It was his first leave, and he wanted to give me a present before he went back to France. And I told him not to be extravagant. And then we were down in the country—and it was all a surprise. He told me to look out of the window, and there you were, dancing up the path on a long lead. The funny little man who brought you, a little man who smelt of dogs. How he talked. 'The goods, that's what he is. Look at him, ma'am, ain't he a picture? I said to myself, as soon as the lady and gentleman see him they'll say: "That dog's the goods!"'

"He kept on saying that—and we called you that for quite a long time—the Goods! Oh, Terry, you were such a darling of a puppy, with your little head on one side, wagging your absurd tail! And Michael went away to France and I had you—the darlingest dog in the world. You read all Michael's letters with me, didn't you? You'd sniff them, and I'd say—'From Master,' and you'd understand. We were so happy—so happy. You and Michael and I. And now Michael's dead, and you're old, and I—I'm so tired of being brave."

Terry licked her.

"You were there when the telegram came. If it hadn't been for you, Terry—if I hadn't had you to hold on to . . ."

She stayed silent for some minutes.

"And we've been together ever since—been through all the ups and downs together—there have been a lot of downs, haven't there? And now we've come right up against it. There are only Michael's aunts, and they think I'm all right. They don't know he gambled that money away. We must never tell anyone that. *I* don't care—why shouldn't he? Everyone has to have some fault. He loved us both, Terry, and that's all that matters. His own relations were always inclined to be down on him and to say nasty things. We're not going to give them the chance. But I wish I had some relations of my own. It's very awkward having no relations at all.

"I'm so tired, Terry—and remarkably hungry. I can't believe I'm only twenty-nine—I feel sixty-nine. I'm not really brave—I only pretend to be. And I'm getting awfully mean ideas. I walked all the way to Ealing yesterday to see Cousin Charlotte Green. I thought if I got there at half-past twelve she'd be sure to ask me to stop to lunch. And then when I got to the house, I felt it was too cadging for anything. I just couldn't. So I walked all the way back. And that's foolish. You should be a determined cadger or else not even think of it. I don't think I'm a strong character."

Terry groaned again and put a black nose into Joyce's eye.

"You've got a lovely nose still, Terry—all cold like ice cream. Oh, I do love you so! I can't part from you. I can't have you 'put away.' I can't. . . . I can't. . . . I can't. . . ."

The warm tongue licked eagerly.

"You understand so, my sweet. You'd do anything to help Missus, wouldn't you?"

Terry clambered down and went unsteadily to a corner. He came back holding a battered bowl between his teeth.

Joyce was midway between tears and laughter.

"Was he doing his only trick? The only thing he could think of to help Missus. Oh, Terry—Terry—nobody shall part us! I'd do anything. Would I, though? One says that—and then when you're shown the thing, you say, 'I didn't mean anything like *that*.' Would I do anything?"

She got down on the floor beside the dog.

"You see, Terry, it's like this. Nursery governesses can't have dogs, and companions to elderly ladies can't have dogs. Only married women can have dogs, Terry—little fluggy expensive dogs that they take shopping with them—and if one preferred an old blind terrier—well, why not?"

She stopped frowning and at that minute there was a double knock from below.

"The post. I wonder."

She jumped up and hurried down the stairs, returning with a letter.

"It might be. If only . . ."

She tore it open.

DEAR MADAM,

We have inspected the picture and our opinion is that it is not a genuine Cuyp and that its value is practically nil.

YOURS TRULY,
SLOANE & RYDER

Joyce stood holding it. When she spoke, her voice had changed.

"That's that," she said. "The last hope gone. But we won't be parted. There's a way—and it won't be cadging. Terry darling, I'm going out. I'll be back soon."

Joyce hurried down the stairs to where the telephone stood in a dark corner. There she asked for a certain number. A man's voice answered her, its tone changing as he realized her identity.

"Joyce, my dear girl. Come out and have some dinner and dance tonight."

"I can't," said Joyce lightly. "Nothing fit to wear."

And she smiled grimly as she thought of the empty pegs in the flimsy cupboard.

"How would it be if I came along and saw you now? What's the address? Good Lord, where's that? Rather come off your high horse, haven't you?"

"Completely."

"Well, you're frank about it. So long."

Arthur Halliday's car drew up outside the house about three quarters of an hour later. An awestruck Mrs. Barnes conducted him upstairs.

"My dear girl—what an awful hole. What on earth has got you into this mess?"

"Pride and a few other unprofitable emotions."

She spoke lightly enough; her eyes looked at the man opposite her sardonically.

Many people called Halliday handsome. He was a big man with square shoulders, fair, with small, very pale blue eyes and a heavy chin.

He sat down on the rickety chair she indicated.

"Well," he said thoughtfully. "I should say you'd had your lesson. I say—will that brute bite?"

"No, no, he's all right. I've trained him to be rather a—a watch-dog."

Halliday was looking her up and down.

"Going to climb down, Joyce," he said softly. "Is that it?"

Joyce nodded.

"I told you before, my dear girl. I always get what I want in the end. I knew you'd come in time to see which way your bread was buttered."

"It's lucky for me you haven't changed your mind," said Joyce.

He looked at her suspiciously. With Joyce you never knew quite what she was driving at.

"You'll marry me?"

She nodded. "As soon as you please."

"The sooner, the better, in fact." He laughed, looking round the room.

Joyce flushed.

"By the way, there's a condition."

"A condition?" He looked suspicious again.

"My dog. He must come with me."

"This old scarecrow? You can have any kind of a dog you choose. Don't spare expense."

"I want Terry."

"Oh! All right, please yourself."

Joyce was staring at him.

"You do know—don't you—that I don't love you? Not in the least."

"I'm not worrying about that. I'm not thin-skinned. But no hanky-panky, my girl. If you marry me, you play fair."

The color flashed into Joyce's cheeks.

"You will have your money's worth," she said.

"What about a kiss now?"

He advanced upon her. She waited, smiling. He took her in his arms, kissing her face, her lips, her neck. She neither stiffened nor drew back. He released her at last.

"I'll get you a ring," he said. "What would you like, diamonds or pearls?"

"A ruby," said Joyce. "The largest ruby possible—the color of blood."

"That's an odd idea."

"I should like it to be a contrast to the little half hoop of pearls that was all that Michael could afford to give me."

"Better luck this time, eh?"

"You put things wonderfully, Arthur."

Halliday went out chuckling.

"Terry," said Joyce. "Lick me—lick hard—all over my face and my neck—particularly my neck."

And as Terry obeyed, she murmured reflectively:

"Thinking of something else very hard—that's the only way. You'd never guess what I thought of—jam—jam in a grocer's shop. I said it over to myself. Strawberry, black currant, raspberry, damson. And perhaps, Terry, he'll get tired of me fairly soon. I hope so, don't you? They say men do when they're married to you. But Michael wouldn't have tired of me—never—never—never—Oh! Michael . . ."

JOYCE ROSE THE NEXT morning with a heart like lead. She gave a deep sigh and immediately Terry, who slept on her bed, had moved up and was kissing her affectionately.

"Oh, darling—darling! We've got to go through with it. But if only something would happen. Terry darling, can't you help Missus? You would if you could, I know."

Mrs. Barnes brought up some tea and bread and butter and was heartily congratulatory.

"There now, ma'am, to think of you going to marry that gentleman. It was a Rolls he came in. It was indeed. It quite sobered Barnes up to think of one of them Rolls standing outside our door. Why, I declare that dog's sitting out on the window sill."

"He likes the sun," said Joyce. "But it's rather dangerous. Terry, come in."

"I'd have the poor dear put out of his misery if I was you," said Mrs. Barnes, "and get your gentleman to buy you one of them plumy dogs as ladies carry in their muffs."

Joyce smiled and called again to Terry. The dog rose awkwardly and just at that moment the noise of a dog fight rose from the street below. Terry craned his neck forward and added some brisk barking.

The window sill was old and rotten. It tilted and Terry, too old and stiff to regain his balance, fell.

With a wild cry, Joyce ran down the stairs and out of the front door. In a few seconds she was kneeling by Terry's side. He was whining pitifully and his position showed her that he was badly hurt. She bent over him.

"Terry—Terry darling—darling, darling, darling—"

Very feebly, he tried to wag his tail.

"Terry boy—Missus will make you better—darling boy—"

A crowd, mainly composed of small boys, was pushing round.

"Fell from the window, 'e did." "My, 'e looks bad." "Broke 'is back as likely as not."

Joyce paid no heed.

"Mrs. Barnes, where's the nearest vet?"

"There's Jobling—round in Mere Street—if you could get him there."

"A taxi."

"Allow me."

It was the pleasant voice of an elderly man who had just alighted from a taxi. He knelt down by Terry and lifted the upper lip, then passed his hand down the dog's body.

"I'm afraid he may be bleeding internally," he said. "There don't seem to be any bones broken. We'd better get him along to the vet's."

Between them, he and Joyce lifted the dog. Terry gave a yelp of pain. His teeth met in Joyce's arm.

"Terry—it's all right—all right, old man."

They got him into the taxi and drove off. Joyce wrapped a handkerchief round her arm in an absent-minded way. Terry, distressed, tried to lick it.

"I know, darling; I know. You didn't mean to hurt me. It's all right. It's all right, Terry."

She stroked his head. The man opposite watched her but said nothing.

They arrived at the vet's fairly quickly and found him in. He was a red-faced man with an unsympathetic manner.

He handled Terry none too gently while Joyce stood by agonized.

The tears were running down her face. She kept on talking in a low, reassuring voice.

"It's all right, darling. It's all right. . . ."

The vet straightened himself.

"Impossible to say exactly. I must make a proper examination. You must leave him here."

"Oh! I can't."

"I'm afraid you must. I must take him below. I'll telephone you in—say—half an hour."

Sick at heart, Joyce gave in. She kissed Terry on his nose. Blind with tears, she stumbled down the steps. The man who had helped her was still there. She had forgotten him.

"The taxi's still here. I'll take you back." She shook her head.

"I'd rather walk."

"I'll walk with you."

He paid off the taxi. She was hardly conscious of him as he walked quietly by her side without speaking. When they arrived at Mrs. Barnes', he spoke.

"Your wrist. You must see to it."

She looked down at it.

"Oh! That's all right."

"It wants properly washing and tying up. I'll come in with you."

He went with her up the stairs. She let him wash the place and bind it up with a clean handkerchief. She only said one thing.

"Terry didn't mean to do it. He would never, *never* mean to do it. He just didn't realize it was me. He must have been in dreadful pain."

"I'm afraid so, yes."

"And perhaps they're hurting him dreadfully now?"

"I'm sure that everything that can be done for him is being done. When the vet rings up, you can go and get him and nurse him here."

"Yes, of course."

The man paused, then moved toward the door.

"I hope it will be all right," he said awkwardly. "Good-bye."

"Good-bye."

Two or three minutes later it occurred to her that he had been kind and that she had never thanked him.

Mrs. Barnes appeared, cup in hand.

"Now, my poor lamb, a cup of hot tea. You're all to pieces, I can see that."

"Thank you, Mrs. Barnes, but I don't want any tea."

"It would do you good, dearie. Don't take on so now. The doggie will be all right, and even if he isn't, that gentleman of yours will give you a pretty new dog—"

"Don't, Mrs. Barnes. Don't. Please, if you don't mind, I'd rather be left alone."

"Well, I never—there's the telephone."

Joyce sped down to it like an arrow. She lifted the receiver. Mrs. Barnes panted down after her. She heard Joyce say, "Yes—speaking. What? Oh! Oh! Yes. Yes, thank you."

She put back the receiver. The face she turned to Mrs. Barnes startled that good woman. It seemed devoid of any life or expression.

"Terry's dead, Mrs. Barnes," she said. "He died alone there without me."

She went upstairs and, going into her room, shut the door very decisively.

"Well, I never," said Mrs. Barnes to the hall wallpaper. Five minutes later she poked her head into the room. Joyce was sitting bolt upright in a chair. She was not crying.

"It's your gentleman, miss. Shall I send him up?"

A sudden light came into Joyce's eyes.

"Yes, please. I'd like to see him."

Halliday came in boisterously.

"Well, here we are. I haven't lost much time, have I? I'm prepared to carry you off from this dreadful place here and now. You can't stay here. Come on, get your things on."

"There's no need, Arthur."

"No need? What do you mean?"

"Terry's dead. I don't need to marry you now."

"What are you talking about?"

"My dog—Terry. He's dead. I was only marrying you so that we could be together."

Halliday stared at her, his face growing redder and redder. "You're mad."

"I dare say. People who love dogs are."

"You seriously tell me that you were only marrying me because—Oh, it's absurd!"

"Why did you think I was marrying you? You knew I hated you."

"You were marrying me because I could give you a jolly good time—and so I can."

"To my mind," said Joyce, "that is a much more revolting motive than mine. Anyway, it's off. I'm not marrying you!"

"Do you realize that you are treating me damned badly?"

She looked at him coolly but with such a blaze in her eyes that he drew back before it.

"I don't think so. I've heard you talk about getting a kick out of life. That's what you got out of me—and my dislike of you heightened it. You knew I hated you and you enjoyed it. When I let you kiss me yesterday, you were disappointed because I didn't flinch or wince. There's something brutal in you, Arthur, something cruel—something that likes hurting. . . . Nobody could treat you as badly as you deserve. And now do you mind getting out of my room? I want it to myself."

He spluttered a little.

"Wh-what are you going to do? You've no money."

"That's my business. Please go."

"You little devil. You absolutely maddening little devil. You haven't done with me yet."

Joyce laughed.

The laugh routed him as nothing else had done. It was so unexpected. He went awkwardly down the stairs and drove away.

Joyce heaved a sigh. She pulled on her shabby black felt hat and in her turn went out. She walked along the streets mechanically, neither thinking nor feeling. Somewhere at the back of her mind there was pain—pain that she would presently feel, but for the moment everything was mercifully dulled.

She passed the Registry Office and hesitated.

"I must do something. There's the river, of course. I've often thought of that. Just finish everything. But it's so cold and wet. I don't think I'm brave enough. I'm not brave really."

She turned into the Registry Office.

"Good morning, Mrs. Lambert. I'm afraid we've no daily post."

"It doesn't matter," said Joyce. "I can take any kind of post now. My friend, whom I lived with, has—gone away."

"Then you'd consider going abroad?"

Joyce nodded.

"Yes, as far away as possible."

"Mr. Allaby is here now, as it happens, interviewing candidates. I'll send you in to him."

In another minute Joyce was sitting in a cubicle answering questions. Something about her interlocutor seemed vaguely familiar to her, but she could not place him. And then suddenly her mind awoke a little, aware that the last question was faintly out of the ordinary.

"Do you get on well with old ladies?" Mr. Allaby was asking.

Joyce smiled in spite of herself.

"I think so."

"You see my aunt, who lives with me, is rather difficult. She is very fond of me and she is a great dear really, but I fancy that a young woman might find her rather difficult sometimes."

"I think I'm patient and good-tempered," said Joyce, "and I have always got on with elderly people very well."

"You would have to do certain things for my aunt and otherwise you would have the charge of my little boy, who is three. His mother died a year ago."

"I see."

There was a pause.

"Then if you think you would like the post, we will consider that settled. We travel out next week. I will let you know the exact date, and I expect you would like a small advance of salary to fit yourself out."

"Thank you very much. That would be very kind of you."

They had both risen. Suddenly Mr. Allaby said awkwardly:

"I—I hate to butt in—I mean I wish—I would like to know—I mean, is your dog all right?"

For the first time Joyce looked at him. The color came into her face, her blue eyes deepened almost to black. She looked straight at him. She had thought him elderly, but he was not so very old. Hair turning gray, a pleasant weatherbeaten face, rather stooping shoulders, eyes that were brown and something of the shy kindliness of a dog's. He looked a little like a dog, Joyce thought.

"Oh, it's *you,*" she said. "I thought afterward—I never thanked you."

"No need. Didn't expect it. Knew what you were feeling like. What about the poor old chap?"

The tears came into Joyce's eyes. They streamed down her cheeks. Nothing on earth could have kept them back.

"He's dead."

"Oh!"

He said nothing else, but to Joyce that Oh! was one of the most comforting things she had ever heard. There was everything in it that couldn't be put into words.

After a minute or two he said jerkily:

"Matter of fact, I had a dog. Died two years ago. Was with a crowd of people at the time who couldn't understand making heavy weather about it. Pretty rotten to have to carry on as though nothing had happened."

Joyce nodded.

"I *know*—" said Mr. Allaby.

He took her hand, squeezed it hard and dropped it. He went out of the little cubicle. Joyce followed in a minute or two and fixed up various details with the ladylike person. When she arrived home, Mrs. Barnes met her on the doorstep with that relish in gloom typical of her class.

"They've sent the poor little doggie's body home," she announced. "It's up in your room. I was saying to Barnes, and he's ready to dig a nice little hole in the back garden—"

THREE BLIND MICE

It was very cold. The sky was dark and heavy with unshed snow.

A man in a dark overcoat, with his muffler pulled up round his face, and his hat pulled down over his eyes, came along Culver Street and went up the steps of number 74. He put his finger on the bell and heard it shrilling in the basement below.

Mrs. Casey, her hands busy in the sink, said bitterly, "Drat that bell. Never any peace, there isn't."

Wheezing a little, she toiled up the basement stairs and opened the door.

The man standing silhouetted against the lowering sky outside asked in a whisper, "Mrs. Lyon?"

"Second floor," said Mrs. Casey. "You can go on up. Does she expect you?" The man slowly shook his head. "Oh, well, go on up and knock."

She watched him as he went up the shabbily carpeted stairs. Afterward she said he "gave her a funny feeling." But actually all she thought was that he must have a pretty bad cold only to be able to whisper like that—and no wonder with the weather what it was.

When the man got round the bend of the staircase he began to whistle softly. The tune he whistled was "Three Blind Mice."

MOLLY DAVIS STEPPED back into the road and looked up at the newly painted board by the gate.

MONKSWELL MANOR
GUEST HOUSE

She nodded approval. It looked, it really did look, quite professional. Or, perhaps, one might say *almost* professional. The T of *Guest House* staggered uphill a little, and the end of *Manor* was slightly crowded, but on the whole Giles had made a wonderful job of it. Giles was really very clever. There were so many things that he could do. She was always making fresh discoveries about this husband of hers. He said so little about himself that it was only by degrees that she was finding out what a lot of varied talents he had. An ex-naval man was always a "handy man," so people said.

Well, Giles would have need of all his talents in their new venture. Nobody could be more raw to the business of running a guest house than she and Giles. But it would be great fun. And it did solve the housing problem.

It had been Molly's idea. When Aunt Katherine died, and the lawyers wrote to her and informed her that her aunt had left her Monkswell Manor, the natural reaction of the young couple had been to sell it. Giles had asked, "What is it like?" And Molly had replied, "Oh, a big, rambling old house, full of stuffy, old-fashioned Victorian furniture. Rather a nice garden, but terribly overgrown since the war, because there's been only one old gardener left."

So they had decided to put the house on the market, and keep just enough furniture to furnish a small cottage or flat for themselves.

But two difficulties arose at once. First, there *weren't* any small cottages or flats to be found, and secondly, all the furniture was enormous.

"Well" said Molly, "we'll just have to sell it *all.* I suppose it *will* sell?"

The solicitor assured them that nowadays *anything* would sell.

"Very probably," he said, "someone will buy it for a hotel or guest house in which case they might like to buy it with the furniture complete. Fortunately the house is in very good repair. The late Miss Emory had extensive repairs and modernizations done just before the war, and there has been very little deterioration. Oh, yes, it's in good shape."

And it was then that Molly had had her idea.

"Giles," she said, "why shouldn't *we* run it as a guest house ourselves?"

At first her husband had scoffed at the idea, but Molly had persisted.

"We needn't take very many people—not at first. It's an easy house to run—it's got hot and cold water in the bedrooms and central heating and a gas cooker. And we can have hens and ducks and our own eggs, and vegetables."

"Who'd do all the work—isn't it very hard to get servants?"

"Oh, *we'd* have to do the work. But wherever we lived we'd have to do that. A few extra people wouldn't really mean much more to do. We'd probably get a woman to come in after a bit when we got properly started. If we had only five people, each paying seven guineas a week—" Molly departed into the realms of somewhat optimistic mental arithmetic.

"And think, Giles," she ended, "it would be our *own* house. With our *own* things. As it is, it seems to me it will be years before we can ever find anywhere to live."

That, Giles admitted, was true. They had had so little time together since their hasty marriage, that they were both longing to settle down in a home.

So the great experiment was set under way. Advertisements were put in the local paper and in the *Times,* and various answers came.

And now, today, the first of the guests was to arrive. Giles had gone off early in the car to try and obtain some army wire netting that had been advertised as for sale on the other side of the county. Molly announced the necessity of walking to the village to make some last purchases.

The only thing that was wrong was the weather. For the last two days it had been bitterly cold, and now the snow was beginning to fall. Molly hurried up the drive, thick, feathery flakes falling on her waterproofed shoulders and bright curly hair. The weather forecasts had been lugubrious in the extreme. Heavy snowfall was to be expected.

She hoped anxiously that all the pipes wouldn't freeze. It would be too bad if everything went wrong just as they started. She glanced at her watch. Past teatime. Would Giles have got back yet? Would he be wondering where *she* was?

"I had to go to the village again for something I had forgotten," she would say. And he would laugh and say, "More tins?"

Tins were a joke between them. They were always on the lookout for tins of food. The larder was really quite nicely stocked now in case of emergencies.

And, Molly thought with a grimace as she looked up at the sky, it looked as though emergencies were going to present themselves very soon.

The house was empty. Giles was not back yet. Molly went first into the kitchen, then upstairs, going round the newly prepared bedrooms. Mrs. Boyle in the south room with the mahogany and the four-poster. Major Metcalf in the blue room with the oak. Mr. Wren in the east room with the bay window. All the rooms looked very nice—and what a blessing that Aunt Katherine had had such a splendid stock of linen. Molly patted a counterpane into place and went downstairs again. It was nearly dark. The house felt suddenly very quiet and empty. It was a lonely house, two miles from a village, two miles, as Molly put it, from *anywhere*.

She had often been alone in the house before—but she had never before been so conscious of being alone in it.

The snow beat in a soft flurry against the windowpanes. It made a whispery, uneasy sound. Supposing Giles couldn't get back—supposing the snow was so thick that the car couldn't get through? Supposing she had to stay alone here—stay alone for days, perhaps.

She looked round the kitchen—a big, comfortable kitchen that seemed to call for a big, comfortable cook presiding at the kitchen table, her jaws moving rhythmically as she ate rock cakes and drank black tea—she should be flanked by a tall, elderly parlor-maid on one side and a round, rosy housemaid on the other, with a kitchenmaid at the other end of the table observing her betters with frightened eyes. And instead there was just herself, Molly Davis, playing a role that did not yet seem a very natural role to play. Her whole life, at the moment, seemed unreal—Giles seemed unreal. She was playing a part—just playing a part.

A shadow passed the window, and she jumped—a strange man was coming through the snow. She heard the rattle of the side door. The stranger stood there in the open doorway, shaking off snow, a strange man, walking into the empty house.

And then, suddenly, illusion fled.

"Oh Giles," she cried, "I'm so glad you've come!"

"Hullo, sweetheart! What filthy weather! Lord, I'm *frozen.*"

He stamped his feet and blew through his hands.

Automatically Molly picked up the coat that he had thrown in a Giles-like manner onto the oak chest. She put it on a hanger, taking out of the stuffed pockets a muffler, a newspaper, a ball of string, and the morning's correspondence which he had shoved in pell mell. Moving into the kitchen, she laid down the articles on the dresser and put the kettle on the gas.

"Did you get the netting?" she asked. "What ages you've been."

"It wasn't the right kind. Wouldn't have been any good for us. I went on to another dump, but that wasn't any good, either. What have you been doing with yourself? Nobody turned up yet, I suppose?"

"Mrs. Boyle isn't coming till tomorrow, anyway."

"Major Metcalf and Mr. Wren ought to be here today."

"Major Metcalf sent a card to say he wouldn't be here till tomorrow."

"Then that leaves us and Mr. Wren for dinner. What do you think he's like? Correct sort of retired civil servant is my idea."

"No, I think he's an artist."

"In that case," said Giles, "we'd better get a week's rent in advance."

"Oh, no, Giles, they bring luggage. If they don't pay we hang on to their luggage."

"And suppose their luggage is stones wrapped up in newspaper? The truth is, Molly, we don't in the least know what we're up against in this business. I hope they don't spot what beginners we are."

"Mrs. Boyle is sure to," said Molly, "She's that kind of woman."

"How do you know? You haven't seen her?"

Molly turned away. She spread a newspaper on the table, fetched some cheese, and set to work to grate it.

"What's this?" inquired her husband.

"It's going to be Welsh rarebit," Molly informed him. "Bread crumbs and mashed potatoes and just a *teeny weeny* bit of cheese to justify its name."

"Aren't you a clever cook?" said her admiring husband.

"I wonder. I can do one thing at a time. It's *assembling* them that needs so much practice. Breakfast is the worst."

"Why?"

"Because it all happens at once—eggs and bacon and hot milk and coffee and toast. The milk boils over, or the toast burns, or the bacon frizzles, or the eggs go hard. You have to be as active as a scalded cat watching everything at once."

"I shall have to creep down unobserved tomorrow morning and watch this scalded-cat impersonation."

"The kettle's boiling," said Molly. "Shall we take the tray into the library and hear the wireless? It's almost time for the news."

"As we seem to be going to spend almost the whole of our time in the kitchen, we ought to have a wireless there, too."

"Yes. How nice kitchens are. I love this kitchen. I think it's far and away the nicest room in the house. I like the dresser and the plates, and I simply love the lavish feeling that an absolutely *enormous* kitchen range gives you—though, of course, I'm thankful I haven't got to cook on it."

"I suppose a whole year's fuel ration would go in one day."

"Almost certainly, I should say. But think of the great joints that were roasted in it—sirloins of beef and saddles of mutton. Colossal copper preserving-pans full of homemade strawberry jam with pounds and pounds of sugar going into it. What a lovely, comfortable age the Victorian age was. Look at the furniture upstairs, large and solid and rather ornate—but, oh!—the heavenly comfort of it, with lots of room for the clothes one used to have, and every drawer sliding in and out so easily. Do you remember that smart modern flat we were lent? Everything built in and sliding—only nothing slid—it always stuck. And the doors pushed shut—only they never stayed shut, or if they did shut they wouldn't open."

"Yes, that's the worst of gadgets. If they don't go right, you're sunk."

"Well, come on, let's hear the news."

The news consisted mainly of grim warnings about the weather, the usual deadlock in foreign affairs, spirited bickerings in Parliament, and a murder in Culver Street, Paddington.

"Ugh," said Molly, switching it off. "Nothing but misery. I'm *not* going to hear appeals for fuel economy all over again. What do they expect you to do, sit and freeze? I don't think we ought to have tried to start a guest house in the winter. We ought to have waited until the spring." She added in a different tone of voice, "I wonder what the woman was like who was murdered."

"Mrs. Lyon?"

"Was that her name? I wonder who wanted to murder her and why."

"Perhaps she had a fortune under the floor boards."

"When it says the police are anxious to interview a man 'seen in the vicinity' does that mean he's the murderer?"

"I think it's usually that. Just a polite way of putting it."

The shrill note of a bell made them both jump.

"That's the front door," said Giles. "Enter—a murderer," he added facetiously.

"It would be, of course, in a play. Hurry up. It must be Mr. Wren. Now we shall see who's right about him, you or me."

Mr. Wren and a flurry of snow came in together with a rush. All that Molly, standing in the library door, could see of the newcomer was his silhouette against the white world outside.

How alike, thought Molly, were all men in their livery of civilization. Dark overcoat, gray hat, muffler round the neck.

In another moment Giles had shut the front door against the elements, Mr. Wren was unwinding his muffler and casting down his suitcase and flinging off his hat—all, it seemed, at the same time, and also talking. He had a high-pitched, almost querulous voice and stood revealed in the light of the hall as a young man with a shock of light, sunburned hair and pale, restless eyes.

"Too, too frightful," he was saying. "The English winter at its worst—a reversion to Dickens—Scrooge and Tiny Tim and all that. One had to be so terribly hearty to stand up to it all. Don't you think so? And I've had a terrible cross-country journey from Wales. Are you Mrs. Davis? But how delightful!" Molly's hand was seized in a quick, bony clasp. "Not at all as I'd imagined you. I'd pictured you, you know, as an Indian army general's widow. Terrifically grim and *memsahibish*—and Benares *whatnot*—a real Victorian *whatnot*. Heavenly, simply heavenly—Have you got any wax flowers? Or birds of paradise? Oh, but I'm simply going to *love* this place. I was afraid, you know, it would be very Olde Worlde—very, very Manor House—failing the Benares brass, I mean. Instead, it's marvelous—real Victorian bedrock respectability. Tell me, have you got one of those beautiful sideboards—mahogany—purple-plummy mahogany with great carved fruits?"

"As a matter of fact," said Molly, rather breathless under this torrent of words, "we have."

"No! Can I see it? At once. In here?"

His quickness was almost disconcerting. He had turned the handle of the dining-room door, and clicked on the light. Molly followed him in, conscious of Giles's disapproving profile on her left.

Mr. Wren passed his long bony fingers over the rich carving of the massive sideboard with little cries of appreciation. Then he turned a reproachful glance upon his hostess.

"No big mahogany dining-table? All these little tables dotted about instead?"

"We thought people would prefer it that way," said Molly.

"Darling, of course you're *quite* right. I was being carried away by my feeling for period. Of course, if you had the table, you'd have to have the right family round it. Stern, handsome father with a beard—prolific, faded mother, eleven children, a grim governess, and somebody called 'poor Harriet'—the poor relation who acts as general helper and is very, very grateful for being given a good home. Look at that grate—think of the flames leaping up the chimney and blistering poor Harriet's back."

"I'll take your suitcase upstairs," said Giles. "East room?"

"Yes," said Molly.

Mr. Wren skipped out into the hall again as Giles went upstairs.

"Has it got a four-poster with little chintz roses?" he asked.

"No, it hasn't," said Giles and disappeared round the bend of the staircase.

"I don't believe your husband is going to like me," said Mr. Wren. "What's he been in? The navy?"

"Yes."

"I thought so. They're much less tolerant than the army and the air force. How long have you been married? Are you very much in love with him?"

"Perhaps you'd like to come up and see your room."

"Yes, of course that was impertinent. But I did really want to know. I mean, it's interesting, don't you think, to know all about people? What they feel and think, I mean, not just who they are and what they do."

"I suppose," said Molly in a demure voice, "you are Mr. Wren?"

The young man stopped short, clutched his hair in both hands and tugged at it.

"But how frightful—I never put first things first. Yes, I'm Christopher Wren—now, don't laugh. My parents were a romantic couple. They hoped I'd be an architect. So they thought it a splendid idea to christen me Christopher—halfway home, as it were."

"And are you an architect?" asked Molly, unable to help smiling.

"Yes, I am," said Mr. Wren triumphantly. "At least I'm nearly one. I'm not fully qualified yet. But it's really a remarkable example of wishful thinking coming off for once. Mind you, actually the name will be a handicap. I shall never be *the* Christopher Wren. However, Chris Wren's Pre-Fab Nests may achieve fame."

Giles came down the stairs again, and Molly said, "I'll show you your room now, Mr. Wren."

When she came down a few minutes later, Giles said, "Well, did he like the pretty oak furniture?"

"He was very anxious to have a four-poster, so I gave him the rose room instead."

Giles grunted and murmured something that ended, ". . . young twerp."

"Now, look here, Giles," Molly assumed a severe demeanor. "This isn't a house party of guests we're entertaining. This is business. Whether you like Christopher Wren or not—"

"I don't," Giles interjected.

"—has nothing whatever to do with it. He's paying seven guineas a week, and that's all that matters."

"If he pays it, yes."

"He's agreed to pay it. We've got his letter."

"Did you transfer that suitcase of his to the rose room?"

"He carried it, of course."

"Very gallant. But it wouldn't have strained you. There's certainly no question of stones wrapped up in newspaper. It's so light that there seems to me there's probably nothing in it."

"*Ssh,* here he comes," said Molly warningly.

Christopher Wren was conducted to the library which looked, Molly thought, very nice, indeed, with its big chairs and its log fire. Dinner, she told him, would be in half an hour's time. In reply to a question, she explained that there were no other guests at the moment. In that case, Christopher said, how would it be if he came into the kitchen and helped?

"I can cook you an omelette if you like," he said engagingly.

The subsequent proceedings took place in the kitchen, and Christopher helped with the washing up.

Somehow, Molly felt, it was not quite the right start for a conventional guest house—and Giles had not liked it at all. Oh, well, thought Molly, as she fell asleep, tomorrow when the others came it would be different.

THE MORNING CAME WITH dark skies and snow. Giles looked grave, and Molly's heart fell. The weather was going to make everything very difficult.

Mrs. Boyle arrived in the local taxi with chains on the wheels, and the driver brought pessimistic reports of the state of the road.

"Drifts afore nightfall," he prophesied.

Mrs. Boyle herself did not lighten the prevailing gloom. She was a large, forbidding-looking woman with a resonant voice and a masterful manner. Her natural aggressiveness had been heightened by a war career of persistent and militant usefulness.

"If I had not believed this was a *running* concern, I should never have come," she said. "I naturally thought it was a well-established guest house, properly run on scientific lines."

"There is no obligation for you to remain if you are not satisfied, Mrs. Boyle," said Giles.

"No, indeed, and I shall not think of doing so."

"Perhaps, Mrs. Boyle," said Giles, "you would like to ring up for a taxi. The roads are not yet blocked. If there has been any misapprehension it would, perhaps, be better if you went elsewhere." He added, "We have had so many applications for rooms that we shall be able to fill your place quite easily—indeed, in future we are charging a higher rate for our rooms."

Mrs. Boyle threw him a sharp glance. "I am certainly not going to leave before I have tried what the place is like. Perhaps you would let me have a rather large bath towel, Mrs. Davis. I am not accustomed to drying myself on a pocket handkerchief."

Giles grinned at Molly behind Mrs. Boyle's retreating back.

"Darling, you were wonderful," said Molly. "The way you stood up to her."

"Bullies soon climb down when they get their own medicine," said Giles.

"Oh, dear," said Molly. "I wonder how she'll get on with Christopher Wren."

"She won't," said Giles.

And, indeed, that very afternoon, Mrs. Boyle remarked to Molly, "That's a very peculiar young man," with distinct disfavor in her voice.

The baker arrived looking like an Arctic explorer and delivered the bread with the warning that his next call, due in two days' time, might not materialize.

"Holdups everywhere," he announced. "Got plenty of stores in, I hope?"

"Oh, yes," said Molly. "We've got lots of tins. I'd better take extra flour, though."

She thought vaguely that there was something the Irish made called soda bread. If the worst came to the worst she could probably make that.

The baker had also brought the papers, and she spread them out on the hall table. Foreign affairs had receded in importance. The weather and the murder of Mrs. Lyon occupied the front page.

She was staring at the blurred reproduction of the dead woman's features when Christopher Wren's voice behind her said, "Rather a *sordid* murder, don't you think? Such a *drab*-looking woman and such a *drab* street. One can't feel, can one, that there is any story behind it?"

"I've no doubt," said Mrs. Boyle with a snort, "that the creature got no more than she deserved."

"Oh." Mr. Wren turned to her with engaging eagerness. "So you think it's definitely a *sex* crime, do you?"

"I suggested nothing of the kind, Mr. Wren."

"But she *was* strangled, wasn't she? I wonder"—he held out his long white hands—"what it would feel like to strangle anyone."

"Really, Mr. Wren!"

Christopher moved nearer to her, lowering his voice. "Have you considered, Mrs. Boyle, just what it would feel like to be strangled?"

Mrs. Boyle said again, even more indignantly, "Really, Mr. Wren!"

Molly read hurriedly out, "'The man the police are anxious to interview was wearing a dark overcoat and a light Homburg hat, was of medium height, and wore a woolen scarf.'"

"In fact," said Christopher Wren, "he looked just like everybody else." He laughed.

"Yes," said Molly. "Just like everybody else."

IN HIS ROOM AT Scotland Yard, Inspector Parminter said to Detective Sergeant Kane, "I'll see those two workmen now."

"Yes, sir."

"What are they like?"

"Decent class workingmen. Rather slow reactions. Dependable."

"Right." Inspector Parminter nodded.

Presently two embarrassed-looking men in their best clothes were shown into his room. Parminter summed them up with a quick eye. He was an adept at setting people at their ease.

"So you think you've some information that might be useful to us on the Lyon case," he said. "Good of you to come along. Sit down. Smoke?"

He waited while they accepted cigarettes and lit up.

"Pretty awful weather outside."

"It is that, sir."

"Well, now, then—let's have it."

The two men looked at each other, embarrassed now that it came to the difficulties of narration.

"Go ahead, Joe," said the bigger of the two.

Joe went ahead. "It was like this, see. We 'adn't got a match."

"Where was this?"

"Jarman Street—we was working on the road there—gas mains."

Inspector Parminter nodded. Later he would get down to exact details of time and place. Jarman Street, he knew was in the close vicinity of Culver Street where the tragedy had taken place.

"You hadn't got a match," he repeated encouragingly.

"No. Finished my box, I 'ad, and Bill's lighter wouldn't work, and so I spoke to a bloke as was passing. 'Can you give us a match, mister?' I says. Didn't think nothing particular, I didn't, not then. He was just passing—like lots of others—I just 'appened to arsk 'im."

Again Parminter nodded.

"Well, he give us a match, 'e did. Didn't say nothing. 'Cruel cold,' Bill said to 'im, and he just answered, whispering-like, 'Yes, it is.' Got a cold on his chest, I thought. He was all wrapped up, anyway. 'Thanks mister,' I says and gives him back his matches, and he moves off quick, so quick that when I sees 'e'd dropped something, it's almost too late to call 'im back. It was a little notebook as he must 'ave pulled out of 'is pocket when he got the matches out. 'Hi, mister,' I calls after 'im, 'you've dropped something.' But he didn't seem to hear—he just quickens up and bolts round the corner, didn't 'e, Bill?"

"That's right," agreed Bill. "Like a scurrying rabbit."

"Into the Harrow Road, that was, and it didn't seem as we'd catch up with him there, not the rate 'e was going, and, anyway, by then it was a bit late—it was only a little book, not a wallet or anything like that—maybe it wasn't important. 'Funny bloke,' I says. 'His hat pulled down over his eyes, and all buttoned up—like a crook on the pictures,' I says to Bill, didn't I, Bill?"

"That's what you said," agreed Bill.

"Funny I should have said that, not that I thought anything at the time. Just in a hurry to get home, that's what I thought, and I didn't blame 'im. Not 'arf cold, it was!"

"Not 'arf," agreed Bill.

"So I says to Bill, 'Let's 'ave a look at this little book and see if it's important.' Well, sir, I took a look. 'Only a couple of addresses,' I says to Bill. Seventy-Four Culver Street and some blinking manor 'ouse."

"Ritzy," said Bill with a snort of disapproval.

Joe continued his tale with a certain gusto now that he had got wound up.

" 'Seventy-Four Culver Street,' I says to Bill. 'That's just round the corner from 'ere. When we knock off, we'll take it round'—and then I sees something written across the top of the page. 'What's this?' I says to Bill. And he takes it and reads it out. '"Three blind mice"—must be off 'is knocker,' he says—and just at that very moment—yes, it was that very moment, sir, we 'ears some woman yelling, 'Murder!' a couple of streets away!"

Joe paused at this artistic climax.

"Didn't half yell, did she?" he resumed. "'Here,' I says to Bill, 'you nip along.' And by and by he comes back and says there's a big crowd and the police are there and some woman's had her throat cut or been strangled and that was the landlady who found her, yelling for the police. 'Where was it?' I says to him. 'In Culver Street,' he says. 'What number?' I asks, and he says he didn't rightly notice."

Bill coughed and shuffled his feet with the sheepish air of one who has not done himself justice.

"So I says, 'We'll nip around and make sure,' and when we finds it's number seventy-four we talk it over, and 'Maybe,' Bill says, 'the address in the notebook's got nothing to do with it,' and I says as maybe it *has,* and, anyway, after we've talked it over and heard the police want to interview a man who left the 'ouse about that time, well, we come along 'ere and ask if we can see the gentleman who's handling the case, and I'm sure I 'ope as we aren't wasting your time."

"You acted very properly," said Parminter approvingly. "You've brought the notebook with you? Thank you. Now—"

His questions became brisk and professional. He got places, times, dates—the only thing he did not get was a description of the man who had dropped the notebook. Instead he got the same description as he had already got from a hysterical landlady, the description of a hat pulled down over the eyes, a buttoned-up coat, a muffler swathed round the lower part of a face, a voice that was only a whisper, gloved hands.

When the men had gone he remained staring down at the little book lying open on his table. Presently it would go to the appropriate department to see what evidence, if any, of fingerprints it might reveal. But now his attention was held by the two addresses and by the line of small handwriting along top of the page.

He turned his head as Sergeant Kane came into the room.

"Come here, Kane. Look at this."

Kane stood behind him and let out a low whistle as he read out, "'Three Blind Mice!' Well, I'm dashed!"

"Yes." Parminter opened a drawer and took out a half sheet of notepaper which he laid beside the notebook on his desk. It had been found pinned carefully to the murdered woman.

On it was written, *This is the first.* Below was a childish drawing of three mice and a bar of music.

Kane whistled the tune softly. *Three Blind Mice, See how they run—*

"That's it, all right. That's the signature tune."

"Crazy, isn't it, sir?"

"Yes." Parminter frowned. "The identification of the woman is quite certain?"

"Yes, sir. Here's the report from the fingerprints department. Mrs. Lyon, as she called herself, was really Maureen Gregg. She was released from Holloway two months ago on completion of her sentence."

Parminter said thoughtfully, "She went to Seventy-four Culver Street calling herself Maureen Lyon. She occasionally drank a bit and she had been known to bring a man home with her once or twice. She displayed no fear of anything or anyone. There's no reason to believe she thought herself in any danger. This man rings the bell, asks for her, and is told by the landlady to go up to the second floor. She can't describe him, says only that he was of medium height and seemed to have a bad cold and lost his voice. She went back again to the basement and heard nothing of a suspicious nature. She did not hear the man go out. Ten minutes or so later she took tea to her lodger and discovered her strangled.

"This wasn't a casual murder, Kane. It was carefully planned." He paused and then added abruptly, "I wonder how many houses there are in England called Monkswell Manor?"

"There might be only one, sir."

"That would probably be too much luck. But get on with it. There's no time to lose."

The sergeant's eye rested appreciatively on two entries in the notebook—*74 Culver Street; Monkswell Manor.*

He said, "So you think—"

Parminter said swiftly, "Yes. Don't you?"

"Could be. Monkswell Manor—now where—Do you know, sir, I could swear I've seen that name quite lately."

"Where?"

"That's what I'm trying to remember. Wait a minute—Newspaper—*Times*. Back page. Wait a minute—Hotels and boardinghouses—Half a sec, sir—it's an old one. I was doing the crossword."

He hurried out of the room and returned in triumph, "Here you are, sir, look."

The inspector followed the pointing finger.

"Monkswell Manor, Harpleden, Berks." He drew the telephone toward him. "Get me the Berkshire County police."

WITH THE ARRIVAL OF Major Metcalf, Monkswell Manor settled into its routine as a going concern. Major Metcalf was neither formidable like Mrs. Boyle, nor erratic like Christopher Wren. He was a stolid, middle-aged man of spruce military appearance, who had done most of his service in India. He appeared satisfied with his room and its furniture, and while he and Mrs. Boyle did not actually find mutual friends, he had known cousins of friends of hers—"the Yorkshire branch," out in Poonah. His luggage, however, two heavy pigskin cases, satisfied even Giles's suspicious nature.

Truth to tell, Molly and Giles did not have much time for speculating about their guests. Between them, dinner was cooked, served, eaten, and washed up satisfactorily. Major Metcalf praised the coffee, and Giles and Molly retired to bed, tired but triumphant—to be roused about two in the morning by the persistent ringing of a bell.

"Damn," said Giles. "It's the front door. What on earth—"

"Hurry up," said Molly. "Go and see."

Casting a reproachful glance at her, Giles wrapped his dressing-gown round him and descended the stairs. Molly heard the bolts being drawn back and a murmur of voices in the hall. Presently, driven by curiosity, she crept out of bed and went to peep from the top of the stairs. In the hall below, Giles was assisting a bearded stranger out of a snow-covered overcoat. Fragments of conversation floated up to her.

"Brrr." It was an explosive foreign sound. "My fingers are so cold I cannot feel them. And my feet—" A stamping sound was heard.

"Come in here." Giles threw open the library door. "It's warm. You'd better wait here while I get a room ready."

"I am indeed fortunate," said the stranger politely.

Molly peered inquisitively through the banisters. She saw an elderly man with a small black beard and Mephistophelean eyebrows. A man who moved with a young and jaunty step in spite of the gray at his temples.

Giles shut the library door on him and came quickly up the stairs. Molly rose from her crouching position.

"Who is it?" she demanded.

Giles grinned. "Another guest for the guest house. Car overturned in a snowdrift. He got himself out and was making his way as best he could—it's a howling blizzard still, listen to it—along the road when he saw our board. He said it was like an answer to prayer."

"You think he's—all right?"

"Darling, this isn't the sort of night for a housebreaker to be doing his rounds."

"He's a foreigner, isn't he?"

"Yes. His name's Paravicini. I saw his wallet—I rather think he showed it on purpose—simply crammed with notes. Which room shall we give him?"

"The green room. It's all tidy and ready. We'll just have to make up the bed."

"I suppose I'll have to lend him pajamas. All his things are in the car. He said he had to climb out through the window."

Molly fetched sheets, pillowcases, and towels.

As they hurriedly made the bed up, Giles said, "It's coming down thick. We're going to be snowed up, Molly, completely cut off. Rather exciting in a way, isn't it?"

"I don't know," said Molly doubtfully. "Do you think I can make soda bread, Giles?"

"Of course you can. You can make anything," said her loyal husband.

"I've never tried to make bread. It's the sort of thing one takes for granted. It may be new or it may be stale but it's just something the baker brings. But if we're snowed up there won't be a baker."

"Nor a butcher, nor a postman. No newspapers. And probably no telephone."

"Just the wireless telling us what to do?"

"At any rate we make our own electric light."

"You must run the engine again tomorrow. And we must keep the central heating well stoked."

"I suppose our next lot of coke won't come in now. We're very low."

"Oh, bother. Giles, I feel we are in for a simply frightful time. Hurry up and get Para—whatever his name is. I'll go back to bed."

Morning brought confirmation of Giles's forebodings. Snow was piled five feet high, drifting up against the doors and windows. Outside it was still snowing. The world was white, silent, and—in some subtle way—menacing.

MRS. BOYLE SAT AT breakfast. There was no one else in the dining-room. At the adjoining table, Major Metcalf's place had been cleared away. Mr. Wren's table was still laid for breakfast. One early riser, presumably, and one late one. Mrs. Boyle herself knew definitely that there was only one proper time for breakfast, nine o'clock.

Mrs. Boyle had finished her excellent omelette and was champing toast between her strong white teeth. She was in a grudging and undecided mood. Monkswell Manor was not at all what she had imagined it would be. She had hoped for bridge, for faded spinsters whom she could impress with her social position and connections, and to whom she could hint at the importance and secrecy of her war service.

The end of the war had left Mrs. Boyle marooned,as it were, on a desert shore. She had always been a busy woman, talking fluently of efficiency and organization. Her vigor and drive had prevented people asking whether she was, indeed, a good or efficient organizer. War activities had suited her down to the ground. She had bossed people and bullied people and worried heads of departments and, to give her her due, had at no time spared herself. Subservient women had run to and fro, terrified of her slightest frown. And now all that exciting hustling life was over. She was back in private life, and her former private life had vanished. Her house, which had been requisitioned by the army, needed thorough repairing and redecorating before she could return to it, and the difficulties of domestic help made a return to it impracticable in any case. Her friends were largely scattered and dispersed. Presently, no doubt, she would find her niche, but at the moment it was a case of marking time. A hotel or a boardinghouse seemed the answer. And she had chosen to come to Monkswell Manor.

She looked round her disparagingly.

Most dishonest, she said to herself, *not to have told me they were only just starting.*

She pushed her plate farther away from her. The fact that her breakfast had been excellently cooked and served, with good coffee and homemade marmalade, in a curious way annoyed her still more. It had deprived her of a legitimate cause of complaint. Her bed, too, had been comfortable, with embroidered sheets and a soft pillow. Mrs. Boyle liked comfort, but she also liked to find fault. The latter was, perhaps, the stronger passion of the two.

Rising majestically, Mrs. Boyle left the dining-room, passing in the doorway that very extraordinary young man with the red hair. He was wearing this morning a checked tie of virulent green—a woolen tie.

Preposterous, said Mrs. Boyle to herself. *Quite preposterous.*

The way he looked at her, too, sideways out of those pale eyes of his—she didn't like it. There was something upsetting—unusual—about that faintly mocking glance.

Unbalanced mentally, I shouldn't wonder, said Mrs. Boyle to herself.

She acknowledged his flamboyant bow with a slight inclination of her head and marched into the big drawing-room. Comfortable chairs here, particularly the large rose-colored one. She had better make it clear that that was to be *her* chair. She deposited her knitting on it as a precaution and walked over and laid a hand on the radiators. As she had suspected, they were only warm, not hot. Mrs. Boyle's eye gleamed militantly. She could have something to say about *that*.

She glanced out of the window. Dreadful weather—quite dreadful. Well, she wouldn't stay here long—not unless more people came and made the place amusing.

Some snow slid off the roof with a soft whooshing sound. Mrs. Boyle jumped. "No," she said out loud. "I shan't stay here long."

Somebody laughed—a faint, high chuckle. She turned her head sharply. Young Wren was standing in the doorway looking at her with that curious expression of his.

"No," he said. "I don't suppose you will."

MAJOR METCALF WAS HELPING Giles to shovel away snow from the back door. He was a good worker, and Giles was quite vociferous in his expressions of gratitude.

"Good exercise," said Major Metcalf. "Must get exercise every day. Got to keep fit, you know."

So the major was an exercise fiend. Giles had feared as much. It went with his demand for breakfast at half past seven.

As though reading Giles's thoughts, the major said, "Very good of your missus to cook me an early breakfast. Nice to get a new-laid egg, too."

Giles had risen himself before seven, owing to the exigencies of hotelkeeping. He and Molly had had boiled eggs and tea and had set to on the sitting rooms. Everything was spick-and-span. Giles could not help thinking that if he had been a guest in his own establishment, nothing would have dragged him out of bed on a morning such as this until the last possible moment.

The major, however, had been up and breakfasted, and roamed about the house, apparently full of energy seeking an outlet.

Well, thought Giles, *there's plenty of snow to shovel.*

He threw a sideways glance at his companion. Not an easy man to place, really. Hard-bitten, well over middle age, something queerly watchful about the eyes. A man who was giving nothing away. Giles wondered why he had come to Monkswell Manor. Demobilized, probably, and no job to go to.

MR. PARAVICINI CAME DOWN late. He had coffee and a piece of toast—a frugal Continental breakfast.

He somewhat disconcerted Molly when she brought it to him by rising to his feet, bowing in an exaggerated manner, and exclaiming, "My charming hostess? I am right, am I not?"

Molly admitted rather shortly that he was right. She was in no mood for compliments at this hour.

"And why," she said, as she piled crockery recklessly in the sink, "everybody has to have their breakfast at a different time—It's a bit hard."

She slung the plates into the rack and hurried upstairs to deal with the beds. She could expect no assistance from Giles this morning. He had to clear a way to the boiler house and to the henhouse.

Molly did the beds at top speed and admittedly in the most slovenly manner, smoothing sheets and pulling them up as fast as she could.

She was at work on the baths when the telephone rang.

Molly first cursed at being interrupted, then felt a slight feeling of relief that the telephone at least was still in action, as she ran down to answer it.

She arrived in the library a little breathless and lifted the receiver. "Yes?"

A hearty voice with a slight but pleasant country burr asked, "Is that Monkswell Manor?"

"Monkswell Manor Guest House."

"Can I speak to Commander David, please?"

"I'm afraid he can't come to the telephone just now," said Molly. "This is Mrs. Davis. Who is speaking, please?"

"Superintendent Hogben, Berkshire Police."

Molly gave a slight gasp. She said, "Oh, yes—er—yes?"

"Mrs. Davis, rather an urgent matter has arisen. I don't wish to say very much over the telephone, but I have sent Detective Sergeant Trotter out to you, and he should be there any minute now."

"But he won't get here. We're snowed up—completely snowed up. The roads are impassable."

There was no break in the confidence of the voice at the other end.

"Trotter will get to you, all right," it said. "And please impress upon your husband, Mrs. Davis, to listen very carefully to what Trotter has to tell you, and to follow his instructions implicitly. That's all."

"But, Superintendent Hogben, what—"

But there was a decisive click. Hogben had clearly said all he had to say and rung off. Molly waggled the telephone rest once or twice, then gave up. She turned as the door opened.

"Oh, Giles darling, there you are."

Giles had snow on his hair and a good deal of coal grime on his face. He looked hot.

"What is it, sweetheart? I've filled the coal scuttles and brought in the wood. I'll do the hens next and then have a look at the boiler. Is that right? What's the matter, Molly? You looked scared."

"Giles, it was the *police*."

"The police?" Giles sounded incredulous.

"Yes, they're sending out an inspector or a sergeant or something."

"But why? What have we done?"

"I don't know. Do you think it could be that two pounds of butter we had from Ireland?"

Giles was frowning. "I did remember to get the wireless license, didn't I?"

"Yes, it's in the desk. Giles, old Mrs. Bidlock gave me five of her coupons for that old tweed coat of mine. I suppose that's wrong—but *I* think it's perfectly fair. I'm a coat less so why shouldn't I have the coupons? Oh, dear, what else is there we've done?"

"I had a near shave with the car the other day. But it was definitely the other fellow's fault. Definitely."

"We must have done *something,*" wailed Molly.

"The trouble is that practically everything one does nowadays is illegal," said Giles gloomily. "That's why one has a permanent feeling of guilt. Actually I expect it's something to do with running this place. Running a guest house is probably chockfull of snags we've never heard of."

"I thought drink was the only thing that mattered. We haven't given anyone anything to drink. Otherwise, why shouldn't we run our own house any way we please?"

"I know. It sounds all right. But as I say, everything's more or less forbidden nowadays."

"Oh, dear," sighed Molly. "I wish we'd never started. We're going to be snowed up for days, and everybody will be cross and they'll eat all our reserves of tins—"

"Cheer up, sweetheart," said Giles. "We're having a bad break at the moment, but it will pan out all right."

He kissed the top of her head rather absentmindedly and, releasing her, said in a different voice, "You know, Molly, come to think of it, it must be something pretty serious to send a police sergeant trekking out here in all this." He waved a hand toward the snow outside. He said, "It must be something really *urgent*—"

As they stared at each other, the door opened, and Mrs. Boyle came in.

"Ah, here you are, Mr. Davis," said Mrs. Boyle.

"Do you know the central heating in the drawing-room is practically stone-cold?"

"I'm sorry, Mrs. Boyle. We're rather short of coke and—"

Mrs. Boyle cut in ruthlessly. "I am paying seven guineas a week here—*seven* guineas. And I do *not* expect to freeze."

Giles flushed. He said shortly, "I'll go and stoke it up."

He went out of the room, and Mrs. Boyle turned to Molly.

"If you don't mind my saying so, Mrs. Davis, that is a very extraordinary young man you have staying here. His manners—and his ties—And does he never brush his hair?"

"He's an extremely brilliant young architect," said Molly.

"I beg your pardon?"

"Christopher Wren is an architect and—"

"My dear young woman," snapped Mrs. Boyle, "I have naturally heard of Sir Christopher Wren. Of course he was an architect. He built St. Paul's. You young people seem to think that education came in with the Education Act."

"I meant this Wren. His name is Christopher. His parents called him that because they hoped he'd be an architect. And he is—or nearly—one, so it turned out all right."

"Humph," Mrs. Boyle snorted. "It sounds a very fishy story to me. I should make some inquiries about him if I were you. What do you know about I him?"

"Just as much as I know about you, Mrs. Boyle—which is that both you and he are paying us seven guineas a week. That's really all that I need to know, isn't it? And all that concerns me. It doesn't matter to me whether I like my guests, or whether—" Molly looked very steadily at Mrs. Boyle"—or whether I don't."

Mrs. Boyle flushed angrily. "You are young and inexperienced and should welcome advice from someone more knowledgeable than yourself. And what about this queer foreigner? When did *he* arrive?"

"In the middle of the night."

"Indeed. Most peculiar. Not a very conventional hour."

"To turn away bona fide travelers would be against the law, Mrs. Boyle." Molly added sweetly. "You may not be aware of that."

"All I can say is that this Paravicini, or whatever he calls himself, seems to me—"

"Beware, beware, dear lady. You talk of the devil and then—"

Mrs. Boyle jumped as though it had been indeed the devil who addressed her. Mr. Paravicini, who had minced quietly in without either of the two women noticing him, laughed and rubbed his hands together with a kind of elderly satanic glee.

"You startled me," said Mrs. Boyle. "I did not hear you come in."

"I come in on tiptoe, so," said Mr. Paravicini, "nobody ever hears me come and go. That I find very amusing. Sometimes I overhear things. That, too, amuses me." He added softly, "But I do not forget what I hear."

Mrs. Boyle said rather feebly, "Indeed? I must get my knitting—I left it in the drawing-room."

She went out hurriedly. Molly stood looking at Mr. Paravicini with a puzzled expression. He approached her with a kind of hop and skip.

"My charming hostess looks upset." Before she could prevent it, he picked up her hand and kissed it. "What is it, dear lady?"

Molly drew back a step. She was not sure that she liked Mr. Paravicini much. He was leering at her like an elderly satyr.

"Everything is rather difficult this morning," she said lightly. "Because of the snow."

"Yes." Mr. Paravicini turned his head round to look out of the window. "Snow makes everything very difficult, does it not? Or else it makes things very easy."

"I don't know what you mean."

"No," he said thoughtfully. "There is quite a lot that you do not know. I think, for one thing, that you do not know very much about running a guest house."

Molly's chin went up belligerently. "I daresay we don't. But we mean to make a go of it."

"Bravo, bravo."

"After all," Molly's voice betrayed slight anxiety, "I'm not such a very bad cook—"

"You are, without doubt, an enchanting cook," said Mr. Paravicini.

What a nuisance foreigners were, thought Molly.

Perhaps Mr. Paravicini read her thoughts. At all events his manner changed. He spoke quietly and quite seriously.

"May I give you a little word of warning, Mrs. Davis? You and your husband must not be too trusting, you know. Have you references with these guests of yours?"

"Is that usual?" Molly looked troubled. "I thought people just—just came."

"It is advisable always to know a little about the people who sleep under your roof." He leaned forward and tapped her on the shoulder in a minatory kind of way. "Take myself, for example. I turn up in the middle of the night. My car, I say, is overturned in a snowdrift. What do you know of me? Nothing at all. Perhaps you know nothing, either, of your other guests."

"Mrs. Boyle—" began Molly, but stopped as that lady herself reentered the room, knitting in hand.

"The drawing-room is too cold. I shall sit in here." She marched toward the fireplace.

Mr. Paravicini pirouetted swiftly ahead of her. "Allow me to poke the fire for you."

Molly was struck, as she had been the night before, by the youthful jauntiness of his step. She noticed that he always seemed careful to keep his back to the light, and now, as he knelt, poking the fire, she thought she saw the reason for it. Mr. Paravicini's face was cleverly but decidedly "made up."

So the old idiot tried to make himself look younger than he was, did he? Well, he didn't succeed. He looked all his age and more. Only the youthful walk was incongruous. Perhaps that, too, had been carefully counterfeited.

She was brought back from speculation to the disagreeable realities by the brisk entrance of Major Metcalf.

"Mrs. Davis. I'm afraid the pipes of the—er—," he lowered his voice modestly, "downstairs cloakroom are frozen."

"Oh, dear," groaned Molly. "What an awful day. First the police and then the pipes."

Mr. Paravicini dropped the poker into the grate with a clatter. Mrs. Boyle stopped knitting. Molly, looking at Major Metcalf, was puzzled by his sudden stiff immobility and by the indescribable expression on his face. It was an expression she could not place. It was as though all emotion had been drained out of it, leaving something carved out of wood behind.

He said in a short, staccato voice, "*Police,* did you say?"

She was conscious that behind the stiff immobility of his demeanor, some violent emotion was at work. It might have been fear or alertness or excitement—but there was *something. This man,* she said to herself, *could be dangerous.*

He said again, and this time his voice was just mildly curious, "What's that about the police?"

"They rang up," said Molly. "Just now. To say they're sending a sergeant out here." She looked toward the window. "But I shouldn't think he'll ever get here," she said hopefully.

"Why are they sending the police here?" He took a step nearer to her, but before she could reply the door opened, and Giles came in.

"This ruddy coke's more than half stones," he said angrily. Then he added sharply, "Is anything the matter?"

Major Metcalf turned to him. "I hear the police are coming out here," he said. "Why?"

"Oh, that's all right," said Giles. "No one can ever get through in this. Why, the drifts are five feet deep. The road's all banked up. Nobody will get here today."

And at that moment there came distinctly three loud taps on the window.

It startled them all. For a moment or two they did not locate the sound. It came with the emphasis and menace of a ghostly warning. And then, with a cry, Molly pointed to the French window. A man was standing there tapping on the pane, and the mystery of his arrival was explained by the fact that he wore skis.

With an exclamation, Giles crossed the room, fumbled with the catch, and threw open the French window.

"Thank you, sir," said the new arrival. He had a slightly common, cheerful voice and a well-bronzed face.

"Detective Sergeant Trotter," he announced himself.

Mrs. Boyle peered at him over her knitting with disfavor.

"You can't be a sergeant," she said disapprovingly.

"You're too young."

The young man, who was indeed very young, looked affronted at this criticism and said in a slightly annoyed tone, "I'm not quite as young as I look, madam."

His eye roved over the group and picked out Giles.

"Are you Mr. Davis? Can I get these skis off and stow them somewhere?"

"Of course, come with me."

Mrs. Boyle said acidly as the door to the hall closed behind them, "I suppose that's what we pay our police force for, nowadays, to go round enjoying themselves at winter sports."

Paravicini had come close to Molly. There was quite a hiss in his voice as he said in a quick, low voice, "Why did you send for the police, Mrs. Davis?"

She recoiled a little before the steady malignity of his glance. This was a new Mr. Paravicini. For a moment she felt afraid. She said helplessly, "But I didn't. I didn't."

And then Christopher Wren came excitedly through the door, saying in a high penetrating whisper, "Who's that man in the hall? Where did he come from? So terribly hearty and all over snow."

Mrs. Boyle's voice boomed out over the click of her knitting-needles. "You may believe it or not, but that man is a policeman. A policeman—skiing!"

The final disruption of the lower classes had come, so her manner seemed to say.

Major Metcalf murmured to Molly, "Excuse me, Mrs. Davis, but may I use your telephone?"

"Of course, Major Metcalf."

He went over to the instrument, just as Christopher Wren said shrilly, "He's very handsome, don't you think so? I always think policemen are terribly attractive."

"Hullo, hullo—" Major Metcalf was rattling the telephone irritably. He turned to Molly. "Mrs. Davis, this telephone is dead, quite dead."

"It was all right just now. I—"

She was interrupted. Christopher Wren was laughing, a high, shrill, almost hysterical laugh. "So we're quite cut off now. Quite cut off. That's funny, isn't it?"

"I don't see anything to laugh at," said Major Metcalf stiffly.

"No, indeed," said Mrs. Boyle.

Christopher was still in fits of laughter. "It's a private joke of my own," he said. *"Hsh,"* he put his finger to his lips, "the sleuth is coming."

Giles came in with Sergeant Trotter. The latter had got rid of his skis and brushed off the snow and was holding in his hand a large notebook and pencil. He brought an atmosphere of unhurried judicial procedure with him.

"Molly," said Giles, "Sergeant Trotter wants a word with us alone."

Molly followed them both out of the room.

"We'll go in the study," Giles said.

They went into the small room at the back of the hall which was dignified by that name. Sergeant Trotter closed the door carefully behind him.

"What have we done, Sergeant?" Molly demanded plaintively.

"Done?" Sergeant Trotter stared at her. Then he smiled broadly. "Oh," he said. "It's nothing of that kind, madam. I'm sorry if there's been a misapprehension of any kind. No, Mrs. Davis, it's something quite different. It's more a matter of police protection, if you understand me."

Not understanding him in the least, they both looked at him inquiringly.

Sergeant Trotter went on fluently, "It relates to the death of Mrs. Lyon, Mrs. Maureen Lyon, who was murdered in London two days ago. You may have read about the case."

"Yes," said Molly.

"The first thing I want to know is if you were acquainted with this Mrs. Lyon?"

"Never heard of her," said Giles, and Molly murmured concurrence.

"Well, that's rather what we expected. But as a matter of fact Lyon wasn't the murdered woman's real name. She had a police record, and her fingerprints were on file, so we were able to identify her without any difficulty. Her real name was Gregg; Maureen Gregg. Her late husband, John Gregg, was a farmer who resided at Longridge Farm not very far from here. You may have heard of the Longridge Farm case."

The room was very still. Only one sound broke the stillness, a soft, unexpected *plop* as snow slithered off the roof and fell to the ground outside. It was a secret, almost sinister sound.

Trotter went on. "Three evacuee children were billeted on the Greggs at Longridge Farm in 1940. One of those children subsequently died as the result of criminal neglect and ill-treatment. The case made quite a sensation, and the Greggs were both sentenced to terms of imprisonment. Gregg escaped on his way to prison, he stole a car and had a crash while trying to evade the police. He was killed outright. Mrs. Gregg served her sentence and was released two months ago."

"And now she's been murdered," said Giles. "Who do they think did it?"

But Sergeant Trotter was not to be hurried. "You remember the case, sir?" he asked.

Giles shook his head. "In 1940 I was a midshipman serving in the Mediterranean."

"I—I do remember hearing about it, I think," said Molly rather breathlessly. "But why do you come to us? What have we to do with it?"

"It's a question of your being in danger, Mrs. Davis!"

"Danger?" Giles spoke increduously.

"It's like this, sir. A notebook was picked up near the scene of the crime. In it were written two addresses. The first was Seventy-four Culver Street."

"Where the woman was murdered?" Molly put in.

"Yes, Mrs. Davis. The other address was Monkswell Manor."

"What?" Molly's tone was incredulous. "But how extraordinary."

"Yes. That's why Superintendent Hogben thought it imperative to find out if you knew of any connection between you, or between this house, and the Longridge Farm case."

"There's nothing—absolutely nothing," said Giles. "It must be some coincidence."

Sergeant Trotter said gently, "Superintendent Hogben doesn't think it is a coincidence. He'd have come himself if it had been at all possible. Under the weather conditions, and as I'm an expert skier, he sent me with instructions to get full particulars of everyone in this house, to report back to him by phone, and to take all measures I thought expedient for the safety of the household."

Giles said sharply, "Safety? Good Lord, man, you don't think somebody is going to be killed *here?*"

Trotter said apologetically, "I didn't want to upset the lady, but yes, that is just what Superintendent Hogben does think."

"But what earthly reason could there be—"

Giles broke off, and Trotter said, "That's just what I'm here to find out."

"But the whole thing's *crazy.*"

"Yes, sir, but it's because it's crazy that it's dangerous."

Molly said, "There's something more you haven't told us yet, isn't there, Sergeant?"

"Yes, madam. At the top of the page in the notebook was written, 'Three Blind Mice.' Pinned to the dead woman's body was a paper with 'This is the first' written on it. And below it a drawing of *three mice* and a bar of music. The music was the tune of the nursery rhyme 'Three Blind Mice.'"

Molly sang softly:

"Three Blind Mice,
See how they run.
They all ran after the farmer's wife!
She—"

She broke off. "Oh, it's horrible—*horrible.* There were three children, weren't there?"

"Yes, Mrs. Davis. A boy of fifteen, a girl of fourteen, and the boy of twelve who died."

"What happened to the others?"

"The girl was, I believe, adopted by someone. We haven't been able to trace her. The boy would be just on twenty-three now. We've lost track of him. He was said to have always been a bit—queer. He joined up in the army at eighteen. Later he deserted. Since then he's disappeared. The army psychiatrist says definitely that he's not normal."

"You think that it was he who killed Mrs. Lyon?" Giles asked. "And that he's a homicidal maniac and may turn up here for some unknown reason?"

"We think that there must be a connection between someone here and the Longridge Farm business. Once we can establish what that connection is, we will be forearmed. Now you state, sir, that you yourself have no connection with that case. The same goes for you, Mrs. Davis?"

"I—oh, yes—yes."

"Perhaps you will tell me exactly who else there is in the house?"

They gave him the names. Mrs. Boyle. Major Metcalf. Mr. Christopher Wren. Mr. Paravicini. He wrote them down in his notebook.

"Servants?"

"We haven't any servants," said Molly. "And that reminds me, I must go and put the potatoes on."

She left the study abruptly.

Trotter turned to Giles. "What do you know about these people, sir?"

"I—We—" Giles paused. Then he said quietly, "Really, we don't know anything about them, Sergeant Trotter. Mrs. Boyle wrote from a Bournemouth hotel. Major Metcalf from Leamington. Mr. Wren from a private hotel in South Kensington. Mr. Paravicini just turned up out of the blue—or rather out of the white—his car overturned in a snowdrift near here. Still, I suppose they'll have identity cards, ration books, that sort of thing?"

"I shall go into all that, of course."

"In a way it's lucky that the weather is so awful," said Giles. "The murderer can't very well turn up in this, can he?"

"Perhaps he doesn't need to, Mr. Davis."

"What do you mean?"

Sergeant Trotter hesitated for a moment and then he said, "You've got to consider, sir, that *he may be here already.*"

Giles stared at him.

"What do you mean?"

"Mrs. Gregg was killed two days ago. *All your visitors here have arrived since then, Mr. Davis.*"

"Yes, but they'd booked beforehand—some time beforehand—except for Paravicini."

Sergeant Trotter sighed. His voice sounded tired. "These crimes were planned in advance."

"Crimes? But only one crime has happened yet. Why are you sure that there will be another?"

"That it will happen—no. I hope to prevent that. That it will be attempted, yes."

"But then—if you're right," Giles spoke excitedly, "there's only one person it could be. There's only one person who's the right age. *Christopher Wren!*"

Sergeant Trotter had joined Molly in the kitchen.

"I'd be glad, Mrs. Davis, if you would come with me to the library. I want to make a general statement to everyone. Mr. Davis has kindly gone to prepare the way—"

"All right—just let me finish these potatoes. Sometimes I wish Sir Walter Raleigh had never discovered the beastly things."

Sergeant Trotter preserved a disapproving silence. Molly said apologetically, "I can't really believe it, you see—It's so fantastic—"

"It isn't fantastic, Mrs. Davis—It's just plain *facts.*"

"You have a description of the man?" Molly asked curiously.

"Medium height, slight build, wore a dark overcoat and a light hat, spoke in a whisper, his face was hidden by a muffler. You see—that might be anybody." He paused and added, "There are three dark overcoats and light hats hanging up in your hall here, Mrs. Davis."

"I don't think any of these people came from London."

"Didn't they, Mrs. Davis?" With a swift movement Sergeant Trotter moved to the dresser and picked up a newspaper.

"The *Evening Standard* of February 19th. Two days ago. *Someone* brought that paper here, Mrs. Davis."

"But how extraordinary." Molly stared, some faint chord of memory stirred. "Where can that paper have come from?"

"You mustn't take people always at their face value, Mrs. Davis. You don't really know anything about these people you have admitted to your house." He added, "I take it you and Mr. Davis are new to the guest-house business?"

"Yes, we are," Molly admitted. She felt suddenly young, foolish, and childish.

"You haven't been married long, perhaps, either?"

"Just a year." She blushed slightly. "It was all rather sudden."

"Love at first sight," said Sergeant Trotter sympathetically.

Molly felt quite unable to snub him. "Yes," she said, and added in a burst of confidence, "we'd only known each other a fortnight."

Her thoughts went back over those fourteen days of whirlwind courtship. There hadn't been any doubts—they had both known. In a worrying, nerve-racked world, they had found the miracle of each other. A little smile came to her lips.

She came back to the present to find Sergeant Trotter eying her indulgently.

"Your husband doesn't come from these parts, does he?"

"No," said Molly vaguely. "He comes from Lincolnshire."

She knew very little of Giles's childhood and upbringing. His parents were dead, and he always avoided talking about his early days. He had had, she fancied, an unhappy childhood.

"You're both very young, if I may say so, to run a place of this kind," said Sergeant Trotter.

"Oh, I don't know. I'm twenty-two and—"

She broke off as the door opened and Giles came in.

"Everything's all set. I've given them a rough outline," he said. "I hope that's all right, Sergeant?"

"Saves time," said Trotter. "Are you ready, Mrs. Davis?"

Four voices spoke at once as Sergeant Trotter entered the library.

Highest and shrillest was that of Christopher Wren declaring that this was too, too thrilling and he wasn't going to sleep a wink tonight, and please, *please* could we have all the gory details?

A kind of double-bass accompaniment came from Mrs. Boyle. "Absolute outrage—sheer incompetence—police have no business to let murderers go roaming about the countryside."

Mr. Paravicini was eloquent chiefly with his hands. His gesticulations were more eloquent than his words, which were drowned by Mrs. Boyle's double bass. Major Metcalf could be heard in an occasional short staccato bark. He was asking for facts.

Trotter waited a moment or two, then he held up an authoritative hand and, rather surprisingly, there was silence.

"Thank you," he said. "Now, Mr. Davis has given you an outline of why I'm here. I want to know one thing, and one thing only, and I want to know it quick. *Which of you has some connection with the Longridge Farm case?*"

The silence was unbroken. Four blank faces looked at Sergeant Trotter. The emotions of a few moments back—excitement, indignation, hysteria, inquiry, were wiped away as a sponge wipes out the chalk marks on a slate.

Sergeant Trotter spoke again, more urgently. "Please understand me. One of you, we have reason to believe, is in danger—deadly danger. *I have got to know which one of you it is!*"

And still no one spoke or moved.

Something like anger came into Trotter's voice. "Very well—I'll ask you one by one. Mr. Paravicini?"

A very faint smile flickered across Mr. Paravicini's face. He raised his hands in a protesting foreign gesture.

"But I am a stranger in these parts, Inspector. I know nothing, but nothing, of these local affairs of bygone years."

Trotter wasted no time. He snapped out, "Mrs. Boyle?"

"Really I don't see why—I mean—why should *I* have anything to do with such a distressing business?"

"Mr. Wren?"

Christopher said shrilly, "I was a mere child at the time. I don't remember even *hearing* about it."

"Major Metcalf?"

The Major said abruptly, "Read about it in the papers. I was stationed at Edinburgh at the time."

"That's all you have to say—any of you?"

Silence again.

Trotter gave an exasperated sigh. "If one of you gets murdered," he said, "you'll only have yourself to blame." He turned abruptly and went out of the room.

"My dears," said Christopher. "How *melodramatic!*" He added, "He's very handsome, isn't he? I do admire the police. So stern and hard-boiled. Quite a thrill, this whole business. 'Three Blind Mice.' How does the tune go?"

He whistled the air softly, and Molly cried out involuntarily, *"Don't!"*

He whirled round on her and laughed. "But, darling," he said, "it's my *signature* tune. I've never been taken for a murderer before and I'm getting a tremendous kick out of it!"

"Melodramatic rubbish," said Mrs. Boyle. "I don't believe a word of it."

Christopher's light eyes danced with an impish mischief. "But just wait, Mrs. Boyle," he lowered his voice, "till I creep up behind you and you feel my hands round your throat."

Molly flinched.

Giles said angrily, "You're upsetting my wife, Wren. It's a damned poor joke, anyway."

"It's no joking matter," said Metcalf.

"Oh, but it is," said Christopher. "That's just what it is—a madman's joke. That's what makes it so deliciously *macabre*."

He looked round at them and laughed again. "If you could just see your faces," he said.

Then he went swiftly out of the room.

Mrs. Boyle recovered first. "A singularly ill-mannered and neurotic young man," she said. "Probably a conscientious objector."

"He tells me he was buried during an air raid for forty-eight hours before being dug out," said Major Metcalf. "That accounts for a good deal, I daresay."

"People have so many excuses for giving way to nerves," said Mrs. Boyle acidly. "I'm sure I went through as much as anybody in the war, and *my* nerves are all right."

"Perhaps that's just as well for you, Mrs. Boyle," said Metcalf.

"What do you mean?"

Major Metcalf said quietly, "I think you were actually the billeting officer for this district in 1940, Mrs. Boyle." He looked at Molly who gave a grave nod. "That is so, isn't it?"

An angry flush appeared on Mrs. Boyle's face. "What of it?" she demanded.

Metcalf said gravely, "*You* were responsible for sending three children to Longridge Farm."

"Really, Major Metcalf, I don't see how I can be held responsible for what happened. The Farm people seemed very nice and were most anxious to have the children. I don't see that I was to blame in any way—or that I can be held responsible—" Her voice trailed off.

Giles said sharply, "Why didn't you tell Sergeant Trotter this?"

"No business of the police," snapped Mrs. Boyle. "I can look after myself."

Major Metcalf said quietly, "You'd better watch out."

Then he, too, left the room.

Molly murmured, "Of course, you *were* the billeting officer. I remember."

"Molly, did you know?" Giles stared at her.

"You had the big house on the common, didn't you?"

"Requisitioned," said Mrs. Boyle. "And completely ruined," she added bitterly. "*Devastated.* Iniquitous."

Then, very softly, Mr. Paravicini began to laugh. He threw his head back and laughed without restraint.

"You must forgive me," he gasped. "But, indeed, I find all this most amusing. I enjoy myself—yes, I enjoy myself greatly."

Sergeant Trotter reentered the room at that moment. He threw a glance of disapproval at Mr. Paravicini. "I'm glad," he said acidly, "that everyone finds this so funny."

"I apologize, my dear Inspector. I do apologize. I am spoiling the effect of your solemn warning."

Sergeant Trotter shrugged his shoulders. "I've done my best to make the position clear," he said. "And I'm not an inspector. I'm only a sergeant. I'd like to use the telephone, please, Mrs. Davis."

"I abase myself," said Mr. Paravicini. "I creep away."

Far from creeping, he left the room with that jaunty and youthful step that Molly had noticed before.

"He's an odd fish," said Giles.

"Criminal type," said Trotter. "Wouldn't trust him a yard."

"Oh," said Molly. "You think *he*—but he's far too old—Or is he old at all? He uses make up—quite a lot of it. And his walk is young. Perhaps, he's made up to *look* old. Sergeant Trotter, do you think—"

Sergeant Trotter snubbed her severely. "We shan't get anywhere with unprofitable speculation, Mrs. Davis," he said. "I must report to Superintendent Hogben."

He crossed to the telephone.

"But you can't," said Molly. "The telephone's dead."

"What?" Trotter swung round.

The sharp alarm in his voice impressed them all. "Dead? Since when?"

"Major Metcalf tried it just before you came."

"But it was all right before that. You got Superintendent Hogben's message?"

"Yes. I suppose—since ten—the line's down—with the snow."

But Trotter's face remained grave. "I wonder," he said. "It may have been—cut."

Molly stared. "You think so?"

"I'm going to make sure."

He hurried out of the room. Giles hesitated, then went after him.

Molly exclaimed, "Good heavens! Nearly lunch time, I must get on—or we'll have nothing to eat."

As she rushed from the room, Mrs. Boyle muttered, "Incompetent chit! What a place. *I* shan't pay seven guineas for *this* kind of thing."

SERGEANT TROTTER BENT down, following the wires. He asked Giles, "Is there an extension?"

"Yes, in our bedroom upstairs. Shall I go up and see there?"

"If you please."

Trotter opened the window and leaned out, brushing snow from the sill. Giles hurried up the stairs.

Mr. Paravicini was in the big drawing-room. He went across to the grand piano and opened it. Sitting on the music stool, he picked out a tune softly with one finger.

Three Blind Mice,
See how they run . . .

Christopher Wren was in his bedroom. He moved about it, whistling briskly. Suddenly the whistle wavered and died. He sat down on the edge of the bed. He buried his face in his hands and began to sob. He murmured childishly, "I can't go on."

Then his mood changed. He stood up, squared his shoulders. "I've got to go on," he said. "I've got to go through with it."

Giles stood by the telephone in his and Molly's room. He bent down toward the skirting. One of Molly's gloves lay there. He picked it up. A pink bus ticket dropped out of it. Giles stood looking down at it as it fluttered to the ground. Watching it, his face changed. It might have been a different man who walked slowly, as though in a dream, to the door, opened it, and stood a moment peering along the corridor toward the head of the stairs.

Molly finished the potatoes, threw them into the pot, and set the pot on the fire. She glanced into the oven. Everything was all set, going according to plan.

On the kitchen table was the two-day-old copy of the *Evening Standard.* She frowned as she looked at it. If she could only just *remember—*

Suddenly her hands went to her eyes. "Oh, no," said Molly. "Oh, *no!*"

Slowly she took her hands away. She looked round the kitchen like someone looking at a strange place. So warm and comfortable and spacious, with its faint savory smell of cooking.

"Oh, *no,*" she said again under her breath.

She moved slowly, like a sleepwalker, toward the door into the hall. She opened it. The house was silent except for someone whistling.

That tune—

Molly shivered and retreated. She waited a minute or two, glancing once more round the familiar kitchen. Yes, everything was in order and progressing. She went once more toward the kitchen door.

Major Metcalf came quietly down the back stairs. He waited a moment or two in the hall, then he opened the big cupboard under the stairs and peered in. Everything seemed quiet. Nobody about. As good a time as any to do what he had set out to do—

Mrs. Boyle, in the library, turned the knobs of the radio with some irritation.

Her first attempt had brought her into the middle of a talk on the origin and significance of nursery rhymes. The last thing she wanted to hear. Twirling impatiently, she was informed by a cultured voice: "The psychology of fear must be thoroughly understood. Say you are alone in a room. A door opens softly behind you—"

A door did open.

Mrs. Boyle, with a violent start, turned sharply. "Oh, it's you," she said with relief. "Idiotic programs they have on this thing. I can't find anything worth listening to!"

"I shouldn't bother to listen, Mrs. Boyle."

Mrs. Boyle snorted. "What else is there for me to do?" she demanded. "Shut up in a house with a possible murderer—not that I believe *that* melodramatic story for a moment—"

"Don't you, Mrs. Boyle?"

"Why—what do you mean—"

The belt of the raincoat was slipped round her neck so quickly that she hardly realized its significance. The knob of the radio amplifier was turned higher. The lecturer on the psychology of fear shouted his learned remarks into the room and drowned what incidental noises there were attendant on Mrs. Boyle's demise.

But there wasn't much noise.

The killer was too expert for that.

THEY WERE ALL HUDDLED in the kitchen. On the gas cooker the potatoes bubbled merrily. The savory smell from the oven of steak and kidney pie was stronger than ever.

Four shaken people stared at each other, the fifth, Molly, white and shivering, sipped at the glass of whiskey that the sixth, Sergeant Trotter, had forced her to drink.

Sergeant Trotter himself, his face set and angry, looked round at the assembled people. Just five minutes had elapsed since Molly's terrified screams had brought him and the others racing to the library.

"She'd only just been killed when you got to her, Mrs. Davis," he said. "Are you sure you didn't see or hear anybody as you came across the hall?"

"Whistling," said Molly faintly. "But that was earlier. I think—I'm not sure—I think I heard a door shut—softly, somewhere—just as I—as I—went into the library."

"Which door?"

"I don't know."

"Think, Mrs. Davis—try and *think*—upstairs—downstairs—right, left?"

"I don't *know,* I tell you," cried Molly. "I'm not even sure I heard anything."

"Can't you stop bullying her?" said Giles angrily. "Can't you see she's all in?"

"I'm investigating a murder, Mr. Davis—I beg your pardon—*Commander* Davis."

"I don't use my war rank, Sergeant."

"Quite so, sir." Trotter paused, as though he had made some subtle point. "As I say, I'm investigating a murder. Up to now nobody has taken this thing seriously. Mrs. Boyle didn't. She held out on me with information. You all held out on me. Well, Mrs. Boyle is dead. Unless we get to the bottom of this—and quickly, mind, there may be another death."

"Another? Nonsense. Why?"

"Because," said Sergeant Trotter gravely, "there were three little blind mice."

Giles said incredulously, "A death for each of them? But there would have to be a connection—I mean another connection with the case."

"Yes, there would have to be that."

"But why another death *here?*"

"Because there were only two addresses in the notebook. There was only one possible victim at Seventy-four Culver Street. She's dead. But at Monkswell Manor there is a wider field."

"Nonsense, Trotter. It would be a most unlikely coincidence that there should be *two* people brought here by chance, both of them with a share in the Longridge Farm case."

"Given certain circumstances, it wouldn't be so much of a coincidence. Think it out, Mr. Davis." He turned toward the others. "I've had your accounts of where you all were when Mrs. Boyle was killed. I'll check them over. You were in your room, Mr. Wren, when you heard Mrs. Davis scream?"

"Yes, Sergeant."

"Mr. Davis, you were upstairs in your bedroom examining the telephone extension there?"

"Yes," said Giles.

"Mr. Paravicini was in the drawing-room playing tunes on the piano. Nobody heard you, by the way, Mr. Paravicini?"

"I was playing very, very softly, Sergeant, just with one finger."

"What tune was it?"

"'Three Blind Mice,' Sergeant." He smiled. "The same tune that Mr. Wren was whistling upstairs. The tune that's running through everybody's head."

"It's a horrid tune," said Molly.

"How about the telephone wire?" asked Metcalf. "Was it deliberately cut?"

"Yes, Major Metcalf. A section had been cut out just outside the dining-room window—I had just located the break when Mrs. Davis screamed."

"But it's crazy. How can he hope to get away with it?" demanded Christopher shrilly.

The sergeant measured him carefully with his eye.

"Perhaps he doesn't very much care about that," he said. "Or again, he may be quite sure he's too clever for us. Murderers get like that." He added, "We take a psychology course, you know, in our training. A schizophrenic's mentality is very interesting."

"Shall we cut out the long words?" said Giles.

"Certainly, Mr. Davis. Two six-letter words are all that concern us at the moment. One's 'murder' and the other's 'danger.' That's what we've got to concentrate upon. Now, Major Metcalf, let me be quite clear about your movements. You say you were in the *cellar*—Why?"

"Looking around," said the major. "I looked in that cupboard place under the stairs and then I noticed a door there and I opened it and saw a flight of steps, so I went down there. Nice cellar you've got," he said to Giles. "Crypt of an old monastery, I should say."

"We're not engaged in antiquarian research, Major Metcalf. We're investigating a murder. Will you listen a moment, Mrs. Davis? I'll leave the kitchen door open." He went out; a door shut with a faint creak. "Is that what you heard, Mrs. Davis?" he asked as he reappeared in the open doorway.

"I—it does sound like it."

"That was the cupboard under the stairs. It could be, you know, that after killing Mrs. Boyle, the murderer, retreating across the hall, heard you coming out of the kitchen, and slipped into the cupboard, pulling the door to after him."

"Then his fingerprints will be on the inside of the cupboard," cried Christopher.

"Mine are there already," said Major Metcalf.

"Quite so," said Sergeant Trotter. "But we've a satisfactory explanation for those, haven't we?" he added smoothly.

"Look here, Sergeant," said Giles, "admittedly you're in charge of this affair. But this is my house, and in a certain degree I feel responsible for the people staying in it. Oughtn't we to take precautionary measures?"

"Such as, Mr. Davis?"

"Well, to be frank, putting under restraint the person who seems pretty clearly indicated as the chief suspect."

He looked straight at Christopher Wren.

Christopher Wren sprang forward, his voice rose, shrill and hysterical, "It's not true! It's not *true!* You're all against me. Everyone's always against me. You're going to frame me for this. It's persecution—persecution—"

"Steady on, lad," said Major Metcalf.

"It's all right, Chris." Molly came forward. She put her hand on his arm. "Nobody's against you. Tell him it's all right," she said to Sergeant Trotter.

"We don't frame people," said Sergeant Trotter.

"Tell him you're not going to arrest him."

"I'm not going to arrest anyone. To do that, I need evidence. There's no evidence—at present."

Giles cried out, "I think you're crazy, Molly. And you, too, Sergeant. There's only one person who fits the bill, and—"

"Wait, Giles, wait—" Molly broke in. "Oh, do be quiet. Sergeant Trotter, can I—can I speak to you a minute?"

"I'm staying," said Giles.

"No, Giles, you, too, please."

Giles's face grew as dark as thunder. He said, "I don't know what's come over you, Molly."

He followed the others out of the room, banging the door behind him.

"Yes, Mrs. Davis, what is it?"

"Sergeant Trotter, when you told us about the Longridge Farm case, you seemed to think that it must be the eldest boy who is—responsible for all this. But you don't *know* that?"

"That's perfectly true, Mrs. Davis. But the probabilities lie that way—mental instability, desertion from the army, psychiatrist's report."

"Oh, I know, and therefore it all seems to point to Christopher. But I don't believe it *is* Christopher. There must be other—possibilities. Hadn't those three children any relations—parents, for instance?"

"Yes. The mother was dead. But the father was serving abroad."

"Well, what about him? Where is *he* now?"

"We've no information. He obtained his demobilization papers last year."

"And if the son was mentally unstable, the father may have been, too."

"That is so."

"So the murderer may be middle-aged or old. Major Metcalf, remember, was frightfully upset when I told him the police had rung up. He really *was*."

Sergeant Trotter said quietly, "Please believe me, Mrs. Davis, I've had all the possibilities in mind since the beginning. The boy, Jim—the father—even the sister. It *could* have been a woman, you know. I haven't overlooked anything. I may be pretty sure in my own mind—but I don't *know*—yet. It's very hard really to know about anything or anyone—especially in these days. You'd be surprised what we see in the police force. With marriages, especially. Hasty marriages—war marriages. There's no background, you see. No families or relations to meet. People accept each other's word. Fellow says he's a fighter pilot or an army major—the girl believes him implicitly. Sometimes she doesn't find out for a year or two that he's an absconding bank clerk with a wife and family, or an army-deserter."

He paused and went on.

"I know quite well what's in your mind, Mrs. Davis. There's just one thing I'd like to say to you. *The murderer's enjoying himself*. That's the one thing I'm quite sure of."

He went toward the door.

Molly stood very straight and still, a red flush burning in her cheeks. After standing rigid for a moment or two, she moved slowly toward the stove, knelt down, and opened the oven door. A savory, familiar smell came toward her. Her heart lightened. It was as though suddenly she had been wafted back into the dear, familiar world of everyday things. Cooking, housework, homemaking, ordinary prosaic living.

So, from time immemorial women had cooked food for their men. The world of danger—of madness, receded. Woman, in her kitchen, was safe—eternally safe.

The kitchen door opened. She turned her head as Christopher Wren entered. He was a little breathless.

"My dear," he said. "*Such* ructions! Somebody's stolen the sergeant's skis!"

"The sergeant's skis? But why should anyone want to do that?"

"I really can't imagine. I mean, if the sergeant decided to go away and leave us, I should imagine that the murderer would be only too pleased. I mean, it really doesn't make *sense,* does it?"

"Giles put them in the cupboard under the stairs."

"Well, they're not there now. Intriguing, isn't it?" He laughed gleefully. "The sergeant's awfully angry about it. Snapping like a turtle. He's been pitching into poor Major Metcalf. The old boy sticks to it that he didn't notice whether they were there or not when he looked into the cupboard just before Mrs. Boyle was murdered. Trotter says he *must* have noticed. If you ask me," Christopher lowered his voice and leaned forward, "this business is beginning to get Trotter down."

"It's getting us all down," said Molly.

"Not me. I find it most stimulating. It's all so delightfully unreal."

Molly said sharply, "You wouldn't say that if—if you'd been the one to find her. Mrs. Boyle, I mean. I keep thinking of it—I can't forget it. Her face—all swollen and purple—"

She shivered. Christopher came across to her. He put a hand on her shoulder.

"I know. I'm an idiot. I'm sorry. I didn't think."

A dry sob rose in Molly's throat. "It seemed all right just now—cooking—the kitchen," she spoke confusedly, incoherently. "And then suddenly—it was all back again—like a nightmare."

There was a curious expression on Christopher Wren's face as he stood there looking down on her bent head.

"I see," he said. "I see." He moved away. "Well, I'd better clear out and—not interrupt you."

Molly cried, "Don't go!" just as his hand was on the door handle.

He turned round, looking at her questioningly. Then he came slowly back.

"Do you really mean that?"

"Mean what?"

"You definitely don't want to—go?"

"No, I tell you. I don't want to be alone. I'm afraid to be alone."

Christopher sat down by the table. Molly bent to the oven, lifted the pie to a higher shelf, shut the oven door, and came and joined him.

"That's very interesting," said Christopher in a level voice.

"What is?"

"That you're not afraid to be—alone with me. You're not, are you?"

She shook her head. "No, I'm not."

"Why aren't you afraid, Molly?"

"I don't know—I'm not."

"And yet I'm the only person who—fits the bill. One murderer as per schedule."

"No," said Molly. "There are—other possibilities, I've been talking to Sergeant Trotter about them."

"Did he agree with you?"

"He didn't disagree," said Molly slowly.

Certain words sounded over and over again in her head. Especially that last phrase: *I know exactly what's in your mind, Mrs. Davis.* But did he? Could he possibly know? He had said, too, that the murderer was enjoying himself. Was that true?

She said to Christopher, "*You're* not exactly enjoying yourself, are you? In spite of what you said just now."

"Good God, no," said Christopher, staring. "What a very odd thing to say."

"Oh, I didn't say it. Sergeant Trotter did. I hate that man! He—he puts things into your head—things that aren't true—that can't possibly be true."

She put her hands to her head, covering her eyes with them. Very gently Christopher took those hands away.

"Look here, Molly," he said, "what is all this?"

She let him force her gently into a chair by the kitchen table. His manner was no longer hysterical or childish.

"What's the matter, Molly?" he said.

Molly looked at him—a long appraising glance. She asked irrelevantly, "How long have I known you, Christopher? Two days?"

"Just about. You're thinking, aren't you, that though it's such a short time, we seem to know each other rather well."

"Yes—it's odd, isn't it?"

"Oh, I don't know. There's a kind of sympathy between us. Possibly because we've both—been up against it."

It was not a question. It was a statement. Molly let it pass. She said very quietly, and again it was a statement rather than a question, "Your name isn't really Christopher Wren, is it."

"No."

"Why did you—"

"Choose that? Oh, it seemed rather a pleasant whimsy. They used to jeer at me and call me Christopher Robin at school. Robin—Wren—association of ideas, I suppose."

"What's your real name?"

Christopher said quietly, "I don't think we'll go into that. It wouldn't mean anything to you. I'm not an architect. Actually, I'm a deserter from the army."

Just for a moment swift alarm leaped into Molly's eyes.

Christopher saw it. "Yes," he said. "Just like our unknown murderer. I told you I was the only one the specification fitted."

"Don't be stupid," said Molly. "I told you I didn't believe you were the murderer. Go on—tell me about yourself. What made you desert—nerves?"

"Being afraid, you mean? No, curiously enough, I wasn't afraid—not more than anyone else, that is to say. Actually I got a reputation for being rather cool under fire. No, it was something quite different. It was—my mother."

"Your mother?"

"Yes—you see, she was killed—in an air raid. Buried. They—they had to dig her out. I don't know what happened to me when I heard about it—I suppose I went a little mad. I thought, you see, it happened to *me*. I felt I had to get home quickly and—and dig myself out—I can't explain—it was all confused." He lowered his head to his hands and spoke in a muffled voice. "I wandered about a long time, looking for her—or for myself—I don't know which. And then, when my mind cleared up, I was afraid to go back—or to report—I knew I could never explain. Since then, I've just been—nothing."

He stared at her, his young face hollow with despair.

"You mustn't feel like that," said Molly gently. "You can start again."

"Can one ever do that?"

"Of course—you're quite young."

"Yes, but you see—I've come to the end."

"No," said Molly. "You haven't come to the end, you only think you have. I believe everyone has that feeling once, at least, in their lives—that it's the end, that they can't go on."

"You've had it, haven't you, Molly? You must have—to be able to speak like that."

"Yes."

"What was yours?"

"Mine was just what happened to a lot of people. I was engaged to a young fighter pilot—and he was killed."

"Wasn't there more to it than that?"

"I suppose there was. I'd had a nasty shock when I was younger. I came up against something that was rather cruel and beastly. It predisposed me to think that life was always—horrible. When Jack was killed it just confirmed my belief that the whole of life was cruel and treacherous."

"I know. And then, I suppose," said Christopher, watching her, "Giles came along."

"Yes." He saw the smile, tender, almost shy, that trembled on her mouth. "Giles came—everything felt right and safe and happy—Giles!"

The smile fled from her lips. Her face was suddenly stricken. She shivered as though with cold.

"What's the matter, Molly? What's frightening you? You *are* frightened, aren't you?"

She nodded.

"And it's something to do with Giles? Something he's said or done?"

"It's not Giles, really. It's that horrible man!"

"What horrible man?" Christopher was surprised. "Paravicini?"

"No, *no*. Sergeant Trotter."

"Sergeant Trotter?"

"Suggesting things—hinting things—putting horrible thoughts into my mind about Giles—thoughts that I didn't know were there. Oh, I hate him—I hate him."

Christopher's eyebrows rose in slow surprise. "Giles? *Giles!* Yes, of course, he and I are much of an age. He seems to me much older than I am—but I suppose he isn't, really. Yes, Giles might fit the bill equally well. But look here, Molly, that's all nonsense. Giles was down here with you the day that woman was killed in London."

Molly did not answer.

Christopher looked at her sharply. "Wasn't he here?"

Molly spoke breathlessly, the words coming out in an incoherent jumble. "He was out all day—in the car—he went over to the other side of the county about some wire netting in a sale there—at least that's what he said—that's what I thought—until—until—"

"Until what?"

Slowly Molly's hand reached out and traced the date of the *Evening Standard* that covered a portion of the kitchen table.

Christopher looked at it and said, "London edition, two days ago."

"It was in Giles's pocket when he came back. He—he must have been in London."

Christopher stared. He stared at the paper and he stared at Molly. He pursed up his lips and began to whistle, then checked himself abruptly. It wouldn't do to whistle that tune just now.

Choosing his words very carefully, and avoiding her eye, he said, "How much do you actually—know about Giles?"

"Don't," cried Molly. "Don't! That's just what that beast Trotter said—or hinted. That women often didn't know anything about the men that they married—especially in wartime. They—they just took the man's own account of himself."

"That's true enough, I suppose."

"Don't *you* say it, too! I can't bear it. It's just because we're all in such a state, so worked up. We'd—we'd believe *any* fantastic suggestion—It's not true! I—"

She stopped. The kitchen door had opened.

Giles came in. There was rather a grim look on his face. "Am I interrupting anything?" he asked.

Christopher slipped from the table. "I'm just taking a few cookery lessons," he said.

"Indeed? Well, look here, Wren, tête-à-têtes aren't very healthy things at the present time. You keep out of the kitchen, do you hear?"

"Oh, but surely—"

"You keep away from my wife, Wren. She's not going to be the next victim."

"That," said Christopher, "is just what I'm worrying about."

If there was significance in the words, Giles did not apparently notice them. He merely turned a rather darker shade of brick-red. "I'll do the worrying," he said. "I can look after my own wife. Get the hell out of here."

Molly said in a clear voice, "Please go, Christopher. Yes—really."

Christopher moved slowly toward the door. "I shan't go very far," he said, and the words were addressed to Molly and held a very definite meaning.

"*Will* you get out of here?"

Christopher gave a high childish giggle. "Aye, aye, Commander," he said.

The door shut behind him. Giles turned on Molly.

"For God's sake, Molly, haven't you got *any* sense? Shut in here alone with a dangerous homicidal maniac!"

"He isn't the—" she changed her phrase quickly "—he isn't dangerous. Anyway, I'm on my guard. I can—look after myself."

Giles laughed unpleasantly. "So could Mrs. Boyle."

"Oh, Giles, *don't*."

"Sorry, my dear. But I'm het up. That wretched boy. What you see in him I can't imagine."

Molly said slowly, "I'm sorry for him."

"Sorry for a homicidal lunatic?"

Molly gave him a curious glance. "I could be sorry for a homicidal lunatic," she said.

"Calling him Christopher, too. Since when have you been on Christian-name terms?"

"Oh Giles, don't be ridiculous. Everyone always uses Christian names nowadays. You know they do."

"Even after a couple of days? But perhaps it's more than that. Perhaps you knew Mr. Christopher Wren, the phony architect, before he came here? Perhaps you suggested to him that he *should* come here? Perhaps you cooked it all up between you?"

Molly stared at him. "Giles, have you gone out of your mind? What on earth are you suggesting?"

"I'm suggesting that Christopher Wren is an old friend, that you're on rather closer terms with him than you'd like me to know."

"Giles, you must be crazy!"

"I suppose you'll stick to it that you never saw him until he walked in here. Rather odd that he should come and stay in an out-of-the-way place like this, isn't it?"

"Is it any odder than that Major Metcalf and—and Mrs. Boyle should?"

"Yes—I think it is. I've always read that these murmuring loonies had a peculiar fascination for women. Looks as though it were true. How did you get to know him? How long has this been going on?"

"You're being absolutely absurd, Giles. I never saw Christopher Wren until he arrived here."

"You didn't go up to London to meet him two days ago and fix up to meet here as strangers?"

"You know perfectly well, Giles, I haven't been up to London for weeks."

"Haven't you? That's interesting." He fished a fur-lined glove out of his pocket and held it out. "That's one of the gloves you were wearing day before yesterday, isn't it? The day I was over at Sailham getting the netting."

"The day *you* were over at Sailham getting the netting," said Molly, eying him steadily. "Yes, I wore those gloves when I went out."

"You went to the village, you said. If you only went to the village, what is this doing inside that glove?"

Accusingly, he held out a pink bus ticket.

There was a moment's silence.

"You went to London," said Giles.

"All right," said Molly. Her chin shot up. "I went to London."

"To meet this chap Christopher Wren."

"No, not to meet Christopher."

"Then why did you go?"

"Just at the moment, Giles," said Molly, "I'm not going to tell you."

"Meaning you'll give yourself time to think up a good story!"

"I think," said Molly, "that I hate you!"

"I don't hate you," said Giles slowly. "But I almost wish I did. I simply feel that—I don't know you any more—I don't know anything about you."

"I feel the same," said Molly. "You—you're just a stranger. A man who lies to me—"

"When have I ever lied to you?"

Molly laughed. "Do you think I believed that story of yours about the wire netting? *You* were in London, too, that day."

"I suppose you saw me there," said Giles. "And you didn't trust me enough—"

"Trust you? I'll never trust anyone—ever—again."

Neither of them had noticed the soft opening of the kitchen door. Mr. Paravicini gave a little cough.

"So embarrassing," he murmured. "I do hope you young people are not both saying just a little more than you mean. One is so apt to in these lovers' quarrels."

"Lovers' quarrels," said Giles derisively. "That's good."

"Quite so, quite so," said Mr. Paravicini. "I know just how you feel. I have been through all this myself when I was a younger man. But what I came to say was that the inspector person is simply insisting that we should all come into the drawing-room. It appears that he has an idea." Mr. Paravicini sniggered gently. "The police have a clue—yes, one hears that frequently. But an *idea*? I very much doubt it. A zealous and painstaking officer, no doubt, our Sergeant Trotter, but not, I think, over-endowed with brains."

"Go on, Giles," said Molly. "I've got the cooking to see to. Sergeant Trotter can do without me."

"Talking of cooking," said Mr. Paravicini, skipping nimbly across the kitchen to Molly's side, "have you ever tried chicken livers served on toast that has been thickly spread with *foie gras* and a very thin rasher of bacon smeared with French mustard?"

"One doesn't see much *foie gras* nowadays," said Giles, "Come on, Paravicini."

"Shall I stay and assist you, dear lady?"

"You come along to the drawing-room, Paravicini," said Giles.

Mr. Paravicini laughed softly.

"Your husband is afraid for you. Quite natural. He doesn't fancy the idea of leaving you alone with *me.* It is my sadistic tendencies he fears—not my dishonorable ones. I yield to force." He bowed gracefully and kissed the tips of his fingers.

Molly said uncomfortably, "Oh, Mr. Paravicini, I'm sure—"

Mr. Paravicini shook his head. He said to Giles, "You're very wise, young man. *Take no chances.* Can I prove to you—or to the inspector for that matter—that I am not a homicidal maniac? No, I cannot. Negatives are such difficult things to prove."

He hummed cheerfully.

Molly flinched. "Please Mr. Paravicini—not that horrible tune."

"'Three Blind Mice'—so it was! The tune has got into my head. Now I come to think of it, it is a gruesome little rhyme. Not a nice little rhyme at all. But children like gruesome things. You may have noticed that? That rhyme is very English—the bucolic, cruel English countryside. 'She cut off their tails with a carving-knife.' Of course a child would love that—I could tell you things about children—"

"Please don't," said Molly faintly, "I think you're cruel, too." Her voice rose hysterically. "You laugh and smile—you're like a cat playing with a mouse—playing—"

She began to laugh.

"Steady, Molly," said Giles. "Come along, we'll all go into the drawing-room together. Trotter will be getting impatient. Never mind the cooking. Murder is more important than food."

"I'm not sure that I agree with you," said Mr. Paravicini as he followed them with little skipping steps. "The condemned man ate a hearty breakfast—that's what they always say."

Christopher Wren joined them in the hall and received a scowl from Giles. He looked at Molly with a quick, anxious glance, but Molly, her head held high, walked looking straight ahead of her. They marched almost like a procession to the drawing-room door. Mr. Paravicini brought up the rear with his little skipping steps.

Sergeant Trotter and Major Metcalf were standing waiting in the drawing-room. The major was looking sulky. Sergeant Trotter was looking flushed and energetic.

"That's right," he said, as they entered. "I wanted you all together. I want to make a certain experiment—and for that I shall require your cooperation."

"Will it take long?" Molly asked. "I'm rather busy in the kitchen. After all, we've got to have a meal sometime."

"Yes," said Trotter. "I appreciate that, Mrs. Davis. But, if you'll excuse me, there are more important things than meals! Mrs. Boyle, for instance, won't need another meal."

"Really, Sergeant," said Major Metcalf, "that's an extraordinarily tactless way of putting things."

"I'm sorry, Major Metcalf, but I want everyone to cooperate in this."

"Have you found your skis, Sergeant Trotter?" asked Molly.

The young man reddened. "No, I have not, Mrs. Davis. But I may say I have a very shrewd suspicion who took them. And of why they were taken. I won't say any more at present."

"Please don't," begged Mr. Paravicini. "I always think explanations should be kept to the very end—that exciting last chapter, you know."

"This isn't a game, sir."

"Isn't it? Now there I think you're wrong. I think it *is* a game—to somebody."

"The *murderer* is enjoying himself," murmured Molly softly.

The others looked at her in astonishment. She flushed.

"I'm only quoting what Sergeant Trotter said to me."

Sergeant Trotter did not look too pleased. "It's all very well, Mr. Paravicini, mentioning last chapters and speaking as though this was a mystery thriller," he said. "This is real. This is happening."

"So long," said Christopher Wren, fingering his neck gingerly, "as it doesn't happen to me."

"Now, then," said Major Metcalf. "None of that, young fellow. The sergeant here is going to tell us just what he wants us to do."

Sergeant Trotter cleared his throat. His voice became official.

"I took certain statements from you all a short time ago," he said. "Those statements related to your positions at the time when the murder of Mrs. Boyle occurred. Mr. Wren and Mr. Davis were in their separate bedrooms. Mrs. Davis was in the kitchen. Major Metcalf was in the cellar. Mr. Paravicini was here in this room—"

He paused and then went on.

"Those are the statements you made. I have no means of checking those statements. They may be true—they may not. To put it quite clearly—four of those statements are true—but *one of them is false.* Which one?"

He looked from face to face. Nobody spoke.

"Four of you are speaking the truth—one is lying. I have a plan that may help me to discover the liar. And if I discover that one of you lied to me—then I know who the murderer is.

Giles said sharply, "Not necessarily. Someone might have lied—for some other reason."

"I rather doubt that, Mr. Davis."

"But what's the idea, man? You've just said you've no means of checking these statements?"

"No, but supposing everyone was to go through these movements a second time."

"Bah," said Major Metcalf disparagingly. "Reconstruction of the crime. Foreign idea."

"Not a reconstruction of the *crime,* Major Metcalf. A reconstruction of the movements of apparently innocent persons."

"And what do you expect to learn from that?"

"You will forgive me if I don't make that clear just at the moment."

"You want," asked Molly, "a repeat performance?"

"More or less, Mrs. Davis."

There was a silence. It was, somehow, an uneasy silence.

It's a trap, thought Molly. *It's a trap—but I don't see how—*

You might have thought that there were five guilty people in the room, instead of one guilty and four innocent ones. One and all cast doubtful sideways glances at the assured, smiling young man who proposed this innocent-sounding maneuver.

Christopher burst out shrilly, "But I don't see—I simply can't see—what you can possibly hope to find out—just by making people do the same thing they did before. It seems to me just nonsense!"

"Does it, Mr. Wren?"

"Of course," said Giles slowly, "what you say goes, Sergeant. We'll cooperate. Are we all to do exactly what we did before?"

"The same actions will be performed, yes."

A faint ambiguity in the phrase made Major Metcalf look up sharply. Sergeant Trotter went on.

Mr. Paravicini has told us that he sat at the piano and played a certain tune. Perhaps, Mr. Paravicini, you would kindly show us exactly what you did do?"

"But certainly, my dear Sergeant."

Mr. Paravicini skipped nimbly across the room to the grand piano and settled himself on the music stool.

"The maestro at the piano will play the signature tune to a murder," he said with a flourish.

He grinned, and with elaborate mannerisms he picked out with one finger the tune of "Three Blind Mice."

He's enjoying himself, thought Molly. *He's enjoying himself.*

In the big room the soft, muted notes had an almost eerie effect.

"Thank you, Mr. Paravicini," said Sergeant Trotter. "That, I take it, is exactly how you played the tune on the—former occasion?"

"Yes, Sergeant, it is. I repeated it three times."

Sergeant Trotter turned to Molly. "Do you play the piano, Mrs. Davis?"

"Yes, Sergeant Trotter."

"Could you pick out the tune, as Mr. Paravicini has done, playing it in exactly the same manner?"

"Certainly I could."

"Then will you go and sit at the piano and be ready to do so when I give the signal?"

Molly looked slightly bewildered. Then she crossed slowly to the piano.

Mr. Paravicini rose from the piano stool with a shrill protest. "But, Sergeant, I understood that we were each to repeat our former roles. *I* was at the piano here."

"The same actions will be performed as on the former occasion—*but they will not necessarily be performed by the same people.*"

"I—don't see the point of that," said Giles.

"There *is* a point, Mr. Davis. It is a means of checking up on the original statements—and I may say of *one* statement in particular. Now, then, please. I will assign you your various stations. Mrs. Davis will be here—at the piano. Mr. Wren, will you kindly go to the kitchen? Just keep an eye on Mrs. Davis's dinner. Mr. Paravicini, will you go to Mr. Wren's bedroom? There you can exercise your musical talents by whistling 'Three Blind Mice' just as he did. Major Metcalf, will you go up to Mr. Davis's bedroom and examine the telephone there? And you, Mr. Davis, will you look into the cupboard in the hall and then go down to the cellar?"

There was a moment's silence. Then four people moved slowly toward the door. Trotter followed them. He looked over his shoulder.

Count up to fifty and then begin to play, Mrs. Davis," he said.

He followed the others out. Before the door closed Molly heard Mr. Paravicini's voice say shrilly, "I never knew the police were so fond of parlor games."

FORTY-EIGHT, FORTY-NINE, fifty."

Obediently, the counting finished, Molly began to play. Again the soft cruel little tune crept out into the big, echoing room.

Three Blind Mice
See how they run . . .

Molly felt her heartbeating faster and faster. As Paravicini had said, it was a strangely haunting and gruesome little rhyme. It had that childish incomprehension of pity which is so terrifying if met with in an adult.

Very faintly, from upstairs, she could hear the same tune being whistled in the bedroom above—Paravicini enacting the part of Christopher Wren.

Suddenly, next door, the wireless went on in the library. Sergeant Trotter must have set that going. He himself, then, was playing the part of Mrs. Boyle.

But why? What was the point of it all? Where was the trap? For there was a trap, of that she was certain.

A draft of cold air blew across the back of her neck. She turned her head sharply. Surely the door had opened. Someone had come into the room—No, the room was empty. But suddenly she felt nervous—afraid. If someone *should* come in. Supposing Mr. Paravicini should skip round the door, should come skipping over to the piano, his long fingers twitching and twisting—

"So you are playing your own funeral march, dear lady, a happy thought—" Nonsense—don't be stupid—don't imagine things. Besides, you can hear him whistling over your head, just as he can hear you.

She almost took her fingers off the piano as the idea came to her! Nobody *had* heard Mr. Paravicini playing. Was that the trap? Was it, perhaps, possible that Mr. Paravicini hadn't been playing at all? That he had been, not in the drawing-room, but in the library. In the library, strangling Mrs. Boyle?

He had been annoyed, very annoyed, when Trotter had arranged for her to play. He had laid stress on the softness with which he had picked out the tune. Of course, he had emphasized the softness in the hopes that it would be too soft to be heard outside the room. Because if anyone heard it this time who hadn't heard it last time—why then, Trotter would have got what he wanted—*the person who had lied.*

The door of the drawing-room opened. Molly, strung up to expect Paravicini, nearly screamed. But it was only Sergeant Trotter who entered, just as she finished the third repetition of the tune.

"Thank you, Mrs. Davis," he said.

He was looking extremely pleased with himself, and his manner was brisk and confident.

Molly took her hands from the keys. "Have you got what you wanted?" she asked.

"Yes, indeed." His voice was exultant. "I've got exactly what I wanted."

"Which? Who?"

"Don't you know, Mrs. Davis? Come, now—it's not so difficult. By the way, you've been, if I may say so, extraordinarily foolish. You've left me hunting about for the third victim. As a result, you've been in serious danger."

"Me? I don't know what you mean."

"I mean that you haven't been honest with me, Mrs. Davis. You held out on me—just as Mrs. Boyle held out on me."

"I don't understand."

"Oh, yes, you do. Why, when I first mentioned the Longridge Farm case, *you knew all about it.* Oh, yes, you did. You were upset. And it was you who confirmed that Mrs. Boyle was the billeting officer for this part of the country. Both you and she came from these parts. So when I began to speculate who the third victim was likely to be, I plumped at once for you. You'd shown firsthand knowledge of the Longridge Farm business. We policemen aren't so dumb as we look, you know."

Molly said in a low voice, "You don't understand. I didn't want to remember."

"I can understand that." His voice changed a little. "Your maiden name was Wainwright, wasn't it?"

"Yes."

"And you're just a little older than you pretend to be. In 1940, when this thing happened, you were the schoolteacher at Abbeyvale school."

"No!"

"Oh, yes, you were, Mrs. Davis."

"I wasn't, I tell you."

"The child who died managed to get a letter posted to you. He stole a stamp. The letter begged for help—help from his kind teacher. It's a teacher's business to find out why a child doesn't come to school. You didn't find out. You ignored the poor little devil's letter."

"Stop." Molly's cheeks were flaming. "It's my sister you are talking about. She was the schoolmistress. And she didn't ignore his letter. She was ill—with pneumonia. She never saw the letter until after the child was dead. It upset her dreadfully—dreadfully—she was a terribly sensitive person. But it wasn't her fault. It's because she took it to heart so dreadfully that I've never been able to bear being reminded of it. It's been a nightmare to me, always."

Molly's hands went to her eyes, covering them. When she took them away, Trotter was staring at her.

He said softly, "So it was your sister. Well, after all—" He gave a sudden queer smile. "It doesn't much matter, does it? Your sister—*my* brother—" He took something out of his pocket. He was smiling now, happily.

Molly stared at the object he held. "I always thought the police didn't carry revolvers," she said.

"The police don't," said the young man. He went on, "But you see, Mrs. Davis, *I'm not a policeman.* I'm Jim. I'm Georgie's brother. You thought I was a policeman because I rang up from the call box in the village and said that Sergeant Trotter was on his way. Then I cut the telephone wires outside the house when I got here, so that you shouldn't be able to ring back to the police station."

Molly stared at him. The revolver was pointing at her now.

"Don't move, Mrs. Davis—and don't scream—or I pull the trigger at once."

He was still smiling. It was, Molly realized with horror, a child's smile. And his voice, when he spoke, was becoming a child's voice.

"Yes," he said, "I'm Georgie's brother. Georgie died at Longridge Farm. That nasty woman sent us there, and the farmer's wife was cruel to us, and you wouldn't help us—three little blind mice. I said then I'd kill you all when I grew up. I meant it. I've thought of it ever since." He frowned suddenly. "They bothered me a lot in the army—that doctor kept asking me questions—I had to get away. I was afraid they'd stop me doing what I wanted to do. But I'm grown up now. Grown-ups can do what they like."

Molly pulled herself together. *Talk to him,* she said to herself. *Distract his mind.*

"But, Jim, listen," she said. "You'll never get safely away."

His face clouded over. "Somebody's hidden my skis. I can't find them." He laughed. "But I daresay it will be all right. It's your husband's revolver. I took it out of his drawer. I daresay they'll think *he* shot you. Anyway—I don't much care. It's been such fun—all of it. Pretending! That woman in London, her face when she recognized me. That stupid woman this morning!"

He nodded his head.

Clearly, with eerie effect, came a whistle. Someone whistling the tune of "Three Blind Mice."

Trotter started, the revolver wavered—a voice shouted, "Down, Mrs. Davis."

Molly dropped to the floor as Major Metcalf, rising from behind the concealment of the sofa by the door flung himself upon Trotter. The revolver went off—and the bullet lodged in one of the somewhat mediocre oil paintings dear to the heart of the late Miss Emory.

A moment later, all was pandemonium—Giles rushed in, followed by Christopher and Mr. Paravicini.

Major Metcalf, retaining his grasp of Trotter, spoke in short explosive sentences.

"Came in while you were playing—slipped behind the sofa—I've been on to him from the beginning—that's to say, I knew he wasn't a police officer. *I'm* a police officer—Inspector Tanner. We arranged with Metcalf I should take his place. Scotland Yard thought it advisable to have someone on the spot. Now, my lad—" He spoke quite gently to the now docile Trotter. "You come with me. No one will hurt you. You'll be all right. We'll look after you."

In a piteous child's voice the bronzed young man asked, "Georgie won't be angry with me?"

Metcalf said, "No. Georgie won't be angry."

He murmured to Giles as he passed him, "Mad as a hatter, poor devil."

They went out together. Mr. Paravicini touched Christopher Wren on the arm.

"You, also, my friend," he said, "come with me."

Giles and Molly, left alone, looked at each other. In another moment they were in each other's arms.

"Darling," said Giles, "you're sure he didn't hurt you?"

"No, no, I'm quite all right. Giles, I've been so terribly mixed up. I almost thought you—why did you go to London that day?"

"Darling, I wanted to get you an anniversary present, for tomorrow. I didn't want you to know."

"How extraordinary! *I* went to London to get *you* a present and I didn't want you to know."

"I was insanely jealous of that neurotic ass. I must have been mad. Forgive me, darling."

The door opened, and Mr. Paravicini skipped in in his goatlike way. He was beaming.

"Interrupting the reconciliation—Such a charming scene—But, alas, I must bid you adieu. A police jeep has managed to get through. I shall persuade them to take me with them." He bent and whispered mysteriously in Molly's ear, "I may have a few embarrassments in the near future—but I am confident I can arrange matters, and if you should receive a case—with a goose, say, a turkey, some tins of *foie gras,* a ham—some nylon stockings, yes? Well, you understand, it will be with my compliments to a very charming lady. Mr. Davis, my check is on the hall table."

He kissed Molly's hand and skipped to the door.

"Nylons?" murmured Molly, "*Foie gras?* Who is Mr. Paravicini? Santa Claus?"

"Black-market style, I suspect," said Giles.

Christopher Wren poked a diffident head in. "My dears," he said, "I hope I'm not intruding, but there's a terrible smell of burning from the kitchen. Ought I to *do* something about it?"

With an anguished cry of "*My pie!*" Molly fled from the room.